THE BURNING ISSUE OF THE DAY

THE BURNING ISSUE OF THE DAY

A Lady Hardcastle Mystery

T E KINSEY

f THOMAS & MERCER

Text copyright © 2019 by T E Kinsey
All rights reserved.

Published by Thomas & Mercer, Seattle

www.apub.com

Amazon, the Amazon logo, and Thomas & Mercer are trademarks of Amazon.com, Inc., or its affiliates.

ISBN-13: 9781542041157
ISBN-10: 1542041155

Cover design by Lisa Horton

Printed in the United States of America

THE BURNING ISSUE OF THE DAY

The Bristol News
Friday, 28 January 1910

ONE DEAD IN SUFFRAGETTE ARSON ATTACK

A fire was deliberately started at the shop of H A Greenham of Thomas Street, Bristol, shortly before midnight on Tuesday. Mr Greenham and his wife live above the shop but were, thankfully, out for the evening. Tragically, their lodger, Mr Christian Brookfield, a highly respected reporter for this newspaper, was apparently asleep in an upstairs bedroom, where he was overcome by the smoke and flames and perished.

Suffragette literature was found scattered in the street, as was a signed note claiming responsibility for the attack which had been pinned to a nearby telephone pole. This is the suffragettes' usual means of claiming responsibility for their criminal damage. On Wednesday morning the police arrested Miss Elizabeth Worrel of Woodfield Road, Redland, on suspicion of arson and murder. She was charged with both offences and appeared before magistrates on Wednesday morning, where she was indicted for trial at the Lent Assizes. She was remanded to the women's wing of Horfield Prison to await trial.

It had been understood that the Women's Social and Political Union, the so-called 'suffragettes', had suspended their campaign of violence during this General Election. It seems that the word of these reckless women cannot, after all, be trusted.

Mr Brookfield, their innocent victim, leaves no family, but this brave young man, whose integrity and industry shone a light into the darkest corners of our society, will be greatly missed not just by those who worked alongside him, but by all the citizens of this great city.

Chapter One

'Be a dear and pass the pepper, would you?' said Lady Hardcastle.

I distractedly did as she asked. It was Friday morning and we were each reading a newspaper. Wherever we had been in the world, Lady Hardcastle liked to take *The Times* as well as a more local newspaper. When we had settled in Littleton Cotterell nearly two years earlier, she had chosen the *Bristol News* as her source of regional tittle-tattle. There was an even more local newspaper, published in the market town of Chipping Bevington, but she preferred to read the news from our nearest big city. The *Bristol News* was published twice a week on Monday and Friday and was always her first choice when there were two newspapers on the breakfast table.

'Anything exciting going on in Bristol?' I asked.

'Much the same as usual,' she said. 'Permission granted to build new commercial premises on . . .' She paused to scan the article. '. . . Thomas Street. A strident call from the sports editor for the sacking of Bristol City's manager after their two-nil loss to Sheffield Wednesday on Saturday. News of a gold shipment coming into Avonmouth, from Chile of all places. And an arson attack on a shop on . . . oh, Thomas Street again. One man dead. Police have arrested the woman responsible.'

'You'd make a rubbish newspaper editor,' I said. 'You should have led with "Arson Murder – Woman Arrested".'

'Then you should contact the newspaper and tell the editor that he's rubbish, too. He led with the General Election. Again.'

'It's not often you hear of a woman arsonist, after all. It's by far the most interesting story.'

'This one was a suffragette,' she said as she reread the article.

'Even more reason to run it as the main story,' I said. 'The *Bristol News* has never made a secret of how much it despises even the idea of women getting the vote, let alone the women campaigning for it.'

'Well, it went with coverage of remarks made by Sir Howell Davis at a Liberal Party meeting in Bedminster.'

'Pfft,' I said.

'Pfft, indeed.' She inspected her breakfast plate, lifting the edge of her fried egg to see what might be concealed beneath. 'Have we run out of haggis?'

'We had the last of it at your impromptu Burns Night celebration on Tuesday,' I said.

'What a pity. An unexpected bonus of our trip. We should have bought more.'

Shortly before Christmas we had made a trip to Scotland, where we had attended the wedding of Lady Hardcastle's brother, Harry, to Lady Lavinia Codrington, sister of the Earl of Riddlethorpe. They had eloped to Gretna Green to escape the seemingly endless bickering over the wedding arrangements that had broken out among the various branches of her family. We wished the happy couple continued happiness after a ceremony at the blacksmith's shop, and then continued to Edinburgh, where we acquired a small supply of haggis after tasting it in the hotel's excellent dining room.

'There's a strict limit on the amount that can be brought out of the country,' I said. 'The Scots are very protective of the haggis.'

'Understandably so,' she said. 'They're quite rare, and a beggar to catch.'

'Not if you know their ways,' I said. 'They live on hillsides and their left legs are shorter than the right to stop them falling over. A clever evolutionary adaptation, but it means they always face the same way and can only run widdershins around the mountain.'

'Making them easier to trap?'

'Exactly,' I said.

'One lives and learns. What are your plans for today, tiny servant?'

'Once again I seem to have some mending to do. Your green dress—' I began.

'Ah, yes, sorry about that. I tripped over in the orangery and it got caught on a nail.'

Lady Hardcastle flitted between hobbies and interests, but her enduring passion was the making of 'animated stories' in the moving picture studio she had built in what had originally been an orangery.

'If you would just let me tidy up in there . . .'

'I have a system, dear,' she said. 'A place for everything and everything in its place.'

'So you keep saying. But "the place" for everything always seems to be the floor.'

'It's only a tiny rip,' she said. 'It won't take you long. What next?'

'After that, I find myself facing an unaccustomed lull in my otherwise ceaseless labours. With Edna and Miss Jones both still working longer hours, I seem to have much less to do. I thought I might read.'

'Has Miss Jones made plans for lunch?'

'I don't think so. What do you fancy? She'll be amenable to anything, I'm sure.'

'Why don't we give her an easy time of it and have lunch at the Dog and Duck?'

'If you like,' I said. 'Although I'm not sure that one of Old Joe's doorstep sandwiches can compete with even the least ambitious of Miss Jones's prandial creations.'

'He might have pie. And he gets his pies from Holman's.'

'Ooh, he might, mightn't he? And it'll give me a chance to catch up with Daisy. All right, then, you've talked me into it. Noon at the foot of the stairs?'

'I'll see you there,' she said.

As I had promised, I was waiting in the hall in my hat and coat at noon precisely. Or 'noon' according to the hall clock, anyway, whose accuracy I was beginning to doubt. As well as a tendency to run fast or slow depending upon its whim, it had also taken to chiming the quarter hour at seemingly random times near the quarter hour, but never quite actually on it.

As I had privately predicted, Lady Hardcastle was late, even allowing for the vagaries of the increasingly eccentric timepiece. I picked up the post from the hall table and leafed through it to pass the time.

I recognized the handwriting and postmarks on letters from two of Lady Hardcastle's regular correspondents. One was the wife of a diplomat whom she had met in the nineties and with whom she had maintained an eager correspondence on subjects as diverse as embroidery, knitting, painting, electronics, chemistry, and Dr Einstein's 'special relativity'. The other was a celebrated concert pianist with passionate views on modern music . . . and gardening. I felt sure Lady Hardcastle would be pleased to receive both letters.

There were also two bills, one of which was from our vintner and was certain to be terrifyingly large.

The final letter was most intriguing. The envelope was of heavy, and unquestionably expensive, paper and it was addressed in an elegant, yet slightly girlish, hand. It was postmarked Bristol. I put it on the top of the pile so that Lady Hardcastle would spot it first and, perhaps, satisfy my curiosity.

Only ten minutes late, she finally exploded through the kitchen door.

'I'm so sorry I'm late, dear,' she said. 'Things just sort of ran away with me.'

'Ran over you, more like,' I said. 'What the devil are you covered in?'

'Fuller's earth, mostly,' she said. 'Although I think that bit might be coffee.' She indicated a splattered stain on her shoulder. 'Lucky I put on the overalls, eh?'

'Fortunate, indeed,' I said.

'Give me ten minutes to wash my face and put a clean dress on and I'll be with you.'

'Right you are, my lady,' I said.

She saw the small pile of post on the table. 'Ooh, post,' she said. 'It's been getting later and later since Christmas. Anything for me?'

I frowned. 'It's all for you,' I said. 'As always.'

'Good-o. Hand it over. I'll have a quick look before I go up.'

She flicked through the small pile. Pleasingly, she was as intrigued by the topmost letter as I had been.

'Hmm,' she said. 'Who can this be from, I wonder?'

She produced a penknife from the pocket of her overalls and used it to slit open the envelope. She walked up the stairs, reading the letter.

'Don't worry,' I said. 'I'll wait here.'

'Right you are, dear,' she said, still reading. 'I shan't be long.'

To give her at least some credit, she actually wasn't long and when she returned – with her dress wonkily buttoned and her hair looking as though it had been styled by a very young child – she was rereading the letter.

'You look enchanting,' I said.

'Nothing seems to be going right for me today,' she said. 'If you could give me a hand to sort things out, I'd be forever in your debt.'

I set about rebuttoning her dress and repairing her hair.

'What is it about that letter that's set you so adrift?' I said.

'We've been asked to help save someone's life,' she said.

'Good heavens. Who?'

'The woman in the newspaper.'

'The suffragette who set fire to the shop?'

'If my correspondent is to be believed, she's the suffragette who definitely didn't set fire to the shop,' she said. 'And she offers one or two compelling reasons why not.'

'It's not just another letter from some buffle who's read about you in the newspaper and thinks you have mystical powers.'

'She might be a buffle for all I know, but she says she knows Simeon so I don't imagine she has any illusions about my powers, mystic or otherwise. He'd have set her straight in no time.'

Dr Simeon Gosling was an old friend of Lady Hardcastle's who was now working as the police surgeon for the Bristol Police Force.

'What does she say that you find so convincing? How can she be so sure that the suffragette didn't do it?'

'Her name is Georgina, Lady Bickle, and she says that she herself is a member of the WSPU. She vouches for this Lizzie Worrel woman personally and says that not only does the WSPU not engage in arson, but there is also a moratorium on all militant action for the duration of the General Election.'

'That much was in the newspaper,' I said. 'But could she not have been acting on her own initiative?'

'Lady Bickle covers that. She says, "I have known Lizzie Worrel for more than a year and I can safely say that no one is more loyal to the WSPU and its aims. It is unthinkable that she would go against the instructions of Mrs Pankhurst and act on her own initiative, most especially when the stakes – that is, the possibility that the men of the country might finally elect a government sympathetic to our cause – are so high." I'm not sure one could be more emphatic than that.'

'It does sound compelling,' I agreed. 'What does she want you to do about it?'

'She wants us – "us", dear, she mentions you by name – she wants us to have elevenses with her tomorrow morning.'

'And what good will that do?'

'She wishes to give us a full briefing in the hope that we might feel able to set off and find the real culprit. Or so she says.'

'And shall we go?'

'I don't think we can refuse, do you? I'll send her a wire while we're in the village for our luncheon. Later, I thought we might drive into Chipping for a quick look round the shops. I need one or two sundries.'

'But lunch is still at the Dog and Duck?' I asked.

'I promised you pie. I can't let you go pie-less.'

'How can you have no pies?' I asked the barmaid, my friend Daisy.

'Calm down,' she said with a laugh. 'It's not like we've run out of cider.'

'No, I know,' I said. 'But I really fancied pie. Lady Hardcastle promised me pie.'

'I can do you a cheese sandwich,' she said.

Daisy Spratt was the butcher's daughter and my best friend in the village. But she was offering me a cheese sandwich instead of a pie. It's easy to go off people.

'What if I nip down to Holman's and buy some pies – could we eat them in here?'

'You could if he had any, my lover,' she said. 'But the reason we don't have none is because he don't have none. And he don't have none because our dad don't have no beef skirt. And he don't have no beef skirt because—'

'Because of a chain of events leading all the way to a farmer with a bad back not being able to get his cattle to market?' I suggested.

'I was goin' to say the wagon threw a wheel and the delivery never got here,' she said. 'Two rounds of sandwiches?'

'Yes, please,' I said. 'And a brandy for Lady Hardcastle. I'll have a glass of ginger beer.'

'It's not like you to abstain.'

'We're driving over to Chipping later. I like to keep my wits about me. I'll be in charge of a deadly machine.'

'I've seen your motor car,' she said. 'Folks is more likely to die laughin' when they sees you drivin' by than from the effects of some what-do-they-call-it? "High-speed collision".'

'I'll have you know that on a good day we can get the Rover up to twenty-four miles an hour. Downhill. With a following wind.'

She laughed and passed me the two drinks. 'You sittin' in the snug?'

'We are. We're ladies of refinement and distinction.'

'I'll bring your sandwiches over when they's ready.'

'Thank you,' I said.

As I was about to make my way back to our table in the other bar a couple of young farmhands clomped into the public bar and approached Daisy. They leered unpleasantly so I put the drinks down and waited to see what happened – just in case.

'Two pints, please, sweetheart,' said the first.

'And a kiss when you're ready,' said the second.

'Two pints comin' up,' said Daisy. 'And you can whistle for your kiss, Davey Witten – I i'n't that kind of girl.'

'That's not what we 'eard,' said the first.

'Oh, yes?' said Daisy. 'And what is it that you heard?'

'We 'eard you was seen kissin' Lenny Leadbetter round the back of the cricket pavilion last week.'

'Well, you heard wrong,' she said. 'I a'n't so much as spoken to Lenny Leadbetter since afore Christmas, much less kissed 'e. Who told you that?'

'It's all over the village,' said the second farmhand. 'Come on, just a quick kiss.'

I returned to the bar.

'Everything all right, Dais?' I said.

'Right as rain,' she said, although she was obviously slightly flustered. 'Just gettin' these two nice young gentlemen their beers.'

'And a kiss each,' said the first farmhand. 'And one from you an' all since you's here.'

He reached out to grab me, but I caught his hand and twisted his thumb into a position it wasn't designed for. He yelped.

'Don't do that, dear,' I said sweetly. 'You might get hurt.' I gave the thumb just a tiny extra push in the wrong direction. 'Now pay for your beers and sling your hook. And if I hear you slandering my pal again, I'll do a sight more than sprain your thumb.'

He glared at me, but wisely decided not to push his luck. I waited until they had taken their drinks to a table well away from the bar.

'What was all that about?' I asked Daisy.

'I i'n't sure,' she said. 'But they i'n't the first to be sayin' it. Someone's spreadin' rumours about me, I reckon.'

'Any idea who?'

'Not yet,' she said. 'But when I finds 'em . . .'

'Let me know if anyone needs a biff up the conk – I'll not have people besmirching my best pal's good name.'

'Thanks,' she said. 'I might hold you to that. But go and sit down now and I'll fetch you those sandwiches.'

I finally made it back to Lady Hardcastle with our drinks.

'Are you starting fights in pubs now?' she asked as I sat down.

'Just a couple of lads trying it on,' I said. 'Nothing to worry about.'

'I'm sure you have it well in hand,' she said. 'What sort of pie did you order?'

I explained the pie shortage and she harrumphed. 'Even I could have made a cheese sandwich,' she said. 'Ah, well. It's nice to be out, I suppose.'

Daisy brought out the cheese doorsteps a few minutes later and we munched contentedly as we discussed our plans for the rest of the day.

◆ ◆ ◆

Back at the house, we prepared ourselves for the trip to the neighbouring market town of Chipping Bevington. Dressing for the motor car was as much of a palaver as dressing for riding, for sport, or for attending a society ball. Sitting in the unenclosed Rover 6 as it trundled along the road was bracing even in the summertime and always required a certain amount of specialist attire to protect us from the elements. In the bitter cold of an English January, that meant heavy waterproof coats, woollen mufflers, sturdy gauntlets, even sturdier boots, warm hats, and, to my eternal amusement, goggles.

When we were finally ready, I set to work cranking the starting handle to bring the little motor car to life.

'There needs to be an easier way to do this,' I said as I heaved the heavy handle round for the third time.

'Some sort of motor to start the motor?' said Lady Hardcastle. 'But what would start that? Another motor?'

'I'm sure it's not beyond the wit of Man to devise a system that doesn't require someone – usually a representative of the downtrodden masses, I might add – to get out and crank the stupid thing to life. What about some sort of spring?'

'Or an electric motor?' she suggested.

'Anything that doesn't involve me risking a wrenched back or a broken arm would get my vote.'

'If only we had a vote, I'd cast mine with yours,' she said.

'You're very kind, but it doesn't inconvenience you in the slightest,' I said as I clambered into the driving seat and engaged low gear. 'I don't remember the last time you started the engine.'

'But I have to listen to you complaining about it every time we go out. I'd pay double for any system that would spare me from that.'

I mumbled mutinously into my muffler and eased the little motor car out on to the road.

The journey to Chipping (all the locals called it 'Chipping', having long since decided that 'Chipping Bevington' was altogether too much of a mouthful) was short and uneventful. We soon parked the motor car on the High Street outside Pomphrey's Bric-a-Brac Emporium.

'Can we go in?' I asked as we dismounted and took off our gloves and goggles.

'I bow to no woman in my admiration of the wonders of Mr Pomphrey's delightful shop,' said Lady Hardcastle, 'but we have quite enough clutter about the house as it is. I think we'll leave him for another day.'

I took a last look at the assemblage of junk in the shop window, admiring – not for the first time – the stuffed moose head wearing a sola topi and smoking a hookah. One day, I thought.

'And we're never going to buy that moose,' she said over her shoulder as she walked across the road to the stationer's. 'Where would we put it?'

I hurried after her, slightly disquieted by her apparent mind-reading ability. This was a new and dangerous development.

The 'one or two sundries' she had so casually mentioned turned out not to be quite so trivial as her offhand tone had implied. After a lengthy perusal of samples, the stationer was delighted to be given an order for a goodly quantity of card of various thicknesses, drawing paper, watercolour paper, writing paper, envelopes, several notebooks, and a rainbow assortment of inks and watercolours. She was also tempted by the new 'Polychromos' coloured pencils and ordered two sets.

From the stationer's we visited the haberdasher's, where she purchased supplies for her model making. Following the enthusiastic reception of her first animated motion picture late the previous year, she had embarked upon a new project. She was irritatingly tight-lipped about the subject matter, but the production seemed to involve the making of a number of tiny costumes for its cast of model characters.

I took advantage of the trip to restock the mending basket. It wasn't nearly so exciting as buying the necessaries for clothing miniature moving picture actors, but with Lady Hardcastle's careless attitude to her clothing it was no less important.

The trip was saved by our final call. At the bottom of the High Street, its windows filled with all the imagined wonders of this world and all those yet to be discovered, was Boxwell's Bookshop, proprietor Mr Dudley Boxwell. I had to be dragged out in the end, but not before I had persuaded Lady Hardcastle to buy an armful of new books.

Most of the day's purchases would be delivered over the coming days, but we still had to find room in the Rover for several small packages from the stationer's and haberdasher's as well as an impressive stack of books wrapped in brown paper. The smaller packages fitted into the lidded storage behind the seats but, try as we might, we couldn't wedge the books into the tiny box.

'I really must make an effort to ask Fishy to design us a more commodious motor car,' said Lady Hardcastle as she stacked the books beneath her legs, leaving her feet crammed uncomfortably against the end of the footwell.

'You promised that on Bonfire Night,' I said. 'Something with an enclosed cabin and a more powerful motor. And yet . . .'

'I know, I know. I'll write to him. But for now, homeward and don't dilly. Nor should you dally – my feet are most uncomfortable.'

I set off for home.

◆ ◆ ◆

While Miss Jones put the finishing touches to dinner, I took care of the mending. Then, once the other two servants had been sent home, Lady Hardcastle and I settled in for a quiet supper, and an evening in front of the fire with our new books.

For reasons unknown to me, Lady Hardcastle had become fascinated by the French philosopher Henri Bergson and had bought three of his works, including *Laughter: An Essay on the Meaning of the Comic*. Not to be outdone, I had bought Sigmund Freud's *The Psychopathology of Everyday Life*. I wasn't entirely sure I was going to enjoy it very much, but one likes to try to keep up with modern ideas.

For light relief I had bought G K Chesterton's new book, *The Ball and the Cross*, and something from an author I'd never heard of before, P G Wodehouse. It was called *Mike*, and Mr Boxwell in the bookshop had recommended it personally.

'It's terribly amusing,' he had said. 'I'm certain you'll love it.'

Lady Hardcastle, meanwhile, had opted for more reliable fare, sticking with G K Chesterton and H G Wells. The latter was a timely novel entitled *Ann Veronica* about the women's suffrage movement. I made a mental note to read it myself when she was done with it.

'Have you had any more thoughts about that arson case?' I asked as I reached the end of a chapter.

Lady Hardcastle put down her book, removed her reading glasses, and looked into the fire for a few moments before answering. 'I've nothing more to go on than you have,' she said at length. 'If the facts reported in the newspaper are accurate, then it seems pretty much cut and dried. The suffragettes never shy away from taking responsibility for their actions – they rely on the resulting hullabaloo to draw attention to their cause, after all. And the scattering of their literature at the scene of the crime very much fits their *modus operandi*. If it weren't for the inconsistencies, and Lady Bickle's letter, I'd think no more of it.'

'It certainly doesn't seem to fit,' I said.

'Not at all. I don't know much about Emmeline Pankhurst other than what I read in the newspapers, but I get the impression she runs a tight ship. I can't imagine any of her followers disobeying her like that while still claiming to be acting in the organization's name.'

'And they've always been careful not to harm anyone.'

'Very careful indeed. It seems most important to them that they're the only ones to suffer, preferably at the hands of the authorities. They all hold that in common, so even a dissenter would have taken care to ensure that the building was empty before she set it on fire. And Lady Bickle insists that this Lily Wardle—'

'Lizzie Worrel,' I corrected her.

'Lizzie Worrel, yes. What did I say?'

'Something else.'

'Did I? Oh, well. This Leonora—'

'Unless you're suffering from one of Dr Freud's unconscious attempts to suppress troubling memories, you're doing it on purpose now. I'm not going to rise to it.'

'Spoilsport. But Lady Buckle . . .' She paused for a reaction, but I just raised my eyebrows and stared at her. '. . . Lady Bickle,' she continued, 'is adamant that Worrel is innocent.'

'Friends, colleagues, and acquaintances of the accused usually stand firm on the subject of their innocence,' I said. 'Often in the face of overwhelming evidence to the contrary. No one wants to believe that their pal is a wrong-un.'

'True, true,' she said. 'We shall have to go to our meeting tomorrow with our eyes and minds wide open. But for now I'm tired of reading and I rather feel that our mouths should be wide open for the drinking of brandy and the singing of songs. Fetch the booze and I'll hunt out something cheering to sing us to bed.'

Chapter Two

By mutual agreement, Edna and Miss Jones always arrived a little later on Saturday mornings. Lady Hardcastle wasn't much of a one for socializing now that we lived out in the country, but we still said that the late start was to allow her to sleep in after Friday-night shenanigans. The real reason was so that Edna – who with her husband, Dan, was the life and soul of Friday nights at the Dog and Duck – had more of a chance to sleep off her own Friday-night shenanigans.

Lady Hardcastle had been introduced to what she insisted on referring to as 'the jentacular delights' of eggs Benedict by an American friend a few years earlier when we were living in London. It was all the rage in New York, we were told, and Lady Hardcastle had adopted it as a breakfast favourite. Making the hollandaise sauce was a bit of a faff so I didn't cook it often, but I enjoyed her reaction enough to want to make the effort from time to time.

I wasn't disappointed.

'Florence Armstrong, you little Welsh marvel,' she said as I put the tray across her lap. 'I haven't had eggs Benedict for simply ever. You win today's award for splendidness above and beyond the call of duty. Thank you.'

I curtseyed exaggeratedly.

'My pleasure, my lady,' I said.

'But what about you? Are you not eating with me?'

'I had some toast downstairs,' I said. 'I didn't want to be too full in case Lady Bickle pushes the boat out for elevenses. No point in slaving away over a hot saucepan if someone else's cook is going to fill my belly for me.'

'Well, now I feel like a pig,' she said. 'Have half with me, then we'll both have room for jam sandwiches and fat wedges of fruit cake.'

It did look nice, so I accepted her offer.

By the time breakfast had been eaten and cleared away, it was time to begin the robing ritual for the journey to Clifton. It was still bitterly cold so there was no possibility of taking shortcuts in our preparations.

'I wonder if Lady Bickle is a stickler for fashion,' said Lady Hardcastle as I laced her heavy driving boots. 'Or gullible, perhaps. Do you think we might persuade her that our clodhopping great boots are actually the height of Parisian chic?'

'A less risky stratagem might be to take more delicate footwear in a bag and change into it when we arrive,' I said. 'I'm no etiquette expert, but I'm not sure it's considered good form to presume ignorance and stupidity in one's host.'

She sighed. 'More fuss and palaver,' she said. 'Ah, well. It's the price we pay for the freedom to come and go as we please, I suppose.'

And so, eventually, we set off with our day boots in a bag stowed in the box behind the seats.

It took the best part of an hour to drive the fifteen miles from Littleton Cotterell to Clifton. The journey passed without too much incident. A milkman shouted angrily at us on Whiteladies Road when the sound of the Rover startled his horse, but we were used to that sort of abuse by now. Lady Hardcastle smiled and waved.

On Queen's Road, I turned right at the City Museum and on to Berkeley Square. We pulled up beside the steps that led up to Berkeley Crescent.

'Perfect timing,' said Lady Hardcastle. 'Thank you.'

I hopped out and rummaged for the bag containing our shoes.

'We're looking for number five,' she said, and we set off up the steps on to the flagstone pavement that ran in front of the crescent of brick-fronted Georgian townhouses.

The first door we passed bore the number six.

'I shall never understand builders,' she said. 'Who on earth numbers a crescent of six houses from right to left? Madness.'

'It was probably to confuse French spies during the Napoleonic wars,' I said. 'They could never invade if they couldn't work out where we lived.'

She tugged smartly on the bell pull of number five and the door was soon opened by a white-haired butler carrying a small silver tray.

'Good afternoon,' said Lady Hardcastle, placing her calling card on the tray. 'I believe Lady Bickle is expecting us.'

The butler glanced discreetly down at the card. 'Yes, Lady Hardcastle, she asks you to wait for her in the drawing room.'

He stepped back to allow us to enter.

'Is there somewhere where we might change our boots?' she asked.

The butler looked down at our heavy boots. 'Yes, my lady,' he said after a brief pause. 'Please follow me.'

He took our coats, hats, gauntlets, and goggles and then took us to the boot room at the rear of the house. He waited outside while we saw to our footwear and then led us back to the drawing room. By the time we arrived, a beautiful, elegantly dressed lady was already waiting for us. She was a good deal younger than I had expected, but carried herself with a confidence that belied her years. She was tall, too. Why was everyone so tall?

'My lady,' said the butler, 'Lady Hardcastle is here to see you.'

'Thank you, Williams,' said the lady. 'We'll take tea in here, I think.'

The butler withdrew.

The lady held out her hand. 'Georgina Bickle,' she said. 'But do call me Georgie. Simply everyone does.'

Lady Hardcastle shook her hand warmly. 'Emily,' she said. 'And this is Florence Armstrong.'

'How do you do?' said Lady Bickle. 'I've heard so much about you both. Simeon Gosling can't stop talking about either of you.'

I returned her 'How-do-you-do?' with a slight curtsey.

'I do hope Simeon hasn't been over-egging it,' said Lady Hardcastle. 'We're not nearly so exciting as you might imagine.'

'I hope he hasn't, too,' said Lady Bickle. 'I so desperately want his tale of being tied up in a deserted cottage to be true. And the chase through the dark in motor cars. He made it all sound so terribly glamorous and exciting.'

'I'm sure he painted quite a picture,' said Lady Hardcastle, 'but don't take him too seriously. It was all rather mundane and everyday, really.'

'Everyday for you, perhaps, but when one is the wife of a surgeon . . . well . . . "mundane" takes on a special new meaning. Do sit down, both of you.'

She waved us into chairs beside the fire.

'What about your work with the suffragettes, though?' said Lady Hardcastle once we had settled. 'That sounds frightfully interesting.'

'Oh, it is. And so important, don't you think?'

'Essential,' said Lady Hardcastle.

'What do you think, Miss Armstrong?'

'I'm all for equal rights for everyone in everything,' I said. 'But my hopes aren't high. Huge numbers of men don't have the vote so I don't rate my own chances even when Parliament does finally wake up. I'm not a property owner, after all.'

Lady Bickle thought for a moment. 'You're quite right, of course. There are many, even within our own ranks, who feel that we should be fighting for universal suffrage, not merely votes for women. But I can't help but think that if we can make a small breach in the wall with votes for *some* women, it won't be long before our lawmakers realize the empty-headedness of disbarring any adult citizen from voting.'

'I certainly think it would be a step in the right direction,' I said.

'Splendid. Ah, here's Williams with the tea. You're just in time, Williams. We were in danger of lapsing into a torpid state of contented agreement. But here you are with the tea, and nothing stirs Englishwomen to heated acrimony more quickly than the matter of pouring tea.'

The butler set the tea tray on the low table in front of the fire. As well as the teapot, cups, saucers, and milk, there was a selection of dainty sandwiches and some extremely delicate cakes. If they were not made by a professional *pâtissier*, then the Bickles had a very accomplished cook indeed.

Williams withdrew without having uttered a word.

'Now, then,' said Lady Bickle, 'Mother always insisted that we put the milk in first, but that seems to be quite the old-fashioned way of doing things. I much prefer to put the milk in last. Do you have a view, Emily?'

'I'm afraid I've been in and out of society so much over the past twenty years that I'm quite unable to keep up with the fads. I can tell you that it affects the taste, though, if that matters to you.'

Lady Bickle seemed impressed. 'Does it really? Well I never. How so?'

'When you put the milk in first, the milk is slowly warmed by the arriving tea and is unlikely to scald. It also accepts the tannins from the tea more evenly, for reasons we need not tarry over. If you put the milk in last, it heats up rapidly as it comes into contact with a cupful of hot tea, which means that it's apt to scald and is also unlikely to react with the tannins quite so evenly. The two taste subtly different but I met one woman who could tell the difference ten times out of ten.'

'I say,' said Lady Bickle, 'I never knew there was so much to it. Simeon said you were a something of a science wallah.'

Lady Hardcastle laughed warmly. 'One picks up a few things here and there,' she said.

'More than a few, from what I've heard. I do hope you can help us.'

'I hope so, too. Please, tell us what you know about your friend's case.'

While we ate our sandwiches (much easier to digest than Old Joe's doorsteps, but not quite as satisfying) and sipped our tea (alternating 'milk in first' and 'milk in last' as part of Lady Hardcastle's improvised experiment – I found myself unable to tell the difference), Lady Bickle explained the details of the case to us.

◆ ◆ ◆

'I presume you've seen the newspaper story,' began Lady Bickle.

'We have,' confirmed Lady Hardcastle. 'It was in the Friday edition of the *Bristol News.*'

'Just so,' said Lady Bickle. 'It outlines the events passably well but, as is so often the case with newspaper reports, it doesn't tell the whole story. And, rather predictably, it paints the WSPU in a rather negative light.'

'They don't seem to like you much, do they?'

'Not at all. Not at all.'

'Might I ask a question?' I said.

'Of course you may,' said Lady Bickle. 'I gather from press reports that you're an important part of the team. Oh, I say. Here I am disparaging the reliability of the press with one breath and relying on them as a valuable source of intelligence with the next. Things are never quite as straightforward as we like to think, are they?' She paused for a moment, staring absently at the ceiling. 'I'm so sorry, you wanted to say something, didn't you?'

'Yes, my lady,' I said. 'I just wanted to clarify from the outset: do you prefer to be the WSPU or "suffragettes"?'

'Oh, that's an interesting one. When that chap in the *Daily Mail* coined the term a few years ago, I think we were a bit put out. I mean, the intention was to belittle us, after all, to make it seem as though we were a witless flock of little girls playing at politics. But, do you know what? We've come to rather embrace it. It sets us apart from the suffragists and it gives us a more . . . a more youthful and . . . what's the word? Dynamic? Yes, dynamic, I like that. It gives us a more dynamic air, don't you think? We girls in the Bristol branch are most definitely suffragettes.'

'Thank you,' I said. 'I didn't want to cause offence by using the wrong term.'

'No offence would have been taken,' she said. 'We're grateful that you've agreed to help us. You will agree, won't you?'

'We're certainly happy to listen,' said Lady Hardcastle.

'Of course, of course,' said Lady Bickle. 'I'm getting ahead of myself as usual. How much do you know about us?'

'Mostly only what we've read in the newspapers. We've been to a couple of meetings, haven't we?'

I nodded in confirmation.

'So you know that we've been making a bit more noise lately. Holding genteel meetings and writing polite letters to MPs can only get one so far – that's why we split from the suffragists in the first place, after all. Sometimes one has to make a bit of a scene. We've always liked to make a nuisance of ourselves, you know, getting ourselves arrested, that sort of thing. But that didn't seem to be gaining their attention, so a couple of years ago we started a campaign of property damage.'

'Window smashing,' I said.

'Exactly so. Never anything more. No one was to be hurt, that was a very strict rule. And only windows were to be damaged. A tiresome inconvenience and extra work for the glaziers, but nothing too serious.'

'No arson?' said Lady Hardcastle.

'Oh my goodness, no. Nothing so drastic. Now, then, where was I? Ah, yes. When Mr Asquith called the General Election, Mrs Pankhurst decreed that for the duration of the election, the WSPU would cease all violent action. We would put all our energies into more conventional forms of campaign, do you see? And the window breaking and suchlike would stop. For the time being, at least. We all agreed that this would be by far the best way to get things done while still keeping everyone on our side, as it were. And we've scrupulously stuck to it.'

'You've done nothing at all of that nature?' asked Lady Hardcastle, who was now, I noticed, taking notes in her pocket notebook.

'Nothing at all,' said Lady Bickle. 'So that's our starting point. No suffragette from the Bristol branch has so much as stamped her foot in frustration, much less broken a window since the start of the election. And no one in any part of the WSPU has ever burned a shop down. Ever.'

'So what happened on . . .' Lady Hardcastle flipped back a few pages in her notebook. '. . . on Tuesday night?'

'Well, that's the thing we need you to find out. The shop burned down, and that poor journalist was killed, but it wasn't anything to do with us.'

'Your literature was found nearby. Is that how you usually announce your involvement? Claim responsibility?'

'It is, indeed,' said Lady Bickle. 'We make sure to drop a few leaflets when we go on a spree – we need people to know it was us. We need them to know how angry we are.'

'Notes, too?'

'Sometimes,' she said. 'If we need to explain the specific reason for picking a particular target.'

'But it definitely wasn't this . . .' Lady Hardcastle consulted her notebook again. '. . . Elizabeth Worrel?'

'Lizzie Worrel. No.'

'Not even if she were acting on her own initiative?'

'She's as loyal as they come,' said Lady Bickle. 'No one knows what goes on in the privacy of a person's own thoughts, but I'm confident that even if she did lose her head and decide to burn down a shop with someone asleep upstairs, she'd not have lain the blame at our door. She would never have brought condemnation upon the WSPU.'

'Do you think she might have lost her head?'

'Honestly? No.'

'Do you know her well?'

'As well as I know any of my fellow suffragettes,' said Lady Bickle. 'We're not quite a family, but we're a tight bunch. We trust each other. We have to.'

'Does she have an alibi?' I asked.

'Oh, I say,' said Lady Bickle. 'An "alibi". It's like the detective stories, isn't it? Clues, and alibis. I'm not certain that she does. She insists she was at home in Redland when the fire started, but she has no one to corroborate her story.'

'Innocent people seldom have alibis to hand,' said Lady Hardcastle. 'Is there any other evidence against her?'

'Not so far as I know. The police haven't said so, anyway.'

'Where did you get your information from?' asked Lady Hardcastle.

'From Lizzie herself. I visited her at once. And I was at her magistrate's hearing.'

'She has legal representation, I presume?'

'We provided her with a brief. We have a couple of sympathetic solicitors in the city and one of them briefed a barrister at once. It didn't do her any good, of course. We'd hoped to get her out on bail, but as you saw in the newspaper she's been locked up in Horfield Prison until the Easter Assizes.'

Lady Hardcastle took a sip of her tea and thought for a moment. She leafed through her notebook before looking up once more at Lady Bickle.

'You make a good case for why it shouldn't be Lizzie Worrel,' she said. 'The WSPU has committed no previous acts of arson and has called a temporary truce, anyway. In Lizzie, you describe a loyal suffragette who would never disobey orders. And you insist she would never do such a thing on her own initiative.'

'I'd bet my jewels on it,' said Lady Bickle earnestly.

'None of that will be any good to a jury, though. You can make them see why it shouldn't be Lizzie, but we need to be able to show that it couldn't be her.'

'So our brief said. I don't think he's much of a suffragist, but he's professionally obliged to argue her case and he's not at all sure there's anything very much he can do. Without a solid alibi, it's rather tricky to prove that someone didn't do a thing just because her friends insist it's unlikely.'

'Well, quite,' said Lady Hardcastle. 'As I see it, then, our task would be to prove her innocence by finding out who actually did burn that shop down, killing Mr Bakersfield.'

'Brookfield, my lady,' I corrected her reflexively.

'Even he,' she said. 'But that's how to prove her innocence: by tracking down the real culprit.'

'And will you?' asked Lady Bickle. 'Oh, do say you will. The police aren't investigating any longer – they have their arsonist. You are, not to put it too melodramatically, all that stands between Lizzie Worrel and the gallows.'

'Well, when you put it like that,' said Lady Hardcastle with a smile.

'We'll cover all your expenses, naturally. The WSPU doesn't have much money, but I'll pay you myself, if it comes to it.'

Lady Hardcastle glanced at me for confirmation before she spoke again. I gave the tiniest of nods and she said, 'Very well, we shall look into it for you. And there'll be no more talk of money. Consider it our contribution to the cause.'

'Oh, thank you,' said Lady Bickle. 'Thank you so much. The rest of the girls will be ever so pleased. You must come and meet them. Do you have any other appointments? Can you come to the shop?'

'We're entirely free for the rest of the day. Is it far?'

'Quite literally just around the corner. I'll get Williams to fetch our coats.'

She walked to the bell pull beside the fireplace and rang for the butler.

◆ ◆ ◆

When Lady Bickle had said '. . . literally just around the corner', I had imagined a twenty-minute meandering walk through the streets of Clifton, during which I would contemplate the text of my forthcoming lecture on the correct use of the word 'literally'.

It was a good job I didn't say anything.

We turned right out of the door, walked down the steps, and then turned left on to Berkeley Square. We passed our little Rover and continued back the way we had driven, out on to Queen's Road. Here we turned our first proper corner. To the right. We passed J B Hamilton's. I could see the Great Western Railway Receiving Office ahead of us, and then a shop owned by Florence Griffiths. What a splendid name. We stopped between Hamilton's and the GWR office.

'Here we are,' said Lady Bickle brightly. 'Number thirty-seven. Our own little shop.'

She was right. The window display was of Votes For Women posters, bedecked with ribbons in the green, white, and purple colours of the WSPU. There was a schedule of meetings and events on the door. This was clearly the headquarters of the Bristol branch of the WSPU and it really was 'literally just around the corner'.

'Come on in and meet the girls,' she said.

We trooped in after her.

It was a small shop with a counter to the rear, behind which a door led to who knew what mysteries and delights. The walls were lined with shelves on which were stacked pamphlets, leaflets, and flyers. A news-paper rack held copies of the suffragette newspaper *Votes for Women*. A tailor's dummy stood to one side of the counter wearing the organiza-tion's customary white dress, adorned with a green, white, and purple sash, along with badges and ribbons in the same colours. A display by 'her' side contained similarly coloured scarves and brooches, as well as, to my slight surprise, a small note suggesting that shoppers should 'enquire at the counter for garters and undergarments'.

The woman behind the counter looked up as we entered and then stepped out to greet us. Dressed head to toe in white, she was a little older and a good deal less terrifyingly good looking than Lady Bickle, although I was pleased to note that she was a much more sensible height. However, there was a blandness about her appearance that made her rather difficult to notice, as though one's eyes simply slid off her and on to something – anything – more interesting instead. She was dressed as though she were on a suffragette march. Even her boots were white, elaborately embroidered with a beautiful daisy motif. They very much looked the part and were by far the most interesting thing about her.

She smiled fleetingly when she saw us and stepped out from behind the counter.

'Georgie!' she said. 'We were wondering when you'd drop in. Is this them?'

'These are indeed they,' said Lady Bickle. 'Lady Hardcastle, please allow me to introduce Miss Beatrice Challenger, manageress of our humble shop and all-round good egg. Beattie, this is Emily, Lady Hardcastle.'

'How do you do?' they both said together.

'Meanwhile, Miss Armstrong, please . . . Oh, I say, this is all just too silly and formal. Florence Armstrong, Beattie Challenger. Miss Armstrong is Lady Hardcastle's lady's maid and right-hand woman.'

We 'How do you do'-ed together, too.

'Where's Marisol?' asked Lady Bickle.

'Upstairs shouting at the filing,' said Miss Challenger.

'Marisol Rojas is our very own Chilean firebrand,' said Lady Bickle. 'Every organization should have one. She's frightfully well organized and an absolute whizz with the paperwork, but she has the shortest fuse of any human being I've ever met. She's a poppet, really, but she does seem to find the world and everything in it terribly frustrating. Come on up, I'll introduce you.'

She turned to lead us through the door behind the counter, but as she reached for the handle it was wrenched away from her. A dark-haired, dark-complexioned lady stood in the doorway, her face set in an angry scowl. She stopped dead when she saw us all there.

'Oh, I'm sorry,' she said in a heavy Spanish accent. 'I did not know we had visitors.'

'Please don't mind us,' said Lady Hardcastle in Spanish. 'We're all friends. We've come to help prove Lizzie Worrel's innocence.'

'Ah,' said the small newcomer. She switched to her native tongue. 'You must be Lady Hardcastle. Georgie said she was going to ask you to help. I am Marisol Rojas. Thank you for coming. The poor girl needs all the help she can get.'

'I can make no promises, but we'll do what we can.'

'Your Spanish is very good,' said Marisol.

'One tries,' said Lady Hardcastle, switching back to English.

'We're going to have to watch out for you two if you're going to be gabbling in Foreign all day long,' said Miss Challenger.

Lady Hardcastle frowned, but said nothing.

'I'm impressed,' said Lady Bickle. 'My French is passable, but I never had the opportunity to learn any other languages. Do you speak many others?'

'One or two,' said Lady Hardcastle. 'It sort of comes with the job when one is a diplomat's wife.'

'I bet you're just being modest. Am I right, Miss Armstrong?'

'A little,' I said. 'To my knowledge she can hold a decent conversation in French, Spanish, German, Italian, Mandarin, Hindi . . . and Latin.'

'And Ancient Greek,' said Lady Hardcastle.

'I'd forgotten that one,' I said.

'And Shanghainese.'

'Ah, yes, and that,' I agreed. 'You can get by in Hungarian and Serbo-Croatian, too.'

'I picked up a little Russian while we were in Moscow.'

'She's stronger than she looks,' I said.

Miss Challenger and Señorita Rojas looked blank, but Lady Bickle gave a chuckle.

'Very droll,' she said. 'But I'm even more impressed than before. That's quite a list.'

'Don't let Armstrong off the hook,' said Lady Hardcastle. 'She has just as impressive a list and she can speak Welsh as well. At least, I think she can. She might just be clearing her throat.'

I used the beautiful language of the Bards to give my colourfully offensive opinion of this slander of my mother's mother tongue.

'You see?' said Lady Hardcastle. 'Either she just said something frightfully rude or she has a touch of bronchitis. My money's on "rude", I have to say, but one can never be certain.'

'You know me too well,' I said.

Miss Challenger continued to regard us with faint disapproval.

'Do I gather from your visit that you've agreed to help us, my lady?' she said.

'We've certainly agreed to try,' said Lady Hardcastle. 'I fear our reputation for sleuthing might have been slightly exaggerated by the press, but we'll give it our best shot, won't we, Armstrong?'

'We shall,' I said. 'Does Miss Worrel work here in the shop, too?'

'Yes,' said Miss Challenger. 'We open six days a week – half-day closing on Wednesday, of course. We try to make sure there's always two of us here so between me, Lizzie, and Marisol we manage to keep the shop open and still have time for other Union business.'

'It's going to be hard work with Miss Worrel gone,' said Lady Hardcastle. 'Can't any of the other members help?'

'That's the problem with a volunteer organization like ours,' said Lady Bickle. 'Almost everyone has other obligations. We've been jolly lucky so far that the four of us have been able to spare so much time. I'll lend a hand with a few extra hours when I can, of course. One or two tedious committees will have to do without me for the duration, and Lady Hooper's Thursday afternoon bridge game might be shorthanded, but some things are more important. And what we're doing here is just such a thing.'

'Do you think you can get her back to us?' asked Miss Challenger.

'I really can't make any promises,' said Lady Hardcastle. 'But that reputation I pooh-poohed a moment ago might open a few doors. We have a good friend in the Bristol CID, for instance. Inspector Sunderland should be able to help us.'

'I wouldn't bet Lizzie's life on it,' said Miss Challenger. 'The police have all the evidence they need and they've told us outright that they're not going to waste any manpower looking for anyone else.'

'Perhaps,' said Lady Hardcastle. 'But it won't hurt to ask. He's a little less hidebound than your average rozzer. And we have a contact at the *Bristol News*, too.'

'We do?' I said. 'You don't mean . . . ?'

'Dinah Caudle, yes.' She addressed the others. 'We met a rather forthright journalist during all that business last year with the moving picture show. I would be lying to say we were pals . . .'

I raised my eyebrows at this – I would be lying to say I didn't want to slap Dinah Caudle in the chops.

'. . . but I think she's the sort of ambitious young lady who would relish the chance to break the big "The Police Got It Wrong But The *Bristol News* Found The Truth" story. We just need to play her the right way.'

'Well, we're jolly grateful for anything you think you might be able to do,' said Lady Bickle. 'Now, then, would you like another cup of tea?'

'Thank you,' said Lady Hardcastle, 'but I think I'd prefer to get started. Strike while the iron's hot and all that. Every day that poor Lizzie Worrel spends in gaol is a day of her precious life wasted. Do you by any chance have a telephone in the shop? If I might be allowed to call Inspector Sunderland, we could well be able to see him straight away.'

Lady Bickle led Lady Hardcastle through the Door of Mystery. I smiled at Miss Challenger and asked about the 'undergarments'.

Chapter Three

Inspector Sunderland was 'at home to callers', as Lady Hardcastle put it. And so, after offering our new suffragette friends our assurances that we would pursue Lizzie Worrel's case with nothing less than our customary vigour, we returned to Lady Bickle's house to retrieve our driving togs and motor car.

It was Saturday lunchtime and Park Street was alive with shoppers. I eased the little Rover carefully down the steep hill between a great many carts and an even greater number of heedless pedestrians, who crossed the road completely oblivious to the danger posed by our mighty machine. The motor car's wheels slipped more than once in the inevitable consequence of making shop deliveries by horse-drawn wagon, while the tram tracks created their own, less organic, hazard. The tracks did at least guide the way to the Tramways Centre and the Floating Harbour, though, and from there it was a short journey to the Central Police Station, the Bridewell. I parked as close to the main door as I could manage, where we dismounted and tried to make ourselves presentable.

I had visited the Bridewell only a few times before and though all of those visits ultimately involved the convivial company of Inspector Sunderland, still my memories of the place were not entirely positive ones. Before we could gain access to our good friend and his CID colleagues, we first had to pass the arcane tests set by the Gatekeeper, in the person of the desk sergeant. On every occasion upon which I had visited the station, the man on duty had been one of the most disagreeable police sergeants it had been my pleasure to meet in a life filled with police sergeants. As we entered the building through the large front door, I found myself hoping he wasn't on duty.

Of course, he was. He was sitting at a desk behind the counter, writing in a large ledger, and my heart sank to see him. Outwardly he was everyone's idea of a jovial man of middle age – crinkly of eye, stout of stature, and wearing the most impressively bushy beard in which small birds and adorable woodland creatures must surely nest. This apparently blithesome exterior, though, clothed a truculently officious soul with no fondness for his fellow man, whose principal pleasure seemed to derive from being as tiresomely obstructive and awkward as he could possibly manage to be.

He ignored us.

There was a bell on the counter. Lady Hardcastle rang it.

He looked up from his ledger. And then returned to the important task of ignoring us.

Lady Hardcastle cleared her throat.

He shook his head.

'I say, Sergeant,' she said.

He grudgingly looked up.

'I'm reasonably certain we could play this game for quite a while,' she continued, 'but one of us would surely tire of it in the end. My money's on me. Would you be good enough to tell Inspector Sunderland that Lady Hardcastle is here, please?'

'Does this Lady Hardcastle have an appointment?' he said.

'She does, indeed,' she said. 'She telephoned him a short while ago.'

'I see. And you are?'

'I am she.'

'She who?'

'Oh, for heaven's sake.' She turned to me. 'You've been to his office. Do you remember the way?'

'Of course, my lady,' I said.

'Lay on, then, McArmstrong.'

I turned towards the open double doors to our right, which I knew led to the staircase and the offices beyond.

''Ere,' said the sergeant, finally getting up from his desk. 'Where do you think you're going?'

'Run over our conversation in your mind, Sergeant. I think you'll be able to work it out.'

We carried on towards the stairs.

'I am obliged to warn you that you will be under arrest for trespassing on police property if you take one more step towards that staircase.'

We paused and exchanged amused looks. A telephone mounted on the wall beside the sergeant's desk began to ring. He answered it.

'Desk sergeant,' he said. 'Yes . . . Yes, sir . . . She's already here, sir . . . A couple of minutes ago, sir . . . I was just about to . . . Right you are, sir . . . Sorry, sir.'

He returned the telephone earpiece to its cradle.

'The inspector is expecting you,' he said as he resumed his seat. 'He says you know the way to his office.'

We were already through the doors and on the stairs.

'Thank you for your help, Sergeant,' called Lady Hardcastle over her shoulder.

Inspector Sunderland's police-issue desk was piled high with manila folders jostling for space with bundles of loose papers tied together with string or ribbon. A half-drunk cup of tea in a chipped, police-issue cup sat precariously atop a particularly thick pile of documents.

Inspector Sunderland himself sat in a battered, police-issue chair. The chair was upholstered in worn, cracked leather; the inspector was upholstered in a neatly brushed and pressed worsted suit. He clenched his always-unlit briar pipe between his teeth as he finished the minute he had been writing in a file.

He placed the pipe on the only empty space on the desk and stood to greet us. Another ridiculously tall person.

'Lady Hardcastle,' he said with a smile. 'And Miss Armstrong. How wonderful to see you both.'

He reached out and shook us by the hand.

'How do you do, Inspector, dear?' said Lady Hardcastle. She indicated the cluttered desk. 'I do hope we're not interrupting urgent work.'

'Not at all,' he said. 'All this is from one case. Would you believe it? Somewhere in that seemingly impenetrable paper jungle is the evidence we need to convict a nasty little man of fraud, embezzlement, and murder. I just have to find all the pieces.'

'Heavens,' she said. 'Well, we shan't keep you from it for too long, but I would value your help if you can spare us a few moments.'

'For you, my lady, anything. Would you care for some tea? There's almost certainly a pot on the go somewhere. The police force runs on tea.'

'If it's not too much trouble,' she said, 'that would be lovely.'

'Never any trouble for me – I have minions. It's the advantage of being an inspector. Excuse me for just a moment.' He went to the door, where he shouted, 'Smith! Tea for three. My office.'

We heard a faint, 'Yes, sir,' from down the corridor.

'There, you see?' said the inspector. 'No trouble at all.'

He fussed about for a few moments, moving yet more paper from two chairs and placing it on the linoleum-covered floor.

'Please,' he said. 'Have a seat.'

'Thank you,' said Lady Hardcastle. 'I've never been in your lair before. It's cosy.'

'An ill-favoured thing, my lady, but mine own. If I'm promoted to chief inspector, I'll get a piece of carpet.'

'It's nice that they give you something to look forward to.'

The tea arrived. Apparently all the station's cups were chipped.

Once Constable Smith had left, taking the inspector's half-drunk cup and closing the door behind him, Inspector Sunderland settled back in his own chair and resumed the contemplative chewing of his pipe.

'So, then, ladies, what can I do for you?' he said.

'How much do you know about the Thomas Street arson?' said Lady Hardcastle.

'It's been mentioned in briefings. One of my colleagues was the investigating officer, but I'm familiar with the nuts and bolts. What's your interest in the case?'

'We've been asked to look into it.'

'Have you?' he said slowly. 'Have you, indeed? By whom?'

'By Lizzie Worrel's colleagues in the WSPU. They're adamant that she's innocent.'

'I see. You believe them?'

'I'm certainly inclined to give them the benefit of the doubt,' she said. 'The evidence in her favour is . . . well, it's virtually non-existent if I'm honest, but they make a good case for the unlikeliness of her guilt. And the police case is circumstantial, at best.'

'I'd have to agree with you there,' he said. 'Anyone can scatter suffragette leaflets about the place. The shopkeeper was known locally as an anti-suffragist – he had a poster in the window advertising a meeting of the Men's League for Opposing Woman Suffrage – so someone who bore a grudge for any sort of reason could burn the place down, blame the suffragettes, and no one would bat an eyelid. Even the so-called "signed note" is written in block capitals, so it doesn't really prove anything. Added together it presents the semblance of a case, but a half-decent brief could cast "reasonable doubt" in the minds of a reasonable jury.'

'Is that what the investigating officer thinks?'

'He has his own doubts, of course – he's a fine and conscientious officer – but he's been told not to waste any more time on it. We've got our murderer and we should get on with solving other crimes, apparently. For my part I don't rate Miss Worrel's chances of getting a reasonable, impartial jury. Not these days – we're a country divided. I rather fear that a jury of anti-suffragists would be inclined to convict on the flimsiest circumstantial evidence, and it's not at all hard to find a jury of anti-suffragists.'

'I think that's the WSPU's worry in a nutshell.'

'What do they want you to do, exactly?'

'They want us to find out who really set fire to that shop and killed Mr Bakersfield.'

'Brookfield, my lady,' I said.

'Quite so,' she said.

'I see. Well, there's nothing I can do officially, you understand,' said the inspector. 'The mood around here is, shall we say, "unsympathetic" to the suffragette cause. What with that and the certainty among my superiors that we already have the culprit, I need to box clever. But I confess I share your misgivings and I do have my sources, so if I can help in any way on the QT you have only to call. It's probably best that you call me at home, though.'

He wrote a telephone number on the back of one of his official calling cards and handed it to Lady Hardcastle.

'You're very kind,' she said as she put the card into her handbag. 'But we don't want you to get into any trouble with your superiors.'

'What they don't know can't hurt them,' he said. 'I'm not going to be able to do much on your behalf, not without making even more trouble for us all, but I'll do what I can.'

'Thank you, Inspector. You can count on our discretion.'

We spent the rest of our visit to the Bridewell in more cheerful conversation while we finished our tea. We once more accepted the inspector's non-specific invitation to 'Come and dine with us one evening – Mrs Sunderland would love to meet you,' before taking our leave. Sergeant Massive Beard didn't even look up.

We drove back to Clifton and parked on Regent Street so that Lady Hardcastle could have 'a quick look round the shops before we head home'.

Our 'quick look round the shops' lasted two hours. Lady Hardcastle's favourite dressmaker, milliner, and boot maker were graced with our presence and several orders were placed. But it was our final stop just before five o'clock that caused by far the most ooh-ing and ahh-ing on the part of my employer. It was a confectioner's and the poor shopkeeper was run ragged fetching jars from shelves as she indulged her fondness for sweets. Time ticked on, and by the time 'just one more thing' had turned into just ten more things, the poor shopkeeper caught my eye and looked at me imploringly. He was glad of the business, I'm sure, but very obviously wanted to go home to his family and put his feet up after a busy week. He filled what he hoped was the last paper bag with a quarter pound of mint humbugs and I discreetly moved Lady Hardcastle to the door before she could ask for the aniseed twists she had just spotted. The shopkeeper smiled weakly at me and we left him to close up.

'Liquorice?' said Lady Hardcastle, offering me one of the many bags she now carried.

I took the proffered sweet as we walked on.

'Mother didn't approve of sweets,' she said. '"They'll rot your teeth and make you fat, Emily," she used to say.'

'She wasn't wrong,' I said.

'Perhaps not, but all things in moderation.'

I looked pointedly at the bagful of bags she carried and raised my eyebrows.

'There must be nearly five pounds of sweets in there,' I said.

'There must be,' she said, 'and you've left me to carry them on my own.'

'The exercise will do you good after eating all those sweets.'

'I'm sure it will,' she said. 'Barley sugar?'

'No thank you, my lady.'

We reached the motor car and readied ourselves for the journey home.

'I've just realized why I'm tucking into these sweets with such gusto,' said Lady Hardcastle. 'We haven't had any lunch.'

'There hasn't been time,' I said. 'And I'm not sure I could have managed much after Lady Bickle filled us up with sandwiches and cake.'

'Nor could I, I'm sure. But that was six hours ago and I'm starving. Shall we find a smart little dining room?'

'I'm sure there are plenty to choose from,' I said. 'We're in Clifton, after all.'

'We are, we are,' she mused. 'Didn't we pass a fish and chip shop earlier?'

'When?' I asked.

'On our way to the police station. Or on the way back. Tudor-looking place near the Guildhall.'

'I know where you mean,' I said. 'You fancy fish and chips, then?'

'Rather!' she said eagerly. 'I haven't had fish and chips for simply ages. We can eat them from the paper in the motor car. We had them once or twice when I was young, you know. Mother wouldn't let us eat them in the street. She insisted we take them home and put them on china plates.'

'The more I hear about your mother,' I said as I fitted the starting handle into its socket, 'the more I like her. No sweets, and no eating in the street. Would that more people followed her example.'

'Oh, pish and fiddlesticks, you diminutive Welsh killjoy. You and your chapel ways. We shall eat fish and chips in the motor car, with toffee and fudge for pudding. Drive me to the fish shop at once.'

We found the fish and chip shop in a half-timbered building at the bottom of Christmas Steps, exactly where Lady Hardcastle had indicated. And, exactly as she had demanded, we ate our battered hake and chips straight from the newspaper as we sat huddled in the Rover on Lewin's Mead. I confess it was one of the best meals I've ever had.

◆　◆　◆

By the time we returned home, Edna and Miss Jones had gone. While Lady Hardcastle stashed her enormous haul of sweets in her study, I set about relighting the fires and loading up the evening tray with brandy, cheese, and crackers.

She called to me from the study.

'We'll need the crime board, I think,' she said. 'Would you be a poppet and fetch it down from the attic? Set it up in the drawing room for now, please.'

I put down the tray and plodded upstairs to find the large black-board and easel that Lady Hardcastle referred to as her 'crime board'. During her time at university she had become accustomed to sharing her workings with her fellow students on blackboards and it remained her favourite way to puzzle things out.

Once it was set up and we were settled in our comfy chairs with our drinks and cheese, Lady Hardcastle began drawing placeholder sketches of the shop on Thomas Street, the late Mr Christian Brookfield, and the suspect, Lizzie Worrel. As time went on and she saw more places and people connected with the case, she would replace the sketches with more accurate portrayals, but for now she pinned them on the board and began to make notes.

'So far we have a burned shop, a dead man, and the most obvious suspect in the history of crime,' she said. 'It's not much to go on, is it? So what are our immediate problems?'

'We don't know whether Mr Brookfield's death was the reason for the fire or just a tragic consequence,' I said.

'You're right,' she said, making a note on the board. 'It's "felony murder", isn't it? Because Brookfield died in the fire and the fire was arson, it becomes murder – there doesn't actually have to be any intention to kill him. Indeed, I get the impression from all that we've heard so far that no one imagines that the intention was to kill anyone at all. They're all taking the suffragette connection at face value and assuming that Brookfield's death was a tragic accident. But what if someone set the fire knowing he was up there?'

'Did Lizzie Worrel have a motive to kill him?'

'We shall have to dig deeper and find out.'

'This could be our way in,' I said. 'If we can find someone who actually did want to do him in, we'll have our real arsonist.'

'Our real murderer,' she said, making another note. 'What else?'

'Was the fire reported?' I said. 'When? By whom? Did the fire brigade attend? Were there any witnesses? Has anyone been questioned? Were—'

'Steady on, old thing,' said Lady Hardcastle as she hurried to scribble everything on the board. 'Give a girl a chance.'

I let her finish her note making.

'We have quite a few things to ask Inspector Sunderland,' she said. 'I may have to take him up on his offer of private help sooner rather than later. What do you think he and Mrs Sunderland do on a Sunday? Would it be impolite to telephone him, do you think?'

'Give them time to have their lunch,' I said. 'Perhaps in the afternoon? There's nothing he can do about it until he gets to work on Monday, anyway.'

'True, true. You take more notice of the minutiae of the newspapers than I. Do you have any recollection of what Mr Bedingfield—'

'Brookfield, my lady,' I said.

'—any recollection of what Mr Brookfield wrote about? Did his name appear on any juicy articles I might have skimmed over?'

'His name doesn't ring any bells,' I said. 'Perhaps Miss Caudle will be able to tell us more about him.'

'Yes, she may be quite an important contact after all. I just wish I didn't find her so . . .'

'Supercilious?' I suggested. 'Obnoxious? Arrogant?'

She laughed. 'I was going to say "abrasive". She's all those things and more, but she's frightfully good at her job. And I'd rather have her with us than against us. I think we can come to some sort of accommodation.'

'Rather you than me,' I said.

'Well, I'll have a go, at least. If I can't talk her round to our side, you can take her into an alley somewhere and do those mystical things you do to our opponents in alleys.'

'Don't tempt me,' I said.

'Your savage whatnot needs calming, I think,' she said with a gentle laugh. 'Music is the key to that, the poets say. Fetch your banjo, I feel some ragtime coming on.'

◆ ◆ ◆

Newly energized as we were by the arrival on our doorstep of a fresh 'case', Lady Hardcastle and I were a veritable blur of activity on Sunday morning. Breakfast was cooked, served, and eaten in record time and Lady Hardcastle retired at once to her study to clear the decks of correspondence and ready her mind for the labours to come. I'm fairly certain there was something in there about stiffening the sinews and conjuring up the blood, and possibly even something about closing up the walls with our English dead . . . I confess my concentration wanders a little when she comes over all *Henry V*.

I was brushing Gloucestershire from our driving coats at around ten o'clock when the telephone rang.

'Hello.' I said. 'Chipping Bevington two-three.'

'Hello?' said a familiar female voice. 'Armstrong? Is that you? I got it right this time, I'll wager.'

'Good morning, Lady Farley-Stroud,' I said. 'You did.'

The Farley-Strouds were the local 'gentry' and had been our friends since we moved in. That is to say, they had been Lady Hardcastle's friends since we moved in – it had taken them a little longer to accept me as part of the 'team', as it were, but there was mutual friendliness there by now.

'We got a telephone chappie out and he worked some sort of wizardry on the thing. No idea what he did but I can hear everything clear as a bell now. Wonder if he can do the same for my ears, what?'

'I think we could all do with that sometimes,' I said. 'A little tweaking here and there would do us all a bit of good. Would you like me to get Lady Hardcastle for you, my lady?'

'No dear, don't worry about that, just get Lady Hardcastle for me, would you?'

I smiled and put the earpiece down on the table.

'Lady Farley-Stroud on the telephone for you, my lady,' I said, once she'd moved the pile of papers that was blocking the door and let me into the study.

'Oh, how lovely. Did she say what she wanted?'

'No,' I said. 'I decided not to ask. It was difficult enough getting her to ask for you, never mind pressing her for further details.'

'Not to worry,' she said. 'I say, you wouldn't mind sort of . . . tidying up in here a bit, would you? It got away from me, somehow.'

Lady Hardcastle had the keenest mind of anyone I'd ever met. She was charming and funny, and quite the best company. She was kind and thoughtful. But she had to rank high in the list of Most Untidy

Humans Ever To Have Lived. She could make a room untidy without seeming to have done anything at all.

'Very few things would give me greater pleasure,' I said. 'I've been begging to be allowed to tidy this tip for months.'

'Splendid,' she said. 'You make a start on that and I'll see what Gertie wants.'

I'd barely begun to sort through the first pile of assorted papers when she returned.

'Sorry to spoil your fun, dear, but I've invited them round for lunch. I'm going to need you to tell Miss Jones that we're four for lunch if she can stretch things, and then I'll need a little sprucing up. Is my burgundy suit presentable?'

'It is,' I said, 'but the white blouse will need pressing. It's been crushed up in the wardrobe for a while.'

'If you wouldn't mind seeing to all that while I have a quick bath, that would be lovely,' she said, and wafted off.

'I'm going to have to steal young Blodwen Jones away from you, m'dear,' said Lady Farley-Stroud as she tucked into her third helping of roast potatoes. 'Mrs Brown is an extremely capable cook, don't get me wrong, but that young gel has a magical touch. Even a humble roast potato becomes a gastronomic masterpiece in her hands.'

'You'll have to excuse the memsahib,' said Sir Hector with a wink. 'The quack's put her on a new diet. She's been eatin' plain fish, clear broth, and steamed vegetables for a week. Let her loose on a roast dinner and she'll wax rhapsodic for hours.'

Lady Farley-Stroud harrumphed. 'It wouldn't be nearly so hard to bear if my beloved husband would join me.'

'He put you on a diet, my little sugar dumpling, not me. Don't see why I should forsake my steamed puddin' just because you've got a touch of the whatever-it-is. I'll tell you what, though, she's right. This is the best meal I've had in ages. How does she make even simple gravy taste like that?'

'She is, as you suggest, something of a magician,' said Lady Hardcastle. 'I don't like to enquire too deeply, though, in case I spoil it. Although, actually, I'm not sure I'd understand even if I did. The kitchen remains a place of arcane wonder, as far as I'm concerned. Flo, on the other hand . . . Our Flo could actually give Miss Jones for a run for her money. I'm sure you understand her mystical ways, don't you?'

'You flatter me,' I said. 'But you're right, I do understand what she does. I'd never have thought of most of it for myself, I have to say, but once she's shown me, it seems like the only way to do it.'

Everyone chomped in silence for a moment, enjoying the food.

'But enough of all this idle chatter,' said Lady Hardcastle at length. 'You indicated on the telephone that you had news of great import to impart. The fatted calf was slain and the board was made to groan just so that I could hear it. So delay me no more. Let's be having it.'

'Think yourself lucky she's given you this long before she blurts it out,' said Sir Hector.

Lady Farley-Stroud smiled almost girlishly. 'I'm going to be a grand-mama,' she said. 'I received a letter from Clarissa yesterday morning.'

'I say,' said Lady Hardcastle, raising her glass. 'Congratulations. And to you, grandpa.'

'Yes,' I said. 'Congratulations to you both.'

Glasses were clinked.

'Never thought it would happen, to tell the truth,' said Sir Hector. 'Wasn't sure she was the motherin' type. Head full of fluff, that girl, never imagined she'd be capable of bringin' up a child, but I can't pretend not to be pleased.'

'He'd fail if he tried,' said Lady Farley-Stroud. 'We're both thrilled.'

'I'm sure you are,' said Lady Hardcastle.

Clarissa was the Farley-Strouds' only child. We had met her only once, at her engagement party, but when that all went disastrously awry she had returned to London, never to be seen again. We heard through her parents that she had quickly married a more suitable gentleman – Adam Whitman, an engineer.

'Thank you, m'dear,' said Lady Farley-Stroud. 'Can't see the gel, though. We'd love her to come home to have the baby, but young Adam's working for Monsieur Blériot just outside Bordeaux. We'll have a French grandchild.'

'*The* Louis Blériot?' I said. 'We read about his channel crossing last summer.'

'The very same,' said Sir Hector. 'Adam's a bit of a whizz with structural whatnots and materials somethin'-or-other. He'll be helpin' build aeroplanes.'

'How exciting,' I said, quite forgetting for a moment that we were supposed to be talking about babies and not aeroplanes.

'When?' asked Lady Hardcastle, saving me from embarrassing myself by asking more questions about the aeroplane factory.

'When what, dear?' said Lady Farley-Stroud. 'Oh, the baby. July.'

'How wonderful. Will you be visiting her?'

'Of course. We'll take the boat train. Make a holiday of it. We haven't been to France since we were young. Do you remember, Hector?'

'How could I forget, m'dear?' he said. 'Beautiful food, beautiful wine, and my beautiful young wife. Who wouldn't hold those treasured memories forever?'

'Oh, Hector, you do talk such utter tosh,' said Lady Farley-Stroud. 'And at the table, too.' But there was a smile in her voice and a twinkle in her eye. To Lady Hardcastle, she said, 'You haven't forgotten our beano next Saturday, have you?'

'Never, dear,' said Lady Hardcastle. 'Not only is it in the diary, but the invitation stands in pride of place on the mantel as an additional reminder. Best bib and tucker already cleaned and prepared. Dancing shoes brushed.'

'Thank you, dear. It was intended to be "just because" but we're turning it into a bit of a celebration now.'

'I'd not miss it for the world. Now, who's for pudding? Flo, dear, would you do the honours? We really do need to get some bells in here.'

I went to the kitchen to get Edna to help clear the dinner plates and to ask Miss Jones to serve her celebrated *tarte Tatin aux poires*.

Chapter Four

The up-and-at-'em spirit persisted into the next morning and we were on our way back to Clifton bright and early. Lady Hardcastle had telephoned Inspector Sunderland as promised on the previous afternoon and they had arranged to meet discreetly at a coffee house not far from the WSPU shop at eleven o'clock.

'In which case,' she had said after explaining the details of the call to me, 'we can get a head start on the day by calling in at the shop first thing. We don't have anything to tell them yet, but we can at least let them know we're making a start.'

And so, at half past nine on that brisk, sunny Monday morning, we drew up outside the shop and parked the Rover.

'Are you sure it will be all right here?' asked Lady Hardcastle as we began removing our gloves and goggles. 'It's on a bit of a slope.'

'The brake should hold it,' I said. 'And if it doesn't, I shouldn't think it will make it as far as Park Street before it hits something that stops it.'

'You're not nearly so comforting as you think you are, you know. But there's nowhere safer so we'll have to take our chances.'

We entered the shop to find both Beattie Challenger and Lady Bickle behind the counter. They were working as a team, with Miss Challenger folding leaflets and Lady Bickle placing them into envelopes.

'Good morning, ladies,' said Lady Hardcastle. 'How are you both?' They looked up from their campaigning work.

'Emily, dear,' said Lady Bickle. 'How lovely. We weren't expecting you.' She paused. 'Were we?'

'No,' said Lady Hardcastle, 'you've not forgotten anything. We just thought we'd drop in.'

'That's such a relief. I'm not nearly so scatter-brained as people like to imagine, but one never knows. I feel sure I would have remembered that you were visiting, though, so I'm glad I haven't completely lost my marbles. Well, not all of them, at any rate.'

'We've no real news, I'm afraid. Not yet, at least. But I wanted you to know that our friend in the police has offered his support. He's not able to help in an official capacity – he confirmed what you said, that the police have their arsonist and have closed the investigation. And he won't break any confidences – he's a very principled officer and loyal to the Force. But he doesn't like to see an injustice done and he'll steer us in the right direction whenever he can.'

'Oh, that is good news,' said Lady Bickle.

'Sounds like typical police laxity to me,' said Miss Challenger. 'Arrest the first person they find, then put their feet up. Pretending to turn a blind eye while one of their own "helps" a pal is just a way to keep the case tightly shut.'

'I don't think you're being entirely fair, Beattie, dear,' said Lady Bickle. 'It sounds like this Inspector . . . ?'

'Sunderland,' said Lady Hardcastle.

'. . . like this Inspector Sunderland is doing this off his own bat. You make it sound as though they're covering things up.'

'Doesn't it look that way to you?' said Miss Challenger.

'Hardly,' said Lady Bickle. 'You vouch for the integrity of this inspector, Emily?'

'We've known him for almost two years. He's a remarkable man,' said Lady Hardcastle.

'One you said was loyal to the Force,' said Miss Challenger. 'You think he's going to put the rights of a suffragette to a fair trial over the reputation of his beloved police force?'

I was wondering about the best way to give this Beattie Challenger character a good tanning and make it look like an accident. Lady Hardcastle was a good deal more self-possessed.

'I can personally vouch for Inspector Sunderland's integrity and his unshakable belief in justice,' she said evenly. 'He'll be beside us in our search for the truth, no matter where the path takes us, even if it leads to the knowledge that the police have it wrong and Lizzie Worrel is innocent. I should warn you, though, that Armstrong and I will continue to search for the truth even if it means finding that Lizzie Worrel is guilty. We're taking you on trust and we're starting from the assumption that she's not the arsonist, but we'll not conceal the truth to free a guilty woman.'

Miss Challenger glared at us both while Lady Bickle shuffled the pile of envelopes on the counter in front of her. She was about to speak when the shop bell rang behind us. We all turned to see who had saved us from the awkwardness and I was slightly dismayed to see that it was someone who was more than capable of bringing her own supply of awkwardness with her. A woman in an expensively tailored suit, wearing an achingly fashionable hat, and with a leather satchel slung across her shoulder stepped into the small shop.

'Good morning, ladies,' said the visitor. 'I wonder if I might . . . Oh.'

'Don't worry, Miss Caudle,' said Lady Hardcastle. 'My presence often provokes that reaction. And that expression, too. I've come to accept it. How the dickens are you?'

'Quite well, thank you,' said Miss Caudle.

'I'm so sorry, I'm being very remiss – I ought to sort out the intro-ductions. Lady Bickle and Miss Challenger, allow me to introduce Miss Dinah Caudle, a journalist with the *Bristol News*. Miss Caudle, this is

Georgina, Lady Bickle, and Miss Beatrice Challenger of the Bristol branch of the WSPU.'

'Oh,' said Lady Bickle brightly, 'so you're Lady Hardcastle's reporter chum? She mentioned you yesterday.'

'Well, I'd hardly say we were ch—' began Miss Caudle.

But Lady Bickle was oblivious. Or determined not to let another conversation turn unpleasant. 'Haven't I seen you before?' she asked. 'Were you at the Royal Infirmary's Christmas Ball? I'm sure you were. You gave it such a jolly write-up in your newspaper.'

'I was certainly there,' said Miss Caudle. 'My fiancé is training to be a doctor and I thought I'd kill two birds with one st—'

'I knew it,' interrupted Lady Bickle again. 'It's lovely to see you. Welcome to our humble shop. How may we help you?'

'Actually,' said Miss Caudle, still evidently baffled by this good-natured barrage, 'I rather thought I might be able to help you. Or help one of your friends, at least. Is there somewhere we might talk privately?' She eyed Lady Hardcastle and me without affection.

'There's an office upstairs if it's a delicate matter,' said Lady Bickle.

'Delicate? No, I shouldn't say so. But I don't think it would do to be overheard by curious ladies stocking up on ribbons and militant literature.' She looked pointedly at us again.

'Don't mind us,' said Lady Hardcastle cheerily. 'We're just offering a little help of our own. We can wait.'

'You? Help? What sort of help can you offer? You're the ones who fancy yourselves as amateur detectives . . . Oh, no. Not you. You can't be.'

'Can't be what, dear?' asked Lady Hardcastle with a smile.

'I've come to talk about the murder of Christian Brookfield,' said Miss Caudle.

'And what have you come to say?'

'I don't think Elizabeth Worrel was responsible.'

'I think you'd all better come upstairs,' said Lady Bickle. 'I'm afraid we'll have to leave you to contend with the hordes on your own, Beattie.'

Miss Challenger looked out at the tiny handful of people making their way past in the chill morning air.

'I think I can manage,' she said.

◆　◆．◆

There were two doors at the top of the stairs. The one to the left opened into the 'office', which took up more than half of the small upper floor of the building. The windows on the Queen's Road side stretched from floor to ceiling, wall to wall. The centre section of the window was set with a huge semi-circular design at the top, making an archway to frame the art gallery opposite. There was a sizeable oak desk against one wall. It was considerably less cluttered than Inspector Sunderland's had been, as were the filing cabinets and bookshelves that lined the other wall. The third wall, facing the window, was home to a long, battered sofa.

Lady Bickle made herself comfortable in the swivel chair at the desk and waved we other three to the sofa. I sat in the middle, perched on the gap between the two overstuffed cushions.

'I can see that you three have some sort of history,' said Lady Bickle, almost sternly, 'but I'm afraid I really don't care. Miss Caudle, I have asked Lady Hardcastle and Miss Armstrong to investigate the case because I believe Lizzie Worrel to be innocent. If you, too, believe her innocent, then you're going to have to put aside your quarrels – no matter how important they might be to you – and share what you know. A woman's life might be at stake and I don't have the time or the patience for any nonsense.'

'Now, look here,' began Miss Caudle, but Lady Hardcastle raised her hand.

'She's right, Miss Caudle. Whatever grudges you bear us over the "Littleton Cotterell Witch Murders" – or whatever melodramatic name you gave them – can be put aside for the sake of this woman whom everyone but the police believe to be innocent.'

'You damn near ruined my reputation,' snapped Miss Caudle.

'We did nothing but reveal the truth. If your reputation could be ruined by something as banal and commonplace as the truth, then it really wasn't much of a reputation in the first place, now was it?'

'You condescending old—' Miss Caudle made to reach for Lady Hardcastle but I batted her hand away and turned to face her, my own hands relaxed but ready.

'Ladies! Please,' snapped Lady Bickle. 'If you want to fight, you can do it later. I'll even hold your coats. But for now, we're talking about Lizzie Worrel. Miss Caudle, you have information, I believe.'

Miss Caudle lifted her satchel from the floor and unbuckled the flap. She reached inside and pulled out a hardbound octavo notebook with a black cover. She returned the satchel to the floor and sat for a few moments with the book on her lap.

After gathering her thoughts, she said, 'Christian Brookfield was a fine journalist. We were friends, he and I, as well as colleagues. He was a man of principle and honour and he made it his mission in life to expose the venality and avarice he saw all around him in public life. He wasn't interested in gossip and marital scandals – not for their own sake, anyway. He didn't cover murders or sensational burglaries.' She looked once more at Lady Hardcastle and me. 'He wrote about corruption in local government, bribery in local business. He sought out the grubby and the greedy at the heart of our society and he exposed their sordid schemes for all to see. He was not, as you might expect, a popular man among the great and the good of Bristol politics and commerce.'

She picked up the black notebook from her lap and held it in both hands as though it were a precious relic.

'Brookfield was not a man given to melodrama, but neither was he complacent about the possible danger his work might place him in. He sometimes joked that one day someone was going to take umbrage at his prying and do him a mischief. I don't think he seriously believed it, but it was certainly at the back of his mind. And so when he was killed in a fire, apparently the accidental victim of political arson, my first thought was that his lighthearted prediction had actually come true. I never believed the suffragette story – I follow your activities with great interest and I knew it wasn't at all your style. But the police clomped in with their hobnail boots, took one look at the superficial evidence, and declared the case closed.'

She opened the book and looked at one of the pages.

'I was at work when I heard of his death. He was as popular among his fellow journalists as he was unpopular at the council offices, and the older hacks took off at once to the local pub to hold an impromptu wake for their fallen comrade. I, naturally, wasn't invited so I went to his desk to see what he was working on. There was nothing really there – a few scrappy notes and a half-finished article about possible shady dealings at Bristol City Football Club with "nothing there – wishful thinking" scrawled at the bottom in his own hand. Then I looked in his desk drawer, where I found this.'

She held up the black notebook.

'It was where he pulled all his information together before breaking a story. He was always up against very powerful men, so he had to be more than ordinarily certain of his story before he committed it to print. This was where he built his arguments, collated his sources, dotted his i's and crossed his t's. If Lizzie Worrel didn't burn down that shop to further the suffragette cause – and I don't believe she did – then it's possible that someone killed Brookfield deliberately. And if that's the case, then it's more than possible that this book holds the key to that person's identity.'

'May I?' said Lady Bickle, leaning forwards in her chair and reaching for the book. Almost reluctantly, Miss Caudle released it from her grasp and allowed her to take it.

Lady Bickle leafed quickly through a few pages. 'Oh,' she said with some dismay. 'It's written in some sort of hieroglyphics. I'm afraid I can't make head nor tail of it.'

She passed the book to me. 'It's Pitman shorthand,' I said, having looked at a few sample pages myself. 'But it's gibberish.'

I passed it to Lady Hardcastle, who was similarly unable to decipher it.

'You know shorthand?' said Miss Caudle with surprise as she took possession of the notebook once more.

'It came in handy for some work I used to do,' I said.

'And what could a lady's maid possibly do that would require the use of shorthand?'

'Oh, you know,' I said. 'This and that. I'm not at liberty to say more.'

'She's really not,' said Lady Hardcastle. 'Official Secrets Act and all that. You wouldn't want the poor girl hanged for treason.'

'Well . . .' said Miss Caudle.

'We'll have none of that,' cautioned Lady Bickle. 'Play nicely. Now, how is it that you recognize it as being written in this Pitman shorthand but you still can't read it? What's going on?'

'The shapes are definitely Pitman,' I said. 'But they're put together in a way that makes no sense in English. May I?' I gestured to Miss Caudle for the book, which she handed over with some reluctance. 'You see here?' I indicated a line at random. 'These squiggles, swoops, dots, and lines should combine to form ordinary English words – they're like our alphabet, but quicker to write. There are a few shortcuts and some common words and phrases are represented by their own special shapes, but it ought to read just like a line of text written in longhand once you know what to look for. But this says, "Doesn't hit dee ezby yoe weff ticket price." Gibberish, as I said.'

'So you're saying that as well as writing in these arcane scribbles, he also used some manner of code?' asked Lady Bickle.

'Yes, that's it,' I said. 'Or partially it. My guess is that some of it is in a private code where particular words and phrases have special meanings. It's virtually impossible to make sense of that without the key. "Ticket" might mean "potato pie" for all we know, and we'd never

55

guess. But part of it is in some sort of cipher, and they can usually be untangled.'

'So a code is where words stand for other words, and a cipher is where letters or other symbols stand for individual letters?'

'Exactly that,' I said.

'Well, hurrah for me,' said Lady Bickle. 'So you can read shorthand, but how are you with ciphers?'

'I'm afraid I have to defer to Lady Hardcastle on the matter of ciphers,' I said.

'I can have a bash,' said Lady Hardcastle. 'There are some techniques I can use. One's initial thought would be that it would be some sort of simple substitution cipher – a Caesar cipher, for instance – or maybe even a complex one, but the Pitman thing rather scuppers that. Pitman's is a phonetic system – it can best represent sounds we can actually make – so some combinations of letters just don't work and ciphers throw up the most unreadable clumps of letters. That makes an ordinary substitution cipher very difficult. On the other hand, it must have been straightforward enough to Mr Brookfield to encipher it as he went along or it would have made the whole thing more trouble than it was worth.'

'So she's a lady's maid who can read shorthand and is bound by the Official Secrets Act. And you're a dilettante widow who can decipher secret messages,' said Miss Caudle. 'Who *are* you two?'

'I'm afraid the Official Secrets Act rather covers the whole sorry story,' said Lady Hardcastle.

'But do you really think you can make sense of it?' asked Lady Bickle.

'I can but try,' she said. 'That is, if you don't mind, Miss Caudle.'

'Any port in a storm,' said Miss Caudle resignedly.

'Then, if you're agreeable, may I borrow the notebook?'

Miss Caudle bent forwards and reached once more into her satchel.

'I'd rather keep the book safely under my own protection,' she said, and handed over several sheets of foolscap. 'But I've transcribed the first few pages. I'll get to work on the rest.'

'Splendid,' said Lady Hardcastle. She glanced at her wristwatch. 'I say, I'm so terribly sorry,' she said. 'We have another engagement nearby at eleven. Would you mind awfully excusing us?'

'Not at all,' said Lady Bickle. 'We're all terribly grateful that you're able to give us any time at all.' She looked at the papers in Lady Hardcastle's hand. 'Would you like a folder for those? Or an envelope, perhaps?'

'Either would be fine, thank you. I shall contact you directly, Miss Caudle, as soon as I've made any progress. Do you have . . .'

Miss Caudle produced a calling card and Lady Hardcastle exchanged it for one of her own.

'Good luck,' said Lady Bickle. 'And thank you again.'

We saw ourselves out.

◆ ◆ ◆

It was a short walk from the WSPU shop on Queen's Road to a small coffee house in what the locals insisted on calling 'Clifton Village'.

'It's not exactly what I'd call a village,' I said as we walked along the busy suburban street.

'No, nor would I,' said Lady Hardcastle. 'But they're not alone. Kensington has a village, after all.'

'Pfft,' I said. 'They'd all have a purple fit if they had to live in a real village. No gas, certainly no electricity, pubs that can't serve pies because a wagon lost a wheel.'

'Do you regret moving to Littleton Cotterell?'

'Actually, no, I really rather like it. I'd kill for electric lights and a gas stove, of course. Although with Miss Jones doing almost all the cooking, the range isn't as much of an inconvenience as it might be.'

'They have electric lights at The Grange,' she said. 'I wonder if their generator could power our little house as well. I'm sure I read an article about transmitting electrical power over long distances. I'll have to ask around. I must surely be acquainted with someone who would know.'

'You surely must,' I said. 'Is this it?'

'Is which what, dear?'

'Is this the coffee house where we're to meet Inspector Sunderland?' I asked, indicating the branch of Crane's Coffee a few yards ahead.

'If it wasn't,' she said, 'it is now.'

I looked at her enquiringly.

'Over the road,' she said, and tilted her head towards the opposite side of the street.

I looked across the road and saw the tall figure of our favourite policeman in bowler hat and overcoat. He was carrying a briefcase, which he raised in salute as he stepped off the pavement. He caught up with us and tipped his bowler hat with his free hand.

'Good morning, ladies,' he said. 'Perfect timing. Shall we?' He opened the coffee house door and entered. We followed him in.

Once we were settled with coffee and buns, the inspector reached into his briefcase and pulled out a manila folder. He passed it across the table to us.

'I'm afraid I can't let you keep that,' he said, 'but I've made a note of the pertinent details for you.' He passed us a sheet of handwritten foolscap.

'I say, Inspector,' said Lady Hardcastle. 'Thank you so very much.' She began to leaf through the file. 'Splendid,' she said. 'There's some background on Mr Brookfield, too. So far he's just been a name, a set of high moral principles, and a notebook.'

'I'm not with you, I'm afraid,' said the inspector.

Lady Hardcastle quickly became engrossed in the file so I told him about our recent meeting with Dinah Caudle.

'Ah, I see,' he said. 'I only met him a few times but I certainly knew him by reputation. We always kept an eye on his pieces in the newspaper and he was a witness in a fraud trial a year or two back. He was younger than I'd imagined from his writing – mid-twenties—'

'Twenty-seven,' interrupted Lady Hardcastle.

'So, in his mid-twenties when I met him,' said the inspector with a smile. 'He was a pleasant enough fellow but he was every bit as serious and . . . and as earnest as you might expect someone like that to be. I liked him well enough, I must say, but I found his company a little hard work after a while. I don't think I ever heard him say anything deliberately funny. Polite, honest, and charming in his own way, but not given to jocular remarks or humorous observations on the absurdities of life.'

'Perhaps he was intimidated by rozzers,' I suggested. 'Maybe he just minded his Ps and Qs when he was with you lot.'

'You might be right,' he said. 'Some people, at least, have a sense of propriety and respect in the presence of officers of the law.'

Lady Hardcastle stuck her tongue out, but carried on reading. It was obvious she wasn't in a hurry to share what she was learning from the file so I decided to ask the inspector directly.

'Did he have any family?' I asked.

'Parents both deceased,' he said. 'There's an aunt in Gloucester but they weren't close and she declined to come to the funeral. There's an older brother in the Merchant Navy and a younger sister working as a nurse at the Royal United Hospital in Bath. The brother is at sea but the sister came to the funeral on Friday. She was rather cut up.'

'I can imagine. You were there, then?' I asked.

'I was. As I say, I'd only met the man briefly but I felt I knew him better than I really did. From his writing, you understand. A few of us who'd had dealings with him went along to pay our respects.'

'Was it well attended?'

'The church was packed,' he said. 'He was a well-liked young man, as it turns out.'

'That must have been some comfort for his poor sister, at least,' I said. 'So what exactly happened on Tuesday night? The newspaper report was light on details.'

'Well,' he said, 'the lads at the Bristol Police Fire Brigade were called to a fire at a shop on Thomas Street not long before midnight. By the time they got there, the whole place had gone up but the local residents were quick thinking enough to douse the neighbouring buildings to stop the fire spreading. The customers from the Court Sampson Inn next door lent a hand, and the fire brigade lads did their best, but the shop was lost and, as it turned out, so was the one man inside.'

'Horrible,' I said. 'Did anyone know at the time that he was in there? Did anyone say anything?'

'No, not a word. The building wasn't searched properly until the next day – it wasn't considered safe to go in there until mid-morning on Wednesday. That's when they found the body.'

'But there were plenty of witnesses to the fire itself?'

'Dozens,' he said. 'It's a popular pub, even on a Tuesday evening. Our lads were there pretty sharpish once the fire brigade boys were called out and they interviewed everyone there and then. But none of them saw anything until the fire had well and truly taken hold. None of them saw anyone or anything suspicious until one of them—'

'Bill Priddy,' said Lady Hardcastle without looking up.

'Until Bill Priddy left to walk home at about a quarter to midnight and saw the flames. He ran straight back into the Court Sampson and raised the alarm.'

'Everyone who had either helped or remained in the pub was questioned,' I said. 'Did anyone think to ask if that was everyone who was there? Might anyone have slipped away unnoticed? Not everyone wants to help put out a blaze or get caught up making witness statements in the middle of the night.'

'We could have done with you down there on Tuesday night,' said the inspector. 'I asked the same question and got a load of mumbling equivocation for my pains. The short answer is, no, no one thought of that at the time. It's more than possible that any number of people could have slipped out into the night to avoid either the danger and hard work of helping or the inconvenience of being called as a witness.'

'That's disappointing.'

'A few of the pavement pounders down at the Bridewell might have that inscribed as a motto on their helmet badges,' he said. '"Bristol Police Force – That's Disappointing". Still, there's nothing to be done now – we just have to work with what information we have.'

I smiled. 'How was the fire started?' I asked.

'They smashed the shop window and threw in a bundle of paraffin-soaked rags. One match and the whole place went up pretty quickly. They're old buildings down there. Plenty of old, dry timbers.'

'You'd have thought someone would have heard that. Or seen it. It would have taken a minute or two to get all that done.'

'Everyone was in bed or in the pub,' he said. 'There are no "passers-by" at that time of night. Not down on Thomas Street, at any rate.'

'And there were suffragette leaflets strewn about the place,' I said. 'The newspaper reported that much.'

'Just so,' said the inspector. 'I did note one strange thing that no one else picked up on. The leaflets proclaimed themselves to be the work of the "Woman Social and Political Union", rather than "Women's". An easy mistake to make on the part of a printer, I suppose, but odd that no one spotted it on a campaign leaflet.'

'Perhaps it was too late to change it,' I said.

'Perhaps. Then there was the "signed note" pinned to a nearby shop door, written in block capitals, as I said before.'

'When was Lizzie Worrel arrested?'

'The next day. We had no record of an E Worrel, and it took a trip to the WSPU shop on Queen's Road first thing on Wednesday morning to find out who she was. She was arrested there and then.'

Lady Hardcastle handed the file back to the inspector. 'They did a very thorough and very professional job,' she said. 'Witnesses were found and interviewed, statements collated, evidence collected. The only accusation that can be levelled at your colleagues is that they didn't trouble to look into the veracity of the so-called confession.'

'That was going to be my next question, actually,' I said. 'They suppose that Lizzie Worrel was so keen to claim responsibility for the arson on behalf of the suffragettes that she left a signed confession at the scene of the crime. But why has she so vehemently denied it ever since?'

'Because when she set the fire it was just arson, but by the time she was arrested it was murder?' suggested Lady Hardcastle.

'I thought that,' said the inspector, 'so I checked the times. The body wasn't discovered until after Lizzie Worrel had been arrested. All anyone knew at the time was that it was arson.'

'And it never occurred to anyone to wonder why someone who was a member of an organization that thrives on being arrested and imprisoned would set a fire, leave self-incriminating evidence, and then deny it nine hours later,' I said.

'I share your doubts,' said the inspector. 'I really do.'

◆ ◆ ◆

With our coffees finished and our cakes eaten, we left the inspector to his official duties and returned to the Rover. To Lady Hardcastle's relief, it hadn't rolled down towards Park Street, and I set about starting the engine while she made herself comfortable in the driving seat.

'My turn to drive, I think,' she said.

I reluctantly conceded that it was, and enjoyed the uneventful ride back to Littleton Cotterell. Once home, I checked with Edna that there were no domestic crises brewing, and with Miss Jones that there was some dinner cooking. Both assured me that everything was in hand and Miss Jones had even made some soup for lunch.

'I didn't know if you'd be eatin' in town, but I thought soup would keep even if you didn't have it today.'

'You're a marvel,' I said. 'Thank you. Have you and Edna eaten?'

'We have, thank you, miss. Edna don't let it go past midday without botherin' me for sommat to eat.'

'Thank you for looking after her,' I said with a smile. 'How's your real mother these days?'

'She's fine, thank you. She'll outlast us all, despite her problems.'

'I'm sure she will. She's a remarkable woman – do give her my regards, won't you.'

'And mine,' said Lady Hardcastle, who had arrived unseen and unannounced.

'Thank you both,' said Miss Jones.

'Sorry to barge in on you,' said Lady Hardcastle. 'I was wondering if there was anything to eat.'

'I was just tellin' Miss Armstrong as how there's some soup.'

'Really? Splendidly wonderful. I'll be in the dining room, salivating.'

'You paint such an attractive picture,' I said. 'Give us a minute or two and I'll bring it through. Bread?'

She was already out the door. 'Yes, please,' she called from the hall. 'And a cloth for the dribble.'

◆ ◆ ◆

Lunch passed in a blur of slurping, interrupted briefly by our recounting of the details of the morning's meetings. Satisfied that our recollections tallied and that we agreed on the facts of the case so far, I was despatched to the drawing room to update the crime board while Lady Hardcastle withdrew to her study to ponder the puzzle of Brookfield's notebook.

I started a 'timeline' on the crime board – something Lady Hardcastle had used to great effect while we were trying to find out who had killed Frank Pickering when we first arrived in the village.

We knew that a regular at the pub, Bill Priddy, had left to walk home at about a quarter to midnight. The fire was already well established so it must have been started anything up to half an hour earlier. I put the time at a quarter past eleven until we knew any different. The fire brigade and the police arrived promptly once they'd been summoned so I put their arrival at no later than a quarter past midnight. All the witnesses who could be found were questioned by, I guessed, one o'clock.

Nothing had happened then until the investigating detective had called at the WSPU shop when it opened at nine o'clock. He arrested Lizzie Worrel immediately. By 'mid-morning' the burned-out building had been searched so I put that at eleven o'clock.

So far, that was all we knew.

I put Christian Brookfield's age and family details next to his placeholder sketch and sat in an armchair to contemplate the case so far. And, so far, there wasn't one. I was about to get up and see if Lady Hardcastle had made any progress when she burst in through the door.

'Eureka!' she exclaimed.

'You can get a bit whiffy yourself on a warm day,' I said.

'Very droll,' she said. 'But shush, I think I've found a way into Brookfield's code. It's childishly simple, really. I half thought it might be, though. It had to be, didn't it? The idea was to make his notes difficult for someone else to read, but the encryption method still had to be straightforward enough that he didn't have to spend all night encoding everything. He also had to be able to read it himself without too much effort. I've been all round the houses trying all manner of complex stratagems. But really it was staring me in the face all along. I had the answer myself when we were talking to Georgie and the Caudle woman, but I was too wrapped up in the imagined complexities to see it.'

She stood in front of me, silently grinning.

'Well?' I said, when it became apparent that there was nothing else on its way.

'What? Oh, yes. The solution. Let's take that bit you read out at the shop.'

She went to the blackboard and wrote, 'Doesn't hit / dee ezby yoe weff / ticket price.'

'Now, when I was explaining things to Georgie – she's a lovely girl, don't you think? A good deal younger than one might expect for an eminent surgeon's wife, but so sharp.'

I smiled and nodded. 'A charming young woman,' I said.

'Ah, yes, sorry, I was talking about the code, wasn't I?' She stood by the board, pointing to her recent scribblings like a schoolmistress. 'So, you can see that the segment you pointed out is two plaintext words, a section of gibberish, and then two more ordinary English words. The gibberish is probably the cipher, but the letter frequencies are all wrong. I couldn't make any sense of it until I was musing on my earlier explanation. Pitman's, I said, is phonetic. And what do you get if you say that section out loud?'

'Dee ezby yoe weff,' I said. 'Ohhhh. D-S-B-O-F.'

'Quite so. And that turns out to be a simple Caesar cipher, a substitution cipher – the sort a busy journalist could do in his head as he went along – for C-R-A-N-E. You see? Just shifting each letter one along.' She wrote 'Crane' underneath the section of gibberish.

'That's rather clever,' I said. 'And it meets all your requirements – he can write it quickly and read it back without getting a notepad out. What about the other parts?'

'They're a little trickier. Or a little easier, depending on your point of view. They're word puzzles. I posited that a journalist like Brookfield must have a facility with words and language. There was a possibility, I thought, that he might be a little bit playful with it – his reported lack of a sense of humour notwithstanding. So, take these first two words: "Doesn't hit". What happens if something doesn't hit?'

'It misses?' I suggested.

'I say, you're much quicker at this than I am. Yes, let's try "Misses".' She wrote the word beneath the 'clue'. 'Now what about the ticket price?'

'Tickets,' I said. 'Tickets . . . Theatre tickets? Bus tickets? Train tickets? Ticket price . . . Cost of admission? The fare?'

'I should have come out here earlier. Let's try "A Fare".' She wrote it down. The line beneath the code now read, 'Misses Crane A Fare.'

'Missus Crane Affair?' I said.

'Without the rest of the entry, it wasn't possible to say for sure, but once you have the context it turns out that that's exactly it. He has quite a bit of evidence in this section about Mrs Crane having an illicit liaison with a man, but sadly he hadn't quite worked out who before he put this bit down on paper. We need more of the notebook.'

'Does it say who this Mrs Crane is?' I asked. 'Might she have wanted to silence him? Or might Mr Crane have feared for his own reputation?'

'Yes, no, and yes. In that order. He makes it plain that the Mr Crane whose wife is out enjoying convivial society with someone other than her husband is the same Crane who owns the coffee-importing business and several coffee houses in the city. One of which, quite by coincidence, we visited this morning. Brookfield suggests in his notes that the scandal, if it broke, would do Mrs Crane little harm but could ruin Oswald Crane. He has, by all accounts, been quite vocal on the subject of marital fidelity and has said that husbands should take the blame if their wives stray.'

'We need to speak to this Oswald Crane chap, then,' I said.

'We do, indeed. Miss Caudle will have to arrange a meeting. I shall telephone her immediately.'

Chapter Five

It took Dinah Caudle just two days to arrange a meeting with Mr Oswald Crane on Thursday morning on the pretext that she wished to write an article about him. So that Lady Hardcastle and I could also attend, she had asked if she could bring her trainee along. He had been reluctant at first until she explained that her 'trainee' was a titled lady 'of middle years' who wished to contribute to the society pages. He had practically fallen over himself to accommodate us once he believed he might be mentioned in the society pages.

'Luckily,' said Lady Hardcastle as we walked along High Street towards our meeting place on Corn Street, 'one can almost always rely on the snobbery of businessmen. They'll do anything to be thought of as part of the smart set.'

'I've seen the smart set at close quarters,' I said. 'I'd rather be associated with cutthroats and streetwalkers any day. Present company excepted, naturally.'

'Naturally,' she said. 'And I can't say I disagree with you, but for today we need to play up to it. I shall be quite the glamourousest, dizziest member of the smart set, and his key to the sort of social recognition he's always thought was his due.'

'Glamourousest?' I said.

'Shush. Did we give you a name?'

We considered that there was a small risk of Lady Hardcastle's name being recognized. She wasn't vain enough to imagine that everyone had heard of her, but she had been mentioned in several newspaper stories over the past two years so her name might ring bells. Consequently, we had decided that she would be Lady Summerford for the day. I hadn't anticipated being introduced by name so I'd not troubled to come up with an alias.

'We didn't,' I said. 'I'm just a 'umble servant girl. We couldn't afford names when I was growin' up. I'm still savin' up for a name of me own.'

'You shall be Nelly Maybee,' she said. 'With two e's.'

'It has possibilities,' I said. 'You rescued me from a life of petty crime in the Cardiff slums. Oh, oh, with hints that I might not have been quite so morally upstanding as a young woman ought to be.'

She simply tutted. We'd played cloak-and-dagger roles many times before in far more dangerous situations than this and she knew me well enough to know that I'd not risk ruining the subterfuge by overdoing things. On this occasion, though, I suspected that a snob like Crane would affect not even to notice me, so I thought I could afford to have a little fun with my character's history. I'd be the only one who'd know, after all.

I had expected our meeting to be held in an ornately oak-panelled boardroom in a grand building in the heart of the business district of the city. There would be portraits of past chairmen on the walls, looking sternly and disapprovingly down at us as we sat at a gleaming mahogany table. I was disappointed, then, when I was told that we were to meet Mr Crane in one of his coffee houses. His first, admittedly, and the jewel of his coffee house empire, but a coffee house all the same.

Dinah Caudle was already seated in the company of a small, spherical gentleman when we arrived. She acknowledged Lady Hardcastle and the man leapt to his feet. It didn't make him much taller.

'Lady Summerford, I presume,' he said. His manner was as puffed up as the absurd moustache that graced his upper lip.

'Lady Summerford,' said Miss Caudle, 'please allow me to introduce Mr Oswald Crane, coffee importer and owner of this magnificent shop. Mr Crane, this is Lady Summerford, the newest freelance writer for the society pages at the *Bristol News*.'

'How do you do?' they both said together.

Mr Crane ostentatiously held a chair for 'Lady Summerford' and, just as ostentatiously, ignored me. I sat at a table nearby, close enough to overhear and far enough away to be forgotten about. I had a book with me which I pretended to read, while earwigging their conversation and embellishing Nelly Maybee's story.

It was a good thing I had something to keep my mind occupied – Mr Crane's dreary conversation did little to hold my attention. He was both a bore and a boor. He was uncommonly well informed on the subject of the cultivation, harvesting, shipping, roasting, distribution, and preparation of coffee. He knew, too, about its advertising and packaging, having recently acquired a printing business for those very purposes.

I knew all this because he was willing to share his knowledge at dismaying length without the faintest awareness of just how dull he was being. This wouldn't have been so bad – enthusiasts can often be charming and fascinating once they warm to their subject – were it not also for his tendency towards the sort of opinionated oafishness that made it fortunate that none of us was armed.

At least, I didn't think Lady Hardcastle was armed. She wasn't wearing the holster hat I'd bought her for Christmas, which had a cunningly concealed compartment in the crown into which a derringer pistol would snugly fit – she'd made a joke about such an item of headwear a while ago, so I thought it would be amusing, and possibly useful, if she were actually to have one. But she did have an alarming tendency to slip her Browning pocket pistol into her handbag 'because one never knows when it might come in useful', so it was impossible to be certain that she was unarmed. Mr Crane's comments about the locals who grew his coffee in Africa and the Americas, his opinions on the poor and needy at home, and most especially his views on women and their role in society, would surely have spelled his doom if she had been. I confess I felt my own sleeve once or twice in case I'd slipped a throwing knife in there and forgotten about it.

Lady Hardcastle managed to appear as though she were hanging on his every word. She had emulated Miss Caudle and was taking copious notes as he spoke.

'. . . and that's another reason women shouldn't be given the vote,' he said, interrupting my daydreams about Nelly Maybee's fledgling career as a pickpocket. 'Too much intuition, d'you see? It's all very well and good having instincts and intuition if you're raising children or managing a household. Those are admirable traits in those circumstances. But politics, just like business, is about sound judgement, it's about pushing aside feelings and fancies and replacing them with reason. I'm afraid women just don't have the capacity for unsentimental, logical thought.'

Miss Caudle had been scowling but, to her immense credit, managed to rearrange her features into a simpering smile by the time he glanced in her direction.

'You're quite right,' she said. 'Women just aren't up to it. I think it would be catastrophic for the country if we got the vote. What do I know about international affairs, after all?'

Lady Hardcastle, meanwhile, seemed to have grown weary of indulging him and proceeded instead to the real reason for the interview.

'Did you hear about the fire last week, down on Thomas Street?' she said.

'I did. Terrible business. Wasn't it one of your chaps who died?'

'It was,' she said. 'Christian Brookfield.'

'Terrible. Terrible. It was a suffragette who set the fire, wasn't it? Which rather proves my point, don't you think? Too much emotion swirling around in a woman's brain. Not enough reason. No thought for the consequences of her actions, d'you see? A man died all because she wanted to get some attention for her "cause".'

'Did you know Christian Brookfield?' said Lady Hardcastle, ignoring these last remarks.

'No, I can't say as I did.'

'Odd that,' she said. 'He knew you. Or knew of you, at any rate.'

'Lots of people know of me, my dear. I have coffee houses all over the city.' He waved his arms expansively to indicate the extent of his magnificent empire.

'Perhaps that explains it. But he knew of your wife, too.'

'Again, lots of people know of my charming lady wife,' he said, slightly less comfortably.

To judge from Miss Caudle's expression, she wasn't too happy with the direction the conversation was going, either. She tried to change tack.

'What are your views on the growing importance of the docks at Avonmouth?' she asked hurriedly. 'Is it a boon to your business to be able to dock larger ships, or is the distance from the city too much of an inconvenience?'

'Well, I have to say—' he began, but Lady Hardcastle wasn't to be put off.

'You see,' she said, looking down at her notebook as though for confirmation, 'Mr Brookfield was working on a story that would reveal that your charming lady wife was having . . . "intimate relations" is the polite phrase, I believe. Yes, intimate relations with someone who most definitely, without wishing to put too fine a point on it, wasn't you. Do you have a statement for the press?'

In the silence that followed, I began to be concerned that Mr Crane might be the one to draw a pistol. His face went an entertaining shade of purple – the first genuinely interesting thing he had done all morning – and his knuckles were white as he grasped the edge of the table.

'This interview is over,' he said through gritted teeth. 'Miss Caudle, get this woman out of my shop. I shall be having words with your editor.'

Miss Caudle stood, but Lady Hardcastle remained seated. 'So you didn't kill him, then? To kill the story? Or maybe you hired someone to do it for you?'

'Out!' he bellowed, his composure finally deserting him.

Trying not to laugh, I followed her out of the shop, protecting her back lest he decide to lash out. The few other customers looked on in scandalized shock or unabashed curiosity, according to their character. The staff cowered in the background, clearly worried that the managing director might take out his anger upon them.

Outside on the pavement, Miss Caudle was equally livid.

'What on earth did you do that for?' she demanded.

'Do what, dear?' said Lady Hardcastle.

'You know perfectly well what. We'll never get the truth out of him now. We'll be lucky if he doesn't sue us for slander.'

'Sue *me*, dear. You were a model of journalistic professionalism – I was the one who levelled baseless and defamatory accusations of wrongdoing.'

Miss Caudle seemed unimpressed, but said nothing.

'I understand that in your line of work it never pays to unnerve people so much that they put up the shutters and stop talking to you,' continued Lady Hardcastle. 'I see the need for blandishments and charm, for lulling them into trusting you and then revealing that which they might otherwise have preferred to keep hidden. But my own experience – and I'm afraid it's extensive and often disagreeable experience – is that murderers aren't nearly so susceptible to flattery. Sometimes the only way to get results is to poke the hornets' nest with a good, stout stick and see what happens.'

'What happens,' said Miss Caudle, 'is that you get badly stung by a gang of extremely angry hornets.'

'Perhaps, dear, but that's a risk we take. The positive thing – from our point of view, at least – is that angry people make mistakes. If you rattle a guilty man, especially a man like Crane, he's liable to flap about in a panic and try to cover his tracks. That's when you can catch him out.'

'A man like Crane?'

'A man like Crane,' said Lady Hardcastle. 'He likes to paint himself as a captain of industry – or a captain of commerce, at any rate – but in reality he's a tedious little man obsessed with coffee. He's all fuss and bluster and he could no more cause trouble for you or me than he could flap his arms and fly to the Americas to check on his precious plantations.'

Miss Caudle had calmed slightly and took a moment to consider Lady Hardcastle's words.

'I reluctantly concede,' she said at length, 'that you might very well have a point. I've done some research of my own and your past exploits as an "agent of the Crown" aren't nearly so hush-hush as you tried to make out. At least, you've been a good deal freer with your stories when talking to other people than you were with me. I bow to your superior knowledge of the behaviour of criminal types. And your assessment of Mr Crane is pretty accurate, too – a tedious little man, indeed. But if you're going to do anything like that again, do please let me know in advance.'

'Right you are, dear,' said Lady Hardcastle brightly. 'Would you care for some lunch?'

'I'd say that was the least you could do,' said Miss Caudle. 'Come on, I know just the spot. I hope you brought plenty of money.'

Miss Caudle's chosen luncheon venue was the same Bristol hotel recommended to us by Lady Farley-Stroud when we had first moved to the West Country. The head waiter made a fuss of pretending to remember Lady Hardcastle rather better than he actually did, and showed us to a table near a large window, from where I was able to watch the city passing by.

'So, tell me, Miss Caudle,' said Lady Hardcastle once we were all seated, 'how did you come to inhabit the murky world of journalism?'

Miss Caudle regarded her coolly for a moment, as though trying to decide whether to engage in such personal chit-chat with a comparative stranger.

'I'm the youngest of four, and the only girl. You know how it goes: eldest son inherits, second son goes into the army, third son the clergy, and any stray daughters you happen to have lying around get married off as soon as possible, preferably to someone else's eldest son so you don't have to pay for her upkeep.'

'And you didn't fancy that?'

'I should say not. So I struck a bargain with them. If I could support myself, they were to stop nagging at me to marry the first chinless oaf who came along, and leave me to make my own choices.'

'How did they react to that?'

'Papa laughed in my face and Mama wept real tears for her lost daughter. So I told them what they could do to themselves – with suggestions as to the appropriate and most effective implements – and set off to the city to seek my fortune.'

'That's the spirit,' said Lady Hardcastle. 'But why the newspapers?'

'I was working as a waitress – here as a matter of fact – and sharing digs with a girl who was a secretary at the *Bristol News*. One day she told me that they were looking for someone to cover "society things". They wanted someone who spoke the language, was acquainted with a few of the right people, and would know what shoes to wear while interviewing a duchess. To cut a tedious story frustratingly short, I got the job.'

'And your parents?'

'Are mortified, yes. Things haven't gone quite so well as they'd hoped with the others, either, it should be noted. Brother Number One is a gullible drunk who managed to lose an absolute packet on some stupidly ill-advised investments. Brother Number Two was cashiered shortly after Spion Kop for "reasons we don't talk about" and is now an assistant bank manager somewhere dreary. Brother Number Three has been posted to a mission in Burma after he was caught carrying on with the wife of the chairman of the parish council. There was also talk of him pinching money from the collection plate, but they couldn't prove it. One would think that my own life being entirely free of scandal would be cause for celebration, but apparently nothing brings more shame on a family than one's twenty-seven-year-old spinster daughter working at a "trade".'

'You seem to be making a go of it, though,' said Lady Hardcastle. 'What is it they say? "Living well is the best revenge." You made a splendid job of covering our moving picture whatnot and the attendant unpleasantness last year, after all. It's not as though you're stuck on the society column.'

'Indeed, no. I try to involve myself in more serious stories whenever I can. It has been pointed out to me that kinematograph films and music hall performances are no more "serious" than the lives and loves of the landed gentry, but I stand firm in my belief that they're both of a great deal more interest to a great many more people. And if I can report the arrest and trial of Brookfield's real killer, they'll have to take notice of me.'

'It seems our short-term ambitions are aligned, then,' said Lady Hardcastle. 'We wish to get to the bottom of all this, too. Shall we be able to form an alliance, do you think? Reach some sort of accord?'

'We two?' said Miss Caudle with a snort that bordered on the derisive. 'Working together?'

'We three, dear,' said Lady Hardcastle. 'Armstrong and I come as a set.'

Miss Caudle looked at me appraisingly. 'Ah, yes, the redoubtable Florence Armstrong. You get fewer mentions in the cuttings, but you're an ever-present figure in the background. I'm still not entirely clear on what your role is, but I'm sure you'll come in handy if one of us needs anything mended.'

I took another bite of my pheasant but said nothing.

'You'll know when you need her,' said Lady Hardcastle, 'and when you do, you'll be glad she was there. For now, I take it you're willing to transcribe and translate Mr Brookfield's notebook? We shall take care of the legwork. I think we've established our credentials in that regard.'

'You certainly know how to needle people, there's no doubt about that. Then again, from the little I know about you I imagine you would have been imprisoned, hanged, or left dead in an alley if you didn't possess certain abilities. How many of the stories about you are true?'

'I don't know which ones you've heard, but I should say no more than half.'

'You owe me more of an answer than that,' said Miss Caudle. 'I've laid my family's shame bare, the least you can do is fill in a little background.'

'Perhaps you're right. Well, now. My late husband was a diplomat, and I worked alongside him as a . . . well, as a spy, I suppose one could say. He was the respectable face of British international relations and I poked around in dark corners for the information our enemies would rather keep to themselves. Our friends, too, on more than one occasion. I needed an assistant, so I recruited my lady's maid. That's the heart of it.'

'When did your husband die?' said Miss Caudle. 'Forgive me for being so blunt.'

'In ninety-nine, in Shanghai. He was murdered by a German agent who thought he was the spy. Armstrong and I fled inland and crossed China on foot. We met a Shaolin monk on the way, who taught Armstrong some impressive fighting skills to go with her knife-throwing prowess – her father was a circus performer, you know. We found our way to Burma, bartered some of our few remaining possessions for a boat, and sailed down the Irrawaddy to Rangoon. From there, a boat to Calcutta, where we landed in, what, spring 1901?'

'1901,' I confirmed.

'Quite so,' said Lady Hardcastle. 'The queen had passed not long before and we found ourselves agents of the new king. We stayed in India for another two years, working on this and that with an old friend of mine, Major George Dawlish. Lovely chap. Family friend. I'd known him since we were children.'

'What sort of work were you engaged in?' asked Miss Caudle, her journalistic instincts awakened.

'Oh, you know, "this and that", as I said. We unmasked a South American merchant as a saboteur – The Poisoned Banana Tree Affair, I think the press called that one.'

I nodded in confirmation.

'We foiled the attempted assassination of a minor member of the Russian royal family who was visiting Calcutta. That was terribly exciting and all very last minute. By the time we worked out what the plot entailed, the assassin was already on top of a building with a high-powered air rifle pointed at the spot where the carriage was due to stop. I couldn't get a clear shot at him so it was left to Armstrong to sprint up a staircase and tackle him in person. You got him with a knife, didn't you, dear?'

'From ten yards,' I said. 'Back of the neck. Died instantly.'

Dinah Caudle smiled uneasily, and I hoped she was beginning to regret her 'if we need anything mending' comment.

'What else did we do there?' asked Lady Hardcastle.

'There was that Austro-Hungarian spy who tried to steal those military plans from the Governor General's offices,' I said.

'Oh, yes, "Der Mungo" he called himself – "The Mongoose".'

'He left empty handed,' I said.

'In more ways than one, as I recall. He left India without the papers and with two fewer fingers than he had arrived with. So that was India. We came home in 1903 and based ourselves in London. We carried on in the same line of work, but after another five years of people shooting at us and trying to strangle us in the dark – well, trying to strangle me, at any rate; I don't think anyone managed to get the drop on Armstrong – I decided enough was enough and we decamped to Gloucestershire. The rest, I think, you know.'

'If even half of that is true, I'd be a fool not to enlist your help,' said Miss Caudle. 'And that's before I add half the other things I've heard.'

'An equal partnership, then,' said Lady Hardcastle. 'We share all our intelligence, and work together to free Lizzie Worrel and see the real murderer convicted.'

'Always assuming Lizzie Worrel actually is innocent,' I added.

'Of course,' they both said together.

'To justice,' said Lady Hardcastle, raising her glass.

'And votes for women,' I said.

'And pudding,' said Miss Caudle, raising her own glass. 'I happen to know they do a rather splendid jam roly-poly. With custard.'

'Three of those, then, please,' said Lady Hardcastle to a passing waiter.

◆ ◆ ◆

We left Miss Caudle to get back to her vital work documenting the lives of the well-to-do, and returned to the Rover. The motor car started first time and I walked round to the driver's side.

'I only had one glass of wine,' complained Lady Hardcastle as I gave her my hardest stare and ordered her out of the driving seat.

'You and Miss Caudle shared the best part of two bottles,' I said. 'And we agreed that we don't drive if we've been drinking. Remember Sir Hector's story about some chap he knew being eaten by a tiger?'

'I think he was mauled, dear, but there are no tigers in Bristol. Well, in the Zoological Gardens, perhaps, but they're unlikely to be able to reach me from there.'

'He was mauled,' I said, 'because he fell off his bicycle. And he fell off his bicycle because . . . ?'

'Because he was, in Hector's own words, "completely pie-eyed". But I'm just mildly squiffy.'

'Don't make me hurt you, my lady,' I said.

She harrumphed, and struggled clumsily into the passenger seat.

'Shall we stop at the zoo?' I asked. 'It's a nice afternoon for a stroll among the animals.'

'Zoos make me melancholy, dear, you know that. Perhaps we should call at the shop, instead. We can apprise Georgie of our progress.'

'What do you make of Lady Bickle?' I asked. 'I can't quite fathom her.'

'She's a bit of a closed book to me, too. As I said before, she's a good deal younger than one would expect the wife of an eminent surgeon to be, but one can't read much into that. We've not really spent much time with her, though, so other than that trifling observation I've nothing really to offer.'

We mused silently on the enigma that was Georgina, Lady Bickle, as the little Rover chugged and wheezed its way up Park Street.

'Have you written to Lord Riddlethorpe yet?' I asked.

'As a matter of fact, I have,' she said. 'He replied at once saying that, quite coincidentally, he had been toying with the idea of building a motor car with two seats, an enclosed driving compartment, and powered by one of his racing engines. He went on for at least another page about chassis and suspension configurations, but engineering was never my strong suit. The long and the short is that he'll be sending me some drawings soon and is keen for us to act as his test drivers. He seems to be thinking of building more of them and selling them to enthusiasts. We'll get a discount in return for our detailed review. And because you saved his sister's life. Obviously.'

'I look forward to it,' I said. 'Oh, bother.'

There were two carts on Queen's Road outside the WSPU shop. Their horses had been given nosebags and were contentedly munching on their afternoon tea. They were going to be there for a while.

'I'll have to park round the corner near the Bickles',' I said.

'Of course,' she said. 'It's not as though it's far.'

I put the Rover in the same spot we'd used on Saturday and we prepared for the walk round the corner.

◆ ◆ ◆

Beattie Challenger was alone in the shop.

'Good afternoon,' she said. 'We were wondering when we might hear from you. How are things progressing?'

'Passably well, thank you,' said Lady Hardcastle.

'Did you make any progress with poor Mr Brookfield's notebook?'

'Lady Hardcastle cracked the code,' I said.

'Did you, indeed?' said Miss Challenger. 'Did you really? We'd heard you were clever.'

'I'd be lying if I said it was terribly complex,' said Lady Hardcastle. 'But between us we did find out how it was done. It turned out to be a simple phonetic Caesar cipher and some wordplay, that's all.'

Miss Challenger said nothing for a moment, merely blinking. 'Well,' she said after a pause, 'it's all well above my head. But what does it say now you've decoded it?'

'We're still working on it, but we have ascertained that it's a record of his ongoing investigations. We've already spoken to his first target, Mr Oswald Crane. We met him this morning with Miss Caudle.'

'The coffee fellow?'

'The very same,' said Lady Hardcastle. 'Not the most impressive chap we've ever encountered, eh, Armstrong?'

'We've certainly met brighter and braver,' I agreed. 'But his lack of . . . well, his lack of anything very much apart from an unjustified sense of his own superiority doesn't necessarily rule him out. More weaselly men than him have killed for less than that.'

'Less than what?' asked Miss Challenger.

'Oh, I'm sorry,' I said. 'Mr Brookfield had evidence that Mr Crane's wife was having an affair.'

'Oh my goodness,' she said. 'And after he made that speech about how it was the husband's fault if the wife strayed.'

'Well, quite,' said Lady Hardcastle. 'He'd be a laughing stock at the very least.'

'Who was the other party?' asked Miss Challenger.

'We've not got to that part yet.'

'Slow going, is it?'

'Miss Caudle is working on it for us, and she does have other calls on her time. But we'll get there, don't worry,' said Lady Hardcastle with a smile.

'That's good, then. Have you told Georgie?'

'No, we came straight here in hopes of being able to tell you both.'

'She's at Lady Hooper's Thursday afternoon bridge game. It's a regular thing with her.'

'I remember her saying. Well, she has our telephone number if she wishes to talk to either of us. Would you pass on the news in the meantime, please, such as it is?'

'Of course,' said Miss Challenger.

'Has anyone visited Lizzie Worrel?' I asked. 'Do we know how she is?'

'No one this week, but I think Georgie is planning to go to Horfield tomorrow morning.'

'Is she?' said Lady Hardcastle. 'You know Miss Worrel well? Would she object to a visit from strangers if we tagged along?'

'I'm sure she'd be delighted, what with you working on her case and all. She needs all the friends she can get at the moment, poor thing.'

'Then I shall telephone Georgie this evening,' said Lady Hardcastle, 'and see what we can arrange. Is that all right with you, Armstrong?'

'I always enjoy a visit to chokey, my lady,' I said. 'As long as I'm on the right side of the cell doors.'

'But you've never been on the wrong side, surely,' said Miss Challenger.

'More than once,' I said. 'There was that time in Serbia, for instance. Belgrade.'

'Oh my word, yes,' said Lady Hardcastle. 'I'd forgotten that one. Was that the time I paid those farmers to pull the bars from your window with their horses?'

'No, that was Bulgaria. Belgrade was where you smuggled me a picklock in a banana and treated the guards to a bottle of rakija with a little something extra in it.'

'That's it,' she said. 'They looked so sweet there, all asleep.'

'Well I never,' said Miss Challenger.

'It was all in a day's work back then,' I said.

'And our day's work tomorrow shall be a visit to the women's wing of Horfield Prison. Have no fear, Miss Challenger, we shall free your friend and set the record straight.'

After yet another 'quick stroll round the shops', it was past teatime by the time we got home and the sun was readying itself for bed. Edna and Miss Jones, too, were readying themselves, if not for bed, then at least a return home to their families. I always enjoyed their company so I spent a while chatting to them.

Miss Jones had made all the preparations for our dinner and, as usual, had left me instructions for finishing it off.

'I thought a nice bit of pheasant would do you both lovely,' she said. 'Fred Spratt had them in and said as how you likes them.'

So much so, I thought, that I ordered pheasant for lunch. I said nothing, of course, and Lady Hardcastle had eaten something muttony, so she'd be delighted.

'Thank you,' I said. 'I think that's everything so why don't you two nip off a bit early?'

'I don't mind if I do, actually. It's our ma's committee night so she likes to eat early.'

'Our Dan can wait for his supper,' said Edna, 'but I'll never say no to an early finish.'

'We'll see you tomorrow, then,' I said. 'Thank you both for another excellent day's work.'

I left them to their hats and coats while I sorted out a tea tray for the lady of the house and carried it through.

'What do we think of today's encounter with the repellent Mr Crane?' I said as I set down the tray in the drawing room.

'I think I should have made arrangements to have him properly followed, that's what I think. The whole point of getting the silly fellow's dander up was to goad him into doing something stupid to try to cover whatever tracks he might think he's left.'

'He doesn't strike me as a man of action,' I said. 'I imagine he'll fret and dither for a bit first. Although, to be fair, we don't know that he's got any tracks to cover. Being a fatuous oaf isn't yet a crime. It will be as soon as I get the vote, mind you, but it's still perfectly acceptable for the moment.'

'The world will no longer be a safe place for oafs and nincompoops when you get the vote.'

'There'll be nowhere for them to hide,' I agreed. 'Where does that particular wump make his nest?'

'He has a grand house in Sneyd Park,' she said. 'North of the Downs. Looks out across the Avon Gorge.'

'When did you find all that out?'

'While you were hobnobbing with the girls in the kitchen, I telephoned Inspector Sunderland. He's had dealings with Crane and happened to remember where he lived.'

'That's handy,' I said. 'And a tiny bit suspicious. What sort of dealings?'

'Nothing helpful to us, I'm afraid. Crane had complained about a couple of roughs prowling about the area after dark. Apparently, there was fear and trembling in the houses of the great and the good, lest they be burgled while they slept. Or worse. But that's to our advantage. The inspector said he'd have a discreet word with the beat copper up there and ask him to keep an eye out for suspicious comings and goings. He can disguise it as following up the earlier report. It's not as good as actually tailing the fellow, but it'll have to do.'

'I think that's the best we can do for now,' I agreed. 'I could shadow him unseen for days, but if he's done nothing it would just be a waste of my time. It's also a bit cold for that sort of work. Best leave it to the rozzers.'

'I quite agree. We've set our cat among his pigeons, though, so we'll just have to wait and see what happens.'

'Did you telephone Lady Bickle?'

'I did. She had just returned from her bridge game. She would be delighted to have us join her tomorrow morning and I said that we would meet her at the gaol at ten o'clock.'

'You've been a busy lady,' I said.

'I have, but that's not all. I also spoke to Dinah Caudle and she claims to be well on the way to deciphering the next story. She hopes to have something useful to tell us tomorrow.'

'Not a bad day's work, then,' I said.

While we had been talking, Lady Hardcastle had been working on a sketch, which she now pinned to the crime board. It was an unkind caricature of Mr Crane as a red-faced football with his waistcoat straining at the seams and one button pinging off at some speed.

'He has a splendid motive,' she said. 'But I do find it hard to imagine him actually doing something about it.'

Chapter Six

Horfield Prison was easy enough to find, just off the Gloucester Road. The main building was a square, red-brick edifice, plain and forbidding. With its clock tower, it looked somewhat like a modern church, but it was clearly not a comforting place of worship. There was a Rolls-Royce parked outside, from which Lady Bickle emerged as we drew up. She had a quick word with her chauffeur and then walked towards us.

'I say,' she said with genuine glee. 'What a delightful little motor car. Good morning to you both.'

We struggled to free our eyes from our goggles and the rest of our faces from our mufflers.

'Good morning to you, too, Georgie, dear,' said Lady Hardcastle. 'You'll have to excuse us for a few moments while we divest ourselves of our travelling togs.'

'Take your time,' she said. 'I'm fully engaged admiring your charming conveyance. Is it difficult to drive?'

'Not at all, my lady,' I said. 'Lever there on the steering wheel for the throttle, gear lever, too. Brake pedal on the floor . . . It all but drives itself.'

'I simply must have one,' she said. 'The Rolls is fine for grand occasions, but Ben sometimes uses it to travel around the place for his work so it's often not at home. I could have one of these and we'd never need to employ another Stanley.'

'Stanley?' said Lady Hardcastle.

'Ben's first chauffeur was called Stanley so it just sort of became the family name for a chauffeur. The current one's an absolute poppet called Alfred. Or Fred, as he prefers to be known.'

By this time we had removed most of our driving clothes and were looking a little more presentable.

'Have you ever visited a prisoner before?' asked Lady Bickle as we walked towards the imposing front door.

'Only Armstrong,' said Lady Hardcastle. 'But never in this country and it was almost always my fault.'

'Gracious,' said Lady Bickle. 'You two are exciting, aren't you? I spent a few hours in a police cell in Lucerne once. It was all just a misunderstanding, though – I hadn't known that the bicycle belonged to a policeman or I'd never have borrowed it. But I asked because it all proved a little too much for poor Beattie. She was quite unprepared for the realities of prison life, I think. She's a gentle soul and I don't think she's seen very much of the darker side of life.'

'Don't worry about us, dear,' said Lady Hardcastle. 'We'll be fine.'

After signing our souls away at the front desk we were led along endless corridors that smelled of disinfectant and echoed with the sound of our boots. The cell doors were all locked, but there were some shouted conversations between neighbours. Eventually, we arrived at a grey door indistinguishable from all the others apart from the number painted above it. Our wardress guide unlocked the door and ushered us in.

'Bang on the door when you're done,' she said. 'I'll be outside.'

We mumbled our thanks and trooped into the dingy cell. A slight woman sat at the table in the corner of the room, dressed in a shapeless grey smock – her prison uniform. Her boots provided the only splash of brightness. She had been arrested in her white suffragette garb, and they had allowed her to keep her white patent leather boots. She began to stand as we entered.

'Don't get up, Lizzie, dear,' said Lady Bickle. 'All friends here.'

The woman sat gingerly down. Her long, mousy hair was pulled back from her face and plaited down her back. The face it revealed was grey and drawn. She looked as though she had barely slept since her arrest over a week ago.

She looked wearily and timidly at us. 'Hello,' she said.

'This is Lady Hardcastle,' said Lady Bickle. 'And her maid, Armstrong. I mentioned them to you the other day.'

'How do you do?' said Lady Hardcastle.

I merely smiled and nodded. The poor woman looked overwhelmed enough as it was without me chiming in.

'How are they treating you?' asked Lady Bickle.

'Like a murderer,' said Miss Worrel.

'Are you eating?'

'I've not been hungry.'

'This isn't a suffragette thing, dear. You'll get no sympathy for starving yourself.'

'Has the Union abandoned me, then?' asked Miss Worrel forlornly.

'Heavens, no,' said Lady Bickle. 'Why do you think we've drafted in Lady Hardcastle? We need to clear your name and save you.'

'I've heard nothing from Head Office.'

Lady Bickle looked discomfited for the first time since we'd met her.

'Well . . . now . . . you see . . .' she began. 'We have heard from the top, and the feeling is that they would prefer to distance themselves from the case for the time being. It's not that they doubt your innocence, it's just . . . well . . .'

'These are delicate times and sensitive matters,' said Lady Hardcastle. 'I imagine they feel that your organization has a chance for the first time in a while to press for real change, and this trumped-up charge against you might be just the distraction your opponents need. If they can get people talking about your trial instead of votes for women, they'll be delighted.'

'So I'm just being left here to rot,' said Miss Worrel.

'Far from it,' said Lady Bickle. 'Lady Hardcastle and Armstrong have already made some progress.'

'You have?'

'We have,' said Lady Hardcastle. 'I would hesitate to overbid on our present hand, but we believe we have a way in. We have Christian Brookfield's coded notebook.'

Miss Worrel looked stricken at the mention of the journalist's name.

'And they're beginning to understand it,' said Lady Bickle enthusiastically. 'Oswald Crane is already a suspect as a result.'

'The coffee man?' asked Miss Worrel. 'Why on earth would he burn down an old shop on Thomas Street?'

'Mr Brookfield was investigating his private life,' said Lady Hardcastle. 'There were allegations of marital infidelity.'

'Him? But I've seen him. He looks like someone's blown him up with a bicycle pump.'

We all laughed.

'No, not him,' said Lady Hardcastle. 'It's his wife who's been having the affair, or so Brookfield thought. After that speech he gave recently about how men should be ashamed of themselves if their wives strayed, or however it was he phrased it, he'd be a laughing stock if word were to get out that his wife were playing at away fixtures.'

'Is it true?'

'We don't know yet,' said Lady Hardcastle.

'But do you think he might be the one who set the fire?'

'We've seen men do worse over less,' I said. It was the first time I'd spoken, and Miss Worrel seemed surprised to hear from me.

'What do you think of all this business, Miss . . . Armstrong, was it?' she said.

'I have an open mind, miss,' I said. 'I'll follow where our investigations lead us, but your friends are all convinced of your innocence and they make convincing arguments in your favour.'

'Do you think I did it?'

'Did you?' I asked.

'No,' she said wearily.

'Then that's my starting point,' I said. 'Is there anything you can offer us to help us prove it? Where were you at the time, for instance?'

'At home in Redland,' she said. 'I have rooms in a house on Woodfield Road.'

'Could your landlord vouch for your whereabouts?' I asked.

'Landlady,' she said. 'And no. She's a lovely old dear, but she's deaf as a post. She lets rooms to two of us "young ladies", as she calls us, but she leaves us to our own devices.'

'Your fellow lodger, then?' I asked.

'She's away visiting her family in Bath.'

'I hope it's not too personal a question,' said Lady Hardcastle, 'but how do you support yourself?'

'I'm an illustrator,' she said. 'Books and magazines, you know the sort of thing. Watercolours, mainly. I like children's adventure books the best, but I've never been known to turn down a commission.'

'How wonderful,' said Lady Hardcastle. 'I dabble – so many people do, don't they? – but I'm always interested to see what people with real talent can produce. You must promise to show me when this is all over.'

Miss Worrel smiled wanly.

There was a loud bang on the door and the wardress shouted, 'Two more minutes in there. This i'n't no social salon.'

'We must be quick,' said Lady Bickle. 'Do you need anything, Lizzie?'

Miss Worrel shook her head.

'And if you can think of anything – anything at all – that might help us, you must get word to us. Hold nothing back.'

The Burning Issue of the Day

Miss Worrel looked sadly up at her, but nodded her understanding.

'And please eat something,' said Lady Bickle. 'We can get food to you, if not a cake with a file in it.'

The door opened, and the sour-faced wardress appeared.

'Time's up,' she said. 'If you . . . ladies will follow me, I'll take you back to the front desk.' She had looked pointedly at me as she said 'ladies', but I denied her the satisfaction of a reaction. 'Worrel,' she continued, 'get your room squared away and be ready to go to the yard for exercise.'

We followed the stout bully back the way we had come and I day-dreamed along the way about whether I could get away with tripping her on the stairs.

As we reached the front desk and prepared to sign ourselves out, the equally sour-faced prison warder responsible for our registration and admission reached into a pigeonhole on his desk and pulled out a piece of folded paper.

'Is one of you' – he looked down at the paper – 'Lady Hardcastle?'

'I am,' she replied.

'This i'n't no post office, "my lady",' he said as he held up the paper.

'No, I'm well aware of that,' she said.

'In that case would you kindly tell your correspondents not to treat it as one?' He handed over the paper, which turned out to be a telegram.

'Thank you,' she said. 'You're most kind. I shall pass on your comments.'

'You do that,' he said. 'Door's that way.' He returned to his work. I wondered if any branch of the justice system employed men to work on their reception desks who actually enjoyed meeting members of the public.

Once we were safely outside in the grey February chill, Lady Hardcastle opened the telegram.

'Tum-te-tum, la-de-da-de-dee, diddly-whippet,' she said as she read it.

'More code?' I asked.

'No,' she said. 'It's from Dinah Caudle – I told her we'd be here this morning. She says that if we can be at the offices of Messrs Churn, Whiting, Hinkley, and Puffett on Corn Street by half past eleven, we can join her as she interviews Mr Redvers Hinkley for her newspaper.'

'Why would we wish to do that?' I asked.

'Unless she has mistakenly divined some sort of fondness on our part for Corn Street, then I presume that the notebook has given up the name Hinkley.'

'To judge by the firm's name, it would seem he's a senior partner in something or other,' I said. 'Exactly the sort of chap Brookfield would go after.'

'I believe he's a property developer,' said Lady Bickle. 'Ben has mentioned him, I'm sure of it. Buys up land, builds things on it, sells it all on at great profit – that sort of carry-on.'

'Just the type of thing Brookfield was interested in,' I said.

'Quite,' said Lady Hardcastle. 'I'm sorry to be dashing off so rudely, Georgie, dear, but if we're to be at Corn Street by half past eleven and looking well kempt and carefree we'd better get our skates on.'

'I perfectly understand. Go. But do let me see how you start this wonderful device. I shall be speaking to Ben about it this very evening.'

Once we had reequipped ourselves with mufflers and goggles, I gave Lady Bickle a brief lesson in starting the Rover's engine. She waved us off as we headed back towards the Gloucester Road and our appointment in the city.

◆　◆　◆

'For heaven's sake, don't poke this particular hornets' nest with your stout poking stick,' said Dinah Caudle as we entered the stone-fronted office building together. 'Hinkley is a sight more canny than Crane and he won't startle nearly so easily. It's also – and I can't emphasize this enough – it's also vitally important to me that I don't give him cause to slam the door in my face for good. Brookfield was on to something with this chap and if he's not responsible for the arson I'll have a chance to skewer him with another story later. But I'll get the best possible results if I can keep talking to him right up to the moment the newspapers start landing on people's breakfast tables.'

'Right you are,' said Lady Hardcastle. 'I shall be church-mouse-like.'

'You can be Lady Summerford again.'

'That makes me Nelly Maybee,' I said. 'With two e's.'

She just looked at me and shook her head.

Mr Hinkley's personal secretary was a harassed-looking man in his early thirties with spectacle lenses like polished glass pebbles. His moustache was as frayed as his coat sleeves, and his fingers as ink-stained as his shirt sleeves. He looked up from his work and blinked slowly. He offered no word nor even a smile of greeting.

'Good morning,' said Miss Caudle. 'I am Miss Caudle, of the *Bristol News*. I have an appointment to see Mr Hinkley at noon.' She looked at the clock on the wall at the precise moment its hands ticked to midday.

'I shall tell him you're here,' said the secretary without making any effort to rise to do so. 'Might I enquire as to the identity of your . . . companions?'

'These are Lady Summerford and Miss Maybee. With two e's. They are associates of mine from the newspaper.'

'Very well,' he said, and slowly unfolded himself from his chair. He walked stiffly, and with a slight limp, towards the large double doors that I now presumed to be the portal to his master's lair. With a flunky's flourish, he opened both doors just wide enough to admit his gangly body and then closed them behind him.

We waited.

After a few moments, he reappeared and beckoned us towards him.

'Mr Hinkley will see you now,' he said, and threw open both doors to bow us in.

Mr Redvers Hinkley was standing behind a desk large enough to sleep a family of four. I'd seen dozens of 'Hinkleys' over the years. Big men in expensive suits who were all smiles and bonhomie, quick to welcome you and put you at ease, and just as quick to stab you in the back – metaphorically or, in one unpleasant case, literally – when you stood between them and their ambition.

'Ladies,' he said, spreading his arms in welcome. 'Do come in and make yourselves comfortable.'

He indicated three high-backed chairs that had been arranged facing the expansive plateau of leather-topped desk. We sat.

'Can I offer you some tea, perhaps?' he said.

'Thank you, that would be most welcome,' said Miss Caudle.

Hinkley nodded over our heads and we heard his secretary close the door. 'Now, then, Miss Caudle,' said Hinkley, 'you I remember from the Mayor's New Year Ball. But your charming friend . . . I'm sure I should have remembered meeting her.' He looked down at a piece of notepaper in front of him. 'Lady Summerford, is it?'

'It is, Mr Hinkley,' said Lady Hardcastle. 'We moved to Bristol late last year. Perhaps you know my husband, Sir Philip? Were you by any chance at the boxing match last Tuesday? The twenty-fifth. You might have seen him there.'

'Sir Philip Summerford,' mused Mr Hinkley. 'No, can't say it rings a bell, and I'm afraid I was working late all last week so I missed the fight. What line is Sir Philip in?'

'He's retired now,' she said. 'But he used to run a tea plantation in Assam.'

'Ah, I see,' he said, his interest evaporating. If this Sir Philip Summerford was no longer active in the world of business or politics, he was of no use to Hinkley and no further effort would be expended on knowing anything about him.

'Lady Summerford is learning the tricks of the trade,' said Miss Caudle. 'She wishes to write articles for the newspaper and so I've taken her under my wing, as it were.'

'Ah,' he said. This was something he could understand. 'So this newspaper business is your little hobby, then, is it? A little something to keep you out from under your husband's feet during the daytime? Jolly good, jolly good. I must say, if I retired I'd have to find something for my wife to do to get her out of the house.'

We all smiled and nodded politely.

'And you, Miss . . . Maybee with two e's?' he said, eyeing my uniform. 'How do you fit into all this? Not many journalists of my acquaintance take their servants to work with them.'

'I assist Lady Summerford,' I said. 'Sometimes it can be handy to have someone to fetch and carry for you.'

Precisely on cue, the secretary returned bearing a tea tray, which he set down on a side table. He poured tea and distributed cups while we talked.

'Well, then, Miss Caudle,' said Mr Hinkley. 'What little story are you writing this time? Surely it's not time for another mayoral ball. My poor bunions have barely recovered from the last one.'

'No, Mr Hinkley, it's not a society story. It's more of a . . . how shall we say . . . more of a social story this time. I understand your firm is behind the proposed development of the new commercial buildings on Thomas Street. I was hoping to write about the rejuvenation of the area and the coming of new jobs. It will be a boon to the immediate area. And the city as a whole, for the matter of that.'

'That old fraud Tapscott down at the *Bristol News* has got women writing business stories now, eh? What a way to run a newspaper.'

'As I say, Mr Hinkley, I'm covering it more from the social angle. How it will benefit the community – change lives for the better – to have these exciting new business premises opening up in what, you would have to admit, is an otherwise rather rundown area.'

'Ah,' he said. 'That makes a good deal more sense. Never met a woman yet who understood commercial matters, but families . . . well, that's another thing entirely. It's the way women's brains work, d'you see? It's like a machine in a factory. You wouldn't expect to be able to make pencils with a machine designed to pump water out of a mine, would you? It's the same with the brains of men and women. Women's brains are made by the Good Lord to raise children and run households. It's common sense.'

We meekly nodded our understanding of this profound truth and smiled our gratitude to the great man for vouchsafing it to us.

'Of course,' said Miss Caudle. 'Which is why I'm concentrating on a different aspect of the story. What will the new premises be used for, for instance? And how many jobs will be created?'

'Well,' he began, settling back in his chair and folding his hands across his waistcoat, 'it will be mainly office buildings, but with some light industrial facilities for handling and processing imported goods from the docks for onward transportation by railway. The site is ideally located between the city's docks and its main railway station at Temple Meads.'

'Oh,' said Miss Caudle, 'that's good. So you'll be able to employ some of the men who have been put out of work as the city docks decline in favour of Avonmouth. How wonderful.'

'I think you misunderstand, Miss Caudle. We're merely a firm of investors and developers. We shan't be employing anybody other than to build the new properties. It will be up to our tenants to decide whom they employ.'

'Ah, yes, of course. But you do think that the development will benefit the nearby communities?'

'All our developments benefit the whole city,' he said grandly. 'That's what we do here at Churn, Whiting, Hinkley, and Puffett, we enrich the city and the people in it.'

Miss Caudle continued in this vein for some minutes more, trying to draw Mr Hinkley into saying something, anything, of substance about the new development. Every attempt was met with the same bland platitudes. Still, she made her notes and smiled at his attempts at joviality, until eventually she politely drew the interview to a close.

◆ ◆ ◆

'That wasn't quite as illuminating as I'd hoped,' said Lady Hardcastle once we were back out on the street.

'Softly, softly, catch the monkey,' said Miss Caudle. 'It was an excellent start.'

'We've presumed that Mr Hinkley is the subject of the next section of Mr Brookfield's notebook,' I said. 'Is it something to do with the Thomas Street development?'

'Mum's the word for the moment,' said Miss Caudle, tapping the side of her nose. 'Walls have ears and all that. We must find somewhere to sit and chat.' She looked about. 'I'd suggest Crane's but you've rather queered the pitch there. Even if dear old Oswald isn't in residence, the staff will undoubtedly recognize us. There will be earwigging and nose poking.'

'We passed a café on St Nicholas Street the other day when we were looking for somewhere to leave the motor car,' said Lady Hardcastle.

'I know it,' said Miss Caudle. 'It'll do nicely. You can treat me to lunch again, although it'll be nothing so luxurious as last time. Faggots, mash, and carrots is more their level.'

'It sounds perfect,' said Lady Hardcastle. 'What say you, Armstrong?'

'Lovely,' I said, almost convincingly.

We turned on to St Nicholas Street and found the café. It was small, but busy, and would serve as a perfect venue for our discussions. As threatened, faggots and mashed potatoes was the most appealing dish on the menu. No carrots were offered.

'Tell all, then, Miss Caudle,' said Lady Hardcastle once the meals had been ordered. 'What has Hinkley been up to?'

'Before we get to that,' said Miss Caudle, 'I need to rant to someone about bloody Christian's bloody notebook, and you're the only people I can tell.'

'Oh dear,' said Lady Hardcastle. 'Is the transcribing not going well?'

'Oh, the text is easy enough to follow now that you've worked out his system. It's time consuming but mostly straightforward. No, what's frustrating me is the chaotic disorganization of the man. When I began, I presumed, or at least hoped, that the notes would be arranged according to some sort of system. Each story in its own section, you see? But not our Christian, oh no. His notes are a stream of consciousness. He wrote down every thought that crossed his mind, in the order he thought it. There's no structure to it. We hop from the beginnings of the Crane investigation to some rambling thoughts about card schools and gambling debts, then on to Hinkley. Interspersing all this are random sentences that mean I know not what. I'm not sure we're going to get the full picture on anything until I've worked my way through the whole wretched mess, and even then it's going to be like completing one of those new jigsaw puzzle things. In the dark. With pieces missing.'

'You seem to be doing a grand job so far,' said Lady Hardcastle. 'We already know that Crane might have wanted him out of the way. And now you have something on Hinkley . . .'

'Yes,' she said. 'Hinkley. It's just half a story at the moment, which is why I don't want to spook him yet. According to Brookfield's notes, there's something shady about that Thomas Street deal but I haven't yet managed to establish what. He's written "council" in the margin in plaintext on several pages, not just these ones, so my intuition is that he might have found some corrupt goings on at the city council.'

'You want to be careful whom you mention "intuition" to,' I said. 'People might start to think Crane and Hinkley are right about women's brains.'

'Those great bumbling oafs and their theories about my brain,' she said.

'Is it merely a coincidence, do you think,' I wondered, 'that Thomas Street has come up again? The shop fire was on Thomas Street, too, don't forget.'

'It's more likely that Christian started poking his nose in because the proposed development was on his doorstep. Something obviously struck him as a bit dodgy. He was sometimes apt to see conspiracies where there were none, but he was right more often than he was wrong.'

'You admired him, didn't you?' said Lady Hardcastle.

'A great deal. He was honest and principled. A good man. I often suggested he should go into politics and sort out the rot from the inside, but he just laughed.'

'What about you?' I asked. 'Have you ever thought of standing for the council?'

'Me?' laughed Miss Caudle. 'Not a chance. I can do a great deal more mischief with my pen then I ever could playing politics.'

The food arrived and talk turned to other matters.

'How did your visit to the gaol go?' asked Miss Caudle between mouthfuls.

'As disheartening as visits to gaols always are,' said Lady Hardcastle. 'Miss Worrel isn't coping at all well. From the look of her, she's not sleeping properly. Nor eating, if my guess is right.'

'I thought that was their speciality, the suffragettes.'

'Not eating? They do it as a deliberate gesture of defiance, yes. But this is different. She seems to be losing the will to fight. And Suffragette HQ, or however they style themselves, seem to have washed their hands of her, so she'd get no praise and support from them if she did starve herself. It's only her friends in the local branch who are standing by her.'

'Do you think she did it?'

'I really don't,' said Lady Hardcastle. 'I had a scientist's open mind before, but now I've met her I'm sure of her innocence.'

'Then I'll redouble my efforts to make sense of Brookfield's ramblings,' said Miss Caudle. 'I'm convinced that the answer is in there somewhere. It must be.'

◆ ◆ ◆

After dinner that evening we sat together in the drawing room sipping brandy and contemplating the crime board. Dinah Caudle had furnished Lady Hardcastle with a photograph of the late Christian Brookfield, from which she had produced a lovely sketch for the centre of the web of connections. Now that we had met Lizzie Worrel, she was able to produce a sketch of her, too, but of a lively and smiling Lizzie, not the pale, sad, hopeless one we had seen in that grim cell.

'And here's Redvers Hinkley,' she said, pinning up the last of the day's drawings and linking it to Brookfield, and Thomas Street.

'How does the betting stand now?' I asked.

'I should say the odds on Lizzie Worrel are lengthening by the day,' she said. 'I know we're staying well clear of intuition, but she does seem by far the least likely candidate. No one knew Brookfield was dead when she was arrested, for a start. If she were the arsonist and had done it in the name of the WSPU, she'd have claimed responsibility at once and yelled her defiance as they dragged her to the Black Maria. Once she learned of the man's death, she'd have been racked with guilt and remorse. I saw none of that, did you?'

'None at all,' I agreed. 'Fear, hopelessness, and bewilderment, but no guilt.'

'So we're agreed that she's the outside bet at the moment, then. As for these others. Hmm. Crane has motive, but no visible backbone. Let's see what Inspector Sunderland has to say about his movements. And Hinkley . . . He's an oily, self-important idiot but that's still not a crime, despite all the letters I've written to our MP. He claims to have been working late on the night of the fire. I know that doesn't mean much, but it's easy enough to check. And we're not yet sure what his motive might be because we don't know what Brookfield thought he was up to.'

'Bribery would be my bet,' I said. 'He seems the type. Miss Caudle was pressing him on the Thomas Street development and there were those unexplained "council" references in the notebook.'

'Just so. We'll keep that as our working hypothesis for now, then, and await further news.'

'Unless . . .' I said.

'Unless what, dear?'

'What if Brookfield's death really was accidental? What if Hinkley's firm needed the land that old shop stood on but the landlord wouldn't budge? Or if it was some sort of insurance swindle? Maybe the landlord worked out that he could get paid twice – once by the insurance company and then again when he sold the vacant land?'

'How very ingenious,' she said. 'But the development deal is signed and sealed. It's at the other end of the road, too, with a good few buildings in between, not least that pub . . .'

'The Court Samson Inn,' I said.

'Yes, there. It sounded like a busy place from the police report so I can't imagine the landlord selling up. I doubt Fandangle, Piffle, and Snood—'

'Churn, Whiting, Hinkley, and Puffett,' I said wearily.

'Even they. I doubt they'd offer a decent price to buy out a business when all they'd want is the land, even if they were looking to expand their doings to the other end of the street.'

'You make a good case,' I said. 'So we're back to coincidence?'

'For Thomas Street? It's more likely that the link is simply Brookfield himself, just as Dinah Caudle said. It was where he lived, after all, so he'd have been disposed to keep an eye on what was going on outside his own front door.'

'Then we're stuck until we get more decipherings from Miss Caudle.'

'We are, indeed. We shall take the weekend off.'

'You might be able to,' I said, 'but one of us has got to make sure the other one's best gown and dancing shoes are spick and span for the Farley-Strouds' do tomorrow evening.'

'Oh my word, I'd completely forgotten. Will you drive me up there, too, please? It's a long walk in dancing shoes.'

'Of course. Carriages at one?'

'It'll be on the invitation, but I'm sure Gertie won't mind if you slip downstairs and wait there. It'll save you sitting here on your own all evening.'

'I might have been looking forward to sitting on my own all evening,' I said.

'Were you?'

'No. I was hoping to spend the evening with Maude Denton. She'll have nothing to do if Lady Farley-Stroud is hosting a soirée so we can have a chinwag in her room. I've not spoken to her for ages.'

'A convocation of ladies' maids. Do you have a collective noun? A mending of ladies' maids? A dressing? Oh, oh, I know, an impertinence of ladies' maids.'

'Might I offer you some friendly and respectful advice, my lady?'

'Of course, dear.'

'Shut your trap before it gets you in trouble. You might end up walking home tomorrow night.'

'Right you are. Shall I play? Some Mendelssohn, perhaps. A couple of *Lieder ohne Worte* would go down well, I feel. And some cheese and crackers if we have any.'

Chapter Seven

I allowed Lady Hardcastle to lie-in on Saturday morning. She was going to have to stay up late being sparkling and wonderful at the Farley-Strouds' soirée, after all. I got on with a few odds and ends, and then helped Miss Jones plan the menus for the coming week so that she could get the orders out before the local shops shut at lunchtime.

Lady Hardcastle ambled blearily into the kitchen shortly before ten o'clock.

'Good morning, household,' she said. 'Am I too late for brekker?'

'Never too late, m'lady,' said Miss Jones. 'But we didn't know when to expect you so I didn't put nothin' on. What would you like?'

'Can I have a couple of poached eggs, please?' said Lady Hardcastle. 'On toast. Did we ever get any of that American stuff, the tomato ketchup? Helston's?'

'Heinz,' I said. 'I'll bring it through.'

'Thank you, dear,' she said as she ambled out again. 'Join me, would you?'

When she had gone, Miss Jones said, 'I don't know how she can eat that muck.'

'Egg on toast?' I said.

'No, that tomato ketchup stuff. Don't taste nothin' like tomatoes. I can make her a lovely tomato sauce if she wants one. Or a mushroom ketchup. It'd take a while, mind, but it'd go lovely with her eggs.'

'I've grown rather fond of it,' I said. 'There are worse crimes committed in the name of food, don't forget. There's a fermented herring dish in Sweden called *surströmming* – it smells so revolting that they only eat it outdoors.'

'That's as may be, but it don't mean I has to like Mr Heinz, or his tomato ketchup.'

'What about the baked beans Lady Hardcastle got from Fortnum's?'

'You got me there,' she said with a grin. 'I loves they.'

'Me too. Can you do me a couple of eggs as well, please? I'll make the coffee.'

A few minutes later I carried the food and the post through to the morning room, where I joined Lady Hardcastle at the table.

'Here you go, my lady,' I said as I gave her a plate of eggs on toast. 'Welcome to Saturday.'

She looked out of the window at the grey wintry sky. 'You're welcome to it,' she said. 'I might go back to bed.'

She started on her breakfast.

'Do you have any exciting plans for the day?' I asked, trying to lift the mood a little.

'Nothing fabulous,' she said. 'If I "had my druthers", as our colonial cousins say, I should prefer to be trying to free Lizzie Worrel from gaol, but we're kicking our heels on that one until Caudle comes up with more of the transcription. I thought I might do some work on the models for the new animation, but even with the paraffin heater it's a bit parky in the orangery. I keep feeling we ought to do something about the garden, too.'

'But you hate gardening,' I said.

'Precisely the reason nothing ever gets done. Perhaps I should make enquiries. There must be a reliable fellow nearby who could take care of a bit of planting and pruning for us.'

'You know who I always thought would make a good gardener?' I said.

'No? Who?' She was distracted now, leafing through the post.

'You remember that chap who helped us out with the Spencer Caradine case? Lived in a caravan in the woods.'

'Obadiah Tuppence,' she said absently.

'Jedediah Halfpenny,' I replied. 'Better known as Old Jed. I bet he knows a thing or two. And I bet he'd be glad of a few bob in his pocket in return for an honest day's toil. He liked you.'

'Everyone likes me, dear,' she said. 'I'm adorable. But if you think he'd be up to the job, you have my permission to seek him out and attempt to engage him. Oh, this one's from Harry. Pass me your butter knife, would you? Mine's covered in something.'

'Butter?' I suggested.

'Yes, please.'

I passed her the knife, which she used to slit open the envelope from her brother, Harry. She began reading.

'Is he well?' I asked.

'Full of the joys,' she said. 'Married life seems to suit him . . . Let's see . . . They're renting a place on Bedford Square. Not terribly handy for Whitehall, but he says the walk will do him good. What else . . . ? Servants have been engaged and he even has a valet now, so he has no excuses for being badly turned out. I must say, it always used to frustrate me so much that he just had a part-time housekeeper at that flat in St John's Wood . . . Lavinia is engaged in the usual round of charities and good causes. Oh, but she's also been appointed to the board of her brother's company. She has a shrewd mind. She'll do well there.'

Lady Lavinia's brother was the 'Fishy' from whom Lady Hardcastle was hoping to buy a new motor car.

She read on for a moment. 'Then he asks after me. Oh, and you. Apparently Lavinia wants to know when we're going to visit . . . There's some stuff about work . . . Oh.' Abruptly, she put the letter down.

'What is it?' I asked.

'Ehrlichmann has been spotted again.'

Günther Ehrlichmann was the German agent who had killed Lady Hardcastle's husband, Sir Roderick, in Shanghai. We knew little about him other than that Lady Hardcastle had shot him dead moments after he murdered Sir Roderick. His very real, slightly messy death notwithstanding, our friends Skins and Dunn – two ragtime musicians – had seen him in a London nightclub before Christmas.

'What does he say?' I asked.

'You remember the boys said Harry had spoken to them at Rag-A-Muffin after their encounter with the man calling himself Ehrlichmann?'

'I do,' I said. 'He said he'd had some men from the Foreign Office following the chap for a while.'

'He did. They lost track of him, apparently, but Harry had also asked Special Branch to keep an eye out and one of their chaps spotted him on Thursday. He was at Paddington Station boarding a train for Penzance.'

'And the trains for Penzance pass through Bristol,' I said.

'They do, indeed. He managed to get a local man to Bristol Temple Meads in time to meet the train and there was no sign of the supposed Ehrlichmann, but it does give one pause, don't you think?'

'It certainly brought him nearer for a while. Although if he went all the way to Penzance, he's further away now than he was when he was in London.'

'True, but what on earth is there at Penzance?'

'A railway station, for one,' I said. 'And a harbour. Perhaps he's leaving the country.'

'Perhaps. It's all a little unsettling, though. I thought all this nonsense was behind us.'

'There's nothing much we can do but keep our wits about us. And some sort of weapon.'

'Excellent. I've been dying to wear that holster hat you got me for Christmas. It shall be my hat of choice in the coming days and weeks. Apart from this evening, where glamour and elegance are required.'

'They are. While you're doing whatever Lady of the House things you get up to while I'm toiling on your behalf, I shall be—'

'You shall be toiling on my behalf?'

'I was actually going to say that I shall be ensuring that your gown, shoes, and jewels are at their elegant and glamourousest best.'

'You spoil me.'

'I bloomin' well do. Are you going to eat that last piece of toast?'

Parties in the country, we had learned, did not start at a civilized hour as they did in the cities. In the city, no one would dream of starting a party much before ten o'clock, but out here in the glorious English countryside they did things differently. They were early-to-bed-early-to-rise types and they thought nothing of starting their gatherings at seven.

And so it was that at a quarter past seven on the dot, I delivered Lady Hardcastle to the front door of The Grange. With a wave to Jenkins, the Farley-Strouds' butler, I pulled away and drove the Rover around to the side of the big house. I parked in front of the converted stables that now served as a garage for their own motor car and made my way back towards the house, guided by the light coming up the stone steps from the servants' door.

I entered without knocking and navigated without incident to Maude's door. I knocked briskly.

'Oh, for the love of . . . What now?' came the voice from within.

'It is I, Miss Denton,' I said. 'A simple traveller from distant lands come to seek shelter within. Or Flo from down the hill, come to seek a cup of tea and a chinwag. Whichever you prefer.'

The door opened, and the beaming face of Maude Denton, lady's maid and All-England Skiving Champion, loomed before me. She was a little older than I – though I'd never established how much – not to mention a smidge taller, and good deal broader about the waist. But she had the mischievously twinkling eyes of a girl half my age and an infectious grin to go with them.

'For goodness' sake get inside before anyone notices us,' she said, grabbing my sleeve and pulling me into the room.

'Good evening, Maude,' I said, producing a cake tin from its hiding place under my coat. 'Got any tea?'

'Tea be blowed,' she said, taking the cake. 'This calls for sherry.'

'No can do, I'm afraid,' I said. 'Driving.'

'Tch, you young Welsh girls and your chapel ways,' she said. 'Take your coat off and make yourself comfortable – I'll get the kettle on.'

I had first met Maude shortly after we moved to Littleton Cotterell. I spent much of the afternoon of Clarissa Farley-Stroud's engagement party hiding out in this very room, lest we be roped into any of the frantic preparations that were then underway. I'd not managed to bump into her for a few months and I anticipated a pleasantly lazy evening in her company.

'Not helping upstairs with the party, then?' I said as she handed me a cup of tea and a slice of the Madeira cake I'd brought with me.

She laughed. 'You're such a card,' she said. 'Imagine it – me helping with the party. As if!'

'I've not seen you for months. You might have suffered a blow to the head and been transformed into a completely different woman for all I knew. These things happen, you know. I've read stories in the newspapers.'

'It'll take more than a blow to the head to persuade me to pitch in with that sort of nonsense. I have quite enough to be getting on with, taking care of "m'lady", thank you very much.'

'And how is life at the big house on the hill?' I asked. 'Is there fresh gossip as yet unrepeated in the village?'

'Hardly. Anything that happens up here is all round the village in moments – so if you've heard nothing, there is nothing. Life continues much as it has for generations.'

'How disappointing. So no footmen are carrying on with any chambermaids? Jenkins isn't secretly embezzling the wine money to fund his retirement at Weston-Super-Mare?'

She laughed again. 'Nothing like that. The nearest we ever get to carryings-on is bloomin' Dora Kendrick.'

'Not my favourite housemaid?' I said. 'What's she been up to now?'

'To be honest, I can't keep up with all her nonsense. There are tales of her being sweet on some young lad in the village and wanting him to take her to some dance in the village hall. But he wouldn't have anything to do with her and said he was going to ask the butcher's daughter—'

'Daisy Spratt,' I said, automatically filling in the missing name.

'Yes, that's her. She's a pal of yours, isn't she?'

'She is, yes. And someone's been trying to besmirch her good name. Well, besmirch her name, anyway. I'm not sure how good it is by now – she's never been the chaste type. But she's a kindhearted soul and, as you say, she's my pal. You don't suppose Dora is behind the rumours, do you?'

'What rumours are they?' she asked.

'Something about her being seen behind the cricket pavilion with Lenny Someone-or-other. I forget the details, but she swears it's not true.'

'Lenny Leadbetter,' she said. 'That's the chap Dora had her eye on. I wouldn't put it past her to start trying to stir up trouble for them both.'

'Keep your ears open for me, would you? I'd like confirmation before I do anything rash.'

'Ooh, are you planning to waylay her and give her what for? A swift punch on the conk?'

'Nothing so direct,' I said. 'But I do think it's time someone settled her hash.'

'It's well overdue, dear. Well overdue. Are you sure I can't tempt you to a sherry?'

'Quite sure, but please don't let me stop you from having one. I'm more than happy with my tea.'

'I'll just have a small one,' she said.

Three sherries later, or perhaps four, Maude was decidedly merry and already well on the way to mischievous. She had a plan.

'One of the disadvantages,' she began, 'of hiding away and refusing to pitch in with the party preparations, is that one doesn't get the opportunity to hang around on the periphery with a tray of vol-au-vents and earwig on the conversations of the great and the good.'

'I've earwigged,' I said. 'One isn't missing anything.'

'Perhaps,' she said. 'But sometimes one might. Unless, that is, one knows the secret door that opens on to the secret passageway that leads to the secret room where the secrets of the secretive can be secretly overheard.'

'And do you?'

'Do I what, dear?'

'Do you know the secret way to the secret room?'

She laughed. 'Of course I do, you silly ass. It would be a pretty poor show to rattle on about secret doors and then say, "But, alas and alack, I know not the whereabouts of the secret portal to the realms of the secret secrets." Put down your teacup and follow me.'

I did as I was bidden and tiptoed carefully behind her up the servants' staircase to the ground floor of the house.

'Why are we tiptoeing?' I asked as we emerged into a familiar passage that I knew led past the library and on to the entrance hall.

'For fun,' she said, and tapped the side of her nose.

We stopped just short of the first library door, opposite an ornate Chinese cabinet that I remembered from previous visits to The Grange. To the left of the door was a shallow alcove fitted with shelves, upon which stood an eclectic selection of knick-knacks – mementoes of the Farley-Strouds' lives. Maude reached past a tasselled cap with a 'First XV' badge embroidered on it and fiddled around under the shelf above it. There was a soft click. At her gentle push, the whole shelf assembly swung inwards, revealing a dark, cobwebbed passageway.

'You're not frightened of spiders, are you?' she asked.

'No,' I said. 'Just cows.'

'You're frightened of . . . ? Oh, never mind. If we meet any cows in here, I'll fend them off while you run for it. Come on. And shut the door behind you.'

I followed her in and pushed the perfectly weighted shelf-door until it clicked shut. The passageway was now completely dark.

'Grab my apron ribbon and follow me,' said Maude. 'We'll have to be quiet from now on.'

She set off at a slow, careful pace with me clutching at the neatly tied bow that held her apron in place. After a good few yards of pitch-black shuffling and a couple of cobweb-bestrewn corners, the tiny passageway seemed to grow a little lighter and filled with the distorted babble of a party. As Maude bobbed about in front of me, I caught glimpses of a grille of some sort, set in a wall a few feet ahead.

We stopped, and I was just able to make out Maude, silhouetted against the dim light from the grille, putting her finger to her lips. She gently took hold of my wrist and pulled me towards the wall.

Once I was close enough, I could make out that the grille was one of the many metal plates I had seen on the walls on previous visits to The Grange. They were drilled with an ornately decorative pattern of holes and I had presumed them to be part of some manner of ventilation system. Perhaps elsewhere in the house, they were, but this one had another purpose. I pressed my face closer and peered through one of the tiny holes. I was looking into the Tudor hall at the heart of the eclectically designed house. I'd heard of Tudor householders building secret rooms from which they could spy on their guests, but I'd never actually seen one. Until now. I was able to see and hear everything that was going on in what had been the original house's great hall but which the Farley-Strouds referred to as 'the ballroom'.

The music, I could now see, was provided by a string quartet – four elderly gentlemen scraping away with reasonable proficiency at what sounded to me like Beethoven. People stood in small huddles, conversational islands around which flowed trays of canapés and drinks borne by the liveried supply ships of the footmen and junior maids. The huddle nearest our 'air vent' was discussing the General Election and was drifting on to the subject of women's suffrage. A man with his back to the wall was speaking.

'. . . should never be given the vote, of course. They know nothing of commerce and industry, for one thing. How could a woman be expected to make a pragmatic, informed decision about international trade, or the laws governing the running of our factories? They're too emotional, for another. Too swayed by sentiment. Too easily persuaded to another's point of view. They simply don't have the temperament for the important decisions the electorate has to make. And heavens forfend we should ever let them take seats in Parliament. The country would collapse.'

There were solemn murmurs of agreement from the rest of the group. Eternal truths, it would appear, had been given voice.

'And what about their hats?' slurred an extremely upper-class voice whose owner I couldn't see.

The group laughed, but more in confusion than amusement.

'What the devil do you mean, Jimmy?' asked the first voice.

'Well, you know,' continued the drunk. 'They wear those huge hats nowadays. Bally enormous things. Imagine two ladies in monumental hats sitting in front of a tiny chap in the House. How would the poor little fellow ever make himself known to the Speaker?'

This time the group guffawed.

'Well done, James, lad,' said a third man. 'Knew we could count on you to cut straight to the heart of the matter. Big hats.' He laughed again. 'Wait till I tell the chaps at the League. Actually, we've a meeting coming up. Tuesday evening. You should come along and tell them yourself. We could do with your brand of insightful wit. Some of the chaps are a mite too earnest for my taste. Especially that bloody chap with the coffee shops. What's his name? Gives me the pip, that one.'

'Sorry, old horse, no can do,' said the one who seemed to be called Jimmy. 'Cards.'

The third man laughed. 'Still playing, eh? Getting any better at it?'

'I'm a dashed good player, I'll have you know. Just having a run of bad luck, is all. I say, I don't suppose you could lend a chap a few quid?'

They all laughed at this.

'Why don't you tap your old man for it?' asked the first voice. 'Surely the earl can spare you a few quid.'

'Pater's threatening to cut me off as it is,' said Jimmy forlornly. 'I'm robbing Peter to pay Paul just to keep afloat. If the gaffer gets wind of how much I already owe, I'll be out on my ear without so much as a brass farthing to my name. Fifty would do it. I've backed a dead cert at the end of the month – I'll be quids in. I can settle up with some other chaps and you'll have your money back in no time.'

'Fifty pounds?' laughed the man. 'Too rich for my blood. School fees due, tailor to be paid – you know how it goes.'

'Do think about it,' said Jimmy. 'If you change your mind, you know where I am.'

He seemed to have walked away because the others immediately began talking about him.

'Do you think you think I should, though?' asked the first voice. 'It might be handy having the son of an earl in my debt.'

'Don't even consider it,' said the anti-suffrage man. 'I know one or two of the chaps he plays cards with and you'd get a better return flushing your money down the drain. At least there's a chance you might be able to get it back at the sewage works.'

There was more laughter and the conversation returned to mundane matters.

We stayed in our secret listening room for another quarter of an hour before Maude indicated that we should head back.

◆ ◆ ◆

'And how was your evening?' asked Lady Hardcastle as I helped her into the little motor car at one in the morning.

'Oh, you know,' I said. 'The usual. I had tea with Maude Denton.'

'And how is Gertie's "lazy maid"?'

'She was in fine form,' I said. 'And knocking back the sherry as though it were about to be rationed.'

'I sometimes think it ought to be, you know. Wretched stuff can't make up its mind whether it's wine or brandy. An indecisive drink for vicars and maiden aunts.'

'You can add "ladies' maids of a certain vintage" to your list. She loves the stuff.'

I started the Rover's tiny engine and we set off back down the hill to the village.

'It doesn't sound like much of an evening,' she said. 'I'm so sorry.'

'Ah, but that's because I haven't told you the best part. Have you heard about the secret rooms that Tudor lords built next to their great halls so they could spy on their guests?'

'I'd heard of them, but I've never actually come across one.'

'I have,' I said. 'There's one at The Grange.'

'Good heavens,' she said. 'It's a higgledy-piggledy hotchpotch of a place, mind you, so I oughtn't to be surprised. Every owner from the seventeenth century onwards seems to have added a bit here and a bit there.'

'Well, it turns out that whoever built the original house had one of these little spying rooms put in, and every subsequent owner has kept it in place. Maude showed me the way in and we had a little listen to what you lot were up to.'

'And what were we up to?'

'Annoyingly, there was a group of very tedious men by the listening grate so we didn't learn much other than that one chap is something to do with an anti-suffrage group and that someone called Jimmy is rubbish at cards. We got bored rather quickly and went back to top Maude up with more sherry.'

'You poor things. They were quite the most dreadful people there, I'm afraid. At one point I was treated to a lecture from one chap from the Men's League for Opposing Woman Suffrage on why women shouldn't be allowed the vote. Something to do with hats, I think. I wasn't listening terribly attentively. Whatever it was, the chap in question seemed to think it was the most hilarious thing he'd ever heard and went off to tell some more people.'

'We overheard the origins of that little gem,' I said. 'The terrible cards player that they were calling "Jimmy" came up with it. The Honourable Jimmy, I should think – someone mentioned something about his being the son of an earl.'

'Ah, yes, I met him, too. James Stamford . . . or something. Son of the Earl of . . . of somewhere beginning with K. Knutsford, perhaps.'

This inability to remember names had always struck me as something of a hindrance to someone who had once made her living as one of the Crown's most valuable intelligence agents. So much so that I had long suspected it to be an affectation. I decided not to challenge her on it, though, but made a mental note that the man's name was almost certainly not Stamford, nor was his father the Earl of Knutsford. I was sure I'd heard of a Lord Knutsford but he was a viscount and definitely not an earl.

'Did you meet anyone of actual interest?' I asked.

'Oh, you know, the usual crowd,' she said. 'I had a hairy moment when I saw Redvers Hinkley on the other side of the room. Luckily, he was deep in a rather serious-looking conversation with the chap with the hat obsession so I don't think he recognized me. That would have been awkward.'

'You'd have bluffed your way out of it,' I said confidently.

'Oh, I'm sure I would. But I rather like Lady Summerford – it would be a shame to burn that particular alias. She might come in useful.'

Despite our heavy coats, we were shivering by the time I parked the Rover in its little shed. We got ourselves back indoors as quickly as we could.

I made some cocoa and we retired, but not before promises had been extracted from me concerning a long lie-in and breakfast in bed.

Chapter Eight

Just as Edna was serving lunch on Sunday, the telephone rang.

'Chipping Bevington two-three,' I said, after taking the earpiece from its hook on the side of the wooden box that housed the gubbins. 'Hello?'

'Miss Armstrong? It's Dinah Caudle here.'

'Good afternoon, Miss Caudle,' I said. 'Would you like to speak to Lady Hardcastle?'

'What? No, you'll do. I have more information from Brookfield's notebook and I'd like to talk to you both. I'll be passing through your delightful little village later this afternoon – would it be too much trouble for me to drop in? Say around four?'

By this time, Lady Hardcastle had emerged from the dining room, expecting the call to be, as it usually was, for her.

I put my hand over the telephone mouthpiece and quietly said, 'Caudle has news. Wants to come at four.'

'That will be fine,' she replied in her normal voice. 'Invite her for tea.'

I took my hand from the mouthpiece and said, 'That will be fine, Miss Caudle. Please stay for tea if you can.'

'Thank you,' said Miss Caudle. 'And tell her to speak more quietly – I could still hear her even with your hand over the mouthpiece.'

'Right you are,' I said. 'We'll expect you later.'

I hung up.

'What did she say?' asked Lady Hardcastle.

'She said you're a loudmouth,' I said.

She harrumphed and we returned to our lunch.

Once we'd eaten, Lady Hardcastle went back to her study and I helped Miss Jones put a few things together for tea. It was supposed to be her and Edna's afternoon off, but she insisted on staying and I welcomed her help.

With that done, there was nothing else needing my attention so I retired to the drawing room to read a book. I must have dozed off, because the next thing I heard was the ringing of the doorbell.

I struggled to consciousness and staggered out to answer the door. The hall clock proclaimed it to be ten minutes past four, but that didn't mean anything these days. All I could say for certain was that it was some time in the afternoon, and that was based solely on my memory of having already eaten lunch.

I straightened my uniform and opened the door. Miss Caudle stood on the step, waving over her shoulder at an expensive-looking motor car, which promptly drove away.

'Good afternoon, Miss Caudle,' I said. 'Do come in.'

I helped her out of her overcoat and showed her through to the drawing room.

'Please make yourself comfortable,' I said. 'I'll let Lady Hardcastle know you're here.'

I didn't quite make it to Lady Hardcastle's study door before she emerged. We smiled and nodded, and I left her to greet Miss Caudle while I carried on towards the kitchen to put the finishing touches on our afternoon tea.

They were already deep in conversation by the time I carried the tray through.

Miss Caudle was talking. '. . . on the wrong foot over all that business with the moving picture show, but I think it would be to everyone's benefit if we just put it all behind us. We agreed to work together on this and we've been rubbing along reasonably well so far . . . but you can't deny that there's an undercurrent of unresolved animosity. I can't help but feel things would be easier if we were to draw a line under it all and move on.'

'I quite agree,' said Lady Hardcastle. 'I can't say I wholly approve of your motives or your methods during "all that business", as you call it, but I have a grudging admiration for your efforts to make a career for yourself. I know it's not easy. What say you, Flo? Shall we call a truce?'

'I'm game if you are, my lady,' I said. 'I always prefer friends and allies to enemies and opponents.'

'Steady on,' said Miss Caudle. 'Let's not get carried away. I was proposing a mutually beneficial halt to hostilities, not making daisy chains and brushing each other's hair.'

Lady Hardcastle smiled. 'Allies, at least, then. We have a common cause.'

'We had a common cause before,' said Miss Caudle.

'Hardly, dear,' said Lady Hardcastle. 'We wanted to catch a killer and you wanted a headline story with your name on it.'

'Yes, and if you—' began Miss Caudle.

'Ladies, please,' I interrupted. 'I know I haven't been party to the whole conversation, but the portion I heard seemed to involve the calling of a truce and working together for a common cause. I didn't hear anything about bickering. Was that in the part of the conversation I missed?'

'You're quite right,' said Lady Hardcastle. 'My apologies, Miss Caudle.'

'And mine, too,' said Miss Caudle. 'Do you always let her boss you about like that?'

'She's gracious enough to allow me to pretend I'm in charge, but she's a fearsome little thing and I find it best to do as I'm told.'

I raised my eyebrows. *That'll be the day*, I thought.

'Well, then,' said Miss Caudle, and reached into her ever-present satchel. 'In the spirit of this new *entente cordiale*, let me tell you of the latest developments.'

She withdrew Mr Brookfield's now-familiar notebook and a sheaf of papers covered in a jumble of notes and diagrams.

'The problem with Christian's efforts to keep his notes secret from the prying eyes of his enemies,' she said as she shuffled through the papers, 'is that they keep them from the prying eyes of his pals, too. Even with the "key" it's taking an age, and some of his cryptic little wordplay clues are excruciatingly tricky. But I'm getting there . . . Ah, here we are.'

She found the sheet she'd been looking for.

'I had a bit of an epiphany on Friday,' she said. 'Somehow, I began to see the pattern in the jumble. We'd thought – well, I'd thought, anyway – that he was working on a random tangle of disconnected stories, that it was just the result of capricious whim as he jumped from one to the other. But they're connected. It was all one big story.'

'How did you work it out?' I asked.

'It was after I'd got to this next part,' she said, tapping the paper. 'The next fellow on his tangled list of weasels and ne'er-do-wells is a gambler. An inveterate cards player who is up to his eyeballs in debt, by the name of James—'

'Stansbridge,' interrupted Lady Hardcastle. 'Third son of the Earl of Keynsham.' She winked at me. I knew she'd been putting it on.

'How did you . . . ?' asked Miss Caudle in astonishment.

'Lucky guess. We both encountered him last night at the Farley-Strouds' place – The Grange. There can't be many card-playing debtors called Jimmy who would attract the attention of a sleuthing journalist like Brookfield.'

'Even when someone else is leading the way, you seem to manage to be one step ahead,' said Miss Caudle. 'Yes, the Honourable James "Jimmy" Stansbridge, third son, as you say, of the Earl of Keynsham, came to Christian's attention as part of what I now know to be a larger investigation. He's a little fish and I'd not ordinarily think him worthy of the ink. Who cares about another titled fool who can't pay his tailor?'

'But we do care who lent him the money,' said Lady Hardcastle.

'Right again. That's exactly who we care about.'

'And do we know?' I asked.

'Well, now . . . "know" is a rather problematic word in newspaper circles. There's often a good stretch of clear water between what we "know" and what we can prove.'

'Much the same is true in the world of international . . . "diplomacy",' said Lady Hardcastle. 'What did Brookfield know?'

'He knew as sure as eggs is eggs that the man funding the Honourable Jimmy's inept gambling is a city councillor by the name of Nathaniel Morefield.'

'We are to presume, I presume, that there is a special significance in this name,' said Lady Hardcastle.

'Not on its own, no,' said Miss Caudle. 'He's a well-known councillor with plenty of money, and friends in high places. He's just the sort of person one might expect to be lending an old pal a few bob to help him out of trouble. The significance comes from his connection to the other names Brookfield had been looking at. He seems to have been sure that Nathaniel Morefield was the man tupping Oswald Crane's wife, and the man whose palm had been greased to ensure the success of Redvers Hinkley's plans for the development on Thomas Street.'

'He's a man with quite a strong motive for doing away with the troublesome journalist who was threatening to blow the gaff on his assorted shady dealings, then.'

'Well, quite,' said Miss Caudle.

'A little stronger than the others,' I said. 'But that still doesn't rule any of them out. Crane stood to lose his reputation, and Hinkley his liberty, if the news got out. Even witless Jimmy had a decent motive. Maude and I overheard him saying that his father would cut him off completely if he found out how serious his debt problems were.'

'If the earl knew what was going on, that would give him a motive, too,' said Miss Caudle. 'He would want to protect his family's reputation, after all. He might have threatened to cut his son off if he found more evidence of gambling debts, but I doubt it was from a desire to protect his son or his own fortune. It seems more likely to me that he'd want to stop the boy's gambling to shield the family from the ignominy of his prodigal son losing everything on a hand of cards.'

'What we need,' I said, 'is to start work on crossing some of these names off the list.'

'Finding and testing alibis would help,' said Lady Hardcastle. 'I rather think that if we were to press Oswald Crane, we might spook him into giving up an alibi just to get rid of us.'

'I'll leave that one to you,' said Miss Caudle. 'You seem to have the knack of getting on his nerves. If any of us can do it, you can.'

'Thank you, dear,' said Lady Hardcastle. 'It's not much of a talent but I shall be sure to add "irking pompous company directors" to my list of accomplishments in *Who's Who*.'

'You do that,' said Miss Caudle. 'Hinkley has already supplied an alibi, hasn't he? That was rather neatly done, by the way, that nonsense about the boxing match.'

'One does what one can,' said Lady Hardcastle. 'It's a bit flimsy as alibis go, but it shouldn't be too tricky to find out whether he really was working late at the office all last week.'

'What about the Honourable Jimmy?' I said. 'Are we counting him as a suspect, and what are we going to do about investigating him?'

'I think that might be one for Georgie Bickle,' said Lady Hardcastle. 'I'd be surprised if she didn't know her way around the world frequented by minor nobles in Bristol. We'll call on her tomorrow.'

'And I'll take a tilt at Nathaniel Morefield,' said Miss Caudle. 'There's a charity function coming up and I'm reasonably certain I've seen his name on the list of honoured guests. I'll see if I can set up an interview – he's the sort who'll want to make sure people know he's a doer of good works. Would you two like to come along, Lady Summerford and Miss Maybee with two e's?'

'I think I'd better sit that one out,' said Lady Hardcastle. 'He's more likely to know that there's no such couple as Sir Philip and Lady Summerford, and I can't be certain he hasn't at least seen me before, though I don't recall ever actually meeting him. You're welcome to go along, though, Flo, if you want to.'

'I'd be happy to,' I said. 'As Nelly Maybee with two e's?'

'I like the sound of her,' said Miss Caudle with a smile. 'I'm sure we can concoct a reason for her being there.'

'That's our plan, then,' said Lady Hardcastle. 'Can we tempt you to some more cake?'

◆ ◆ ◆

Lady Hardcastle telephoned Lady Bickle first thing on Monday morning and arranged to meet her at the shop. We arrived in Clifton just after eleven to find Lady Bickle, Beattie Challenger, and Marisol Rojas – all in their finest white dresses – behind the counter of the WSPU shop. They greeted us warmly.

'Do you have news?' asked Lady Bickle when the round of cheek-kissing had finally come to an end.

'Some,' said Lady Hardcastle. 'Should we talk upstairs? I don't want to be overheard by casual shoppers.'

'Of course,' said Lady Bickle. 'Oh, but that means one of you will have to miss out. We'll tell you everything, I promise.'

'I don't mind staying down here,' said Marisol.

'Nor do I,' said Miss Challenger.

'Grab a coin from the till and we'll toss for it,' said Lady Bickle. 'Marisol, you call.'

'Heads,' she said.

'Tails, I'm afraid,' said Lady Bickle as she looked at the coin. 'But we really will tell you everything.'

We trooped upstairs and into the office. I looked out of the window at the City Art Gallery opposite and wondered why we never visited it. Lady Bickle took the swivel chair at the desk while Lady Hardcastle and Miss Challenger sat on the sofa. I'd been very uncomfortable squashed in the middle of the sofa last time so I opted instead to perch on its arm, next to Lady Hardcastle.

'What's been happening?' said Lady Bickle. 'We've been on ten-terhooks since you went into town on Friday. Did Miss Caudle have anything useful to tell you?'

Lady Hardcastle succinctly recounted the details of Miss Caudle's discoveries and of our meeting with the property developer, Redvers Hinkley. Between us we told of the party on Saturday evening and my earwigging on the Men's League members while they rebuffed the Honourable Jimmy's pleas for financial help. I let Lady Hardcastle explain the link between everyone we'd met so far and the corrupt councillor, Nathaniel Morefield.

'That's astonishing,' said Lady Bickle when we had finished.

'Remarkable,' agreed Miss Challenger. 'He was quite the blood-hound, this Christian Brookfield, wasn't he? That's quite a nest he uncovered.'

'He does seem to have been rather dogged, doesn't he?' said Lady Hardcastle.

'That notebook seems to have been a bit of a treasure trove,' said Miss Challenger. 'It's a pity he didn't record more details before he . . . you know . . .'

'Oh, we're nowhere near the end of it – there's still so much more to come,' said Lady Hardcastle. 'Miss Caudle is working as fast as she can in between her other obligations, but it's still slow going.'

'I'll bet,' said Lady Bickle. 'What happens next?'

'I'm glad you asked that,' said Lady Hardcastle. 'We'd rather like you to lend a hand.'

'Me?' said Lady Bickle with some surprise. 'Oh, I say, how exciting. Hugger-mugger stuff? Will I need dark clothes and a jemmy?'

Lady Hardcastle laughed. 'I'm afraid not,' she said. 'We need your social connections. More specifically, your card-playing connections. You told us you have a regular bridge game with . . .'

'Lady Hooper,' I said.

'Thank you. With Lady Hooper. Do you by any chance know of any, shall we say, less genteel card schools in your part of town? Something discreet and suitable for the minor nobility, but where the stakes are a little higher?'

'If such places exist,' said Lady Bickle with a mischievous glint in her eye, 'I should be breaking the rules of discretion were I to confirm their existence . . .'

'But?' said Lady Hardcastle.

'But it happens that I know Jimmy Stansbridge personally, so I don't have to betray anything. Do you want me to have a word?'

'That would be most helpful,' said Lady Hardcastle. 'If you could somehow bring your conversation round to where he was on the evening of Tuesday the twenty-fifth, we might be able, as our constabulary friends put it, to "eliminate him from our enquiries".'

'Or put him squarely in the middle of them,' said Lady Bickle. 'We can't assume he's innocent just because he's one of the nobs.'

'Quite so,' said Lady Hardcastle. 'For good or ill, we need to know where he was that night.'

'I think I can do it without arousing suspicion,' said Lady Bickle. 'I haven't been to one of those card schools – whose existence I can neither confirm nor deny – for some weeks. If I've ever been at all. I could say I'd been at a particular game that night and was disappointed not to see him. He'll most likely give up his whereabouts while expressing his regrets at having missed me.'

'As long as you don't pick the game he actually attended,' I said.

'Ah, yes,' she said. 'That would be awkward, wouldn't it? I'll need to double-check before I make my approach. It's all right – I know a few people.'

'People who may, or may not, be involved in card games that may, or may not, exist?' I said.

'Yes,' she said, 'those ones.'

I happened to glance at Beattie Challenger during this exchange and she seemed to be struggling to mask her distaste – I began to suspect that she disapproved of Lady Bickle's flippant attitude to rule-breaking. It was not the way, I surmised, that she believed proper ladies should behave.

'Splendid,' said Lady Hardcastle. 'That's one thing off the list. Thank you.'

'What else is on your list?' asked Lady Bickle.

'More prodding and poking,' said Lady Hardcastle. 'I have been given the enjoyable task of attempting to goad Mr Oswald Crane into offering up either a confession or an alibi.'

'And I shall be joining Miss Caudle in her attempts to get some useful information from Councillor Nathaniel Morefield.'

'He's a nasty little man,' said Lady Bickle. 'On top of everything else, he's a member of the Men's League for Opposing Woman Suffrage. Not that that makes him a nasty little man, of course. But it doesn't help.'

'What are you doing about the other chap?' asked Miss Challenger.

'Which other . . . oh, Redvers Hinkley?' said Lady Hardcastle. 'The property chap?'

'Yes,' said Miss Challenger. 'Don't you need to check him again?'

'We do need to check his alibi, yes,' said Lady Hardcastle. 'The trouble is, he says he was working late at the office all that week and we've not yet come up with a solid way of checking whether that's true. All ideas are welcome on that one.'

'I'm sure you'll come up with something,' said Lady Bickle. 'A couple of clever old sticks like you.'

'I'm sure we shall,' said Lady Hardcastle. 'But for the moment, we'll have to take him at his word.'

'What are you up to next?' asked Lady Bickle.

'To tell the truth, we're rather at a loose end. Until our various meetings have been arranged, there's not a lot for us to do. I don't suppose anyone fancies joining us for coffee?'

'That would be a lovely idea, but we regretfully have to decline, I'm afraid. We have rather a lot of leaflets to distribute and I have to make sure that all the arrangements are in place for our regular "at home" meeting this evening.'

'Some other time, then,' said Lady Hardcastle.

'We should love to,' said Lady Bickle. 'I say, you're most welcome to come along to the meeting this evening if you wish. I'm sure you'd enjoy it. Seven o'clock at the Victoria Rooms.'

'We'll check the diary over coffee,' said Lady Hardcastle.

We left them to their leaflets and walked up into Clifton village in search of coffee.

◆ ◆ ◆

Despite our growing familiarity with Clifton and its environs, we decided not to hunt for an alternative coffee shop and opted, instead, for the familiarity of the local branch of Crane's. A waitress showed us to a table and took Lady Hardcastle's order: 'A pot of coffee for two, and two of the most enormous, stickiest, most wickedly indulgent cream-filled buns in the place, please.'

While Lady Hardcastle fussed about in her handbag looking for her notebook, I cast an eye about the room. I'd long since stopped feeling the need to scan our surroundings for possible threats, and no longer bothered to make certain we had a clear escape route, but the quick appraising look round the room was a hard habit to break.

The two elderly ladies at the next table seemed to be old friends, listing the names of recently lost contemporaries and lightening the mood by sharing increasingly boastful news of the achievements of their grandchildren. The couple sitting behind Lady Hardcastle were obviously very much in love and, even more obviously, very much married to other people.

The two men in the far corner were . . .

'Did you spot the two men at the table by the window when we came in?' I said quietly.

Without looking round, she said, 'Tallish chap with his back to the door; nervous, ratty fellow with him? Tall one neatly but not expensively dressed; ratty is unshaven and his clothes have seen better days. Ratty keeps touching his jacket pocket – probably a knife or a cosh. Why?'

'The tallish one is Inspector Sunderland.'

'Is it, by George? I wonder what he's doing up here.'

'Having a discreet chat with an informant, I should imagine,' I said. 'This doesn't seem like the sort of place the ratty one would ordinarily visit, so it's also not somewhere he'd be at risk of bumping into someone who knows him.'

'Sounds reasonable to me,' she said. 'We shall have to ask the inspector the next time we see him.'

Our coffee arrived, accompanied by gargantuan sticky buns that far exceeded Lady Hardcastle's facetious specifications.

'Do you think we should have ordered one to share between us?' I said.

'Nonsense. Fortitude, young Florence. Brace yourself and dig in.'

We began the not wholly unpleasant task of tackling the monumental pastries as we discussed the arson case. It wasn't long before we moved on to the difficulties of checking our suspects' alibis without having any authority to compel anyone to do anything, much less tell us the truth.

We were about to merry-go-round our way through the same objections to the same ideas for the third time when the two men by the door rose to leave. Ratty scuttled out as fast as his spindly legs would carry him, and the inspector lingered for a while until he was out of sight. Once his coffee companion had gone, he turned back inside the shop and approached our table.

'Good morning, ladies,' he said.

'How do you do, Inspector?' said Lady Hardcastle. 'What a surprise to see you. Fancy you dropping in here just as we were enjoying our coffee and cake. Join us, won't you?'

'Don't give me that.' He laughed. 'You saw me when you came in.'

'I saw your companion,' she said. 'It was Flo who spotted you.'

'I might have known I'd bump into you, though,' he said, drawing up a chair that he'd taken from a neighbouring table. 'What with the WSPU shop being nearby and this being one of the best coffee shops in the area.'

'Did we interrupt anything?' I asked.

'No, don't worry. Weasel didn't notice you and I didn't let on that there was anyone here I knew.'

'Weasel?' said Lady Hardcastle. 'We had him down as Ratty.'

'Jesse "Weasel" Weaver,' he said. 'Housebreaker of this parish and part-time copper's nark.'

'A handy fellow to know,' she said. 'Did he have any enticing titbits to share?'

129

'Sadly not. I was hoping he might have heard some whispers about a particular case we're working on. That I'm working on, I should say – there's not a lot of enthusiasm for it down at the station.'

'Sounds intriguing,' I said. 'Is there anything we can do?'

'I doubt you move in the right circles,' he said with a chuckle. 'It's not got anything to do with house parties and stolen gems, nor dead farmers, or racing cars, or moving picture shows, for that matter. If I'm right, this is going to be the work of some very serious criminals.'

'You're doing little to lessen the intrigue,' I said.

'And you know little of the circles we move in,' said Lady Hardcastle. 'We ran with some very shady types in our day.'

'I'm sure you did,' he said. 'I've heard you tell the stories.'

'At least half of them are true, too,' I said.

'Did you ever come across any gold thieves?' he asked.

'Well, now,' said Lady Hardcastle. 'Let me see. We smuggled a box of gold coins out of Bratislava that time, didn't we, dear?'

'We did. And they weren't exactly ours to start with, so in a sense . . .'

'So in a sense you're gold thieves yourselves,' he said. 'Perhaps I should just arrest you both now to be on the safe side.'

'Many have tried and failed,' said Lady Hardcastle. 'But what gold is there in Bristol worth stealing? The city's jewellers could barely muster a whole ingot between them, I should have thought.'

'It's not in Bristol yet,' said the inspector. 'It's due to arrive at the Avonmouth docks at the end of the month.'

'From foreign parts?' I asked.

'The foreignest,' he said. 'If you happen to hear anything as you go about your business, do please let me know. Weasel knows nothing and I'm keen for all the intelligence I can get.'

'As are we,' I said.

'Ah, yes,' he said. 'How is the Worrel case coming along?'

I quickly outlined our progress so far, with Lady Hardcastle providing additional details and observations.

'You're doing well,' he said when we'd finished. 'And so was Brookfield. I've often said we need to set up a police unit to deal with the likes of that lot. We're chasing all over town nicking petty villains for their tuppenny-ha'penny crimes, while the likes of' – he dropped his voice – 'Redvers Blooming Hinkley and Nathaniel Blessed Morefield are skimming off hundreds – probably thousands – of pounds with their dodgy deals. I couldn't care less about Lord Whatnot and his card games, though, I must say. And if I were married to Crane, I'd be looking elsewhere for love and companionship, too. But those other two . . .'

'I know what you mean,' said Lady Hardcastle. 'If you want to help us nail Hinkley, you could press him for his whereabouts on the night of the fire. By his own account he was "working late at the office" and we have no way to check that.'

'I'd love to help,' he said. 'But there's not a lot more I can do than you've already done. He's not officially under investigation so he's got no reason to tell me anything, either, I'm afraid. I'll put the feelers out and see if we can get him on fraud and corruption charges, though. Morefield, too.'

'Thank you, Inspector,' she said.

'I'm going to be taking a run at Morefield myself – or, I should say, with Miss Caudle – as soon as she's arranged an interview,' I said.

'Taking your thumbscrews, eh?'

'I've rather gone off thumbscrews, lately,' I said. 'They weigh down my pockets and ruin the line of my dress. To be honest, I've never really needed mechanical assistance to make a man scream for his mother, anyway, so I tend to leave them at home nowadays.'

The inspector smiled. 'I've said it before, Miss Armstrong, and I'm sure to say it again, but I'm exceedingly glad you're on the side of the angels.'

I smiled sweetly.

'Well, then,' said the inspector, rising to his feet. 'On that mildly alarming note, I shall take my leave – crimes to prevent, villains to nab, you know how it is. It was a delight to bump into you both.'

'And into you, Inspector, dear,' said Lady Hardcastle. 'Do take care of yourself, won't you? And give our regards to Mrs Sunderland.'

'I shall, indeed,' he said. 'Thank you. Though I should warn you that once I mention your name at home, I shall be nagged once more into inviting you to dine with us.'

'Then we shall have to resolve to take her up on her offer. We can't have you being nagged, even if it is for the most convivial of reasons.'

He nodded a farewell and navigated his way between the tables to the hatstand by the door. Putting on his bowler, he stepped out into the chill air and was gone.

We lingered for a few minutes more over the dregs of our coffee while we tried to decide on our next course of action.

'Oh, and we never did talk about the WSPU meeting this evening,' asked Lady Hardcastle. 'What do you think? Shall we go?'

'I'd be happy to go along if you want to,' I said.

'Which means "no", really, doesn't it?'

'Well, I'd have been more likely to say, "No, thank you, my lady," but the sentiment would be the same. We've been to suffragette meetings before and I don't really need to be further convinced of the need for women to get the vote. For every adult to get the vote. They're not going to say anything we've not heard before, are they? The only reason I can think of for going would be as a show of solidarity.'

'You're right, of course,' she said. 'It has the potential to be stultifyingly tedious, but it couldn't do us any harm to be seen to be supporting the cause. We might need those ladies on our side.'

'As I said, my lady, I'm happy to go if you want to. It'll be well lit – I can take some sewing.'

'How about we stay until they break for tea and biscuits and then slip out? We can get fish and chips on the way home.'

She left a few coins on the table to cover the cost of our snack and a generous gratuity, and we began to gather our belongings. We were about to stand to leave when the bell above the door tinkled and in waddled the spherical form of the shop's owner, Mr Oswald Crane.

A waitress hurried to fawn over him while he surveyed his empire. His smug, proprietorial smile faded when he saw me.

'What are these two women doing here?' he demanded.

The waitress was taken aback by the harsh tone, and slightly baffled by the question itself.

'Drinking coffee and eating sticky buns, Mr Crane,' she said uncertainly. 'They spoke to one of the other customers briefly. He came over to them when his companion had left.'

'Don't be impertinent,' he snapped. 'Get them out.'

'Don't worry, dear,' said Lady Hardcastle. 'We've finished and we're on our way. Thank you for the wonderful service. You've been most attentive.'

'Lady Hardcastle and her maid – yes, that's right, "my lady", don't think I don't know who you really are – are not welcome in any of my establishments,' said Mr Crane. 'Do you understand?'

'Yes, sir,' said the waitress with an embarrassed curtsey.

Mr Crane seemed to become aware that he had missed some important information.

'Wait a moment. One of the other customers?' he said. 'Which other customer?'

'Inspector Sunderland of the Bristol CID,' she said, proud of her knowledge. 'He's a lovely gentleman. Comes in regular, like. Always polite.'

Mr Crane's florid complexion paled a little.

'Don't worry, Mr Crane,' said Lady Hardcastle. 'He was only asking us where you were on the evening of Tuesday the twenty-fifth. And we don't have the first idea. I'm sure he'll contact you in due course.'

Mr Crane drew us hastily into an unoccupied corner of the shop. It offered no more privacy than he'd had before, but he seemed to think it made our conversation inaudible to the other customers.

'Now listen here, Hardcastle,' he said with a lot less forcefulness than I imagined he intended. 'You have no proof whatsoever that this Brookfield's foul insinuations about my wife are true, and if you're repeating them to this Inspector . . .'

'Sunderland, sir,' I said.

'. . . to this Inspector Sunderland, then I shall sue you for slander.'

'We'll see about that,' said Lady Hardcastle. 'But, as I say, it wasn't your wife he was interested in. It was your own whereabouts on the night Christian Brookfield died.'

'On the night . . . Now, look here. I had nothing to do with that terrible fire and you have to tell him that.'

'But we don't know where you were any more than he does,' she said. 'We can't really tell him anything.'

'I was at home that evening, and you can tell him as much.'

'Can your wife corroborate this?'

'My wife was . . . out that evening.'

'Your servants, then?'

'Yes, yes, I'm sure they can. Why don't you ask them? I had nothing to do with any of this.'

'Thank you, Mr Crane,' said Lady Hardcastle. 'If we see the inspector before you do, we'll be certain to pass the information on. And we have your permission to question your servants?'

'By all means,' he said. 'I have nothing to hide.'

'Thank you, Mr Crane. Good day.'

With that she turned towards the door with me behind her. It was only when the hubbub of conversation resumed that I realized how quiet the shop had become during our conversation.

Chapter Nine

On Monday evening we drove back to Clifton to the WSPU meeting at the Victoria Rooms, not far from the shop. Lady Bickle greeted us warmly and introduced us to a few of the regular attendees. We took seats near the back and settled in.

Lady Bickle opened the meeting, welcoming the regulars and introducing Lady Hardcastle and me. She reassured the members that we were making every effort to clear Lizzie Worrel's name and that we were hopeful of a resolution in the near future. I didn't share her optimism, nor her assessment of Lizzie herself, who, she said, had been in good spirits when we had visited her on Friday. Nevertheless, I understood the need to put a brave face on things – despondency would get us nowhere.

The first speaker was the wife of a prominent Bristol lawyer, who offered a summary of recent events from a suffragette perspective. She recounted press reports of political speeches and offered her own commentary on the opinions expressed by the newspapers' leader writers. She was well informed and surprisingly funny, with a knack for undercutting the less encouraging news with a well-pitched joke, usually at the expense of the original speaker. She left the stage to an enthusiastic round of applause from the assembled women – I estimated there to be getting on for fifty of us – and returned to sit with Lady Bickle.

Administrative notices from the branch secretary followed, covering the need to make sure that membership subscriptions were paid on time, and reminding ladies of the importance of wearing WSPU colours during the General Election.

'And don't forget,' she said, 'if you're short of a sash or a badge, or you think your husband's views might be swayed by the sight of a pair of white, green, and purple bloomers, get yourself along to the WSPU shop on Queen's Road. Georgie, Beattie, and Marisol will be happy to supply you with anything you need.' She paused for an unexpected round of applause for the shop team. 'And speaking of Marisol, it is my great pleasure to introduce our next speaker, all the way from Chile, Miss Marisol Rojas.'

Marisol stepped on to the stage to another ripple of applause. Despite having met her a couple of times already, I was somewhat unprepared for the confidence with which she addressed us, and the forthright nature of her opinions. She was a passionate lady.

'Mine is a young country,' she said at one point. 'There are many in Chile who remember what it is like to live in a land where no one has the vote. Within my lifetime there has been a civil war to bring to us the sort of parliamentary rule that you enjoy in Europe. We fought. And we won. Or we thought we had. But it was an illusion. Still power rested in the hands of the rich men. In England you think you have more rights, more power, but even here the true power is in the hands of the rich men. We fight for votes for women, but there are men here with no say in their own futures.'

She continued on this theme for a while and I became convinced that she would call for a revolution before the night was out. Such was her passion, I'm sure more than half of us would have followed her if she had. By the time she had finished whipping us into a mutinous frenzy, the hall was abuzz with renewed enthusiasm for the cause.

It was time for the interval – a chance for the members to discuss the issues she had raised over a nice cup of tea. As discussed, though, we slipped discreetly away at the tea break and made our way out of the hall.

There were two ladies positioned by the doors who ushered us out into the cold night air.

One said, 'Goodnight, ladies. Mind how you goes.'

The other made me pause when she said, 'There's some lads outside come to cause trouble. Just shout out if they bothers you.'

I turned back. 'Lads?' I said.

'Nothin' to worry about,' said the second lady. 'Just a few students, I reckons, come to have a laugh at the silly women tryin' to get the vote. They won't hurt you.'

'If they tries, mind,' said the first woman, 'just you yell out and we'll give 'em what for.'

I was intrigued. 'You're suffrajitsus?' I said. 'I've read about your training.'

They laughed. 'Not us, my lover,' said the first one. 'We just likes a punch-up. But we's hopin' to get some trainin' soon.'

'"Suffrajitsu"?' said Lady Hardcastle.

'Sorry, my lady,' I said. 'I meant to read you the article a couple of weeks ago, but I must have forgotten. The WSPU are training interested ladies in jiu-jitsu – one of the Japanese fighting arts. The principles are similar to some of the things that Chen Ping Bo taught me in China – one uses one's opponent's strength and size against him. It's ideal for smaller women and it's starting to help in their confrontations with more . . . "enthusiastic" policemen.'

'You knows it, then?' said the second lady.

'Not jiu-jitsu,' I said. 'I learned my fighting skills in China, not Japan. But I can teach you a few tricks to keep you safe until you get your proper suffragette training.'

'That would be wonderful,' she said.

T E Kinsey

'I'm Florence Armstrong,' I said, offering her my hand. 'Lady Bickle knows how to get in touch with us. Tell her I offered to take a class with as many of you as wish to learn.'

'We will,' she said. 'I'm Cissie and this is Ida.'

'It's a pleasure to meet you,' I said. 'And this is my employer, Lady Hardcastle.'

They both bobbed a curtsey. 'Pleased to meet you, ma'am,' they said.

'And you, ladies. Thank you for looking out for us.'

'A pleasure, m'lady,' said Cissie, and held the door open for us.

Once outside, I said, 'You didn't mind my offering, did you? It all happened so quickly that I didn't get a chance to ask you.'

'You're not an indentured serf, dear,' she said. 'You're free to do as you please. And I'd have been most disappointed if you hadn't offered – I think it's a wonderful idea. I'm very proud of you and your skills, you know. I don't say it often enough, but I am.'

'Thank you,' I said. 'You're very—'

'Oi!' shouted a voice from the dark. 'Get home and look after your husbands.'

'Did someone just "oi" me?' said Lady Hardcastle. 'How very uncouth. I haven't been "oi"-ed for years.'

'I believe he was "oi"-ing both of us,' I said. 'Shall we remonstrate?'

'I don't think it's worth the effort, dear,' she said. 'Like the ladies said, it's probably just some students having a lark.'

As we approached the gates, we saw by the light of the streetlamp that it was, indeed, a group of young men in university scarves. There were empty beer bottles on the ground at their feet.

'Good evening, gentlemen,' said Lady Hardcastle affably. 'No studying for you this evening?'

'Field studies, madam,' said one of them with an exaggerated bow. 'We're observing the species *mulieres stulta* in their natural habitat.' He resumed his previous pose, leaning casually against the lamppost.

138

'Foolish women, eh?' she said. 'I look forward to reading your paper.'

'We've found a Latin-speaker, lads,' he said. 'You see what happens when you let them have access to a little learning? One minute they're stumbling through Ovid, the next minute they begin to imagine that they're clever enough to vote.'

He pushed himself upright and took a couple of steps towards us. His companions, still about five yards away, arranged themselves to block our path.

I sighed.

'You see,' said the ringleader, 'there's only one thing worse than a woman who thinks she should have the vote, and that's a woman who thinks she's clever. And we think it's high time someone taught you your proper place.'

A sudden movement to my right caught my eye. One of the young men had stooped to pick up one of the empty beer bottles and was readying himself to throw it.

'Beer bottle on the right,' I said quietly.

'I've seen him,' said Lady Hardcastle. 'I do hope nobody gets hurt.'

This made the young men laugh.

'We'll only hurt you a little bit,' said the ringleader. 'To teach you some manners.'

The bottle wielder lobbed his missile in a high, graceful arc towards us. I caught it easily and put it gently on the ground.

'Don't do that,' I said. 'It's not nice.'

'It's not nice for uppity women to think they should be entitled to vote,' said the ringleader. 'But it doesn't seem to stop you.'

I wasn't entirely certain how we were going to resolve the situation, which now seemed to be at a rather tense stalemate. The boys – it was obvious by now that these were boys, not men – seemed somewhat nonplussed by our calm reaction to their half-hearted aggression. They had clearly expected more in the way of flap and panic on our part and

139

appeared unsure of what to do next. They hadn't, I thought, expected to get as far as actual violence and didn't seem to want to engage us, but I couldn't believe they would be able simply to back down and let us past, either.

Luckily, the ringleader proved a bit more decisive and his decision, though woefully stupid, did at least give us the chance to end things. He rushed towards me and threw a wild punch. At last, I thought, something I could deal with.

I dodged the clumsy swing and stepped inside his reach, landing a better-aimed blow of my own on the poor lad's chin with my open palm. As he began to stumble, I helped him on his way by sweeping his feet out from under him. I grabbed his wrist as he fell, and lowered him gently to the ground to protect him from smashing his head on the pavement. He was out cold.

The others took a step back. Good.

'You'd better help your pal,' I said. 'He might be a little embarrassed when he comes round, but we'll leave it up to you how much you rag him over being floored by a five-foot woman. He'll have a sore jaw for a few days but he should be fine. If he blacks out again, or starts throwing up, take him to a doctor at once.'

The bottle thrower had picked up another empty bottle and was holding it uncertainly in the manner of a club. I stepped over to him and pushed the bottle downwards.

'Don't do that, dear,' I said. 'I told you once it's not nice, and look what happens when you start trying to play rough with the big boys and girls.'

I swept my arm to indicate his fallen comrade, who was beginning to rise woozily to a sitting position.

He let the bottle fall to his side and two of the others rushed to help the groggy ringleader.

'I think you'd all better get back to your digs,' said Lady Hardcastle. 'Before anyone else gets hurt.'

'I'll bally well get you,' slurred the ringleader from the floor. 'You've not heard the last of this. My father's a KC, you know. I'll bally well sue you for . . . for . . .'

'Well, you work it out, dear, and we'll expect your summons in due course,' she said.

We left them to soothe his bruised chin – and even more badly bruised ego – and went to find the Rover.

◆ ◆ ◆

The Rover, bless its little carburettor, started first time. I hopped into the passenger seat beside Lady Hardcastle.

'Well, that was bracing,' she said.

'Starting the engine?' I said. 'It's always an invigorating experience, yes. Gets the old heart pumping.'

'No, silly, I meant walloping those university boys. Although starting the engine does look like fun.'

'You should try it sometime,' I said. 'I won't mind.'

'No, dear. I wouldn't want to spoil your enjoyment.'

She pulled away from the kerb and we set off up Whiteladies Road.

'Why this way?' I asked. 'I thought we were going to get fish and chips in town.'

'I thought since our blood was up, we might visit Mr Crane's house and question his servants.'

'I'm not going to wallop any doddering old butlers,' I said.

'I shouldn't think you'll need to do any more walloping. But he's really starting to get on my nerves, that Crane chap. I honestly doubt he's got murder in him, but we can't ignore him until we've checked his alibi. And I do so long to ignore him. Dreadful little man.'

'Do you know the way?'

'Inspector Sunderland gave me his address. It shouldn't be too hard to find.'

We crossed the Downs and began searching.

An hour later, we found a policeman on his beat and asked him for directions. He pointed to a road two streets away, past which we had already driven at least four times.

'There, you see?' said Lady Hardcastle as she stopped the engine. 'Not too hard to find at all.'

I said nothing as I clambered down and took off my goggles.

The house was a large, stone-built affair, no more than twenty years old. It was set back from the road behind a substantial hedge and its front garden seemed, by the dim light of the streetlamps, to be well tended.

Lady Hardcastle rang the doorbell. Some moments later the door was opened by a slightly doddering butler of uncertain vintage.

'Yes?' he said, in a tone that said, quite emphatically, 'No!'

'Is Mr Crane at home?' asked Lady Hardcastle as she handed the butler her card.

He examined the card. He tried first to read it by holding it as far away from his face as possible. Still unable to make it out, he grudgingly pulled a pair of smudged spectacles from the breast pocket of his jacket and put them on. He adjusted them. He moved the card back and forth again to bring it into focus. At last he spoke.

'Good evening, my lady,' he said. 'Mr Crane is not at home but he told me to expect your visit and to answer your questions truthfully.'

'Did he, indeed?' she said. 'We shan't take up too much of your time, Mr . . . ?'

'Russett, my lady.'

'We shan't take up too much of your time, Mr Russett. In truth we have only one main question: where was your master on the evening of Tuesday the twenty-fifth of January?'

My heart sank when Russett fished about in his inside pocket and produced a small diary. We'd be there all night while he tried to read it.

'Let me see,' he said, licking his thumb and riffling through the pages. 'The twenty-fifth . . . Ah, yes, here we are.' He tromboned the tiny book a little to get it properly into focus. 'He was at home.'

'All evening?' she asked.

'I believe so,' he said. 'He retired at around half past nine complaining of a headache. I took him two aspirin tablets with his cocoa and then retired myself.'

'Was anyone else in the house?'

'The rest of the staff. But we are an efficient household and there was no more work for anyone to do until the morning so everyone was in their own room by no later than ten o'clock.'

'Where was Mrs Crane?'

'She was . . . out for the evening.'

'Did you or anyone else hear Mr Crane leave the house after you had retired?'

'No, my lady. But it is a large house and it is possible for the owners to come and go without disturbing the staff.'

'Does Mr Crane own a motor car?'

'He does.'

'Might the chauffeur have taken him out?'

'Mr Crane does not employ a chauffeur. He much prefers the excitement of driving himself.'

'I see,' she said. 'Thank you, Mr Russett, you've been most helpful.'

'Happy to oblige, my lady,' he said. 'Goodnight.'

He closed the door.

We walked back along the drive to the waiting Rover.

'That was most unhelpful,' said Lady Hardcastle once I had started the engine and clambered in beside her. 'He was in, but he could have gone out. He has a motor car so he could easily have driven to Thomas Street in time to start the fire and been back in bed with no one any the wiser.'

'Or he might have stayed in bed all night with aspirins and a head-ache,' I said.

'Precisely. Stupid man. Ah, well. Fish and chips from the bottom of Christmas Steps?'

'Unless you'd prefer to take me for an expensive meal at that hotel,' I said.

She eased the motor car forwards.

'Fish and chips it is, then,' she said.

The hake was as good as before and the chips even better. By the time we got home, I was sleepy and contented, and more than ready for bed. But the drive had enlivened Lady Hardcastle, who bounced into the house and set about updating the crime board.

'Would you mind awfully putting some cocoa on?' she said. 'That fellow Redmond—'

'Russett,' I said reflexively, cursing myself for being tricked into it again.

'That's the chap,' she said with a grin. 'He mentioned the Crane creature retiring with cocoa, and now I have a hankering.'

'We can't have unsated hankerings,' I said, 'It interferes with the balance of the humours. I shall attend to your cocoa cravings at once.'

'Bung a good glug of brandy in it while you're at it, there's a good girl.'

When I came back with the fortified cocoa, she was sitting in an armchair examining the board.

'We've learned absolutely nothing to move us along. All we have are more questions,' she said.

'We have learned something,' I said.

She raised an eyebrow. 'Oh?'

'We've learned that Crane – whom we had previously believed to be muddling drearily along in his own humdrum, coffee-filled world – has been talking to people.'

'How do we know that?'

'Because he knew who you are. He was very proud of the fact. "Don't think I don't know who you really are," he said. He met you as Lady Summerford last week, but since then he's learned that that was a lie. I doubt he has the gumption to make enquiries of his own. Someone told him.'

'You're right, tiny one. You're right,' she said, sitting up. 'I'd missed it in all the puffed-up bombast, but that's exactly what he said, isn't it. He knows who I really am. I didn't think twice about giving Ridpath . . .'

I didn't react. She sighed.

'. . . giving Russett my calling card, and the man didn't bat an eyelid. He was expecting a call from Lady Hardcastle. So who is it? Who's talking to whom?'

'Perhaps the city really is being run by a sinister cabal after all,' I said. 'I must say I was beginning to think that Brookfield was suffering from some sort of persecution mania – seeing conspiracies everywhere, linking all those men into one big story. But perhaps he was on to something.'

'We shall know more once you others have made your enquiries. I do hope we don't have to wait too long. For us it's merely a frustrating puzzle, but poor Lizzie Worrel is stuck in that miserable little gaol cell.'

'We'll have her out in no time,' I said.

'We shall,' she said, slapping her thighs and rising to her feet. 'Fancy a game of cards before bed?'

'To tell the truth, I'm done in. Would you be awfully upset if I declined?'

'Not at all. You go up. I'll sit down here and read. On my own. In the gloom. With only a cup of cocoa for company.'

'Goodnight, my lady,' I said, and went to bed.

◆ ◆ ◆

The next few days passed without incident, nor even any news. We were both becoming ever so slightly agitated by the lack of progress, so much so that when the telephone rang on Friday morning, Lady Hardcastle answered it herself.

I came through from the kitchen, where I had been helping Miss Jones check the bills we had received from Weakley the greengrocer and Spratt the butcher. I arrived in the hall just as the call was ending.

'Right you are, dear,' said Lady Hardcastle. 'No, you can't miss it. Just turn left off the village green and head up the lane. We're the only house there. A modern one. Red brick . . . No, opposite side from the church . . . If you get lost just call in at the pub, they know where we are . . . Righto. See you later.'

She hung up.

'That was Georgie Bickle,' she said. 'She has news of the Honourable Jimmy, apparently. She's going to brave the Gloucester Road to come and see us for lunch. She'll be here at noon.'

'On her own?'

'No, Fred is driving her, I believe.'

'I meant is she bringing any of the other suffragettes with her?'

'Oh,' she said, 'I see. No, she's coming alone. But with Fred.'

'I'll make sure we have something to offer them,' I said. 'Though it won't be as grand as those pastries she served us.'

'Miss Jones's food is always splendid. Beyond splendid. And don't worry about Fred. I'm told he prefers to wait in the Rolls with his sandwiches and a Thermos of tea.'

I advised Miss Jones that we'd be one extra for lunch and she excitedly set about doing something clever with a few mackerel. While this magic was being performed in the kitchen, I helped to make certain that Lady Hardcastle – who had been working in the studio in her overalls all morning – was in a fit state to receive a visitor.

'Do I look all right?' she asked, checking her reflection in the large glass on the wardrobe door.

'You look splendid,' I said. 'Understated elegance with just a hint of batty old widow.'

'It's the hair, isn't it?'

'No, the hair is fine. You just have a certain air of approachable eccentricity about you.'

'Cultivated over many long years, let me tell you. You've no idea how helpful it can be to make people believe that one is nothing more or less than an amiable ninny.'

'There's no need to tell me,' I said. 'I've seen the effect at first hand. So many big, strong, clever, confident men have given up so many secrets because they so badly underestimated you. Don't you ever wish people would just take you – us – seriously, though? Don't you ever tire of having to pretend to be stupid so as not to upset people?'

'If wishes were horseradish, beggars would eat beef more often. I think that's how it goes. And yes, of course I mind – the whole thing is preposterous. As though being a woman makes one incapable of . . . well, of anything, really, other than gestating offspring.'

'We'll show 'em,' I said.

'Do you know, I don't believe we shall in our lifetimes. But I don't think that matters as long as we show each other. As long as we all know what we can achieve, who cares what anyone else thinks?'

I nodded my agreement as I tugged at the hem of her navy blue jacket to make it lie flat, and proclaimed her ready for public display. She returned to her study to catch up with her correspondence while we waited. I offered my services in the kitchen and was told to sit down, have a cup of tea, and keep out of the way. Edna was already doing that very thing so I did as I was told and the three of us gossiped the rest of the morning away.

◆ ◆ ◆

Lady Bickle arrived at half past twelve.

'I'm terribly sorry to be so late,' she said as I took her coat in the hall. 'We got a little lost, I'm afraid. We found the village all right but we missed the turning for your little lane and found ourselves going up a hill to a big house with a charming mishmash of styles. A little bit of Tudor, a little bit of Regency, a little bit of Victorian gothic. It was quite charming but it was most definitely not the modern house you'd described on the telephone.'

'That was The Grange,' said Lady Hardcastle. 'Our friends Hector and Gertie Farley-Stroud own the place. It's where Flo and I encountered your acquaintance, the Honourable Jimmy.'

'Yes, I met Sir Hector as we turned around at the end of his drive. He was walking three boisterous spaniels. Or they were walking him. It was hard to tell. Anyway, he pointed us in the right direction and sends his regards. Apparently "the memsahib" will contact you soon to invite you for "tiffin".'

'How lovely,' said Lady Hardcastle. 'I shall await her call. Do come through to the dining room. Miss Jones has done something ingenious to some mackerel, I believe.'

It was, indeed, ingenious. And quite delicious. As we ate, we tried to get to know each other better by sharing a few details of our lives. Lady Bickle had already heard something of our adventures, so it was all rather one-sided as we asked her more and more questions.

She was, as we had surmised, a good deal younger than her husband, whom she had met on a skiing holiday in the French Alps. I guessed she was in her late twenties, but I was too polite to ask.

'I adore skiing,' she said. 'One of the few advantages of an outrageously expensive Swiss finishing school is that they tend to be in the mountains. I'd always been a little . . . rebellious, I suppose one might say. I found almost all of the things I was supposed to be interested in to be so frightfully boring. I really wasn't terribly interested in how to alight gracefully from a carriage or how properly to address the maiden aunt of a grand duchess, so I used to hop the wag and go into the village. I met an absolutely darling young Swiss boy, who taught me how to climb and how to ski. So a few years later, I'd gone out to Grenoble with some chums and I came a cropper one day – ended up unconscious in a tangle of limbs and splintered skis. When I came to I was looking into the eyes of quite the most gorgeous man on the mountain. He told me he was a surgeon and that I should lie still until some more chaps arrived with a stretcher. They got me to the local hospital and patched me up. Nothing broken, thank goodness, but lots of sprains and bruises. Ben – that was the surgeon's name – oversaw my treatment and looked after me while I sat on the hotel balcony watching my chums on the snow. It was only once we were home in England that I discovered that he's a brain surgeon who knows nothing about orthopaedics and shouldn't have been allowed within ten feet of me while I was being treated. But I was in love by then so it didn't seem to matter. Do you ski?'

'I don't think so,' said Lady Hardcastle. 'Did the shenanigans in Norway count as skiing, do you think?'

'No,' I said, 'that was more of an improvised sledge. Although I do remember you standing up at one point.'

'Not for long. I quite forgot Newton's third law – the recoil from my pistol nearly upended us both. Winged our pursuer, though, so it was worth the momentary terror.'

'We shall have to go skiing together before the season ends,' said Lady Bickle. 'I absolutely insist.'

I prefer my mountains green, with coal mines at the bottom, but I smiled and 'Mmm'-ed nonetheless. Lady Hardcastle was similarly noncommittal.

Lady Bickle laughed. 'All right, then, perhaps not skiing. But we should do something fun when all this is over.'

'We should,' we both agreed, massively relieved to be spared a week of yodelling and falling over, or whatever happened in the Alps.

When lunch was done, Lady Hardcastle suggested that we retire to the drawing room with our coffee so that we might examine the crime board and hear Lady Bickle's news.

'It took me a while,' she began, 'but I managed to track down Jimmy Stansbridge's favourite card game. It's at a club in Clifton, not an awfully long way from our house.'

'That's splendid news,' said Lady Hardcastle. 'And does he have an alibi?'

'He has half of one. Either an ali or an ibi, I'm not sure which. He wasn't there himself – no one's seen him for days – but I spoke to several swaggeringly self-important young gentlemen. They were confident that he was there until at least ten o'clock.'

'And after that?'

'No one is entirely certain. One or two think they might have seen him. Another couple don't know. And one chap thinks he saw him leave the club, but wouldn't swear to it.'

'But they're all sure he was there until ten? Are they reliable witnesses? Do you trust their testimony?'

'Collectively I'd say they are as unreliable as witnesses get. They were all pie-eyed for a start – theirs is more of a drinking club with occasional card games than the other way round. And they're the most self-absorbed creatures you're ever likely to meet. If something is going on that doesn't actually involve them – even if it's in their direct line of sight – they'll probably not notice. As for trusting them . . . I'm not so sure. They have little reason to lie. I have it on good authority that he owes money to most of them, so it does them no good if he gets into trouble. On the other hand, they have every reason to lie – he owes money to most of them, so it might give them some satisfaction to see him get into trouble.'

Lady Hardcastle was writing notes on the board, including making additions to the timeline I had started the week before.

'So far we can account for both Crane's whereabouts only until nine o'clock, and the Honourable Jimmy up to around ten. Either, both, or neither of them could have got to Thomas Street in time to set the fire and be home in bed before anyone missed them. But it's a start, at least. We just need to find out where they were between ten and midnight.'

'What about the other two?' asked Lady Bickle.

'We're still awaiting word from Miss Caudle about her possible interview with Councillor Morefield, and we've got nowhere with Hinkley. We asked our police inspector friend if he could press Morefield for proof of his whereabouts, but since he's not officially under any suspicion, there's little he can do to help us.'

'Ah, well,' said Lady Bickle. 'We're making some progress, at least. I say, don't think me too much of a pig, but is there any more of that delicious cake left?'

I retrieved the cake from the kitchen and conversation turned once again to less murderous matters.

'I've been thinking about your motor car, you know,' said Lady Bickle after her third slice. 'I wonder . . . would you let me have a go?'

'At driving it?' said Lady Hardcastle. 'Why, of course. Your coat should be warm enough. Flo, dear, you don't mind lending Georgie your gauntlets and goggles, do you?'

'Of course not. I'll even start the engine for you.'

'Would you? I was hoping you might.'

So we got Lady Bickle togged up and Lady Hardcastle showed her the controls. When she was happy that she understood, I started the engine for them, and they sputtered off down the lane towards the village. I could still hear Lady Bickle's whoops of joy even once they had disappeared from view.

Chapter Ten

On Monday morning Lady Hardcastle received a telephone call from Dinah Caudle inviting us both to meet her once more at the WSPU shop. She had one or two things to sort out, she said, but she would see us there at ten o'clock.

We arrived shortly after ten and were met by Lady Bickle, Beattie Challenger, and Marisol Rojas. Of Miss Caudle herself, there was no sign.

While we waited for her, we brought Miss Challenger and Señorita Rojas up to date with all the latest news on the case. Lady Bickle recounted the tale of discovering the Honourable Jimmy's half-alibi and Lady Hardcastle explained that Oswald Crane was in a similar position.

'So you haven't managed to speak to the other two again?' asked Miss Challenger.

'No,' I said. 'There doesn't seem much point in trying Hinkley again – he's already said he was working late all that week – and we've not yet managed to get an appointment to see Councillor Morefield.'

'We're hoping that's why Miss Caudle asked to meet us,' said Lady Hardcastle. 'She and Armstrong are going to talk to him about a charity do that he's attending. They're going to try to establish his whereabouts on the twenty-fifth while they're at it.'

'Do you suspect these men?' asked Marisol.

'Yes, and no,' said Lady Hardcastle in Spanish. 'Mr Brookfield suspected that they were linked to each other and his investigation links them all to him. Whether one or more of them is involved in his death, we have yet to discover.'

'Thank you,' said Marisol, still in Spanish.

At that moment, the bell above the door gave its merry tinkle as Dinah Caudle came in.

'Good morning, ladies,' she said as she closed the door behind her. 'Sorry I'm late. My flat was burgled last night and I had to wait in for the police. I thought they'd be quicker.'

'Goodness,' said Lady Hardcastle. 'Were you there at the time? Are you all right?'

'I'm fine, thank you. I'd been away for the weekend visiting an old chum in London. My housekeeper doesn't live in so she was safe, too. Got back this morning to find the lock busted and the door swinging open.'

'That's awful,' said Miss Challenger. 'Was anything taken?'

'A few obvious things – a pair of silver candlesticks, a darling little enamelled box with a few sentimental bits and bobs in. It was hard to tell if anything more had gone, though – the place had been thoroughly and messily ransacked. I left a detective fussing about looking for fingerprints while my housekeeper nagged him about the mess he was making. I'll know more when she's tidied up.'

'What about Mr Brookfield's notebook?' asked Miss Challenger. 'That's not gone, has it?'

'No, thank goodness,' said Miss Caudle. 'I took it with me for something to do on the train. Although I can't see that a burglar would have taken it even if it had been out on the drawing room table. He'd be more likely to take my jewels. Though if he did, he'd be disappointed – I doubt he'd get five bob for the lot. I've never been one for baubles.'

'It could have been much worse,' said Marisol. 'Just think of what might have happened if you had been there with the robbers in your house.'

'She was in no danger,' said Miss Challenger. 'The burglar obviously waited until she was out. It's not like back home in Timbuktu with bandits on every street corner.'

'Timbuktu is in West Africa,' said Marisol crossly. 'Not South America. I am sure you pretend to be ignorant to annoy me.'

'It's all the same to me,' said Miss Challenger. 'It's all foreign. If it isn't part of the Empire, it can't be important.'

'Now look here—' said Marisol.

Lady Bickle slammed her hand loudly on the counter and they both stopped at once.

'It's still horrid,' said Lady Bickle as though nothing had happened. 'Will you be all right there on your own tonight? You're more than welcome to stay with me if you'd like. At least until you've had your door repaired.'

'You're very kind,' said Miss Caudle. 'I might take you up on that. I'll check with my housekeeper this afternoon and then I might just lock the door and leave it. I'm more shaken by it than I imagined I would be.'

'Of course,' said Lady Bickle. 'Think nothing of it.'

Miss Challenger didn't look too pleased at this generous offer of hospitality to a comparative stranger, but Lady Bickle immediately went up in my estimation.

'But anyway,' said Miss Caudle. 'Enough of all that. The real reason for my visit wasn't to tell my tale of petty larceny and woe, but to invite you, Miss Armstrong, to accompany me on a trip to the council offices. We have an appointment with Councillor Nathaniel Morefield.'

'I say. Well done,' said Lady Bickle.

'Well done, indeed,' said Lady Hardcastle.

'The thing is,' said Miss Caudle, 'I was happy to stroll down here from Redland, and the walk from here to the council offices on Corn Street is also pleasingly downhill. But the walk back . . . well. Would it be altogether too cheeky to ask if we can use your pretty little motor car?'

'Of course not,' said Lady Hardcastle. 'I was about to offer. And you must take my goggles and gauntlets, too. It's quicker than walking, but it can get rather chilly.'

'Thank you,' said Miss Caudle. 'You're certain you don't mind?'

'Not at all. I'm sure I can find a way of making myself useful here.'

'Ra-ther,' said Lady Bickle. 'We have more leaflets to put in the post. And there are some . . . some plans to be made now that the election is over. I think you might have some skills we can make use of.'

'Language skills?' said Lady Hardcastle innocently.

'I was thinking more of your . . . your practical skills. We shall have to talk upstairs.'

'I'd better get my handbag down from up there if you're going to be having a secret confab,' said Miss Challenger. 'I need to get away at lunchtime to see to my mother and I don't want to interrupt a War Council.' She scooted out the back to the stairs.

Miss Caudle and I, meanwhile, readied ourselves for the short drive into the middle of the city.

Miss Caudle, it turned out, was an enthusiastic and knowledgeable passenger.

'I am engaged,' she said, 'to a fellow who's absolutely batty about motor cars. It's endearing at first, but when one learns that it's a chap's only topic of conversation, it does wear a little thin. I might have mentioned that he's training to be a doctor, and I was quite prepared for gruesome accounts of a day spent rummaging about in someone's innards, but the reality is quite different – he never stops talking about motor cars. The dismaying result is that I now know more than a person would ever want to know about the blessed things. This Rover 6, for instance, has a single cylinder, water-cooled engine developing six horsepower.'

'I believe you're right,' I said. 'You know your stuff.'

'Oh, but how I wish I didn't. He's a charming chap, but he's going to have to go. I can't spend the rest of my life pretending I'm interested only in motor cars. One has one's limits. He's handy for getting about the place, mind you. Always keen to offer a girl a lift.'

'Lady Bickle has expressed an interest in buying one of these for herself,' I said. 'I think she wants to be free from relying on her husband's chauffeur.'

'Actually, that's not a bad idea. I used to get around on a bicycle when I was younger, but everywhere in this blessed city seems to be uphill. You set off on a journey thinking, "Blast this stupid hill. Still, at least it'll be downhill on the way home." When it comes to home time you find that the journey home is uphill, too. It's like a lost chapter from *Alice's Adventures in Wonderland* where hills only go upwards and a talking badger explains how it's a metaphor for life's struggles or something. I could definitely do with a motor car of my own.'

'I have a feeling Lady Hardcastle is thinking about replacing this one so it might be for sale soon. I think you'd have to fight Lady Bickle for it, though.'

'Georgie Bickle, eh? There's more to that woman than meets the eye. What do you make of her?'

I had to think for a moment. What exactly did I make of her? 'Honestly?' I said.

'Yes, completely honestly. Forget all your deference and your "Yes, my lady" and tell me what you really think. It'll go no further.'

'When I first met Lady Hardcastle, she was around Lady Bickle's present age – in her late twenties. Lady Bickle puts me very much in

mind of a young Lady Hardcastle. There's the same mischievous attitude, the same irreverence, and the wilful desire to do whatever she
jolly well pleases and hang the consequences. Lady Hardcastle might
have had the better education, and more opportunities to show off her
talents, but I see definite similarities.'

'I take it you approve, then?'

'Wholeheartedly,' I said. 'It's all tempered with kindness and
compassion – she very much cares about Lizzie Worrel's welfare, and
all her mischief and naughtiness has been directed to an important
cause. The world would be a better place with more people like those
two in it.'

'Hmm,' she said. 'Perhaps. Do you trust her?'

I paused again. 'Yes,' I said at length. 'Yes, I do.'

'I think I do, too,' she said. 'What about Miss Beatrice Challenger,
spinster of this parish and runner-up in the West of England Mediocrity
Challenge Cup?'

I laughed. 'She's a bit of a plodder,' I said. 'But she seems committed, too.'

'And do you trust her?'

'I hadn't wondered whether I needed to,' I said. 'She's given me no
cause to distrust her.'

'Hmm. And here's me thinking your mistress was the one with the
diplomatic training.'

'Well, what do you think of her?' I asked. 'Do you trust her?'

'I make it a rule never to trust anyone,' she said. 'But there's something about her. She's dim, but she always seems a little sly to me.'

'Are you certain it's not just your own prejudices?' I asked. 'You can't
believe that there could be so little going on beneath that unfashionable
hat, so you imagine there must be plots and schemes being hatched in
there. Maybe she really is just dull and ordinary.'

'Maybe,' she said. 'Maybe. What of Señorita Marisol Rojas of
Chile?'

'She's an odd one,' I said. 'She's bright and sharp. She has a temper on her, I'm told. I think we saw the beginnings of it when Challenger was ragging her about being foreign. Actually, that was odd in itself, now I come to think about it. Perhaps there's more to Challenger than meets the eye. But Marisol . . . ? I think she's sound.'

'Probably. I think I'm starting to be affected by the notebook. Everyone's a suspect.'

'So you suspect her?' I asked.

'Not as such. Perhaps I'm as much of a jingoist as Challenger after all. Anyone who's not from the Empire can't be trusted and all that. I'd hate to think I was like that, but one never knows what lurks in the subconscious.'

'You've read Dr Freud?'

'I have as it happens,' she said. 'Have you?'

'I'm staggering through some at the moment.'

'Well, well. There's more to you than meets the eye, too. Ah, look, here we are. Pull round on to Small Street and we can park right outside.'

I did as I was asked.

'Might we need to make a quick getaway?' I asked.

'I shouldn't think so. It's just that it seems rather to defeat the point of bringing the motor car if we then commit ourselves to a lengthy journey on foot once we've arrived. If we find ourselves in a position where we might have to flee, I'm rather relying on you being able to fight our way out.'

'I'm sure I don't know what you're talking about,' I said as I took our goggles and gauntlets and stowed them in the Rover's little storage box.

'I have several contacts at the Bridewell,' she said. 'The constable on the Queen's Road beat came upon some bruised and battered university students last Monday evening outside the Victoria Rooms. He was about to run them in for roughhousing in the street but when they claimed they'd been set upon by "one of those dreadful suffragette women and her wretched little servant", he laughed so much that they scarpered before he could do anything more. You're saying that wasn't you?'

'Ah . . . well . . . now . . . you see . . .' I said.

'I thought so. Well done, you.'

'I only actually hit one of them,' I said.

'Pity. They're always out there trying to stop ladies from going in and then harassing them as they come out. It's about time someone gave them a pasting.'

'It was thoroughly wrong, and a complete failure of English society's agreed conventions of polite discourse,' I said. 'But it was very satisfying indeed, and he really did deserve it.'

'Those vile little boys will be running the country in a few years' time,' she said. 'God help us.'

We approached the oversized doors of the offices of Bristol City Council.

Following the directions of the porter on the door, we found a large room at the end of a long corridor on the first floor. From there, half a dozen doors led – I presumed – to councillors' offices.

Being a city councillor and humble servant of the people of Bristol, Mr Nathaniel Morefield did not have an obsequious assistant to guard the entrance to his office. Instead there was a lone, slightly bored, typist who seemed to be at the beck and call of several councillors. She would have struggled to try to appear less interested in the comings and goings in the offices around her and didn't look up from her work when Miss Caudle and I approached her.

'Good morning, I'm Miss Dinah Caudle.'

'Are you, indeed?'

'From the *Bristol News*.'

'Good for you, dear,' said the typist.

'Miss Maybee – with two e's – and I are here to see Mr Morefield.'

'That's nice.'

'He's expecting us.'

'I dare say he is,' said the typist.

'Would you be kind enough to let him know we're here?'

The typist stopped typing and looked up at us properly for the first time. 'Why the devil would I want to do that?' she asked with genuine astonishment.

Miss Caudle stopped to consider this surprising question. After a moment's thought she said, 'Actually, I've no idea why you'd want to do it. I presumed it was part of your duties.'

'You're not alone,' said the typist. 'There's a lot of presumin' goes on round here. They presumes I'll make their tea. They presumes I'll keep their diaries. They presumes I'll show people in. It never happens, though. They's all as disappointed as you're gonna be. I'm paid to type. And type I does.'

'There's no arguing with that,' said Miss Caudle. 'Can you at least tell us which office is his?'

But the typist had already returned to her typing. 'Names is on the doors,' she said without looking up again.

We split up and started on opposite sides of the room. The names were typed on two-inch by one-inch cards in brass holders on the door jambs. I found one labelled 'Mr N. Morefeild' – it was close enough. I coughed to attract Miss Caudle's attention. I beckoned her over.

She knocked and opened the door without waiting for a reply.

'For heaven's sake, Elsie,' said the expensively dressed man behind the rickety desk, having also failed to look up. 'How many times do I have to tell you to wait to be invited in? What's the point of even knocking if you're just going to barge in anyway? I mean— oh, I do beg your pardon. I thought you were my assistant.' He had finally noticed us.

'Good morning, Mr Morefield,' said Miss Caudle. 'I'm Dinah Caudle from the *Bristol News*. I spoke to you on the telephone earlier.'

He stood, revealing himself to be almost excessively tall. 'So you did, so you did.'

He waved us into two dilapidated wooden chairs.

'This is Miss Maybee – with two e's,' said Miss Caudle. 'She's working with me.'

'How do you do?' I said.

The cramped office gave new meaning to the word 'shabby'. The walls were an insipid shade of green, and the paint was scuffed and chipped where the furniture of previous occupants had been scraped against it. The furniture itself might once have been rather pleasing – nothing grand or ostentatious, but good, honest, hardwearing furniture for the representatives of the people. Sadly, decades of careless treatment by those representatives had left it scarred and scruffy. The only smart thing in the room was Mr Morefield, whose weekly barber's bill alone could have furnished half a dozen offices to this squalid standard.

'Now, what can I do for you, Miss Caudle?' he said. 'You're writing a piece about the forthcoming Chamber of Commerce Winter Ball, I think you said.'

'That's quite right,' said Miss Caudle. 'I know it's the C-of-C's big charity bunfight and I think our readers would love to know a little more about the selfless men who work so hard to raise so much money for philanthropic causes.'

'It's true, actually,' he said. 'I know people are a little cynical these days about businessmen and politicians – even humble local politicians like myself – but we really do care a great deal about the city we live and work in. We like to give a little back, you know. To help those less fortunate than ourselves.'

And so began one of the most shamelessly self-serving interviews in the history of newspapers. Miss Caudle played her part well and allowed the preening, pompous buffoon to explain in the most patronizing terms just what an absolutely spiffing fellow he was while I pretended to make notes. When he had finished extolling his own virtues, he moved on to those of his dear, dear friends.

My attention began to wander until he said, '. . . good old Redvers Hinkley. Do you know him? His firm is going to transform the Thomas Street area with their new development, you know. He'll be there, too, of course. At least I hope so. I've not seen him for a couple of weeks . . .' He broke off and consulted his desk diary. 'Good lord. The twenty-fifth of last month. Well I never. At his office, too. I say, there's another thing you can put in your article. We were at his office thrashing out the details until gone midnight. I'll wager the public doesn't know how hard we chaps work, you know.'

And then he was off again. For another ten minutes he wittered on and on about how marvellous he was. When he had finally run out of steam, Miss Caudle thanked him very much for his time and we said our goodbyes. We gave Elsie a cheery goodbye, too, and showed ourselves out. She didn't look up.

We made small talk as we left the building, but once we were in the Rover and threading our way once more through the narrow streets in the oldest part of town, Miss Caudle cut straight to the heart of the matter.

'He knew exactly what we were up to,' she said.

'It would appear so,' I replied. 'He'd never make it in the spying world. That pantomime with the diary was shockingly transparent. Giving himself and Hinkley an alibi for the night of the fire, all "natural"-like, without even being asked.'

'Indeed. We need to tell the others that we've been tumbled.'

◆ ◆ ◆

By the time we got back to the shop, Lady Hardcastle and Lady Bickle had gone. Marisol Rojas was behind the counter.

'Ah, Miss Armstrong, Miss Caudle,' she said. 'How wonderful to see you. How are your . . . your enquiries going? Are you having some success?'

'Some,' I said. I couldn't quite say why, but I felt disinclined to elaborate.

'That is good,' she said. 'Georgie has gone to her home with Lady Hardcastle. She says for you to join her. She is making lunch for you all.'

'Lady Bickle is making lunch?' said Miss Caudle with some amusement. 'I'd pay double to see that.'

'I have said something wrong?' asked Marisol.

'No,' I said, having given Miss Caudle a raised-eyebrow look of reproach. 'Not at all. Take no notice of Miss Caudle.'

'Is Beattie with them?' asked Miss Caudle.

'No,' said Marisol. 'She is upstairs cooking the books.'

Miss Caudle laughed again. 'Making up the books?'

'Yes, that is what I thought was the right word, but she always says, "I am off upstairs to cook the books." It is another joke, I suppose?'

'I'm afraid so. We keep the books, or make up the books, but when we're up to no good, we cook them. Making up the books is good. Cooking the books is fraud.'

'But when you cook the books you are "making up" the entries,' said Marisol.

'Just so. Isn't English wonderful?'

'That is not the word I would use,' said Marisol.

Miss Caudle laughed once more. 'No, I think you're probably right. Thank you for your help, though. We'll see you later, I'm sure.' She turned to me. 'Do we know where Georgie lives?'

'We do, indeed,' I said. 'Follow me.'

I led the way out of the shop and round the corner to Berkeley Crescent.

'Talk about living above the shop,' said Miss Caudle when I indicated the Bickles' front door. 'She doesn't have far to walk to work, does she?'

I let her ring the bell.

Williams the butler answered the door and had ushered us inside before either of us could say anything.

'Lady Bickle and Lady Hardcastle are waiting for you both in the dining room. If I may take your coats . . .'

After hanging up our overcoats, he led us along a short passage to a half-open door from which issued the sound of conversation.

'. . . and then Flo said, "If you do that again, I'll snap it off."'

Laughter ensued.

Williams knocked on the door.

'Your other guests are here, my lady,' he said, and stood aside to allow us to enter.

'Ah, there you are,' said Lady Bickle. 'Do come in and make yourselves comfortable. Williams? Please tell Cook that we're ready for lunch.'

'Of course, my lady,' said Williams as he buttled off.

We sat down at the table and Lady Bickle offered us some wine. I declined apologetically, but Miss Caudle eagerly accepted the proffered glass.

'Flo never drinks when she's driving,' said Lady Hardcastle.

'Very commendable,' said Miss Caudle, raising her glass in salute. 'Did you know that it's an offence to be drunk in charge of horses, carriages, cattle, and steam engines, but not – because they hadn't been invented when the law was passed – motor cars? I wrote a piece about it for the newspaper but the editor spiked it. "No gentleman likes to be told what he can and can't do in the privacy of his own motor car, Miss Caudle," he said. So that was the end of that little campaign.'

'Well, you have an ally in Armstrong,' said Lady Hardcastle. 'I was just telling Georgie the story of—'

'I know which story you were telling, my lady,' I said. 'It's funny how the stories you tell never end with you in an awkward situation with a subaltern from the Household Cavalry.'

There was more good-natured laughter and we were saved from hearing further details of the encounter by the rearrival of Williams, this time accompanied by a footman, both bearing trays of food.

As we ate, Miss Caudle and I recounted the details of our meeting with Morefield.

'. . . all of which led us to the presumption,' she said by way of wrapping up, 'that he knew we were coming, that he knew what we were after, and that he knew that Miss Armstrong wasn't really Miss Maybee with two e's.'

'This really is most aggravating,' said Lady Hardcastle. 'Flo and I reached much the same conclusion after speaking to Oswald Crane's butler. These chaps are definitely talking to each other.'

'That much doesn't really surprise me,' said Miss Caudle. 'They're all in it up to their necks and they're all linked through Morefield. But how do they know who you are?'

'Hinkley was at the Farley-Strouds' party,' I said. 'The Honourable Jimmy was definitely there, too.'

'True,' said Lady Hardcastle. 'But the Honourable Jimmy has never met me anywhere else and I don't think Hinkley saw me. He was deep in conversation with that fellow from the Men's League for Opposing Woman Suffrage and I managed to keep out of his way.'

'The League?' said Miss Caudle. 'Did he introduce himself as the leader of the group, by any chance?'

'I believe he did, as a matter of fact,' said Lady Hardcastle.

'Then you, my dear lady, have already met Mr Nathaniel Morefield. Extremely tall chap, looks like he spends more on clothes than even I do?'

'That's him. He had quite the neatest moustache I've ever seen. "Dapper" doesn't seem to do him justice.'

'He certainly likes to look after himself,' said Miss Caudle.

'That might explain it, then,' I said. 'If we suppose that Hinkley noticed you, after all, then it's not many steps from there to him telling

Morefield all about it and them both finding out that you're not Lady Summerford at all.'

'Blast,' said Lady Hardcastle. 'Oh, well, it was good while it lasted. Or goodish, at any rate. All we've actually managed is to get some partial – or flimsily self-corroborating – alibis out of them by nefarious means. I can't really see that we'll do much worse if we have to be more brazen about it.'

'What should be our next move?' asked Lady Bickle.

'I think we have quite a list of next moves,' said Lady Hardcastle. 'I know we fancy these four charming gents because they were all under investigation by Christian Brookfield, but I think we have to keep in mind the possibility that none of them has anything to do with it. So our first order of business is to pin down those alibis once and for all. So what do we have?'

'Crane was at home,' I said. 'But his servants can't swear he was there after ten.'

'Right, so we need to speak to his wife. She's having an affair with Morefield and if she's got any sense at all, she almost certainly can't stand her husband. If she vouches for him, he must be in the clear.'

'Jimmy Stansbridge was playing cards in Clifton but went out at ten,' said Lady Bickle.

'So we need to find out where he went,' said Lady Hardcastle. 'Could you contrive to bump into him and just ask him? You're pals, are you not?'

'The best of card-playing chums. I'll track him down.'

'Meanwhile Morefield and Hinkley alibi each other,' said Miss Caudle. 'They were working together in Hinkley's office "until gone midnight", or so says Morefield.'

'A place like that would have a night porter on the door,' said Lady Hardcastle. 'Especially if the partners regularly work late. Someone will have seen Hinkley and Morefield leave. I'm sure a few bob and a bit of the old Hardcastle charm will get the story. So that sorts all that out, but there's someone we're forgetting in all this.'

'Oh?' we all said, almost in unison.

'Poor old Lizzie Worrel,' she said. 'We need to pay her another visit to let her know how we're getting on. She must think we've left her to rot.'

'I've been popping in when I can,' said Lady Bickle. 'But I'm sure she'd love to see you for a full report. She's putting a lot of faith in your abilities – she's certain you won't let her down.'

'Then we definitely need to make that trip as soon as possible. Can I leave it to you to arrange it?'

'Of course,' said Lady Bickle. 'I'll telephone you with the details.'

'And in the meantime,' said Miss Caudle, 'I need to crack on with that notebook. I'm sure it holds the key.'

'Splendid,' said Lady Hardcastle. 'We seem to have a plan.'

Chapter Eleven

By the time Edna and Miss Jones left for the day on Tuesday afternoon, we had already received telephone calls from Lady Bickle and Dinah Caudle. Lady Bickle had organized a prison visit for us all on Friday morning, and had managed to arrange to meet the Honourable Jimmy at the cards club that evening. Miss Caudle, meanwhile, had made some discreet enquiries and had found that the night porter at the offices of Messrs Churn, Whiting, Hinkley, and Puffett rejoiced in the name of Gordon Horden and was on duty every day except Sunday, from seven o'clock in the evening until seven o'clock the next morning.

'Did Miss Caudle say anything more about her burglary?' I asked when Lady Hardcastle had conveyed the gist of her message.

'Ah, yes, she did,' she said. 'By the time they'd tidied up, she was short one pair of pearl earrings, her favourite pen, two silk scarves, and about fifteen shillings in change – give or take a couple of farthings – that she was saving in an old jam jar in her kitchen. That's in addition to the candlesticks and trinket box she'd already spotted.'

'So it was just a common-or-garden housebreaking, then,' I said.

'It certainly seems to have been, which means that we can focus on more immediate matters. Our confederates have made great strides while we've been sitting complacently on our backsides.'

'Speak for yourself,' I said. 'I've been working my dainty little socks off.'

'And don't think I don't appreciate it,' she said. 'But we ought to do our bit to help with the investigation. I propose a trip to Sneyd Park at our earliest convenience, to try to beard Mrs Crane in her lair. She's a bit of a one for going out of an evening, so if we wish to catch her at home, we'd better go soon.'

'We've a pretty shrewd idea of where she goes, though,' I said.

'Well, yes, we do. But can you imagine the fuss, furore, hubbub, and, indeed, hullabaloo that would ensue were we to pitch up on Mr Morefield's doorstep and ask to speak to Mrs Crane? Not to mention the brouhaha, carry-on, and kerfuffle.'

'There would certainly be some manner of scene,' I said. 'I can see that. Shall I get our driving togs?'

'Yes, please, dear. And then we must fire up our wingèd chariot. There's no time to lose.'

'You know you have two potential buyers for your wingèd chariot now, don't you?'

'I know Georgie's interested,' she said. 'Who's the other?'

'Miss Caudle. She's been relying on her beau to chauffeur her around but she's about to give him his marching orders and she's wondering how she's going to get about.'

'I shall have to prod Fishy in that case. The sooner we have a replacement, the sooner those two can fight over who gets dear old Hortense.'

'You named the motor car "Hortense"?' I said. 'When did that happen?'

'Just then. It came to me all of a sudden. She lives in the garden, after all. And one of my governesses was called Hortense. Slow-moving little woman with a red face. Never did as my mother instructed.'

'Well, that sums up the Rover,' I said.

'I thought so. Now let's get cracking or our quarry will be off on her nocturnal manoeuvres.'

◆ ◆ ◆

We found Crane's house much more quickly on this second visit and had parked on the road outside less than an hour after leaving home. We approached the front door, where, once again, Lady Hardcastle rang the bell.

Russett, the doddering butler, once again answered the door. This time, though, there was no hesitation before he said, 'Mr Crane is not at home.'

'That's quite all right,' said Lady Hardcastle. 'We've come to see Mrs Crane. Is she at home?'

'I shall find out,' said Russett, and shut the door.

'It's all right,' I said quietly. 'We'll just wait here.'

We didn't have to wait long. Barely a minute passed before the door reopened and the butler stood aside to usher us in.

'Mrs Crane will see you in the drawing room,' he said, indicating the half-open door a few feet along the passageway.

I kept to one side of the passage to allow him to pass and show us in, but he had already disappeared into another room. He clearly considered his buttling obligations to have been fully discharged.

Lady Hardcastle knocked on the door and entered. I followed.

In my thirty-two years on the planet I had seen many, many people – tall ones, short ones, fat ones, thin ones, attractive ones, and ugly ones. But never had I seen anyone quite so exquisitely beautiful as the woman standing by the fireplace. She looked as though she had been handcrafted by the most skilled artists – every part of her was perfect. Almost every part, that is.

'Hardcastle?' she said in a voice that sounded like a small child with a sore throat.

'Emily, Lady Hardcastle, yes. And this is my associate, Miss Florence Armstrong. You're Mrs Crane?'

'I am,' said the woman. 'Your "associate" appears to be dressed as a maid.'

'A girl has to earn a living,' I said.

'Are you always this impertinent?'

'Almost always. Are you always this rude?'

After glaring at me for a moment, she turned back to Lady Hardcastle. 'You're here to find out whether dear old Oswald's . . . alibi stands up,' she said.

'We are. We know he had a motive for setting the fire that killed Christian Brookfield and so far we can only be certain of his whereabouts until ten o'clock on that night. Your man Russett says that Mr Crane retired at nine o'clock with a headache and that the rest of the household turned in at ten. From then on he was free to come and go as he pleased.'

'You know, I believe, that I was out for the evening,' said Mrs Crane.

'Russett told us as much,' said Lady Hardcastle.

'But he didn't say where I was?'

'He drew a discreet veil over your whereabouts.'

'I was having dinner with Nathaniel Morefield,' said Mrs Crane.

'I'm sure that's none of our business,' said Lady Hardcastle. 'When did you return home?'

'I was home by a quarter past ten. Nathaniel was unable to stay out. He had taken a quick break from his work to see me, but he had to return to the office just before nine. I stayed at the restaurant for a while on my own and then came home to find Oswald asleep in bed.'

'You share a bed?'

'For appearances' sake, yes. So I can confirm that he was dead to the world and didn't rise until morning.'

'I see,' said Lady Hardcastle.

'It would be very much to my advantage to see Oswald disgraced and imprisoned. I might finally be free of him then. Sadly, though, he hasn't got the gumption to burn anyone's house down and he was most definitely sleeping the sleep of a just man – or of just about a man, at least – when I came home. He's not your arsonist.'

'Then we shall cross him off our list. Thank you for being so frank.'

'Merely honest. I see no profit in pretending to be other than I am. But now that you know, I don't expect to see either of you again.'

'Now that we know, there'll be no need to see either of us again,' said Lady Hardcastle.

'I also know that you're harassing Nathaniel, and I expect you to leave him alone, too.'

'You choose to characterize it as harassment, but we see it as looking for the truth in order to free an innocent woman. And in that matter, at least, I'm afraid your expectations will be thwarted. We shall continue to press for justice, and if that means asking further questions of your lover, then those questions will be asked.'

'I don't think you fully understand who you're dealing with,' said Mrs Crane. 'But you can't say you haven't been warned.'

'We've received far more impressive threats from people far more powerful than you and Mr Morefield,' said Lady Hardcastle. 'And yet somehow we're still here. One doesn't like to get sucked into these nursery squabbles, but to put it into your own terms, I'm not at all certain that you fully understand who you're dealing with, either. We'll show ourselves out.'

We turned and left.

◆ ◆ ◆

The journey home was as uneventful and swift as the journey there, and we were back at the house before eight o'clock with an evening of quiet reading in prospect. At least, it would be quiet until Lady Hardcastle began to get fidgety and started playing the piano.

Miss Jones had left a delicious stew in the oven, topped with the fluffiest dumplings known to humankind. I vowed to ask Lady Hardcastle if she might consider giving her cook a rise. Whatever she was paying her was certainly not enough. I dished up two hearty portions and took them through to the dining room.

'Wine?' I asked as I put down the plate in front of her.

She made a whining noise. 'Like that?' she said with a self-satisfied grin.

'Yes, exactly like that,' I said. 'And would you like a glass of wine to drink?'

'Something robust and hearty,' she said, 'to match this delicious-looking stew. Is there any of that Saint-Émilion left?'

'A couple of bottles, I think.'

'Bring them both,' she said. 'We've been uncommonly abstemious lately – I think we deserve a treat.'

'Would you like me to decant it?'

'There's no time for that. Just bring it and we'll glug it straight into the glass as though we were at a café in the backstreets of Bordeaux itself. We can run the dregs through a tea-strainer if the sediment bothers you.'

'You are a lady of class and refinement,' I said, and went off to the cellar.

The food was delicious, and the wine close to perfect. A mood of silliness and tomfoolery began to set in soon after the second bottle had been opened and I abandoned my plans for a relaxing evening with a book. We had begun composing limericks when the telephone rang.

'A freshly minted fiver for the girl who can suggest what the man called Nathaniel might have been doing with the spaniel,' said Lady Hardcastle to my retreating back as I went out into the hall to answer it.

It was Lady Bickle.

'Hello, Florence, dear,' she said. I wasn't sure when I'd become Florence rather than Miss Armstrong, but it betokened a certain level of acceptance that I found oddly pleasing. 'How are your enquiries getting along?'

'Not too badly, my lady,' I said. 'We paid a visit to the Crane household to see Mrs Crane this evening.'

'And how was she?'

'Rude and with an unwarrantedly high opinion of her own importance,' I said.

'Yes, I think I met her at something Ben dragged me along to. If I'm thinking of the same person, she has a paradoxical face.'

'How's that?' I asked.

'It's beautiful to look at and one could stare at it in rapt admiration for hours, but as soon as it begins to speak one's strongest desire is to slap that gorgeous face until her teeth rattle.'

'That's the one,' I said with a chuckle. 'But once we'd overcome the urge to punch her, she did tell us what we needed to know. Crane isn't our man. He was at home all night.'

'That's a shame,' she said. 'I rather wanted it to be him. Ah, well. I, meanwhile, met Jimmy Stansbridge. I stood him supper and a glass or two of the club's least offensive red, in return for which he blushingly told me what he'd been up to when he disappeared from the club that night.'

'And what was that?' I asked.

'He was visiting what my dear mother was wont to call a "fallen woman". There is, I now know, an establishment in a house in Cotham that provides "certain services" to discerning gentlemen.'

'Do you have the address?'

'I do, yes. Why?'

'We'll pop along and ask her if she can corroborate his story,' I said. 'Did he give you her name?'

'Molly,' she said. 'But you're not going to, are you? Not really?'

'Of course. Most of them are sweethearts if you treat them with respect. The madams can get a bit boisterous, but none of them has ever managed to hurt us. In our previous line of work, we always found brothels to be an excellent source of intelligence. They had a healthy disrespect for the regular forces of law and order, but they were always very helpful to us. I'll tell Lady Hardcastle and we'll pop round there and have a word.'

'Tell Lady Hardcastle what?' said a loud voice behind me. 'Is that Georgie Bickle?'

'It is, my lady,' I said. 'Would you like to talk to her?'

'Rather,' she said.

'Lady Hardcastle has materialized from the dining room,' I said into the telephone. 'Thank you for the information, it was lovely talking to you.'

'And to you, dear,' said Lady Bickle.

'I'll pass you over,' I said, and handed the earpiece to Lady Hardcastle.

I left them to chat and returned to the wine.

She poked her head through the door a few minutes later.

'I think we should withdraw to the withdrawing room,' she said. 'Could you rustle up some cheese and biscuits? And perhaps some port for when the wine runs out. We need to set some of these limericks to music.'

We retired to the drawing room with our cheese and our booze and had a hilarious evening singing slanderous songs about the men in Brookfield's notebook.

The next morning we received a surprise visit. Inspector Sunderland was 'just passing' and thought he'd 'drop in' to see how we were getting on. I settled him in the drawing room with the crime board while I enjoined Miss Jones to put a pot of coffee on. Of Lady Hardcastle there was no sign.

'Has she passed this way?' I asked.

'Lady H?' said Miss Jones. 'She went out to her studio about half an hour ago. She asked what sort of hat I thought a hedgehog might wear and was out the door before I could answer.'

'What sort of hat did you choose?'

'I always thought hedgehogs was fussy little fellows. Quite prim. I saw him in a little waistcoat and bowler hat. But by the time I'd thought of it, I heard the orangery door slammin'.'

'Thank you,' I said. 'I'll go and fetch her. We really need a telephone out there, you know. It's a pleasure to nip out there in the summer, but this time of year you can freeze to death before you're halfway across the garden.'

And so it was that three minutes later, with the lady of the house in tow, I returned to the warmth of the kitchen to try to get some life back into my frozen fingers.

'I put the inspector in the drawing room,' I said. 'Do you want to change before you sit down for coffee?'

She looked down at her grubby overalls. 'No,' she said. 'He's a copper, after all. I'm sure he's seen worse.'

I left her to go and greet our visitor while I helped Miss Jones put a tray together.

I found them a few moments later, standing by the crime board. Inspector Sunderland was pointing with the stem of his pipe.

'So Crane and Stansbridge are in the clear,' he said. 'While Hinkley and Morefield alibi each other.'

'That's the simplified version, yes,' said Lady Hardcastle. 'Although Stansbridge's alibi isn't confirmed yet – we need to see the tart he spent the evening with.'

'Do I want to know about that?'

'I'm not sure. Do you already know about the brothel on Cotham Road?'

'We're well aware of the establishment,' he said with a chuckle. 'We turn a blind eye. Partly because it's one of the more orderly of the city's disorderly houses, but mostly because we're likely to run into any number of civic dignitaries and senior members of the Force there, enjoying the facilities.'

'That's all right, then. We'll be visiting Molly later. At some point we need to talk to Gordon Horden, too, but I'm not sure when to do that.'

'He's a nice old chap,' said the inspector.

'You know him as well?'

'I'm a rozzer, my lady. It's my job to know everyone.'

'Quite so, Inspector, dear, quite so.'

'There's coffee here,' I said. 'And some of Miss Jones's ginger cake.'

'Good morning, Miss Armstrong,' said the inspector. 'I'm so sorry, I hadn't noticed you there.'

'That's how it always is for us poor serving girls. Ignored while the toffs talk about important things as though we weren't there.'

'You poor love,' said Lady Hardcastle. 'Is there anything you wish to add now that we've noticed you?'

'No, thank you,' I said. 'I think you've got it pretty much in hand. It's all a bit frustrating, though, isn't it?'

'How's that?' asked the inspector.

'Well, all we have to go on are Mr Brookfield's notes, and the only suspects they've given us so far seem to be non-starters.'

'Welcome to the world of policing,' he said. 'Most of the time we don't even get a handy list of potential suspects. You're doing well, I should say. And you've helped the late Mr Brookfield shine a light underneath a couple of the city's grubbier rocks. I shall be looking into the business affairs of Mr Redvers Hinkley myself in due course. As for Councillor Morefield . . . well. I dare say there'll be plenty of fine upstanding members of the community finely standing up in my way, but his dealings need a fair bit of scrutiny, too.'

'At least something good will come out of it,' I said.

'Perhaps. But it does lead me on to the main reason for my visit. Did you say there was ginger cake?'

'Miss Jones's finest,' I said. 'Is that the main reason for your visit?'

'Of course not. But I am very partial to a bit of ginger cake. May I?'

'Help yourself,' said Lady Hardcastle.

We sat down and waited for the inspector to finish his mouthful.

'Are you aware of an organization known as the Men's League for Opposing Woman Suffrage?' he asked eventually. 'And my compliments to Miss Jones – this is an excellent cake.'

'We've heard of them,' said Lady Hardcastle. 'Georgie Bickle tells us that your favourite councillor is their local leader.'

'Nathaniel Morefield is the branch chairman, yes,' he said. 'They hold their meetings on Tuesday evenings and one of our lads went along last night. We don't see eye to eye on political matters, but we get along well enough and he sought me out this morning. He knows of my acquaintanceship with you—'

'Friendship by now, I hope,' interrupted Lady Hardcastle.

'You're very kind,' he said. 'But knowing of our connection, he felt he ought to tell me that you were mentioned by name at the League's meeting.'

'Me?' she said. 'Whatever for?'

'Both of you. The meeting was told that you're on some sort of quest to discredit members of the League and that they should all be on their guard.'

'I say, how exciting. And slightly slanderous.'

'Were any threats made?' I asked.

'They'd not be stupid enough to make actual threats at a min-uted public meeting, but my colleague did overhear some of the less thoughtful members discussing ways they might "settle your hash". Did I understand right – did you have a set-to with some students recently?'

'There was a small altercation,' I said.

'So that was you,' he said with a chuckle. 'I thought it must have been. It was all over the station – the lads thought it was side-splitting. The boy was known to us, you see. He'd been given a stern talking-to on a number of occasions for coming the bully-boy and it was a genuine pleasure to find out that he'd been knocked on his backside by a five-foot woman.'

'I didn't just knock him down,' I said. 'I knocked him out. Although if he wants to press charges, I was nowhere near the Victoria Rooms last Monday night, I've never socked a student on the jaw, and I have no idea what he's talking about.'

'There's no fear of that,' he said. 'But the story has made its way to the League and there seemed to my colleague to be one or two who might want to teach you a lesson.'

'I don't think there's much they can teach me,' I said, 'but thank you for the warning.'

He turned to Lady Hardcastle. 'I don't doubt she's right,' he said, 'but they might think you're an easier target. You should both be careful.'

'We shall, inspector, dear, we shall.'

We tried to persuade Inspector Sunderland to stay for lunch but he declined. There were, apparently, other cases to be dealt with and he shouldn't really have been in Littleton Cotterell at all. So we ate alone and tried to decide when best to visit the Cotham 'fancy house'.

'The brothels in London always seemed to have a vibrant lunchtime trade,' said Lady Hardcastle. 'So I expect we'd not be too unwelcome in the mid-afternoon, once the lunchtime rush has died down and before the evening trade picks up.'

'Sounds like a plan to me,' I said. 'Do you remember that place in Mayfair where we cornered that chap from the German embassy? That was busy at eleven in the morning.'

'I do. That was a fun morning, I must say. I'm sure they could have held a cabinet meeting there with the number of senior politicians we saw. I'm not certain it was typical, though. So what say we get there for about four? That should give the girls time to be finished with the lunchtime rush, but still be early enough not to disrupt their evening business.'

And so that's what we did. Cotham Road was a beautifully wide thoroughfare with ample space to park the Rover and still leave room for the traffic to pass. The address we'd been given was a perfectly ordinary house on a respectable residential street. We approached the door and rang the bell.

Almost instantly, the door was answered by a fashionably dressed woman of about Lady Hardcastle's age. Her tone was polite, but wary.

'Good afternoon, ladies,' she said. 'What can I do for you?'

'My name is Lady Hardcastle, and this is Miss Florence Armstrong. We're here on a delicate matter – or potentially delicate, at any event. Would it be possible to talk privately inside?'

The house's proprietress looked us up and down while she considered the request. 'Very well,' she said at length. 'Come in. But I should warn you before we begin that I have no idea where your husband is.'

'That's quite all right,' said Lady Hardcastle brightly. 'He was buried in Shanghai a little over ten years ago. At least I assume he was. I was unable to attend the funeral.'

The woman led us past the house's drawing room, where I caught a glimpse of a couple of similarly well-dressed young ladies sitting on a huge sofa. They were chatting amiably and gave me a little wave as we passed by. We proceeded down a newly painted passage to a small parlour near the back of the house.

'Tea?' said the woman after inviting us to sit.

'If you're having one, then yes, please. But don't go to any trouble,' said Lady Hardcastle.

'It's no trouble,' said the woman. She pulled a bell rope beside the fireplace and a maid arrived moments later. With the tea ordered, the woman sat down opposite us.

'I'm sorry,' she said, 'I don't seem to have introduced myself. I'm Jemima Tooks, but most people call me Madam Jemima.'

'How do you do?' said Lady Hardcastle and I in unison.

'You'll forgive me if this sounds impertinent,' said Madam Jemima, 'but if you two are ever looking for work, please come and see me first. I have a number of regulars who would just love you.'

'That's most flattering,' said Lady Hardcastle. 'We shall most certainly bear it in mind.'

'But that's not why you're here,' said Madam Jemima. 'And you're not looking for an errant husband . . . so what brings you to my door? Do say you're not here to save my girls.'

'Nothing like that,' said Lady Hardcastle. 'But we would like to speak to one of them if she's willing.'

'Oh? And who might that be?'

'The name we've been given is Molly.'

'We certainly have a Molly. What do you want with her?'

Quickly and succinctly, Lady Hardcastle outlined the case so far. Starting with the fire, and Lizzie Worrel's arrest, and ending with our disappointing list of suspects and the Honourable Jimmy's alibi. She finished just as the maid arrived with the tea tray.

'For obvious reasons I have to steer well clear of politics,' said Madam Jemima. 'Imagine the red faces and flustered mumblings I'd have to endure if I met any of my regulars at the meeting hall. But I've made some discreetly anonymous contributions to the WSPU coffers. If there's anything I can do to help free an innocent suffragette from gaol, you have my support. But I can't compel any of my girls to help you. They're "independent contractors" and they're under my protection, not my orders. I shall tell Molly what you told me and she can make up her own mind whether she wishes to speak to you. I can do no more than that.'

'We can ask no more of you,' said Lady Hardcastle. 'Thank you.'

'If you don't mind waiting here on your own for a few minutes, I'll go upstairs and speak to her. If she agrees, I'll send her down. I should warn you of something, though . . .'

'Oh?' said Lady Hardcastle.

'Molly is one of our specialists. Don't be confused by her dress.'

She left, closing the door behind her.

'I wonder what that might mean,' I said once we were properly alone.

'It could be anything,' said Lady Hardcastle. 'I'm sure I saw one girl in the Mayfair house dressed as a pantomime cow.'

We didn't have too long to wonder before the door opened again. A bespectacled governess entered the room, her high-collared blouse stiffly starched and her boots clicking menacingly on the flagstone floor of the parlour.

'Hello, my loves,' said a warm, friendly voice, completely at odds with the stern appearance. 'Madam Jemima says I might be able to help you.'

'We certainly hope so,' said Lady Hardcastle. 'Please sit down.'

The young woman sat in the chair recently vacated by her employer. She took off her spectacles.

'They's not real,' she said as she put them into the pocket of her long tweed skirt. 'Just a little prop. Now what can I do for you?'

'It's about one of your clients,' said Lady Hardcastle. 'So we understand if you'd rather not say – I imagine you must value discretion. But he was the one who named you, so you'd not be giving away anything he hasn't already said himself.'

'Who is it?' said Molly.

'You might know him as Jimmy.'

'The Dishonourable Jimmy?' she said. 'I knows him. He's one of my naughty boys.'

'Splendid,' said Lady Hardcastle. 'On the night of the fire – the twenty-fifth of last month – he says he left his club at about ten o'clock to come and see you. I don't suppose you can remember seeing him?'

The girl fished in the other pocket of her skirt and produced a small, black diary. She began to riffle through the pages. 'The twenty-fifth?' she said. 'That were a Tuesday, weren't it?'

'It was.'

'Yes, here we are. The Dishonourable Jimmy, a quarter past ten. He was here.'

'I don't suppose you have a record of when he left?'

'Let's see. Well, I had . . . Actually, better not say who . . . I had another naughty boy to see at eleven so he was definitely gone by then.'

'Before eleven o'clock?' I said. 'That gives him plenty of time to get to Thomas Street, even if he were walking.'

'He wouldn't have wanted to sit down for a bit, so he might have preferred to walk,' said Molly with a twinkle.

'That really is most helpful,' said Lady Hardcastle. 'Thank you very much indeed.'

'My pleasure,' said Molly brightly. 'Always happy to help the suffragettes. Is that all you wanted?'

'It is, thank you, yes,' said Lady Hardcastle.

'I'd better get back to the nursery,' said Molly.

Moments later Madam Jemima returned.

'Do you have what you need?' she said.

'We do,' said Lady Hardcastle. 'You've been much more helpful than we had any right to expect. Thank you very much indeed. And thank Molly again for us, would you?'

'Of course. Now, I don't wish to appear inhospitable, but the after-work rush starts soon and our clients are a skittish lot.'

'Of course. They don't want the likes of us milling about the place.'

'Well . . .' said the brothel-keeper slowly, looking at us both again. Thankfully, she left the thought unfinished.

Chapter Twelve

Lady Bickle telephoned early the next day – Thursday – to confirm the arrangements for the visit to Lizzie Worrel the following morning. I thought that would be it for the day, but just after lunch, the telephone rang again.

It was Dinah Caudle.

'I'll see if Lady Hardcastle is available,' I said once the introductions were done.

'Oh, don't bother with that. You're as much a part of all this as she is. I'll tell you and then you can pass it on.'

'As you wish,' I said. 'What's the news?'

'That's the girl,' she said. 'I've just deciphered a section about our friend Nathaniel Morefield. A little financial revelation.'

'Financial?' I said. 'Fraud?'

'Nothing so glamorous,' she said. 'Just some banking information.'

'It's reassuring to know that our banks are so discreet,' I said.

She laughed. 'No one is discreet,' she said. 'You of all people should know that. You must have had helpful contacts in your previous line of work. Some sympathetic soul on the inside who slips you a few juicy titbits from time to time.'

'I'm familiar with the concept,' I said. 'Brookfield knew someone at the bank?'

'They played football together. Been pals for years. I was introduced to him once. Nice chap. Good at his job but he has a conscience – he was as angry as Brookfield about some of the goings-on in the city council so he passed on anything he thought suspicious.'

'I see,' I said. 'And what did he pass on?'

'Morefield was in debt up to his eyeballs.'

'Is that suspicious?' I said. 'Lots of people are in debt.'

'Not like this. He owns several properties as well as his home – all mortgaged to the hilt. He has loans secured against his interests in several companies, and a substantial overdraft. He lives as though he's the richest man in town, but the harsh truth is that he's barely got a pot to piddle in, and is struggling to repay the debts. According to Brookfield's notes he's "about an inch and a half from bankruptcy" and his creditors are circling.'

'How does that help us?' I asked.

'I don't know yet,' she said, somewhat deflatedly. 'But it's certainly juicy, and Brookfield thought it important enough to make a note of.'

'I'll pass it on and see what Lady Hardcastle has to say.'

'You do that,' she said. 'I'll press on and see if the next section is any help.'

We said our goodbyes, and I hung up the telephone.

'What have I missed?' asked Lady Hardcastle as she came out of her study into the hall.

I recounted the details of the telephone conversation as succinctly as I could.

'It's not enough to hang the man on its own,' she said when I was done. 'But the more we find out, the blacker it looks against him. She's making good progress, our Dinah.'

'She is,' I said.

'Our visit to Lizzie Worrel tomorrow should be a little less bleak. I'm not dreading it quite so much now. Perhaps we can take her a treat.'

◆ ◆ ◆

And so it was that at ten o'clock on Friday morning we were sitting outside Horfield Prison, shivering and sipping tea from a flask, with one of Miss Jones's magnificent Madeira cakes in a tin at our feet.

'Whatever other features Fishy includes in this new motor car he's building us,' said Lady Hardcastle as she handed me her cup for a refill, 'I shall have to insist that he provides some means of heating the passenger compartment. I haven't been this cold since Prague in '04.'

'Are you keeping him up to date with your list of requirements?' I asked.

'We are in regular contact,' she assured me. 'He's fascinated by the whole thing, it seems. He says he's only ever had to think of things to make a motor car go faster. The driver's comfort and convenience have never been of any concern. But now he's having to design a machine that will not only "spank along at a decent clip" but which must also "meet the needs of the world's most demanding driver".'

'It sounds like we'll both be in our dotage by the time it's ready.'

'That's what I thought,' she said. 'What I didn't know was that he'd already built most of it before we began speaking of it. He's planning to come down in it in a couple of weeks.'

'How exciting,' I said. 'So we need to arrange a series of heroic tasks for Miss Caudle and Lady Bickle to see which of them is worthy of the Rover.'

'I was just going to ask them to sort it out between themselves, but your plan has merits. Could you include some sort of weed-hacking challenge, do you think? That might solve our garden wilderness problem.'

'I told you we should just find Old Jed and employ him.'

We were interrupted by the silkily burbling arrival of Lady Bickle's Rolls-Royce. It was time to go in.

We passed through the familiar formalities of admission and were led by the same sour-faced wardress down the same drab corridors to the same bleak cell. We were given the same sullen instruction to bang on the door when we were done, and were then let inside.

Lizzie Worrel looked dreadful, and smelt slightly worse. She was not looking after herself at all.

'Good morning, Lizzie,' said Lady Bickle brightly. 'We've come to see how you're getting on.'

'That's kind,' said the wraith in the corner, whose skin seemed to be the same shade of grey as her prison dress.

We spoke for a while of practical matters. We gave her the cake in the hopes that it might inspire her to eat properly. As gently as we could, we also tried to encourage her to take better care of herself. Eventually the conversation turned towards the investigation. Lady Hardcastle and I outlined the events of the past couple of weeks and there seemed to be a glimmer of something that might develop into hope in Miss Worrel's eyes.

'So I should say we're making quite good progress,' said Lady Hardcastle. 'We're beginning to think it all has something to do with the Men's League for Opposing Woman Suffrage. Everywhere we turn we find one of their members up to no good.'

'I've heard of them,' said Miss Worrel. 'Load of old windbags, as far as I could make out. Christian said they—' She stopped abruptly.

'Christian said they what, dear?' asked Lady Bickle.

Miss Worrel said nothing and Lady Bickle appeared to be about to ask again, but Lady Hardcastle held up her hand to stop her. There was a more important question to be answered.

'Christian?' said Lady Hardcastle. 'Christian Brookfield?'

Still no answer.

'You knew Christian Brookfield?' asked Lady Hardcastle.

'We were . . . we were . . . engaged to be married,' said Miss Worrel desolately.

The silence lasted for a good half a minute before Lady Bickle said, 'Why on earth didn't you tell us, dear? You must have been devastated.'

After another lengthy pause, Miss Worrel finally spoke. 'I was,' she said. 'I am. At first I was too shocked to say I even knew him. But then as time went on and I learned what everyone was saying about me, I thought it would look even worse for me if I let on. I'd be accused of killing him over some lover's quarrel. I just thought I'd best keep it to myself.'

'How long had you been seeing him?' asked Lady Hardcastle.

'Since last summer,' said Miss Worrel.

'So you knew of his work?'

'He didn't talk about his work much. But I knew he was looking closely at the League and what they were up to. And he did say something about having some juicy stories about some of the city's more prominent men. But never details.'

'I can't say this is the most encouraging revelation of the week,' said Lady Hardcastle. 'Although perhaps it would have coloured our thinking if we'd known sooner. Are there any more little titbits of vital information we ought to have?'

Miss Worrel looked more forlorn than ever. 'I'm sorry,' she said.

'Can't be helped,' said Lady Bickle briskly. 'No use crying over the water under the bridge and all that. At least we know now.'

The other two hadn't noticed, but I knew Lady Hardcastle well enough to see that she was fuming. She was as calm and polite as ever, but there had been a steeliness to her tone that didn't bode well for Miss Worrel, whose withholding of this important fact had very obviously disappointed her. It was time to leave.

I banged on the door without asking for anyone's approval and we said our frosty goodbyes as the wardress opened the door. We followed her out.

'Trouble in paradise?' she said as she led us back through the labyrinth. 'You do-gooders are all the same. Murderers like her will let you down every time, but you keep comin' back. You're only foolin' yourselves.'

'Oh, do shut up, you spiteful little harpy,' I said. 'That's quite enough from you.'

She turned towards me with a snarl, and her hand reached for the short truncheon in her skirt pocket.

'Just try it,' I said, meeting her gaze. 'I could do with a laugh.'

We completed the rest of our journey to the front door in silence.

◆ ◆ ◆

Once we were outside, Lady Hardcastle stopped and turned.

'You swear you didn't know anything about this?' she said.

'About what?' asked Lady Bickle. 'About Lizzie and Brookfield? Of course not. I'm as surprised as you.'

'Very well,' said Lady Hardcastle. 'You can see why I might be irritated, though? We've been on this case for three weeks now and suddenly we hear, "Oh, I've been wondering how to tell you I was engaged to the victim and I already knew about most of the things you've found out." Do you still vouch for Worrel? Or are we wasting our time?'

'She's innocent,' said Lady Bickle. 'I believe it in my heart.'

'Then we'll say no more about it. I'll telephone you when we have news.'

Lady Hardcastle walked to the Rover and sat in the passenger seat. I followed and began the tedious process of starting the engine. We left Lady Bickle standing by the side of the road.

We travelled in silence. When we arrived home, Lady Hardcastle hopped out and went immediately indoors while I manoeuvred the little motor car into its shed. I found her in the drawing room, staring at the crime board.

'Have we been wasting our time?' she asked.

'It depends how you define "wasting time",' I said. 'We've certainly spent more time than we needed to in chasing information we might already have had. But was it wasted? We have a more thorough picture of things thanks to our own efforts than we might have had if we only had Lizzie Worrel's vague recollections to go on.'

'I can't gainsay you there. But overall? Is it a fool's errand? Is that stupid girl guilty after all?'

'I still think not. She doesn't have an obvious motive for killing Brookfield, or even just burning the shop down as an act of vandalism. In fact, since she almost certainly knew it was his home and that he was fast asleep upstairs, she has even less reason just to start a fire to prove a point.'

'Again, all true,' she said. 'But everyone we've found so far who might have an excellent motive for killing Brookfield also has an alibi.'

'Except James Stansbridge,' I said.

'Except him, yes. And, actually, we still need to see if the night porter at Bilious, Fandango, Wallop, and Thud can back up the other two. But I'm pretty certain he will. Even if it's just out of loyalty to one of the partners, I'm sure he'll swear blind the two of them were there discussing important matters until the small hours.'

'Perhaps we should go down there later, anyway,' I said. 'I'm sure we'll think of something.'

'I confess I was on the verge of giving up a little while ago. But you're right – we've come this far so we ought to see it through. Since the Honourable James Stansbridge still has no clear alibi, I think I'd like to know a little more about him. I'll telephone Inspector Sunderland at home later and ask him to have a dig around for us. As for the other two, though, I stand by my assertion that Gordon Horden will just say whatever his masters have told him to say. They seem to know about our every move before we've made it, so I'm sure they'll have preempted that one.'

'We might not get anything from the man himself,' I said. 'But I'll wager they have a log book of some sort to keep track of the comings and goings. We just need some sort of ruse. Nothing too elaborate. We've done it before.'

'Istanbul?'

'Istanbul,' I agreed. 'Shall we give him until eight, let him get settled in?'

'Let's do that. I'm still not best pleased by today's turn of events, but we'll press on regardless. I'm off out to the studio as soon as I've changed. You couldn't bring me out some coffee and sandwiches in a little while, could you?'

'Of course,' I said. 'I'll get started on that straight away.'

At a little after eight o'clock that evening we drew up on Small Street and I hopped out of the motor car. Lady Hardcastle allowed me enough time to stow my goggles and gauntlets, and to swap my boots for black plimsolls before she drove off and turned the corner on to Corn Street. I heard the engine stop and knew that she would be several yards beyond the front door of Messrs Churn, Whiting, Hinkley, and Puffett.

I moved towards the corner and listened. I would have been better off on the other side of the road, but the porticoed front door of the council offices was on the corner of Corn Street and Small Street at exactly my preferred spot. The offices were still occupied, even at this late hour, and a woman lurking at the door would certainly have drawn unwanted attention.

After a few moments, I heard Lady Hardcastle's distinctive voice as she told her tale of woe to the night porter she had so conveniently found at work when her motor car had unaccountably broken down just outside his office. The clank of the bonnet being raised was my cue.

I stole silently towards the front door of Hinkley's office building on rubber-soled feet. Checking once that Lady Hardcastle had thoroughly engaged Horden in the entirely pointless task of examining the engine for signs of malfunction, I slipped through the front door and into the spacious entrance hall. My shoes squeaked a little on the polished marble floor as I crossed to the enclosed porter's desk.

As I had hoped, there was a big fat visitors' log book on the desk. It was open at today's page and showed that two of the partners – Mr Whiting and Mr Puffett – were still in the building, but that everyone else had gone home for the night. I riffled backwards through the pages until I came to the entries for the twenty-fifth of January. Mr Hinkley had arrived at nine in the morning and had been signed out by Gordon Horden at ten minutes after midnight. Further down the list I saw that Mr N Morefield had arrived to see Mr Hinkley at nine o'clock. He, too, had been signed out by Horden at ten past midnight. Disappointingly, their alibis appeared to be confirmed.

I was about to flick the book back to today's page when the last entry for the twenty-fifth caught my eye. I had to look twice to make sure I hadn't misread it. I was still goggling at it when I heard a door open. I just had time to duck under the desk before I heard footsteps crossing the hall and a cheery voice saying, 'Night, Horden. Not too late for me this evening. Oh, I say. I wonder where he's got to.'

The next sound was the front door swinging open. The footsteps disappeared into the night.

I reemerged from my hiding place and quickly put the log book back exactly as I'd found it. I stealthily crossed the hall and had almost made it to the glass-panelled inner door when I saw two figures approaching. The door opened as I ducked into the corner and hid behind a marble plinth supporting a bust of one of the firm's founders.

'I really am most dreadfully sorry for dragging you away from your work,' said Lady Hardcastle. 'Your help has been invaluable, but I do hope I didn't get you in trouble.'

'No, madam,' said a man's voice. 'Don't you worry about it at all. That was Mr Puffett. He's a proper gentleman – he'd most definitely have wanted me to help a lady in distress. I just needs to make a proper note of his leaving time, is all. I'm most particular about it. We keeps a very strict record of comings and goings. You never know when there might be a fire – or worse – we has to have a clear record of who's in the building and who i'n't.'

I peeked out and saw that she had positioned herself so that Horden had his back to the door as he talked to her. I caught her eye as she looked over his shoulder to see where I was. I indicated that I was going to try to get out through the door.

'You really have been an absolute poppet,' she said. 'I insist that you take this for your trouble. I don't know what I would have done without your help.'

I caught a glimpse of money changing hands as I slipped out through the door as quietly as I could.

The Rover's engine was running. I grabbed my driving gear from the storage box and sat in the passenger seat putting my boots back on. It was far too cold to be wearing tennis shoes. Lady Hardcastle joined me just as I did up the last button.

'All done?' she asked as she pulled away.

'All done and more,' I said. 'I'll tell you when we're clear.'

◆ ◆ ◆

We drove back up the hill and found a bijou eatery in Clifton, where we ordered a light dinner and a bottle of wine. I poured two glasses – unlike me, Lady Hardcastle allowed herself one glass when she was driving – and sat quietly, smiling beatifically.

'You can be exasperating sometimes, Florence Armstrong.'

'Me, my lady?' I said, still smiling innocently. 'Whatever do you mean?'

'You know full well. You come haring out of the office and we rocket off up the street as though we've just robbed a bank. You say something enigmatic about what you might have found out and then remain silent for the rest of the journey. You are, as I say, exasperating.'

'Oh, that,' I said. 'Before we get to that, might I address a couple of points? First, I didn't hare out of the office – that would have drawn unwanted attention. I walked casually but quickly. Secondly, the Rover would be incapable of rocketing anywhere, even were we to attach actual rockets to it. It puttered away from the kerb at a sedate walking pace. And thirdly . . . Actually you're quite right on the last part. I have been exasperatingly enigmatic, but I feel it's my turn – it's one of your favourite tricks, is this. A girl likes to get her own back and cultivate an air of mystery of her own once in a while.'

'Well, that's quite enough mystery for now. The cat must be let out of the bag, the gaff blown, and the show given away. Your mouth, while it is still free of our forthcoming repast, should shoot off. Blab, sister.'

'I learned two things from the well-kept ledger. Both the day porter and night porter have an extremely neat hand. They are to be commended on their penmanship. Or pencilmanship, at least. It's rare to find a working man whose handwriting is so pleasing. I should think that—'

'I know I'd come off worse in the end, but I'm not above giving you a smack in the chops, you know. Get on with it.'

I grinned. 'Well,' I said. I paused. She glowered. I continued. 'If we are to trust the ledger – and I think from Horden's flustered response to his master's undocumented departure that we would be safe to do so – then Messrs Hinkley and Morefield were, as they claim, both in the building until ten minutes past midnight.'

'Is that it? I waited the best part of half an hour for you to tell me what we already thought we knew anyway?'

'Of course that's not it. Not by a long chalk. The intriguing new development is that at twenty minutes past eleven that night, they were joined by none other than—'

'The Honourable James Stansbridge,' she interrupted.

'Well, it's no wonder I have to work so hard to cultivate an air of intrigue if you're going to steal my thunder every time. Yes, the arrival of the Honourable Jimmy was noted at twenty past eleven and he is shown as visiting Mr Hinkley. His departure was recorded as ten after midnight. I think it's safe to assume that he was in the company of the other two since they all left at the same time. How did you guess it was him?'

'The timing,' she said. 'We already knew that Jimmy left Cotham just before eleven. It's about a twenty-minute walk to Corn Street, so he would arrive at twenty past. I'm not clairvoyant or anything. Just . . . well . . . just terribly clever.'

'I can't argue with that,' I said.

'You'd be foolish to try,' she said. 'But that's most intriguing. If a little frustrating. Much like yourself. All alibis are now confirmed, but somehow those three are connected. But if not in the murder of Christian Brookfield, then what?'

'League business?' I suggested.

'No, not that. You said that you and Maude overheard Morefield inviting Jimmy to a League meeting while you were eavesdropping at Gertie's party. He was nothing to do with the League then.'

'We keep coming back, then,' I said, 'to Brookfield's coded notebook. He must have had a reason for grouping them all together like that. I mean, I know three of them were orbiting Nathaniel Morefield, but that can't be all there is to it.'

'No,' she said. 'No, it really can't. Perhaps Inspector Sunderland has some ideas. He promised to have something for us tomorrow morning and asked that we meet him at "the usual place".'

'Crane's?' I asked.

'Let's hope so. If it's not there, then I've no idea where to meet him. We'll just have to hope that waitress ignores Crane's instruction to kick us out.'

Just then, our meals arrived and conversation drifted to less murdery matters.

◆ ◆ ◆

'And that,' said the inspector, putting down his coffee cup, 'is why I can no longer play cricket.'

We had braved light but persistent rain to get to Clifton, and the coffee shop was heavy with the humidity of drying overcoats and softly dripping umbrellas. The inspector had arrived on foot, wearing a waterproof mackintosh and carrying his briefcase close to his body to protect it from the all-pervading drizzle. We plied him with coffee and cake, and allowed him to dry out a little before hounding him for the new information he had promised us. Lady Hardcastle, of course, was unable to wait too long.

'Enough of your manly sporting exploits, Inspector,' she said. 'It's time to talk of other things. Of shoes and ships and . . . whatnot. Of cabbage-heads, and the delinquent third sons of local earls.'

'The Honourable James Stansbridge,' said the inspector as he reached into his briefcase and produced, as was becoming customary, a manila folder, 'is a far more interesting character than is commonly portrayed in the popular press. Everything you need is in here.' He tapped the folder. 'But it's easy to summarize. Most of the city seems to know "Jimmy" Stansbridge as an affable drunk and incorrigible – and dismayingly inept – gambler. And so he is. But he wasn't always thus. It seems our James was something of a hero. Major James Stansbridge, as he was once known, distinguished himself in the Transvaal when he led a small raiding party and thoroughly walloped a much larger group of Boers, who had been engaged in what they called "guerrilla raids". He beat the Boers at their own game, apparently – sneaked in, caused mayhem, and sneaked out again. He was quite the hero – they awarded him the Distinguished Service Order.'

'So he's Major The Honourable James Stansbridge, DSO,' said Lady Hardcastle. 'That makes his fall from grace all the more tragic. Poor chap.'

'It does,' said the inspector, 'But it also means that he's exactly the sort of character to sneak about in the dead of night and burn a man's house down with him still in it.'

'He would certainly have moved up our list if it weren't for the fact that last night we confirmed his alibi. He was playing cards till ten, visiting Molly the "Governess" until eleven, and then – and this is the part you'll really love – spent the remainder of the time during which we presume the fire was started in the company of Mr Redvers Hinkley and Mr Nathaniel Morefield at Hinkley's office on Corn Street.'

'Do I want to know how you learned that?' asked the inspector.

'It's probably best you don't,' she said.

'No actual laws were broken,' I said. 'But you know how huffy these people get when you go poking around their office buildings – even the public areas.'

'So I suppose you have no idea what he was doing there,' he said.

'He owed Morefield money. Perhaps he was making a payment.'

'Perhaps,' I said. 'Although Morefield was very discreet about Stansfield's indebtedness at the Farley-Stroud party. Not to mention his own. Stansfield made some comment to one of the others about borrowing a few quid and Morefield said nothing about any existing debt. He advised them not to lend him any money, as though it were the sort of thing only a fool would consider. I'm not sure he would have discussed it in front of Hinkley.'

'Just a moment,' said the inspector. 'Did you just say that Morefield has debts?'

'Oh, yes, sorry,' I said. 'Dinah Caudle found a reference to some serious debts in Brookfield's notebook. Morefield is all but bankrupt.'

'That's a turn-up,' said the inspector. 'But it still doesn't tell us what the devil they were all doing there together.'

'Perhaps they wanted some card-playing tips,' I said. 'A few high-stakes games might get Morefield out of trouble.'

'From what I've heard, you'd have to be pretty desperate to seek advice from the Honourable Jimmy,' said Lady Hardcastle. 'It's more likely they want access to the earl for some reason.'

'Maybe,' said the inspector, draining his cup. He reached for the coffee pot.

'Perhaps they needed someone with a little military experience,' I said, not entirely seriously.

The inspector, who had been concentrating on pouring himself another cup of coffee, looked up sharply.

'What did you say?' he asked.

I reached out and tilted the coffee pot before his cup overflowed. 'I said that they might need someone with a little military experience.'

'Might they, indeed?' he mused.

'I was joking,' I said.

'Many a true word, Miss Armstrong. Many a true word.'

'What has your sleuthing sense detected?' asked Lady Hardcastle.

'It's far too fanciful to say out loud at this juncture,' he said. 'But I might end up owing Miss Armstrong a rather large drink.'

'I'm intrigued now,' she said.

'I'm afraid I would feel foolish to say any more.'

'You and Flo are very alike, you know,' she said. 'She torments me with tantalizing titbits, too. "Just you wait, my lady," she says, all sweetness and innocence. "All will be revealed in the fullness of time." All will be revealed when she feels I've suffered enough, she means.'

He laughed. 'I remember that rather better as one of your tricks,' he said. 'If it comes to anything, I'll share it at once. If it doesn't, I'd rather not look a fool for even thinking it in the first place.'

She harrumphed. 'Very well,' she said. 'Shall we get another pot?'

He pulled his watch from his waistcoat pocket and flipped open the cover.

'Why not?' he said. 'I've got plenty of time. Mrs Sunderland is coming into town later to buy a new hat, but I'm not required until then.'

Chapter Thirteen

On Monday morning, nearly four weeks after the fire on Thomas Street and Lizzie Worrel's arrest, the mood in the Hardcastle household was despondent. We'd been chasing our tails for almost a month, learning little other than that the fire's victim was an energetic and principled journalist who had spent his final few months on earth attempting to uncover the misdeeds of a grubby handful of greedy and dishonourable men. But none of them, as far as we could see, was directly responsible for the fire and the death of Christian Brookfield.

Lady Hardcastle was in her study when I came out of the kitchen bearing the coffee tray. Her door was open so I hailed her as I passed.

'There's coffee and cake in the morning room if you'd like to take a break,' I said. 'Or there will be, soon.' I raised the tray to let her see.

'Splendid,' she said. 'Just give me a few moments to finish this letter and I'll join you.'

I set two places at the table and had just poured myself a cup of coffee when she shambled in.

'Lovely,' she said. 'Is that mine? Thank you.'

I passed the cup across to her and poured myself another.

'What have you been up to this morning?' I asked as I cut two slices of fruit cake.

'Beyond moping over our lack of progress with the case, you mean? Just a little correspondence,' she said. 'It does rather get on top of one if one doesn't . . . keep . . . on top . . . of it.'

'That was a much more elegant thought while it was still in your head, wasn't it?'

'It was rather. I'm afraid my linguistic powers have been exhausted by my morning's labours.'

'And how stand the far-flung corners of Empire?'

'Not flung quite as far as you might hope,' she said. 'It's all been local news. I've heard from Betsy Leftwich in Norwich, who remains a martyr to her gout and is troubled by an increase in the number of starlings roosting in her eaves. Then there's Colonel Sawyer – do you remember him from that to-do at the Russian embassy? He wonders if I can recommend a decent gunsmith in Liverpool. Apparently his usual chap has been arrested. And Harry wants an address for Barty and/or Skins. It seems he and Lavinia are throwing a party and would like something a bit more lively than the usual string quartet to entertain their guests.'

'Are we invited?' I asked.

'As a matter of fact, we are. Early April. Would you like to go?'

'In my best clobber, with ragtime music, free booze, and someone else doing the washing up? Do you even have to ask?'

'I'll let him know. What have you been up to?'

'This and that.'

'A woman of mystery, eh?'

'Mystery and intrigue,' I said. 'But mostly sewing.'

'And answering telephones,' she said through a mouthful of cake as the telephone began to ring in the hall.

I did my maidly duty and answered the telephone. I returned a few moments later with a message.

'That was Dinah Caudle,' I said. 'She asks that we be kind enough to meet her at the Hog and Ass on Midland Road at our earliest convenience.'

'Did she say why?'

'She did not,' I said. 'She had about her an air of mystery and intrigue.'

'There's a lot of it about,' she said. 'We'd better get down there if we wish to find out more. Did she give directions?'

'Clear and precise,' I said. 'We can be there in less than an hour.'

◆ ◆ ◆

The pub was next to the newspaper building and had been as easy to find as we had been promised. It was absolutely packed, even at midday on a Monday, and we had to look around for a while before we saw Miss Caudle waving to us from a table in the corner. I waved back but her attention had already been diverted by the need to aggressively defend the table and its highly prized empty chairs from predation by a man in a square printer's cap.

'Good morning, ladies,' she said once we had fought our way to her. 'Sorry about the crush – I'd forgotten how busy this place gets between shifts.'

'It does seem very lively,' said Lady Hardcastle. 'These are all news-papermen, I take it.'

'Yes, the printers come off shift after cleaning everything down for tonight's run. They're having a drink and a bite before going home. The typesetters are going in any minute. They're having a drink and a bite to fortify themselves for their day's toil. The journalists . . . Well, I'd swear some of them lived in here. Can I treat you to lunch? It's nothing grander than a pie and a pint, but it's good hearty nosh.'

'That would be delightful,' said Lady Hardcastle. 'Thank you.'

'And for me, please,' I said.

'Wish me luck,' said Miss Caudle. 'And defend my chair with your very lives. I had to kill a man to get this table.'

She disappeared into the throng.

We positioned ourselves with the empty chair between us and against the wall. It earned us a few resentful glares from men bearing laden plates and brimming glasses, but they left us alone and went to look for somewhere else to eat their lunch. Miss Caudle returned a few minutes later and we made room for her to sit.

'I sweet-talked the barman into bringing our food and drink over,' she said. 'He won't be long.'

'It's interesting to see you in your natural habitat,' I said.

'The Hog and Ass? Hardly. I'm more of a "tea at the Ritz" sort of a girl. Well, I would be if I had the oof – these days you're more likely to find me at Crane's. But I thought you might enjoy a taste of the newspaper life at a real newspaper pub.'

'This is the real thing, then, eh?' said Lady Hardcastle. 'Despite the agricultural name?'

'As real as real can be,' said Miss Caudle. 'The pig and donkey on the sign belie the true origins of the name. In days of yore, you see, the compositors and typesetters had little regard for printers and called them "hogs". Much aggrieved by this calumny, the printers returned the favour and called the compositors "asses". At the Hog and Ass, they come together, forget their age-old rivalries, and complain about the writers over a companionable pint.'

'How wonderful,' said Lady Hardcastle. 'Whereas the Dog and Duck in Littleton Cotterell is named after dogs. And ducks.'

'Ah, no,' I said. 'That name, too, has a more interesting derivation. In the time of King John, "dogs" were tax collectors and avoiding them was known as "ducking". Our village pub actually celebrates a long history of West Country tax evasion.'

They both frowned at me.

'I'm not entirely certain I believe you,' said Miss Caudle.

'Nor I,' said Lady Hardcastle.

'Ah, well,' I said. 'It was worth a try. You're right, my lady. It's named after hunting dogs and the dead ducks they retrieve on hunting trips. I see it was an act of ambitious folly to attempt to deceive you.'

Our pies and beers arrived and we tucked in.

'So tell us,' said Lady Hardcastle between mouthfuls. 'Why have we been summoned across county borders to this charmingly quaint den of iniquity and vice?'

'I've decoded the next section of Brookfield's notebook,' said Miss Caudle. 'And I've arranged a meeting with my editor, Mr Charles Tapscott, to confirm a few things. This lunch is by way of fortifying us for the encounter.'

'He's a formidable fellow?' asked Lady Hardcastle.

'He's a periphrastically inclined old windbag. We'll need all our strength to keep him to the point.'

'And you're not going to tell us anything now?' I said.

'Heavens, no,' said Miss Caudle. 'Where would be the fun in that?'

We followed Miss Caudle through the *Bristol News*'s front door and past the porter, who greeted her with a cheery, 'Afternoon, Miss Caudle. 'E's waitin' for you in his office.'

We went up the stairs to the noisily busy newsroom on the first floor, where those journalists not currently enjoying the hospitality at the Hog and Ass were shouting loudly at each other for no readily evident reason.

The editor's office was in the corner of the room furthest from the door and we negotiated our way past the desks of journalists and typists, who each greeted Miss Caudle cheerily. There was one exception. A short man with ill-fitting spectacles and a misbuttoned waistcoat sneered at her, tutted, and returned to his work.

'Take no notice of him,' said Miss Caudle. 'That's Aubrey Holcomb, our sports editor. A woman's place is in the home. Isn't that right, Aubrey?'

He ignored her.

Lady Hardcastle, though, was unfazed. 'I'm delighted to finally meet you, Mr Holcomb,' she said. 'I read your piece about Bristol City's woes. Very insightful. Although I do wonder if sacking the manager might be a bit drastic. I think it's the formation that's wrong – I'm not at all sure the pyramid is fully effective. If they drop the two outside midfielders back to form a four-man defensive line, then drop the wingers and one of the inside forwards back to midfield, they'll have two impenetrable four-man lines of defence.'

'And only two forwards,' scoffed Holcomb.

'Ah,' she continued. 'But the former wingers can work both in attack and defence. And you could push one of the other midfielders forwards, too. The other one can hang back to shield the fullbacks. So in attack, you still effectively have your five-man attacking line with your two centre forwards, two outside-halves and a nimble midfielder. But as soon as the ball comes adrift, the three midfielders who have been helping the attack fall back into their defensive front line. Set up like that, they should be able to run rings around a team like Sheffield Wednesday.'

'What?' said Holcomb, somewhat too aggressively for my taste. 'What on earth makes you imagine you know the first thing about football?'

'It's quite simple, really.'

'I've never heard such tommyrot,' he said, and returned to angrily flicking through his notebook.

When we were out of his earshot, I said, 'What was all that about? Is that a real thing or were you just trying to irritate him?'

'A little of both, to be honest,' she said. 'We watched a match while we were in London, do you remember? And I kept thinking about how much better it would be if they played it all slightly differently. It would never catch on, though. You know what stick-in-the-muds men are.'

Miss Caudle rapped smartly on the editor's door. She opened it without waiting for a reply.

'Miss Caudle,' said the man behind the desk jovially as we all trooped in. 'Oh, and two guests. Welcome all. Sit ye, sit ye.'

We sat us. The office wasn't as large or luxurious as I had expected the office of the editor of a major provincial newspaper to be. But the man himself exuded a quiet authority and gave the room an air of grandeur that the dilapidated furniture and flyblown lamps could not have managed on their own. A large window afforded him an emperor's view of the editorial office but did little to block out the clamour of his exuberantly shouty staff.

He looked to Miss Caudle for introductions.

'Lady Hardcastle,' she said, 'may I introduce Mr Charles Tapscott, editor of the *Bristol News*? Mr Tapscott, this is Emily, Lady Hardcastle, and her friend and colleague, Miss Florence Armstrong. They've been helping me with a story.'

We all how-do-you-do'd.

'I have your notes here, Miss Caudle,' said Mr Tapscott, tapping some papers with the end of his pen. 'You've been hard at work, it seems.'

'We all have,' said Miss Caudle, indicating Lady Hardcastle and me. 'But the bulk of the early legwork was done by Christian Brookfield. He left a coded notebook.'

'I knew broadly what he was working on,' said Tapscott. 'I was on at him for detail, though. It's all very well and knowing that these slimy chaps are up to no good, it's proving it that's the hard thing. Let's face it, we all pretty much knew that men like that would have skeletons in their cupboards. I mean, you've met them, haven't you? You've only to take one look at them to know there's something fishy about the lot of them. They—'

'Yes, quite,' interrupted Miss Caudle. 'We tried hard to talk to the men, to find out more about them. At first we tried to do it clandestinely – assumed identities and all that. But within days they knew exactly who we were. And now I think I know why.'

'Well,' said Mr Tapscott, 'they're all from the whatsitsname, the League of Fuddy-Duddies, or whatever they call themselves. Anti-suffrage types. And they've got someone "on the inside" with the WSPU. A spy. Never met a spy. Sounds like a thoroughly fascinating job. I remember a fellow I went to school with saying that his father was involved in espionage. Never believed him. Chap was an absolute tick. But then years later what do you know but I was covering a story up by the Khyber Pass and—'

'Indeed,' interrupted Miss Caudle again. 'You knew about this?'

'Of course. Brookfield had to clear it with me before he carried out the next stage of his investigation.'

'The next stage?' said Miss Caudle. 'I've only decoded up to the section where he was musing on the possibility of there being a spy in the WSPU.'

'Yes,' said Mr Tapscott. 'He needed my approval – or, at least, he needed me to be aware of what he was doing in case there were any repercussions – because he intended to woo the woman he suspected.'

'Lizzie Worrel?' we all said together.

'The one the police have got for the arson and murder? Perhaps. Her name definitely came up in conversation, but to tell the truth, I can't be certain it was that particular conversation.'

'Do you have any record of the meeting?' asked Miss Caudle.

'Brookfield definitely sent me a memo. I've got it somewhere. I'll get Mary to look for it.'

At that moment, a woman entered the room without knocking. She was bearing a fully laden tea tray.

'Ah, Mary, there you are,' said Mr Tapscott. 'Brookfield sent me a memo on the WSPU story he was working on. Could you dig it out for me, please?'

'Certainly, Mr Tapscott,' she said. She set down the tray and left the room.

'Gives me the creeps, that woman,' said Mr Tapscott, handing us each a slightly chipped and scarred cup full of dauntingly strong tea. 'Just materializes out of nowhere whenever you mention her name. Pretty sure we'd have burned her as a witch in the Middle Ages. Not sure there's many here who would try to stop me if I ordered it now, to tell the truth. Damn fine secretary, mind you. Efficient, but unnerving.'

'You mentioned the Men's League for Opposing Woman Suffrage as though you disapproved of them,' said Lady Hardcastle.

'I do,' he said. 'Most heartily.'

'But your newspaper is strongly opposed to women's suffrage.'

'It might appear to be, to a supporter of the cause. To the opponents of women's suffrage, it most definitely appears to be in favour of it. But as for the newspaper, I take the view that we should report the news entirely without prejudice – it's up to our readers to make up their own minds about which side to support. I proudly regard it as a sign of our neutrality that we manage to attract claims of bias from both sides of any debate.'

Mary returned at that moment with a sheet of paper. She placed it on Mr Tapscott's desk and left without saying a word.

'Thank you,' said Mr Tapscott to the closing door. 'Let's see now,' he said, picking up the paper. '"To Mr C Tapscott, from C Brookfield,"' he said as he read the memo. '"Further to our conversation . . . alleged infiltration of the WSPU . . . important to have it on record . . ." Ah, here we are . . . "It is my intention to form a romantic liaison with the woman whom I suspect . . ." Oh, I'm terribly sorry, listen to this: "I feel it would be inappropriate at this stage to record the woman's name in formal correspondence. If my suspicions are unfounded, it would be unfortunate to have made a defamatory accusation that might damage an innocent woman's reputation." An honourable and conscientious chap, old Brookfield. We could do with more like him. But I'm afraid it doesn't help you – I have no idea who the woman was.'

'We shall have to dig a little deeper ourselves,' said Miss Caudle. 'Thank you.'

'I'm sorry I can't be of any more help,' said Mr Tapscott. 'Was there anything else?'

'Not from me,' she said. 'Ladies?'

'Not for the moment,' said Lady Hardcastle.

'No, sir,' I said. 'But we've made at least half a step forwards. Thank you for your time.'

'Yes,' said Lady Hardcastle. 'Thank you.'

'Entirely my pleasure,' said Mr Tapscott with a smile. 'Before you go, though – I rather think you two may have stories to tell. If ever you've a mind to tell them, do please come to me first. I'll pay top rates for the inside story on any of your cases. Or any of your other adventures, for the matter of that. Rumours abound about your exploits – I often wonder if I may have met a spy after all.'

'Thank you,' said Lady Hardcastle. 'We'll most definitely keep you in mind.'

'Please do,' he said.

'Thank you again,' said Miss Caudle. 'Unless you object, I'm going to carry on working on this. I think it would be a feather in the newspaper's cap if we can find the answers the police haven't bothered with, even if the end result is the same.'

'No objections at all, Miss Caudle,' said Mr Tapscott. 'I said we need more like Brookfield and you have the makings. Keep up the good work.'

We exchanged another round of farewells and left him to running his newspaper.

◆ ◆ ◆

Back in the editorial office, Lady Hardcastle asked Miss Caudle if there were a telephone she might use. Miss Caudle directed her to a desk in the far corner of the office and she left to make her call while Miss Caudle and I waited at an empty desk.

'You're working wonders with that notebook,' I said.

'Thank you,' she said. 'But Tapscott could have saved me a lot of work if he'd told me everything he knew when I began. I suppose it's my fault for not letting him know sooner what I was up to, but still.'

'What about these latest developments?'

'I was rather surprised when I decoded Brookfield's suspicions about the spy, but suddenly things did make a little more sense. It had seemed odd to me that Hinkley and co. knew so quickly what we were up to and I had definitely begun to wonder if that's how they were doing it. But I confess it's something of a surprise to find that Brookfield not only knew there was a spy, but also had an idea of who it might be.'

'And infuriating that he didn't mention her name.'

'It has to be Worrel, though, don't you think?' she said. 'It fits so well. She was the spy, he suspected her, he wooed her, she found out it was a sham, she killed him.'

'She killed him, and left a note claiming responsibility.'

'She claimed responsibility for the fire, which damages the WSPU's reputation. She must have imagined that simply saying she had no idea that there was anyone there would get her off any murder charge.'

'And why would she tell us that they were engaged to be married?' I asked.

'She did? When?'

'We saw her in the gaol on Friday.'

'It still fits. Now she's moved on to denying responsibility for everything and she's trying to strengthen her case by saying that she'd have no reason to kill the man she loved. In reality she was trying to silence him before he could write his story.'

'I don't know,' I said. 'It still doesn't feel right, somehow.'

'What doesn't feel right?' asked Lady Hardcastle as she returned from making her telephone call.

'That Lizzie Worrel is engaged in an elaborately desperate double bluff,' I said.

'I can see pros and cons,' she said. 'I think Georgie Bickle might be able to tell us more. I telephoned expecting to leave a message but I caught her at home. She's invited the three of us up to Clifton to discuss the current state of play.'

'What are we waiting for?' asked Miss Caudle. 'Let's go.'

'The Rover's only a two-seater, I'm afraid,' I said. 'Shall I make two trips?'

'Two trips be blowed,' said Miss Caudle. 'Will that box thing on the back take my weight?'

'I should think so,' I said. 'You're not terribly heavy. The engine might struggle to pull us all, but if we go up past the hospital and along Park Row it's not too steep.'

'That's settled, then,' said Lady Hardcastle. 'We're off to Berkeley Crescent.'

◆ ◆ ◆

Lady Bickle welcomed us as we were shown into the drawing room and invited us to sit.

'I've asked cook to make us a pot of tea,' she said, 'but Emily tells me you've only just had your lunch so I didn't ask for any food. Do speak up if you fancy something, though – she does make devilishly good cakes.'

'I meant to remark on it before, my lady,' I said. 'She's an extremely skilled *pâtissier*.'

'She trained in Paris,' said Lady Bickle proudly. 'She ought to run her own shop, or at least be working in one of the grand hotels, but we've got her for now. She's sweet on one of our footmen and I think her heart is ruling her head. I keep telling her she should spread her wings but she smiles and says, "Yes, my lady," and then carries on regardless. Still, she's young – there'll be plenty of time for fame and fortune. And he is a handsome cove. I can very well see the attraction.'

'Well,' said Lady Hardcastle, drawing out the word over at least three syllables, 'if she's made cakes anyway, it would be a terrible shame to let them go to waste.'

'Almost an insult to her talent,' agreed Miss Caudle.

Lady Bickle laughed and when Williams appeared moments later, she asked him to tell the cook that we'd like some pastries after all.

'Now, then,' she said as she poured the tea. 'What's been going on since last we spoke?'

Between us, we filled in the details gleaned from the notebook and our meeting with Mr Tapscott at the *Bristol News*.

'A spy?' she said when we had finished. 'In our ranks? Posing as one of our own? That's a serious accusation to level at anyone. Did Brookfield have any proof? Did he have a suspect?'

'We're not certain yet what proof he had – I'm still deciphering the notebook,' said Miss Caudle. 'But he definitely had a suspect.'

'Who, then?'

'We don't know,' said Lady Hardcastle. 'He was loathe to say for fear of accidental defamation.'

'But we do know,' I said, 'that he set out to get close to the woman he suspected. Romantically close.'

'Lizzie Worrel?' asked Lady Bickle.

'They were certainly walking out,' said Lady Hardcastle.

'Wait a moment,' said Lady Bickle. 'Brookfield's suggestion was that the Men's League for Being a Shower of Utter Dunderheads employed a woman to do their dirty work?'

'That stumped me for a little while,' I said. 'But then I remembered that there's a Women's National Anti-Suffrage League. It's possible that they're working together. Actually, it would be stupid of them not to be. They're both working towards the same end, after all. I'm sure the irony of the realization that they'd be better off working together will be entirely lost on them when they band together to stop women getting the vote.'

'When did Lizzie join you?' asked Lady Hardcastle.

'Last year,' said Lady Bickle. 'Early in the summer, I think.' She paused for a moment, trying to remember exactly when. 'Yes, that was it,' she said eventually. 'Last June. We had quite a little flurry of new members then – that's when we welcomed Beattie Challenger and Marisol Rojas, too. And a handful of others, as well, but most of them have fallen by the wayside since then.'

'So any of those three could secretly be members of the Women's National Anti-Suffrage League,' said Miss Caudle. 'They could have been feeding your plans to the other side for months.'

Lady Bickle was lost in thought for another moment or two. 'You know, now you come to say it, we have noticed a few strange things of late. We put them down to bad luck at the time – batches of leaflets going missing, the police just happening to be patrolling when we were planning to smash a few council windows, that sort of thing. But it could just as easily have been coincidence and misfortune as deliberate sabotage.'

'The burglary at my flat was almost certainly an attempt to get the notebook,' said Miss Caudle. 'And no one outside our group knew of its existence. Someone tipped off . . . well, someone or other – my money's on Morefield – and they had my place turned over looking for it.'

'Exactly,' I said. 'They've known about everything. Given that Mr Brookfield has been right about everything else so far,' I said, 'I'm inclined to believe him on this one. I believe you have a cuckoo in your nest, Lady Bickle.'

'I really don't want to believe it,' said Lady Bickle, 'but I'm forced to concede that it's the most reasonable explanation. Questions remain, though. The two uppermost in my mind are who is it, and what do we do about it?'

'I think we can mitigate the effects by keeping our plans to ourselves for the time being,' said Lady Hardcastle. 'We're assuming it isn't you, by the way. I shan't insult your intelligence by pretending I didn't consider the possibility that it might be, but on balance you seem the least likely suspect.'

'I appreciate your candour,' said Lady Bickle. 'Thank you. And I agree. We shall keep any further plans and discoveries among ourselves. Even Lizzie Worrel must be kept in the dark. I've been telling her what we've been up to, so she's been as well informed as the other two and there's no reason she couldn't have passed things on, even from her gaol cell.'

'I think that's fair,' said Lady Hardcastle. 'Not knowing what we're up to will put additional strain on her, I'm sure, but I think she'll understand. If she really is innocent and we can help to prove it, she won't mind a few days of enforced ignorance.'

'It's all rather academic for the moment, anyway,' said Miss Caudle. 'There's not a great deal we can do until I've deciphered more of this blessed notebook.'

'In that case allow me to fortify you with tea and cake,' said Lady Bickle. 'Then I shall send you all on your merry way and you can get your thinking caps on.'

Chapter Fourteen

With nothing more to do on the case until Miss Caudle could provide
more clues from the notebook, Tuesday passed in a blur of catching
up with domestic matters. Lady Farley-Stroud called round with news
of the comings and goings of several village committees. She was, of
course, angling for Lady Hardcastle's support, but my employer played
the innocent and feigned a complete inability to read between the
lines. Lady Farley-Stroud's heavy-handed hints fell, so she thought,
on deaf ears.

Over lunch, I was grilled on my preferences for a birthday outing.

'It's only a month away, you know,' she said. 'We should make plans
now or we'll leave it till the last minute and end up doing something
you don't really want to do, just for the sake of doing something.'

'I always enjoy dinner and a show,' I said. 'Something light and
frivolous.'

She groaned.

'Your snobbish disdain for popular entertainment does you no
favours, you know,' I said. 'You think it makes you seem sophisticated,
but you just come across as condescending.'

'But . . . I mean . . . really. There's a flower girl, or a waitress,
or a shop girl who sells pretty things for young men to buy for their

sweethearts. And she meets a handsome young duke, or army officer, or something important in the city. He falls head over heels in love with her, forsaking the girl he thought he'd been in love with since they were children. He woos her. She falls in love with him. And then . . . Oh no, he's only gone and done something catastrophically stupid that makes her never want to see him again. She mopes. He mopes. But wait. What's this? It was all a silly misunderstanding? Oh, thank goodness for that. True love prevails and they live happily ever after. Oh, and underscoring all that are some of the soppiest, tritest, most thoroughly syrupy and awful songs ever to escape into the wild from whatever foul pit of musical horror these things are conceived in.'

'You're not keen, then?' I said.

'For you, dear, I would endure even the worst of them, especially on your birthday. As long as there were a slap-up feed and a couple of bottles of fizz at the end of it all, of course.'

'Naturally,' I said. 'I shall ponder, then – thank you. Perhaps there'll be a show to change your mind.'

'That's the spirit,' she said. 'Never be afraid of a challenge.'

After lunch we went our separate ways, she to her mysterious studio-based labours and I to more mundane wardrobe maintenance. That didn't take long, though, and once I had checked that Edna and Miss Jones were well and happy, I was soon able to settle in the drawing room with a book.

Teatime came and went without incident. By the time Edna and Miss Jones had left for the day, the lamps were lit, there were fresh logs on the fires, and I was thinking seriously about locking the doors and settling down for a quiet evening at home. Inspector Sunderland, it seemed, did not approve of my plans.

Just before six there was a ring at the doorbell. I answered it to find a cheerful police inspector on the doorstep.

'Good evening, Miss Armstrong,' said Inspector Sunderland. 'Do you think I might come in for a moment? I have news.'

'I think Lady Hardcastle prefers visitors who have presents,' I said. 'But news will do. Please, come in.'

I took his drizzle-dampened hat and coat to reveal a much shabbier suit than I was used to seeing. I made no comment but led him through to the drawing room, where Lady Hardcastle was experimenting with her latest piano composition – a complicatedly syncopated tune in the ragtime style.

'The inspector is here, my lady,' I said.

She played to the end of the phrase before turning to greet him. 'Good evening, Inspector,' she said warmly. 'What a wonderful surprise to see you. Do make yourself comfortable. To what do we owe this unexpected pleasure?'

'I'm sorry for not telephoning but I bring news of the Thomas Street arson,' he said as he sat down. 'Or news of where news might be found, at least.'

'You are a gift from the gods, my dear chap,' said Lady Hardcastle. 'We have been confounded at every turn and were beginning to think that Miss Elizabeth Worrel of Redland might very well be guilty after all. What is this news? Where may it be found? When can we get it? Does anyone need doing over? My associate here specializes in biffing ne'er-do-wells on the conk.'

He chuckled. 'I believe I may have inadvertently stumbled on one of the missing witnesses from the night of the attack,' he said. 'You remember that the local boys rounded up and questioned everyone who had hung around at the scene? And you remember asking me if I thought anyone might have scarpered before questioning could begin?'

'We do,' I said.

'Indeed. Well, one of my regular informants drinks at the Court Sampson and I believe he was there that night. Knowing Weasel, he'd have hopped it as soon as anyone mentioned summoning the Police Fire Brigade. I reckon he'd have been out the door halfway through the word "police". But he got word to me that he knows something.'

'Is this the same Weasel we saw you with at Crane's the other day?' I asked.

'Ah, yes, it is,' he said. 'I'd forgotten about that. Jesse "Weasel" Weaver.'

'Is he a reliable witness?' asked Lady Hardcastle.

'I wouldn't trust him any further than I could throw your piano,' he said, 'but he seldom steers me wrong. He has no one's interests at heart but his own, and he recognizes that it makes sound financial sense to keep supplying me with accurate intelligence. If he saw anything useful, he'll tell us. For a price.'

'Then we must meet him at once,' she said. 'If he were there before the fire and noticed anything helpful, he might be the key to unravelling this whole thing. Where will he be? At the Court Sampson?'

'We should, he might, and he definitely will be,' said the inspector. 'I've arranged to meet him there. But I'm afraid I must respectfully request that you don't come, my lady. I'd like a second pair of eyes and ears with me, but I think Miss Armstrong would fit in much better on Thomas Street. I adopt a different name and character myself when I meet Weasel in public.'

He indicated his shabby suit and scuffed boots.

'Of course, of course,' she said. 'That's precisely why she and I were so successful in our espionage days – we could each slip unnoticed into places where the other would attract unwanted attention. What say you, tiny one? Are you game?'

'Always,' I said. 'Should I change?'

'Something a little more . . .' the inspector seemed at a loss for the right word.

'Trollopy?' I suggested.

'I scarcely imagine that you have anything trollopy in your wardrobe,' he said, blushing slightly. 'But a little more . . . proletarian, perhaps.'

'Leave it to me,' I said.

'Would it be possible for you to follow us in your own motor car, my lady?' said the inspector. 'I have business to attend to in town after this and it would be a great help not to have to deliver Miss Armstrong home after the meeting.'

'I say, what fun,' she said. 'I shall be your procuress come to pick you up and take you to your next client.'

'I'm not entirely sure how I went from being the inspector's additional pair of eyes and ears to being a "girl of the pavement",' I said. 'Does your snitch-meeting persona pick up professional girls, Inspector?'

'I wouldn't put it past him,' he said with another chuckle. 'But I think we'd both be more comfortable if you were his new sweetheart.'

'I can do that,' I said. 'He'll think himself the luckiest man in town to have Nelly Maybee – with two e's – on his arm.'

'Nelly who?' he said.

'It's her latest alias,' said Lady Hardcastle. 'Don't encourage her too much or you'll get swept along by whimsical tales of petty crime and prostitution in the slums of Cardiff. I believe there was even pickpocketing at one point.'

'She's a reformed character now,' I said in my best Welsh Valleys accent. 'She is clean and wholesome, and working as a seamstress.'

'You see?' said Lady Hardcastle. 'Never one to stint on a character's full life story, our Flo.'

'One should never neglect the details,' I said. 'Do you need help getting into your driving togs?'

'I think I can manage,' she said. 'I'll bring yours with me. Why don't you two tootle off as soon as you're ready and I'll wait for you on the Bristol Bridge.'

'That sounds like a plan,' said Inspector Sunderland.

'Just give me five minutes to change into something less servanty,' I said, 'and we can go whenever you wish.'

◆ ◆ ◆

The journey into the city with Inspector Sunderland made Lady Hardcastle's reckless driving look like that of a nervous maiden aunt taking a Sunday School class on an outing to the seaside. The police motor car was a great deal more powerful than our own and he drove with an urgent aggression that had me clutching at the dashboard and door handle for support.

'Are we in a rush?' I asked innocently as the tyres scrabbled for grip on an unexpectedly sharp bend.

'Not especially,' he said, swerving violently to avoid a man walking on the road carrying a lantern in one hand and a bulky sack in the other. 'Why?'

'Nothing,' I said. 'Just as long as Lady Hardcastle can keep up.'

'She was holding her own for a little while,' he said, looking in his rearview mirror. 'But we've lost her now. She's quite the driver, though.'

'Hmm,' I said, and decided not to pursue the matter further.

The journey took a great deal less time than I was used to and I began to see the possible benefits of a more powerful machine. Being more enclosed was also a treat and we arrived at the Bristol Bridge feeling a good deal warmer than I was used to, too.

To better maintain our cover, we had parked the motor car a few streets away from the pub and completed our journey on foot – arm in arm and staggering a little. Just another tipsy couple on a night out.

'I forgot to ask,' I said as we neared the burned-out shop on Thomas Street. 'What's your name?'

'My name?' he said. 'You know my na— Oh, I'm with you. Sorry. I'm Eddie when I'm working under cover. Eddie Marsh.'

'I just thought your new sweetheart was quite likely to know your name, that's all. Pleased to meet you, Eddie.'

We arrived at the door of the Court Sampson Inn. The building was old, and badly in need of a lick of paint. The sign outside proclaimed it to be owned by 'Bristol United Breweries Ltd' and promised 'Pale Ales, Old Beer, and Stout'. We pushed our way inside.

It was a thoroughly down-at-heel city pub, like dozens of others I'd been in all over the country. The sawdust-strewn floor was scarred by the hobnails of a thousand boots. The once-white ceiling was stained brown by the smoke of a thousand pipes. The men sitting at the tables nursing their drinks were rough and rumpled. The women who accompanied some of them were even rougher but their rumples were smoothed out by their plumpness.

We attracted little obvious attention as we walked in, but I noticed several pairs of suspicious eyes discreetly turning our way. We were strangers, but we seemed to be the right sort of stranger and the eyes slid off us as everyone returned to their games and conversations.

The inspector nudged me. 'There's Weasel,' he said quietly, nodding towards a table at the back. I recognized the man we had seen talking to the inspector at Crane's in Clifton. He was playing dominoes with an older man and had already spotted us.

As we approached he said, 'Go on now, Bernie, sling your hook, I've got a bit of business to attend to.' He wasn't a local. I put his accent somewhere towards the East End of London.

The old man stroked his prodigious grey beard, but made no effort to leave.

'Don't worry,' said Weasel, 'I won't look at your 'and. Eddie 'ere will look after your dominoes for you, won't you, Eddie?'

The inspector nodded as he grunted his assent.

'Can't say fairer than that, can you?' said Weasel, and the old man reluctantly withdrew, taking his glass of rum with him.

'Take a seat, Eddie,' said Weasel. 'And your lady friend, too. I don't think as I've had the pleasure.'

'This is Nelly,' said the inspector. 'Nelly, this is Jesse Weaver.'

'But my friends calls me Weasel,' he said, holding out his hand.

'Charmed, I'm sure,' I said, cranking up my accent.

'A Taffy, eh?' said Weasel. 'There's a lot of you about round 'ere.'

'Better opportunities for work,' I said.

'Horizontal work?' he said with a leer.

I leaned towards him and said quietly, 'I don't want to get off on the wrong foot, my love, what with you bein' a friend of Eddie's and all, but one more insinuation like that from you and it'll take an extremely skilled surgeon to extract those dominoes from where I shove them. Are we clear?'

He laughed – a harsh cackling sound. 'You've got a spirited one 'ere, Eddie boy.'

'You don't know the half of it,' said the inspector. 'Treat her nice, Weasel, or she'll have you crying for your mother quicker than you can blink.'

Weasel grinned and nodded.

'Let me get you another drink,' said the inspector. 'What are you having?'

'I'll have another of their "old beers",' said Weasel. 'When in Rome an' all that.'

'Brandy as usual for me, please, *bach*,' I said.

'Not only fiery, but classy with it,' said Weasel. 'Why can't I ever meet a lass like you?'

'Who knows?' I said. 'You seem like such a lovely bloke.'

He laughed again.

We said nothing further to each other until the inspector returned with our drinks.

'Getting to know each other?' he said with a frown as he set down the glasses.

'Getting along famously, we are, aren't we, darlin'?' said Weasel.

I raised an eyebrow.

The inspector sat. He put a few shillings on the table, as though it were his change from the bar. He toyed with the coins as he spoke.

'What have you got for me, Weasel?' he asked calmly.

'You in a rush?' asked the informant.

223

'People keep asking me that,' said the inspector. 'I suppose I must be. I've always got better things to be doing than chasing round after you. And you know how much I hate wasting my time. So, yes, let's say I'm in a rush.'

'All right, all right, keep your hair on. Just messin' about. I ain't never steered you wrong, now 'ave I? I don't waste your time. Old Weasel always comes up with the goods.'

'Eventually,' said the inspector, tapping a coin on the beer-stained table.

'All right,' said Weasel, putting up his hands. 'I 'eard you was lookin' into the fire next door. I 'eard you upset a few people down at the Bridewell who reckon they've got it all wrapped up in a neat little bow already.'

'Are they right?'

'About that suffragette woman?' asked Weasel slyly. 'I reckon they are.'

'How so?'

'I saw her in 'ere that night. Dark coat, big hat. She sat over there in the corner where the light don't shine. But I could see she had a white dress and white boots like they all wear. You know?'

'I know,' said the inspector.

'She had a big bag with her. Like a sailor's duffel. Then about quarter past eleven she drinks up, hoists her big bag on her tiny shoulders, and slopes off into the dark.'

'Did you see her face at all?' asked the inspector.

'No, she kept to the shadows and kept her head down. Couldn't see nothin' but her hat.'

'Did anyone talk to her?'

'No, she just sat there on her own for about half an hour, then got up and went.'

'It certainly could be Worrel,' said the inspector.

'It could be any suffragette,' I said. 'A woman in a white dress and white boots whose face no one saw could be any one of thousands of women.' I sat for a moment, lost in thought. After a while I said, 'Describe her boots to me.'

'They was white,' he said. 'White boots like some of the suffragettes wear.'

'Plain white?' I said.

'What? Yes, they was plain . . . No, hang on a minute, you're right. No, they wasn't. They had flowers embroidered on 'em. Daisies. I was watchin' her as she walked out and I caught 'em then. White boots with daisies.'

◆ ◆ ◆

Inspector Sunderland added a few coins to the small pile of change and we let Weasel return to his dominoes.

Back out on the street, the inspector said, 'You know who the woman was, don't you?'

'I certainly know who wears white boots embroidered with daisies,' I said. 'She's on our list of suspected cuckoos.'

'Your what?'

'One of the recent recruits to the suffragette cause is actually a member of the Women's National Anti-Suffrage League and has been feeding details of the WSPU's plans both to the Women's League and the Men's League for Opposing Sense and Reason.'

'The Men's League for Opposing Woman Suffrage, surely,' he said with a slight laugh.

'It amounts to the same thing,' I said. 'Of all the women who joined the WSPU towards the end of last year, only three remained committed to the cause: Lizzie Worrel, Beattie Challenger, and Marisol Rojas. One of them, we knew – or thought we knew, at any rate – was the cuckoo. The smart money was on Lizzie Worrel, with an each-way bet on the Chilean – none of us knows anything about South American politics, so who knows what her motivations are? But the rank outsider – in my mind, at least – was a pasty lump of nothing by the name of Beatrice Challenger. A woman so bland and unassuming that it's often difficult to remember that she's even there. The only spark she's ever shown was when she was criticizing the police. Other than that she's a woman about whom the only interesting thing is that she wears extremely pretty boots of white leather embroidered with daisies.'

'And the motive for the fire?'

'At the very least, to discredit the WSPU by breaking their cease-fire,' I said.

'It's a bit flimsy,' he said. 'Have you any evidence other than Weasel remembering the daisies?'

'At this stage, none at all,' I said. 'And all the evidence we have so far comes from the dead journalist's encoded notebook.'

'It certainly adds up, though. I'd been wondering how the chief superintendent came to find out I'd been moonlighting on the case. I've been extremely careful to make certain that all my enquiries have been discreet, and I kept our meetings as scarce and as short as possible. I was sure no one knew I was taking any interest in it at all. But Weasel was right – I've been leaned on quite heavily. And now I know where the information came from.'

'Thank you for going to so much trouble on our behalf,' I said. 'And thank you for taking me along this evening.'

'You and Lady Hardcastle are never any trouble,' he said. 'Well, never very much trouble, anyway.'

'We try not to be,' I said. 'The problem we have now, though – as I'm reasonably sure you must have told us more than once – is that knowing a thing and being able to prove that thing are two completely different . . . things.'

'I'm very much afraid they are. But if anyone can work out how to trap this Challenger character and find the proof we need to secure her conviction, I'd always put my money on you and Lady Hardcastle.'

'You're very kind,' I said. 'Although getting Lizzie Worrel released remains our priority.'

'Of course, but the one follows the other. Here we are.'

We had arrived at Bristol Bridge, where the little Rover was parked beneath a streetlamp. A well-dressed man was leaning drunkenly on the front wing. He had apparently been talking to Lady Hardcastle.

'Ah,' she said as we approached, 'here she is. This gentleman was wondering how much you'd charge for an hour of your company.'

'Tell him he can't afford me,' I said, stepping around him to get into the motor car.

'I did, dear, but he's really rather insistent.' She was very evidently enjoying herself.

I'd almost made it to the motor car when the man grabbed my arm and said, 'Come on, sweetheart. Just a kiss, at least. Don't be so coy.'

The word 'coy' was actually delivered as 'c—oyyyyyyoof' as I threw him on to his back. I still had hold of the hand that had grabbed me and I used it to twist his arm.

'Don't do that, my love,' I said in Nelly's broad Valleys accent. 'It's not nice. You should treat women with a little more respect, you should.'

'I'll . . . I'll . . . I'll bloody well get you for this. You saw what she did,' he said to the inspector. 'You saw. I'll be calling you as a b-b-bloody witness.'

I twisted a little harder, making him yelp.

'I've no idea what you're talking about,' said the inspector. 'I didn't see a thing. But she's right, you know – you should treat women with a great deal more respect.'

I dropped the man's arm and clambered into the Rover while the inspector graciously cranked the engine to life for us. The man was hauling himself to his feet by gripping on to the side of the Rover with his good arm.

'I mean it,' he said. 'I'll have you. I'm going to find a copper and I'll bloody have you.'

The inspector had pulled out his warrant card.

'You've found one,' he said, holding up the card. 'Now unless you want to be taken down to the Bridewell and charged with causing a public nuisance, I suggest you sling your hook.'

'But . . . but . . .' stammered the man, now more bewildered and frustrated than ever. 'You saw her assault me.'

'I also saw you slander a titled lady and her maid by suggesting that they were common prostitutes. If you insist on pressing charges, I shall have to tell the truth, the whole truth, and nothing but the truth.'

The man made a half-hearted lunge at me, but the inspector blocked him.

'I really would be on my way if I were you, sir. I'd hate to see what she might do to the other arm if I let her get at you.'

Muttering a few choice oaths, the man sloped off, massaging his recently wrenched shoulder.

'You two ought to sling your hooks, too,' said the inspector with a smile. 'Before you cause any more trouble.'

With a cheery wave, we set off towards the High Street and the middle of town.

◆ ◆ ◆

In defiance of all the tediously restrictive rules of etiquette, we decided to see if Lady Bickle was at home. It was far too late to be paying unannounced social calls, and there was a fair chance she would be out anyway, but we thought it was worth trying. I had told Lady Hardcastle what we had learned from Weasel and she was keen to share the news at once.

We rang the doorbell and were only slightly astonished when Williams welcomed us in and said that we should go straight through to the drawing room. He led the way, opened the door, and ushered us in without introduction.

Lady Bickle was sitting at the piano and got up as soon as we entered. There were two men relaxing in armchairs, one of whom I knew – it was Lady Hardcastle's friend Dr Simeon Gosling.

'How extraordinary and wonderful to see you both,' said Lady Bickle. 'Welcome. We were just talking about you, and here you are.'

'Hello,' said Lady Hardcastle. 'You can't possibly have been expecting us, though. Surely not.'

'What do you mean, dear? Oh, Williams. No, not specifically. I just made sure he knew that if ever you were to call, he should let you in and lead you to me without delay.'

'That's a relief – I suddenly wondered if there might be another spy.'

'No,' said Lady Bickle. 'Don't be silly. But listen to me chattering on. I haven't done the introductions. The heart-meltingly handsome individual on the sofa is my husband Ben. Ben, dear, this is Emily, Lady Hardcastle and her . . . her friend. I was going to say lady's maid, but I've known them for nearly a month now and she's so much more than that. Oh, and I've not mentioned her name. She's Florence Armstrong. Or do you prefer Flo?'

'Either is fine, my lady,' I said. 'Actually my mother calls me Flossie, but most people call me Flo.'

'Then good evening, Emily, and good evening, Flo,' said Sir Benjamin. He was, as we had suspected, a good deal older than his wife, but he had the same boyish air about him as his friend, the police surgeon sitting next to him.

'And the other reprobate you know, I think.'

'Hello, old girl,' said Dr Gosling. 'Fancy seeing you here.'

'Fancy,' said Lady Hardcastle.

'To what do we owe the pleasure?' asked Lady Bickle. 'Is it exciting news?'

'Interesting, I should say, more than exciting,' said Lady Hardcastle. 'But news there is.'

'Then we must retire at once to another room and leave the boys to their own devices for a few moments. Do excuse us, gentlemen.'

She led us out of the door and into what appeared to be a sitting room.

'I'm afraid we've already eaten,' she said, 'but do please stay and spend the rest of the evening with us. Ben and Simeon get a bit silly when they're together so it would be good to have an ally or two.'

'We're hardly dressed for it,' said Lady Hardcastle. 'But if you'll take us as we are, I'd definitely love to. Flo?'

'Of course,' I said. 'It would be a wonderful way to spend the evening.'

'That's settled, then,' said Lady Bickle. 'Now, what's this news?'

'Flo has just been to the Court Sampson Inn,' said Lady Hardcastle, 'in the company of our dear friend, Inspector Sunderland. This is the reason for her uncustomary scruffy appearance.'

'Trollopy, was the word used, I believe,' I said.

'Only by you, dear. All of this is by the by. There they met one of the inspector's informants, from whose eyewitness account of the evening of the fire they have discovered that the person responsible – and almost certainly the cuckoo in your suffragette nest – is . . .'

There was an annoyingly long pause.

'I've already come close to dislocating a man's shoulder this evening, my lady,' I said. 'I'm clearly not in the mood to be trifled with. And Lady Bickle has a guest, so she certainly has better things to do.'

'I was trying to build an air of dramatic tension,' she said. 'The cause of all your misfortunes is Beattie Challenger.'

'I can't say I'm overly surprised,' said Lady Bickle. 'Hugely disappointed, but not surprised. I don't know why, but I couldn't really see it being either of the other two.'

'Really?' said Lady Hardcastle. 'I was sure it would be one of the other two. Challenger is so . . . so . . .'

'Bland?' I suggested.

'The very word,' she said. 'Thank you.'

'I think it's for that selfsame reason that I've never quite trusted her,' said Lady Bickle. 'How can someone be so drearily ordinary? There's no spark to the woman. None visible, anyway. It's obvious now that it was just an act. The question remains, though: what are we going to do about it?'

'I had the same conversation with the inspector,' I said. 'We need to find proof of her guilt or to devise some way of trapping her into a confession. It's not going to be easy.'

'Not at all,' said Lady Hardcastle. 'I suggest that our very first move be not to move at all. Whatever happens, we absolutely must not let on that we know what she's up to.'

'Actually,' I said, 'Since we don't know the full extent of what she's up to, it's doubly important. We can't tip her off before we know everything there is to know.'

'Agreed,' said Lady Bickle.

'We have a little experience in finding out what people are up to,' said Lady Hardcastle. 'So perhaps we should retreat to our country lair and see what we can come up with. If you have any ideas in the meantime, please telephone us.'

'I most certainly shall,' said Lady Bickle. 'For now, though, shall we rejoin the boys? I'm sure they've been missing us terribly.'

We rejoined 'the boys', who had barely noticed that we weren't there.

As we walked in, Sir Benjamin was saying, '. . . trying to put it back in with a pair of Elliot forceps.'

This, apparently, was hilarious, and rendered the two men helpless with laughter.

'Hello, darling,' said Sir Benjamin when they had calmed down. 'Have you had your confab?'

'We have. The game – as that chap in the books always says – is afoot.'

'Foot,' said Dr Gosling, and they were off again.

'I invited Emily and Flo to stay a while,' said Lady Bickle. 'I thought we might play something.'

'Know any five-handed card games?' asked Dr Gosling.

'A few,' said Sir Benjamin. 'But a word of advice for you all: never gamble with my wife. You'll lose your shirt.'

'I think I might,' said Dr Gosling. 'But I'm not sure about our Emily. Didn't you tell me you'd won a German brothel in a poker game, old girl?'

'Free use of a brothel, dear,' said Lady Hardcastle. 'And a huge pile of cash.'

'There you are, then,' said Dr Gosling. 'I think we ought to play for matchsticks.'

And so we did. It was past midnight by the time we stepped out into the cold night and shivered our way home in our open motor car.

Chapter Fifteen

First thing on Wednesday morning, Lady Hardcastle began trying to contact Dinah Caudle by telephoning the newspaper office. She was told that Miss Caudle hadn't been in that day and that she had left a message saying that she would be out all day researching a story. Lady Hardcastle left a message of her own, asking Miss Caudle to contact us as soon as she was able.

We took our elevenses in the drawing room, where we began rearranging the crime board. We were sure now that Lizzie Worrel was innocent of the arson, and that she was probably not involved in any of the other shenanigans that Brookfield had uncovered. It seemed unlikely that Marisol Rojas was mixed up in anything, but we kept her on the board for completeness. And, lack of actual evidence notwithstanding, Beattie Challenger now took centre stage as our likely arsonist and murderer.

'I don't think we should discount the men,' I said as Lady Hardcastle rearranged her sketches and added more notes. 'The Men's League for Opposing the Twentieth Century was definitely involved at some level.'

'I agree,' she said. 'Even if all they did was stand on the touchline and cheer her on, they're part of it. I wonder how far their grubby influence reaches, though. If there's someone high enough to obstruct us, it could be that we never get an opportunity to bring them to justice. Although, if we can get Harry to point us at the right people, we might yet see them punished. I doubt their influence stretches as far as London.'

'That's something for us to look forward to, then,' I said.

'I'll make some circumspect enquiries the next time I write to him,' she said. 'There's no point in being related to someone who works in Whitehall if one doesn't make use of the connection once in a while. And I'm sure it would do him some good, too. I imagine his standing in the Foreign Office could only be helped by making pals in the Home Office.'

'Unless they're all in on it,' I said. 'The Men's League for the Continuing Oppression of Women might have members in Whitehall, too.'

'I doubt they have to,' she said. 'That rather seems to be Whitehall's standing policy – no need for special lobbying on that issue. Do you know, I sometimes think—'

Her sometimes thought was interrupted by the doorbell.

'How rude,' she said. 'Just as I was about to start pontificating.'

'I'm thankful for small mercies,' I said as I left the room to answer the door.

It was, to my surprise, Dinah Caudle. I stepped aside to allow her to enter.

'Good morning, Miss Caudle,' I said. 'Do, please, come in. Lady Hardcastle has been trying to get in touch with you at the newspaper office.'

'Did they not pass on my message?' she said as I took her hat, coat, and gloves.

'Only that you were out working on a story.'

'I despair sometimes. I left clear and specific instructions that if Lady Hardcastle called, they were to tell her I was on my way to see her.'

The lady herself appeared in the hall.

'I'm afraid I didn't get that message,' she said. 'But you're here now, anyway, so it's all turned out for the best. Come through to the drawing room. We were just having our elevenses – can I offer you a little something?'

'A cup of tea would be most welcome,' said Miss Caudle. 'Thank you.'

I fetched the teapot and took it through to the kitchen to be refreshed. Edna was there, taking a break from dusting the bedrooms.

'Ah, Edna,' I said. 'Could you be an absolute treasure and make a fresh pot of tea and bring it to the drawing room, please? I'll take a cup and saucer through.'

'Certainly, m'dear,' she said. 'Is it that newspaper woman?'

'It is.'

'I thought we didn't like her.'

'We didn't used to,' I said. 'But we seem to have arrived at a tense truce. It always feels to me that hostilities might resume at any moment, but for now we're managing to rub along without too much unpleasantness.'

'Right you are, then,' she said. 'A nice cup of tea always helps. There i'n't no one as could start a war over a nice cup of tea.'

'I dare say you're right, Edna. Thank you.'

Back in the drawing room, they were still discussing Miss Caudle's journey.

'. . . and I said, "Well, Michael, dear, since you're going to Cardiff on the train, you'll have no need for your motor car. Can I borrow it?" He's too polite to say no, even though he hates the idea of me driving his precious machine. I shall really have to see if I can tap Papa for a few guineas to buy me one of my own.'

'Edna will bring a fresh pot through in just a moment,' I said as I put the cup and saucer on the table beside Miss Caudle's chair.

'Thank you,' she said. 'Now that you're here, we can get on. You'll forgive my getting straight to business, but I've some rather exciting news.' She reached into her satchel and pulled out Brookfield's note-book. 'I know who the cuckoo in the WSPU's nest is.'

Lady Hardcastle gave a rueful smile. 'Ah,' she said.

'You already know, don't you?' said Miss Caudle. 'I should have guessed.'

Lady Hardcastle gestured to the crime board, where Beattie Challenger now had pride of place in the centre.

'How did you find out?' asked Miss Caudle. 'When?'

'I went to the Court Sampson yesterday evening with Inspector Sunderland to meet one of his informants. Weasel – the informant's name is Weasel – was in the pub on the night of the fire but scarpered when he realized the police would be called. He saw a woman with a big bag. He didn't see her face, but he did see her boots. They were Beattie Challenger's boots.'

'I tried to tell you first thing this morning,' said Lady Hardcastle. 'Hence the telephone call to the newspaper.'

'Ah, well,' said Miss Caudle. 'Can't be helped. But I do know a little something that this Weasel character didn't know. Brookfield did walk out with Beattie Challenger as a way of trying to find out what she was up to. He confirmed that she was a fully paid-up member of the Women's National Anti-Suffrage League and that she had been co-opted by the Men's League to wheedle her way into the WSPU and keep an eye on things. She got rather attached to him, it seems, but he threw her over almost as soon as he met Lizzie Worrel. According to his notes, Challenger was furious with the pair of them.'

'More than enough motive to kill him and frame her,' I said, 'even without the bonus of disgracing the WSPU.'

'Quite,' said Miss Caudle. 'Tapscott is going to have to work over-time to retreat the *News* from its position of condemning the suffrag-ettes for breaking their truce. He does like to stir things up, no matter what he might say. But he also values the truth above everything.'

'With another hung parliament, I'm not sure people are taking much notice of what the suffragettes are up to at the moment,' said Lady Hardcastle. 'All the talk is of whether Asquith will get his budget past the Lords this time.'

'Nevertheless, he'll want to set the record straight.'

'But not yet,' said Lady Hardcastle. 'We've yet to come up with any hard evidence and I think it's still important that we don't show our hand until we do. I don't want her to scarper before we can get her arrested and tried.'

'I might be able to help you there,' said Miss Caudle. 'Or, looking at it another way, I might need you to help me.' She flipped open the notebook to a page near the back. 'The rest of the book is written in the style you helped to fathom out when I first showed the book to you. It's devilishly frustrating at times – his wordplay can be tortuous – but it's quite straightforward once you get the hang of it. But this . . .' She turned the book to face us. Unlike the rest of the notebook, which was written in shorthand, this was a block of seemingly random ordinary letters. 'I tried your trick of shifting the letters. Nothing. So I shifted them again. And again. I went all the way through all the possible . . . What did you call them? "Caesar ciphers"? Nothing. I'm completely stumped. But I thought a woman who even knew the term "Caesar cipher" might know where to go next.'

Lady Hardcastle took the notebook and stared at it for a moment.

'You might think you've wasted your time,' she said, 'but you've done good work. If you've eliminated all the simple shift ciphers, it might be another simple substitution cipher – I can check that with a frequency analysis.'

Miss Caudle looked at her blankly.

'Sorry, dear,' said Lady Hardcastle. 'It's not terribly interesting – I'm just thinking out loud. If that doesn't work, then the next step would be to wonder if it's a "Vigenère cipher".'

'And what's that?' asked Miss Caudle.

'Made famous by a French chap called . . .'

'Vigenère?' I suggested.

'Well, yes, but I was trying to remember the rest of the blessed chap's name. Sixteenth-century fellow. Anyway, he perfected a cipher that was so cunning it was known as *le chiffre indéchiffrable* – the indecipherable cipher.'

'And how does that help us?' asked Miss Caudle. 'If it's indecipherable, how do we . . . you know . . . decipher it?'

'It was only called *le chiffre indéchiffrable*, it wasn't actually *indéchiffrable*.'

'You know how to *déchiffre* it?'

'It's long-winded and tedious,' said Lady Hardcastle, 'but, yes, I know a way.'

Edna arrived at this moment with the fresh tea and a plate of scones.

'I thought you might need some sustenance,' she said as she poured a cup of tea for Miss Caudle. 'My Dan always says a fella can't think on an empty stomach. Mind you, he says he can't do nothin' on an empty stomach. Actually, now I comes to say it out loud, he never has an empty stomach. Always eatin', that man.' She offered round the plate of scones. 'Will there be anythin' else, m'lady?'

'No, thank you, Edna. You've done us proud as always.'

'It was Miss Jones as made the scones, mind,' said Edna. 'I can't take credit for that.'

'Then take her our grateful thanks,' said Lady Hardcastle.

Edna left, closing the door behind her.

'I don't suppose you—' began Lady Hardcastle.

'Painstakingly copied out the letters and checked them three times to ensure I hadn't made a mistake? Of course. Here you are.'

She handed over a foolscap sheet where the letters had been arranged in a grid just as in the original but much neater.

'You have a lovely hand,' said Lady Hardcastle absently as she took the paper.

'I can't claim all the credit,' said Miss Caudle. 'It's largely down to Miss Wyatt, the unfortunate woman who served as my governess.'

'Were you not a good pupil?'

'I was beastly. But somehow I managed to learn a few things, one of which was penmanship.'

'I shall have to study this,' said Lady Hardcastle.

'Of course. It will take time?'

'A few hours, at least. It's all rather unglamorous, I'm afraid. If I pull it off, you'll be amazed at my skills – you might even think me possessed of arcane powers. But mostly it's just counting.'

'Then count away,' said Miss Caudle. 'I shall leave you to your endeavours. Although if I might impose on your hospitality for long enough to finish this delicious scone, that would be grand. But then I must away – I wasn't fibbing to the office when I said I was working on a story.'

'Anything fun?'

'Fun? No, not really. But it's a step or two away from society gossip, so it's definitely more satisfying.'

'Will you telephone this evening?' asked Lady Hardcastle. 'Just in case I've made any progress.'

'Of course. Around seven?'

'Splendid. I'll try to have something useful by then. But in the meantime, would you like a little jam on that?'

While they fussed about with their scones, I took the foolscap sheet and looked carefully at the blocks of letters:

xgcdi vpask qdkqd hnczc zqmvp ichvk ephrq xxcrs jimmb
zcwpq

lhvkl wknzm ymwht itlnm batag swlld dswxs qmjif zcshb
ffbhl

icpdd mjiom zcqqr tzcgs fnntv hephr vsema nwolv cspee gntcr

omqrb szllx tedbm nbiew xnccz czqmx smjdg mvvdv gsflf dbmei

rxwys iudip cmzcg wpmme zsxbg dzidb neblt amnbi mwnjt edbxd

ivtjd firhw qjqrr wmzax zzxzj sfbsg mgzzq txxtw mhvsf zbhbc

ttdzz rplne irtvr hlmzc rvmfz naqqf pzxat enslz qplvc ggtzk

qhacl unmox smfqm eeimc blpon nlmwm zqvio wezbx puosa fjzhb

peylo neicn tkuiy bnrcf gmqsb lpkzt aitvv gqgsg ntiro vnvqw

zxzra mzvzs mpjjd kqigm hecpw ghmbi yldcb spfon aieph rovfj

axksc ztobm zvhmu cymvr xeamq bwpfu mqmgp vskgx swtfp mdbtl

jpplt owrlk qhumy ikots ebgda igmmz tqpvz qmtwi mmqrr bnrbi

ltzrp maudm bsqkg htilv fntht vsdvh plzrx ejudm bjzzl hvmyo

dpcma udmbz tbzkb sepzs ksfvs qgwaz nrxic qsxqh zvsgi zpbgd

nywtr swvjg dsiro qedmp xgshu itaqt vrtvf rpscb rnqql gmnbj

tvcnc xpddq gxsqm fjiqw qdqxd bnnte emokm edmlx lecth moasi

sddic pzrpe axdmm hewld qfpox ncxzj qhvke pdlbs ucrsq gpbzj

mxsqr hvjzz lzbmz vsnbl pxnkq gpbgq wyrps ztotv fswht afqcr

etdcm qatnx midim ccrom qkqrr azmlf janlm enbrn ntpbs xjyco

kzzcq wqvpm nphli cjmsg izpbn eigpb gdksy adpci ykdrq llddk

mecvd cuynp numve pdoiw eedds wmcss piqqm dliei hkall dddty

omclm xsmrd ivpkz tbmzc rlmrm csvpe eqcns rzehr blta: mzbll

vhdtq zzdeq iwlhr qrnpz qoilv chagz vsqwp wqmfb lpxkn bsdez

klgci mdiro zdcdi caghv owmxz ziazn uqhtv fspix wmdgr pmcdl

xzntm lxsms gmjer zlmwd bzmaf cqcfm mdbzj qrrkz
qmsqb zbbmn

azmla ttkrc tatxd fxcil dvedv ddlio gntzt ltadi xeqdb pewtd

moicq rhvzz tudlw zudgw atbgh vodpd vqpwk ztaid wldas
cbnel

mdbqz kxtwm spirw kcalt xldvx lzqhd idisz dsyun tblow
bjasy

bgdte dbczg sqnda zylzx heedv dumvl jkdbs paszj ptagd
fenbk

xpshb gdgtw immmh ewrsm ewbgd tszba tbmvm osksx
qmfig cwrrb

lpenq lwhqs bpmww udgsf ehspe wtsgi xtilz vhhqk kzixi
hmiph

ixrgs fzbgz mdbhz vxxxx

Lady Hardcastle might know the trick of it, but for now I was as
stumped as Miss Caudle.

◆ ◆ ◆

Dinah Caudle wafted out with the same nonchalance as she had wafted
in. Lady Hardcastle retired to her study, only communicating briefly
at one o'clock to request sandwiches, and at four to ask for tea and
cake. I dealt with both requests myself and she was distracted. Polite

and friendly, to be sure, but her mind was most definitely elsewhere. As was mine. There seemed to be a lot riding on this encrypted note. For all we knew, it might have been nothing more significant than Brookfield's shopping list, but neither of us thought so. He had taken so much trouble to conceal its contents with a special cipher that it must be extremely important.

By six o'clock, Edna and Miss Jones had gone home. They left me with only last-minute things to do to prepare the evening meal, which I'd planned for eight, to allow plenty of time for Miss Caudle's call at seven. There was no one to talk to now.

The clock ticked. I tried to settle in the sitting room to read a book. I read the same paragraph five times and didn't understand a word. I stood. I went through to the drawing room to examine the crime board. I sat at the piano and picked out a tune, wishing I'd been more diligent with my practice. I wondered where my banjo was. Perhaps if I . . .

The telephone rang.

'Hello? Chipping Bevington two-three,' I said.

'Miss Armstrong? It's Dinah Caudle. Is there news from the team's resident clever clogs?'

'I was hoping it might be you,' I said. 'I don't know why but I've been on tenterhooks all day while she's been working on that code and I was looking forward to having someone to talk to about it.'

'So, no, then.'

'Not yet, sorry.'

'No, please don't apologize. To tell the truth I've been as anxious as you. I can't help feeling that there's something exciting in that coded note.'

'Is there anything more after that?' I asked.

'No, that's where it ends. I've been wondering if whatever's in that last note is what got him killed. Unless it's his shopping list.'

'I was worried it might be that, too.'

She laughed. 'I'm not certain it's worth going to that much effort to conceal one's fondness for tinned sardines,' she said.

'I don't know. People can be very judgemental over tinned sardines.'

Lady Hardcastle emerged from the study, looking a little the worse for wear but grinning broadly. 'Is that Dinah Caudle?' she mouthed.

I nodded, and then said into the telephone, 'She's just come out of her study. She seems pleased with herself.'

'Put her on, would you?' said Miss Caudle. 'I'm dying to hear this.'

I offered Lady Hardcastle the earpiece. She took it in one hand while holding a sheaf of papers in the other.

'Hello, Miss Caudle,' she said. 'How are you, dear? . . . How's your new story coming along? . . . Yes, Flo always says that . . . Not in those exact words, no. She says I'm "Absolutely infuriating" . . . Well, quite . . . Yes, of course, hold on.' Still grinning, she offered me the earpiece. 'She wants another quick word with you, dear.'

'Hello?' I said.

'Slap her in the face for me, would you?' said Miss Caudle.

'You're playing right into her hands,' I said. 'She does this all the time, and the more frustrated you get with her, the more she grins and drags it out. She's bursting to tell us what she's discovered, but we just have to let her have her bit of fun first.'

Miss Caudle let out a load grunt of frustration and then said, 'All right, then, put her back on.'

'She asked me to slap you in the face, my lady,' I said as I handed the telephone earpiece back to her. 'You need to stop teasing her or I might accede to her request.'

'Spoilsports,' said Lady Hardcastle, the grin still very much plastered across her face. 'Very well. I made the right guess – it is a Vigenère cipher and I have deciphered it. It took me a while to work out the key – I used Babbage's method, of course. Or is it that German chap? Anyway, I worked it out the hard way, but any of us could have guessed the key.

He probably chose it especially so that we could. It was LIZZIE. His true love's name. Isn't that sweet? I was kicking myself by the time I worked it out the long way. I should have just—'

My threatening glare cut her short.

'Ah, yes,' she said. 'The note. One moment. Hold this, dear.' She gave me the papers and flipped open the lorgnette that she wore round her neck. She held the reading glasses up to her eyes and said, 'Keep it steady, I can't quite . . . Ah, there we are. I had to spend quite a while fathoming out the punctuation, but I think I have it. It says, "My dearest Lizzie. If you are reading this, it must be because I'm in gaol or in exile. I don't wish to have to think about it, but I may even be dead. I'm glad you found this notebook and that you understood my last note to you. 'You are the key.' I knew you'd get it. As you have already seen from the rest of this notebook, last year I began working on a story about the corruption in our city. I learned of an insidious web of bribery, blackmail, and hypocrisy among the great and the good. I learned of attempts by rich and powerful men to subvert the cause in which you – and now I – so passionately believe. I fully intended to expose this grubby corruption in my newspaper column. Recently, though, I stumbled upon a criminal plot. These venal men are planning to steal a shipment of Chilean gold intended as payment for mining equipment vital to that country's prosperity. I don't have the full story yet and I feel my time is running short so I may not find out everything before it's too late. Please, my darling, whatever has happened to me, I beg you to bring them to justice. Take this information to the police. Through talking to disgruntled employees and underlings, and by some acts of petty burglary for which I may yet have to face the consequences, I have learned much over the past weeks, but the fine details have eluded me. These are cautious men. But what I do know is this: Nathaniel Morefield is in charge and is controlling the plot. Oswald Crane and Redvers Hinkley are providing the money needed to fund the theft. James Stansbridge is taking care of tactics and will supply extra men as needed. Your pal Beattie Challenger is involved, somehow. I think she will cause some sort of distraction. The gold shipment arrives at Avonmouth docks on the last day of February. I was never able to establish exactly how they planned to steal the loot but I kept coming across the word 'switch'. I love you with all that I am, and will remain always, your Christian." It must have taken him an absolute age to encrypt it, but it was obviously very important to him to write to his sweetheart one last time.' She held the telephone earpiece so that we could both hear.

'That's oddly touching,' said Miss Caudle. 'And at the same time oddly disappointing. He knew so much, but without those final details it's really of very little use. What on earth are we going to do with all that?'

'We're going to take up where he left off and find out exactly what's going on, that's what we're going to do,' said Lady Hardcastle. 'I'll call Georgie Bickle to arrange things, but unless you hear differently, we'll meet at her house tomorrow morning at nine to plan our next steps.'

We said our goodbyes and hung up.

'We need to call the inspector, as well,' she said. 'He's already looking into rumours about the possibility of a gold robbery, so he needs to be with us tomorrow morning, objections from his superiors or not. Oh!'

'Oh?'

'He suspected this all along. Do you remember? At the coffee shop. He nearly spilled his coffee when he put it all together, but he was afraid to say anything in case we thought him stupid. I shall be able to tell him he was right all along. I think I'll call him first.'

'Right you are,' I said. 'Dinner will be on the table in ten minutes.' I left her to make her calls.

◆　◆　◆

On the dot of nine we were parking the Rover on Berkeley Square. Inspector Sunderland was leaning against a lamppost reading a newspaper.

'You look like the most disreputable of loafers, standing there like that,' said Lady Hardcastle as we approached him.

'You're not the only one to think so,' he said as he stood up straight. 'The local bobby has already tried to move me on.'

'Oh dear. Have you been here long?'

'Ten minutes or so,' he said. 'I strolled up the hill somewhat more quickly than I anticipated. But all is well – I have my newspaper. And now you're here. Good morning.' He folded his newspaper and doffed his hat.

'And good morning to you,' she said. 'Shall we go up? Have you met Lady Bickle before?'

'Only briefly. Gosling is a friend of her husband's. I had need of Gosling's services one evening and I had to drag him from a dinner with his pals. She seemed like a charming young lady.'

'She's an absolute poppet. She reminds me of a young me in many ways.'

'I don't remember you ever being a poppet,' I said.

'I was winsome charm personified,' she said. 'Absolutely adorable. Everyone thought so.'

'It must have been before I met you.'

'Number five, is it?' asked the inspector as we reached the top of the steps.

'Yes,' I said. 'But they're numbered from the right.'

'I know,' he said. 'This used to be my beat.'

'Did it really? How delightful. I can imagine you in a tall hat, carrying a truncheon, with a whistle on a chain,' said Lady Hardcastle.

'I'll have you know I looked extremely dashing in my blue serge,' he said. 'I still have a whistle on a chain – we all do. And I often carry a detective's truncheon. I met my wife while I was in uniform – she'll tell you how handsome I was back then.'

'I don't doubt it for a second,' she said. 'Here we are.'

Williams answered the door so quickly that I wondered if he'd been positioned behind it, waiting for our ring at the bell. With a polite, 'Good morning,' he took our coats and led us straight to the drawing room.

Miss Caudle was already there and was pouring herself a cup of tea.

Lady Bickle welcomed us, and Lady Hardcastle dealt with the introductions.

'It's wonderful to meet you properly at last, Inspector,' said Lady Bickle. 'I don't count that time you dragged Simeon away from us. But Emily sings your praises at every opportunity and we're all delighted that you've been helping us on the QT. I do hope it hasn't caused you any difficulties.'

'None at all, my lady,' he lied.

'That's a relief,' she said.

Dinah Caudle and the inspector were old sparring partners, but they both seemed to appreciate the expediency of getting along. They greeted each other with curt civility.

'It's over to you, Emily, I think,' said Lady Bickle once we had all been supplied with tea and somewhere comfortable to sit.

'Thank you,' said Lady Hardcastle. 'I think we're all up to date with the latest information. Yes? Good. As I see it, we have two missions. Our first priority, now that we're absolutely certain of her innocence, is to free Lizzie Worrel and arrest Beattie Challenger in her place. In order to do that, we need to find some actual evidence. Secondly, we need to finish what Christian Brookfield started and find out enough about the planned gold theft that we can simply present everything to the inspector's superiors on a plate. I don't think it's our place to foil a robbery, but in the current climate I also don't think the higher-ups at the Bridewell will take the word of a handful of suffragettes over that of men of standing and substance like Morefield, Crane, and Hinkley. I'm sure most people would believe anything of the Honourable Jimmy, but even then his father would probably step in.'

'Why isn't it our place?' asked Miss Caudle. 'What's to stop us going to the docks and rounding them all up?'

'Numbers, mostly,' said Lady Hardcastle. 'I bow to no woman in my admiration of Flo's skills, and I'm not a bad shot myself when it comes to it, but the four of us against who knows how many toughs under the command of a decorated former soldier? I wouldn't rate our chances, honestly.'

Miss Caudle frowned, but said nothing further.

'So what do you want us to do?' asked Lady Bickle.

'It's the twenty-fourth today, and the gold is arriving on Monday, the twenty-eighth. With only four days to go, my bet is that our conspirators will be on the move. We have no idea what they're planning, but it's certain that men and equipment will have to be moved up into forward positions soon. There should be signs of activity, and with careful surveillance we might manage to tumble their plan in time to alert the authorities. So. Miss Caudle, I'd like you to keep an eye on the comings and goings at the council offices. You can see the front door from Crane's on Corn Street. Set yourself up at a table by the window and watch. Pretend to be writing – no one will bother you. One of us might be able to relieve you later in the day if you find that you're outstaying your welcome.'

'Right you are,' said Miss Caudle. 'Although in the past they've conducted their meetings at night so I might not see anything.'

'That's true,' said Lady Hardcastle. 'But as the time for action approaches, they're likely to have to take more chances. It's definitely worth your while.'

Miss Caudle nodded her assent.

'Georgie,' continued Lady Hardcastle, 'I'd like you to keep a close eye on Beattie Challenger. Do you think you might be able to shadow her when she leaves the shop?'

'Rather,' said Lady Bickle. 'It was a game we played at my awful finishing school. I was never caught.'

'Splendid. We need to know where she goes and whom she meets. Anything that might give us a clue as to what her part is in all this. Meanwhile, I'll keep an eye on the Honourable Jimmy – you have his address, don't you, Georgie? He's a military man so he should be a sight more aware of being followed than Beattie and it might take some of our old skills to keep from being tumbled. I'll need your help, Flo, but you have another job first.'

'Let me guess,' I said. 'Do you by any chance want me to break into Beattie's flat while she's at the shop and see what I can find?'

'That's precisely what I would have had in mind if the inspector weren't here, yes,' she said.

'Don't mind me,' he said, 'I've always had terrible hearing. And I'm not here, anyway.'

'Good man,' said Lady Hardcastle. 'While you're not here, would you mind keeping a weather eye on Hinkley and Crane? Brookfield says they're the money men, but they might do something to give the game away. Particularly Crane – the man's an idiot.'

'My pleasure,' said the inspector. 'Don't forget that I'm working on this case in an official capacity already so I'll shake a few more trees to see what falls out.'

'Thank you. Which reminds me – we're all excited about a "gold shipment" but we've no idea how much there is, in what form it's being transported, where it's going, nor whence it comes. I'm sure it's all terribly secret and I'd never have asked otherwise, but if it can help . . .'

'Of course,' he said. 'The gold is a payment from certain mining interests in Chile for essential equipment from a number of British engineering companies. It's being transported in the form of thirty gold bars, weighing a little over twenty-seven pounds each, with a total value of about a quarter of a million pounds.'

There were oohs of appreciation and a 'Well strike me pink!' from Lady Bickle.

'Indeed,' continued the inspector. 'The whole shipment weighs over seven hundredweight and is being accompanied by a platoon from the Chilean army until it arrives at Avonmouth. Once there it will be transferred into the loving care of a group of heavily armed men privately hired especially for the job. We've verified their bona fides – they're good men.'

'And from there?' asked Lady Hardcastle.

'The gold will be transferred to a train that will take it to London, where bankers will do whatever mystical things it is that bankers do to transform gold into credits in the engineering firms' accounts ledgers.'

'Robbing a moving train on the mainline from Bristol to London wouldn't be impossible,' I said. 'But it wouldn't be easy, either. I'd say the vulnerable time would be at the docks while it's being manhandled from the ship to the train.'

'Getting away would be a problem, surely,' said Miss Caudle.

'It would,' agreed Lady Hardcastle. 'But there's this business of the "switch" that Brookfield mentions in his note. I wonder if they're trying to steal it without anyone knowing it's gone until it's far too late to do anything about it.'

'Which makes it doubly important for us to find out how they're going to do it,' said Lady Bickle.

'Quite so,' said Lady Hardcastle. 'Now, we all have our assignments. Is everyone happy?'

There were murmurs of agreement.

'Any other suggestions? Anything I've forgotten?'

We all shook our heads.

'Time is not on our side,' she continued. 'I suggest we get cracking. Would it be all right if we met back here at, let's say, six o'clock, Georgie?'

'Of course,' said Lady Bickle. 'You're all invited to stay and eat with us, if you're able.'

A round of 'Oh, how lovely, thank you' preceded an orderly stampede towards the door.

Chapter Sixteen

I should like to be able to tell the tale of the daring burglary of Beattie Challenger's rooms. Dressed in black and carrying my tools in a knapsack, I would have shimmied up a drainpipe in dead of night and let myself in through a skylight. There would have been a moment of peril when I lost my footing, then more tension as a policeman on his beat passed mere feet below me as I clung motionless to the wall, hardly daring to breathe.

The reality was a good deal more prosaic.

Miss Challenger had rooms in a house on a back street in Redland, a respectable area of the city divided from the more fashionable Clifton by Whiteladies Road. Lady Bickle had visited Miss Challenger at home and had described the layout of the house to me. It was owned by a widow, who occupied the ground floor, using one of the rooms as a bedroom. A partition wall with a door had been built in the hall to provide a separate entrance to the widow's flat, but leaving open access to the staircase. Thus Miss Challenger had the whole of the first floor to herself and her comings and goings need never disturb her landlady.

The widow, I was told, was a creature of habit, and always left the house promptly at ten to visit a friend who lived a short walk away. She returned at three to be served afternoon tea by her housekeeper.

And so, at ten minutes past ten, Lady Hardcastle parked the motor car round the corner from Challenger's home. I took the plimsolls – which had been left in the Rover after our adventures at Hinkley's offices – and put them on. I walked along the quiet street, discreetly checking whether I was being observed, and then in through the widow's wrought-iron gate, trying not to wince as it squealed on its hinges. There was a moment of suspicious delay while I took out the picklocks concealed in my brooch and used them to open the front door. And then I was in. I relocked the door behind me.

As silently and stealthily as I could manage, I crept up the stairs in my rubber-soled shoes. The housekeeper and maid were almost certainly about their business elsewhere in the house but they would no doubt notice unexpected footsteps on the stairs while Miss Challenger was supposedly at work in the shop.

Her rooms had originally been bedrooms and so they all led off from the landing. I tried the first door at the back of the house and found that it had been furnished as a sitting room. It was neat and ordered, and largely free of personal trappings. There was a book on the little table beside the rather severe-looking armchair, lying open, face down, its spine broken. It looked wounded, and an unhelpfully sentimental part of me wanted to rescue it from its pain. Aside from a fat tabby cat asleep on the chair and an extremely pleasant view across the city, there was nothing of interest to be seen. I would return to the room later if the rest of my search came to nought.

The next room was Challenger's bedroom. Again it was prissily neat, and again there was a broken-backed book on the nightstand. If we couldn't get her for the arson, we should at least be able to secure a conviction for cruelty to books. There was a wardrobe against the wall opposite the bed so I stole in for a better look.

The wardrobe was locked and there was no sign of a key, but the lock was a simple one, which quickly yielded to my trusty picklock. A few dowdy dresses hung from the rail along with a couple of plain jackets. The shelves held the expected collection of underthings and sweaters, all neatly folded.

At the bottom of the cupboard were a pair of 'best' shoes, a pair of summer shoes, and a pair of boots, whose soles were coming away from their uppers. There was also, crumpled up and stuffed at the back, a large canvas bag. It looked like a sailor's duffel.

I noted its exact position, and that of the shoes and boots around it, before carefully lifting it from the wardrobe. Something inside it clinked as I placed it on the floor. Inside, I found two tightly stoppered bottles wrapped in a rag, and a few loose sheets of quarto-sized paper. The interior of the bag smelled of paraffin and a quick sniff after uncorking one of the bottles revealed that it still contained a dribble of that familiar flammable oil. I took out one of the sheets of paper.

It was a printed leaflet headed 'Votes for Women', which succinctly outlined the aims of the Women's Social and Political Union. Nothing remarkable there – Challenger was the manager of the WSPU shop on Queen's Road. I looked again and saw that it didn't say 'Women's' at all. This was a leaflet for the 'Woman Social and Political Union' – the same misprint that had appeared on the leaflets scattered at the scene of the arson attack.

I double-checked the bag to make certain that it contained nothing else of interest. There were at least half a dozen more of the leaflets strewn about the bottom of the duffel, along with a battered box of matches. The leaflet I had removed wouldn't be missed so I folded it and put it in my pocket before replacing the bag in the wardrobe exactly as I had found it. I had a moment of frustration when the lock spurned the tender advances of my picklock and refused to reengage itself. It took a few moments of silent cursing and some increasingly agitated agitation of the mechanism, but it eventually agreed that it was in everyone's best interests if it locked itself again.

I glanced about, but there was nothing else in the room. Why are criminals never considerate enough never to leave details of their plans lying about? Better yet, a signed confession. But if Challenger had a journal or notebook of any kind, she almost certainly kept it with her. There wasn't even anything concealed under the bed.

I left the bedroom and returned to the sitting room, but it was as emptily unhelpful as I had first presumed so I stepped back on to the landing and turned to descend the stairs.

At that moment, I heard the door to the landlady's apartment open. A pair of boots clopped into the tiled hall. I remained stock-still and waited for the sound of one of those boots on the stair. I might have to duck back into the bedroom and conceal myself beneath the bed if the housekeeper or maid needed to come up to Challenger's rooms for any reason. At least I knew there was space for me under there.

But the next sound was the front door being unlocked, opened, and relocked. One of the servants had gone out, and to save themselves the walk up the outside steps from the basement, they had used the front door. I heard the scream of the front gate even from upstairs and marvelled that no one had heard me coming in.

I gave her a minute to get on her way down the road before I tip-toed back down the stairs and out the way I had come, painstakingly relocking the door behind me. I considered vaulting the noisy gate, but opted instead to lift it slightly on its pin hinges to minimize the racket. It squeaked plaintively, as though frustrated at being denied its chance to sing out, but I congratulated myself on making a largely stealthy exit.

I rejoined Lady Hardcastle and changed back into my boots in the motor car as she drove us across to Clifton. Our next stop was at the fashionable Royal York Crescent, where the Honourable James Stansbridge made his home. We parked at the western end of the road and made ourselves comfortable – he was a night owl so we were pre-pared for a long wait. Even on a day when he almost certainly had much to do to prepare for the gold theft, he probably wouldn't rise much before midday.

The long terrace of Regency houses opened on to a broad pavement built on top of the basements that ran beneath them, meaning that the front doors were a good fifteen feet above the road. From where we sat we couldn't see the doors of the houses, just the vaulted fronts of the basements, many set with doors of their own. Lady Bickle had assured us, though, that Stansbridge's front door was close to the first flight of steps leading back down to the road and that, for reasons she didn't understand, it was his habit to descend the steps rather than walk past the houses of his neighbours.

I offered Lady Hardcastle a cup of coffee from the Thermos flask that had been stowed beneath my seat.

'Thank you, dear,' she said. 'I'm glad it's a little milder today, I must say.'

'I'm just thankful it isn't raining,' I said.

'Well, quite. But it's debrief time – what did you find at Cheattie Ballenger's gaff?'

'Her home is as boring as she is,' I said. 'But she does own a very distinctive sailor's duffel, in which she keeps bottles of paraffin, matches, and suffragette leaflets.' I pulled the leaflet from my pocket. 'Does anything strike you?' I asked as I gave it to her.

She took out her lorgnette and examined it closely. 'Aha,' she said. 'It's got the same misprint as the ones on Thomas Street. She's definitely our girl. I say, do you think Crane's printing business made them? His league is opposed to "Woman" suffrage, isn't it? Perhaps he drafted it. Anyway, as soon as we find out a little more about this gold business, the police can conduct an official search of the place and find all that for themselves. It's still not conclusive proof, but with the inspector's informant's eyewitness account of seeing her boots, they must surely have enough to throw a hearty shovelful of doubt on Lizzie Worrel's guilt. Especially with Brookfield's notes to back it all up.'

'Let's hope so,' I said. 'Although Lizzie is well liked – I'm sure we'd have no shortage of volunteers to beat a confession out of Challenger.'

'No doubt. But we'll leave those sorts of brutal tactics to the continental police forces, I think. I'm sure we can persuade her to do the right thing.'

'If we can catch her before she does a moonlight flit with her share of the gold.'

'I've been thinking about that. If we're assuming that they're trying to pinch the gold by "switching" it, they clearly hope to get away without anyone knowing it's gone. If they're doing that, we have also to assume that they're not going to want to draw attention to themselves by hopping on to the next boat train to the south of France to live high on the hog on the proceeds. They're going to carry on as usual until the furore has died down a bit and then slyly convert their ill-gotten gains into cash. I don't think she's going anywhere for a while.'

'Nor are we by the looks of things,' I said. I reached once more beneath my seat. 'Cheese and chutney sandwich?'

'Good choice. How did you know to pack all this?'

'Years of experience,' I said. 'I've lost count of how many times you've said, "And that's my plan – I suggest we start straight away." It was odds-on you were going to have us traipsing about the city all day.'

'I don't know what I'd do without you.'

'Nor do I,' I said, and took a bite from the sandwich. I thought for a moment. 'If you were going to steal seven hundredweight of gold bullion,' I said, 'and you planned to "switch" it, what would you do? Substitute lead bars?'

'I've been mulling that one over ever since I finished decoding the message. If one's operation were properly funded, it would be a simple matter to make up thirty lead bars of the right size, cover them with gold leaf to give them the proper colour and shine, and then look for an opportunity to substitute them for the real thing. The problem is that for all its apparent heaviness, a lead bar is still only just over half the weight of a gold bar of the same size. Let's say the gold is boxed up to keep it together and safe on the voyage. You'd want your guards to be able to manhandle the boxes for loading and unloading so you'd perhaps pack the bars in seven boxes of four and one box of two. The heavier boxes would weigh a bit over a hundred and nine pounds. It wouldn't be the easiest thing they did that day, but two men could carry that. Four lead bars of the same size would weigh just over sixty-four pounds. Even the most dull-witted of guards would notice a forty-five pound difference in their burden.'

'I had no idea the difference was so great,' I said.

'It's not something one has to think about very often. Somehow one has to make a box of four lead bars weigh as much as a box of four gold bars.'

'So . . .' I said as I thought it through, 'if you can't make the lead weigh more, how about making the box weigh more? They have to move the gold inside the boxes, so all they ever really know is the combined weight of the gold and the box. It's unlikely anyone's ever going to take a bar out of the box.'

'We'll make a scientist of you yet, young Armstrong,' she said. 'That was exactly my thinking. If they can somehow add another forty-five pounds of lead to the box itself, only a proper inspection would give them away. Lining the box with a thick enough layer of lead would do the trick if they disguise it right.'

'They'd have to know exactly how the gold was being shipped, and exactly what the procedure at the docks was going to be. It's a ruse that would only survive the most cursory inspection.'

'Crane ships his precious coffee halfway round the world all the time. If anyone has bribable contacts in ports all over South America as well as at home, it's him. He could easily have had spies on the docks in Chile to tell him how it was packed, and at Avonmouth to tell him how it's going to be transferred. Armed with that knowledge, our boy Jimmy Stansbridge could easily formulate a plan to make it disappear from under the guards' noses. And speaking of Stansbridge, is that him coming down the steps?'

I looked where she was pointing. A man in a shiny top hat and a long black coat was loping carelessly down towards a waiting brougham.

'Astrakhan collar and a scarlet feather in his hatband?' I said. 'That's the description Lady Bickle gave us.'

I hopped out of the motor car and cranked the engine to life. We gave the cab a few moments' head start and then set off to follow.

◆ ◆ ◆

The brougham was easy to see and easy to follow, but we had one minor problem: it turns out that motor cars can travel much more quickly than horse-drawn cabs. In its lowest gear, our little Rover was able to travel at eight miles per hour, which just so happens to be roughly the speed of a trotting horse. Things were fine until the cab came up behind a slow-moving cart, or the driver chose to slow the horse to a walk to negotiate an obstacle. When that happened – as it did annoyingly often – we were forced to stop and wait for the horse to pull away again. Fortunately, neither Stansbridge nor the driver was inclined to look behind them and so, somewhat astonishingly, we managed to follow them without being spotted.

His first stop was in a back street near Old Market, not far from the Empire, Bristol's most famous music hall. The cab pulled up outside a shop with dusty windows which proclaimed itself to be Montague Mallick & Sons – Theatrical Costumiers & Propmakers. We stopped a safe distance away and watched as he went inside. He was there for no more than five minutes and emerged bearing two large, squashy brown-paper packages fastened with string.

And we were off again. His next stop was just a short drive away, outside the Sheldon Bush and Patent Shot Company Limited in

Redcliffe. Again he disappeared inside, this time for nearly half an hour, but he emerged empty handed.

The tensest moment came shortly after this visit to the lead works. The cab threaded its way back towards the business and banking heart of the city around Corn Street. It appeared that he might simply be returning home – this was as good a route to Clifton as any – and Lady Hardcastle became a little complacent in her following technique. She had been keeping a safe, unobtrusive distance from our quarry, and allowed the cab to turn out of sight on to St Nicholas Street before turning left to follow it. Unbeknown to us, the cab had stopped less than ten yards from the junction and we all but ran into it.

We carried on past, not looking at the rangy gentleman in the black coat and top hat who unfolded himself from the brougham and paid the driver. We were unable to avoid being seen by the man walking along the road towards him – Nathaniel Morefield – but we were hopeful that our driving garb rendered us more or less unrecognizable. The scarlet motor car was rather distinctive, but there was no reason Morefield should have known to whom it belonged.

Yet another ten yards further on was another familiar figure in an exquisitely tailored coat, carrying a leather satchel. Miss Caudle, it seems, had left her observation post in Crane's to follow her target round the corner. I saw her eyes flicker towards us as we passed, but she was canny enough not to acknowledge us.

We had no choice but to carry on and try to find somewhere unobtrusive to park.

'Shall we try to do it on foot?' I asked as we pulled up on Clare Street.

'We could,' said Lady Hardcastle, 'but I'm not sure what we'd learn. Stansbridge and Morefield are probably meeting for lunch to go over the last-minute details and there's little we could achieve by trying to earwig on that conversation other than getting ourselves caught. I hope

Dinah doesn't follow them into wherever they're going – Morefield definitely knows her.'

'Stansbridge was empty handed when he got out of the cab,' I said. 'And he sent it on its way, so he's probably going to be here a while. Should we follow the cab and see where the packages end up, perhaps?'

'I think it's all that's left us,' she agreed. 'Although he's probably going to drop them off back at York Crescent.'

'It's worth a try, though,' I said. 'Miss Caudle will let us know what happens after their luncheon.'

By this time the cab had passed us and was about to get lost in the bustle of carts and trams around the Tramway Centre. We set off in hot pursuit and were just in time to see it disappearing slowly up Park Street. It was beginning to look as though the packages were going to be dropped off at home after all.

But the cabbie ignored all the turnings towards Clifton. He carried on up Whiteladies Road and Blackboy Hill, and set off across the Downs. It was becoming increasingly difficult to remain unobserved as the traffic thinned almost to nothing, but the cabbie did much of our work for us and continued not looking behind himself with a pleasingly helpful determination.

Nevertheless, we stayed further back, reasoning that we'd easily be able to pick up his trail if we briefly lost sight of him, especially since we could travel, if we chose, at three times his speed.

He carried on.

'Where are we now?' asked Lady Hardcastle.

'I'm not sure,' I said. 'We've never been out this way. Do you think we might be heading towards Avonmouth?'

'It seems the most likely destination,' she said, 'given what we already know. We just have to keep going and hope we can find our way back.'

After many tediously slow miles we began to see civilization ahead. There were glimpses of the derricks of the dock cranes between the huge warehouse buildings, and then the funnels of a ship. We were, indeed, approaching the Avonmouth docks.

There was a small terrace of three old cottages on the outskirts of the site. They looked abandoned – the windows of the first two had been boarded up. Our guess was that the occupants had been forced out many years ago by the arrival of the docks, perhaps to live in the newly built streets of houses nearby, but that the land was not yet needed for any expansion of the port.

The cab pulled up outside one of the cottages and the driver stood up on his seat to look around, as though puzzled that the address he'd been given was of an empty, rundown cottage. I thought he was about to give up and leave, perhaps imagining himself to be the victim of a rich man's prank, when the cottage door opened and a stocky man emerged. He had a brief conversation with the cab driver while another man watched from the doorway. The cabman handed over the brown paper packages in exchange for what was presumably the balance of his promised fee.

We had observed all this from a safe distance and remained at the side of the road while the cab turned around and drove past us, on its way back to the city. The driver was as oblivious to our presence on the way out as he had been on the way there. He didn't even look at us.

Lady Hardcastle took a notebook and pencil from her bag and made a quick sketch of the cottage and its position on the road. She made a few notes before saying, 'I think we should get back to Georgie's and report in, don't you?'

'Can we take her up on her invitation to stay for dinner?' I said. 'I'm starving.'

◆ ◆ ◆

We arrived at Berkeley Crescent shortly before six to find that the other three were already there. Where previously the atmosphere had been polite but somewhat cold, now the two ladies were chattering like old pals.

'As you can tell,' said Lady Bickle as she welcomed us in, 'Dinah and I are rather excited to tell our tales. I'm not entirely sure I could have held on much longer but the inspector was very insistent that we wait for you.'

'I'm so sorry we delayed you,' said Lady Hardcastle. 'Our poor motor car did the best it could, bless its little heart, but it still took us an absolute age to get back.'

'Where did you end up?' asked Miss Caudle. 'The last I saw of you, you were tootling along St Nicholas Street trying not to be noticed.'

'All in good time,' said Lady Hardcastle. 'We held you up, so one of you should go first.'

Both Lady Bickle and Miss Caudle began speaking at once. They stopped. They laughed. They each gestured that the other should go first. They both began speaking. They laughed again.

The inspector, who looked as though he had been enduring this level of girlish excitement for a while, rolled his eyes.

'Georgie,' said Lady Hardcastle. 'Why don't you start? Then our tale can follow Dinah's.'

'Righto,' said Lady Bickle with a grin. 'Well, let me see. I strolled down to the shop after you were all safely on your way. We had a quiet morning. Beattie was unusually animated. She's such a quiet soul most of the time, but she was very chatty. We sold a few bits and bobs – the bloomers with the green and purple ribbons have been surprisingly popular lately. I suppose it's a form of domestic protest. But anyway. It was getting on for lunchtime, and Beattie asked if I wouldn't mind staying on for another hour while she went on one or two errands. I usually only work in the shop during the mornings, you see. So I said it would be fine, and off she toddled. Marisol was upstairs sorting out some paperwork, so I asked her to mind the shop instead – I said I had to pop home to organize some things with the servants. It all took just a few moments, but by the time I hurried out, I could just see Beattie about to disappear up Whiteladies Road.

'She was probably on her way home, I thought, so I didn't panic. I trotted after her, and sure enough she turned right towards Redland. By this time I was about fifty yards behind her so I would still have been in trouble if she'd been going anywhere else, but she kept on towards her flat.

'It suddenly dawned on me that if she went in, I'd be scuppered. How could I watch her front door without her seeing me when she came back out? I was so intent on solving this little conundrum that I almost bowled straight into her as she came out of a little hardware shop just round the corner from her home. I'd lost sight of her completely, you see, so I didn't notice her going in. As it was, I just about managed to duck into the newsagent's next door. I have a quarter of mint humbugs if anyone wants one.

'By the time I thought it safe to leave the shop, she was gone. But I did see what she'd bought from the hardware shop: a huge can of paraffin.'

'That's very interesting, given what Flo found in Challenger's flat when she searched it,' said Lady Hardcastle.

'Well, now Flo has to go next,' said Miss Caudle. 'You can't just leave that dangling there.'

I quickly recounted my search of Beattie Challenger's flat, with special reference to the arsonist's duffel and empty paraffin bottles.

'It seems she's quite the one for setting fire to things,' said Miss Caudle. 'Do we think that's the "distraction" that Brookfield mentioned in his notes? A well-timed fire at the docks would draw a lot of attention away from a certain gold shipment.'

'It certainly would,' said Lady Hardcastle. 'Your turn next. What were Stansbridge and Morefield up to? Tell me you didn't follow them to lunch.'

'As a matter of fact,' said Miss Caudle with no small amount of smugness, 'I did precisely that. I'm not quite as green as I'm cabbage-looking, you know. I've done my share of surreptitious earwigging, even as a social correspondent. More so, I dare say – when one earns one's daily crust peddling gossip, it pays to be able to go unnoticed while still being able to eavesdrop.'

'And what did you hear?' asked Lady Bickle.

'My first shock was learning that, when he's sober, the Honourable Jimmy isn't quite the amiable duffer he pretends to be. Sharp as razors, as it turns out – one wonders how he manages to be quite so rubbish at cards. But he was there to report to his CO, as it were. Evidently the men have been moved up to their forward positions and the matériel is being delivered today and tomorrow, whatever that means. Morefield sidestepped his questions about the distribution of the loot, saying only that it required great circumspection and would take time.'

'I think we can help you on the men and matériel problem,' said Lady Hardcastle. She told them about Stansbridge's errands and our trip to Avonmouth. 'My guess,' she said when she had finished, 'is that the men in the cottage took delivery of some uniforms from the costumier. They could be either Chilean army or local security men, depending upon exactly how their deception is to work.' She went on to outline her thoughts on swapping lead bullion for the gold. 'If I'm right, then that would be the reason for the visit to Sheldon Bush. Short of stealing it from church roofs, buying it from a lead shot factory would seem to be the quickest and easiest way to get one's hands on seven hundred-weight of lead. I wonder at them leaving it so late, though. Unless . . . perhaps Mallick & Sons have already made up the fake gold ingots and he was just making sure that the order for the box linings was going to be ready in time.'

The inspector had remained silent throughout, merely making occasional notes in his ever-present notebook.

'This is all very helpful, ladies,' he said when we'd finished. 'Between you I think you might have cracked the case. Well done.'

You could almost taste the pleasure in the room as he said this.

'You know where the gang are hiding out. You've almost certainly hit upon the method of the "switch" – I'd imagined swapping the gold for lead myself, but I hadn't considered the difference in weight. Yours is a good solution, my lady. Very good indeed. My day wasn't nearly so productive, I'm ashamed to say – once again, my informants came up with nearly nothing. But armed with all this new intelligence, I've a better idea of the questions I should be asking and of whom I should be asking them. Thank you very much.'

'You're quite welcome,' said Lady Hardcastle. 'So, what's next?'

'Ah,' he said. 'I was worried you might ask that. Now, I know how much you've enjoyed yourselves today, and I know you're all champing at the bit to get on and help, but I must ask you just to sit tight now and let me and my colleagues on the Force do some ordinary policing. This gang is a good deal more organized and ruthless than I think anyone has given them credit for. Don't forget they've already killed one man for getting too close. I've got enough information to be able to mount a proper police operation now, so just bask in the glory of your achievement.'

There was the briefest moment of absolute silence before Lady Bickle and Dinah Caudle both started remonstrating with the inspector in the most strident tones. Lady Hardcastle let them vent just a little steam before she brought the meeting to order once more.

'I'm sure,' she said quietly and calmly, 'that we can find ourselves something useful to do, police operation or not.' Her glance told the inspector not to interrupt. 'Don't forget that our mission is, and has always been, to free Lizzie Worrel. Saving a few pounds' worth of gold from being stolen by one group of robbers while it's on its way from a second group of robbers to a third is all terribly exciting, but it's not what we're here for. And don't try to persuade me that businessmen aren't just robbers in expensive suits, I simply shan't listen.'

The two ladies mumbled mutinously like school children after a telling off.

'Inspector. Do you think you could solve our problem for us by arranging an official search of Beattie Challenger's flat? If you could arrest her, it might also put a spanner in the works for the gold robbery.'

'And that's exactly why I'm unwilling to do so,' he said. 'For the first time in weeks, I find myself a step ahead of the gold thieves. If I force them into a position where they're having to implement contingency plans – or, worse, improvise – then I lose my advantage. I'm afraid my interests are best served by letting things play out in the way we predict and nabbing them all in one go.'

'Then there's nothing for it but for us all to have a drink before dinner,' said Lady Bickle. 'Dinner is at seven so we've time for a livener before Ben gets home from work.'

There was nothing much any of us could do but agree.

Chapter Seventeen

We made a great show of heeding Inspector Sunderland's instructions to sit tight and let the police take care of the robbers. When we parted after dinner on Thursday night, we had all reassured him that we had absolutely no intention of going anywhere near the docks nor anyone whom we knew to be involved in the plot.

And we all went quietly about our business on Friday. Lady Hardcastle and I, for instance, undertook a little bit of shopping – a few sundries here and there about town.

It was on Saturday that things began to deviate from the inspector's orders. There was a strategy meeting at Lady Bickle's house, led by Lady Hardcastle, where we four ladies fomented our plans for disobedience.

'I know I said I was opposed to the idea of our trying to thwart the robbery on our own,' said Lady Hardcastle once we had all agreed a course of action for Monday morning, 'but there'll be dozens of policemen there so we shan't be on our own. And I, for one, don't want to miss out on the excitement – not after we put in all the hard work on the boring stuff.'

We gave Lady Bickle and Miss Caudle a package each from Friday's shopping trip and agreed to meet at Berkeley Crescent at six o'clock on Monday morning.

We spent Sunday doing Sunday things (that is to say, nothing very much at all) and rose abominably early on Monday to drive to Clifton in the dark.

With only the housemaid actually up and working at Berkeley Crescent, Lady Bickle herself let us in and we trooped into the drawing room to wait for Miss Caudle. When she arrived, we spent an entertaining quarter of an hour changing our clothes and readying ourselves for the day ahead.

In order that we might move around the docks relatively unnoticed, Lady Hardcastle and I had made a note of everyone's measurements and had bought some essential clothing from various shops in Bristol. We had four sets of workman's overalls, four pairs of heavy work boots, four heavy sack coats, and four workman's caps of various styles. Once we were suitably attired, my job – as the only one who actually knew what she was doing – was to secure the other ladies' hair so that it could be concealed in the saggy caps. My own hair was stuffed into my cap more or less competently by Miss Caudle.

'There,' said Lady Hardcastle once we were done. 'I think we'll pass muster. From a distance, at least.'

'As long as nobody sees us all tumbling out of Lady B's Rolls,' said Miss Caudle. 'Not many dock workers travel to work in a chauffeur-driven Rolls-Royce Silver Ghost.'

'I'll be driving, actually,' said Lady Bickle.

'Oh, well, that makes all the difference. Perhaps you won it in a pub raffle?'

Lady Bickle stuck her tongue out.

'We'll be parking out of sight in the trees and walking the last mile or so,' said Lady Hardcastle. 'No one will see the Rolls.'

'A mile in new boots?' said Miss Caudle. 'You're braver than I gave you credit for.'

'It'll be more than that once we're done. I don't actually know where the ship will be docking or where the Customs shed is. To be

honest, I don't even know if the ship arrived last night as it was supposed to.'

'Last night?' said Lady Bickle. 'Everyone's been saying it would
arrive today.'

'It will dock today,' said Lady Hardcastle, 'but it has to wait for the
tide. If everything went well for them, they'll have arrived during the
night and anchored in the middle of the estuary. At high tide, they'll be
able to approach the docks.'

'And when is high tide today?' asked Miss Caudle.

'Shortly before midday.'

'Then we'd better get a move on if we're going to scout the place
out and be in position to watch the fun at midday,' said Lady Bickle.

Continuing the topsy-turvy theme of the day, the Ladies Bickle and
Hardcastle sat in the front of the Rolls-Royce, in the open seats, while
Miss Caudle and I relaxed in the comparative warmth and comfort of
the enclosed back seats. We were aware of some bickering in the front,
accompanied by a certain amount of pointing and gesticulating, but for
the most part the journey was calm and peaceful.

We passed the village of Shirehampton and then headed away from
the docks towards a wooded area nearby. Here, as promised, we parked
the motor car, partly concealed by a stand of trees. We continued our
journey on foot.

We seemed to have arrived during the middle of a shift and there
were very few men walking about. Our first stop was at the small group
of cottages where Lady Hardcastle and I had watched the cab driver as
he had delivered the packages. As before, there was no sign of life in the
two boarded-up cottages, and we approached the third with caution.

'Who wants to take a peek inside?' asked Lady Hardcastle.

Lady Bickle and Miss Caudle put their hands up like eager school children.

'Flo, can you do the honours?' she said.

'Of course,' I said. 'This way, ladies. Be quiet, and stay clear of the windows until I say it's all right. If anyone challenges us, get behind me and make a run for it – I'll fend them off.'

'What with?' asked Miss Caudle.

'I shall reason with them,' I said.

'No fisticuffs?' said Lady Bickle, sounding a little disappointed.

'Of course, my lady. When reason fails, a swift kick in the trousers can be very persuasive.'

'I don't think you should be calling me "my lady" while we're in disguise. I think my character is more of a Bill.'

I rolled my eyes but said nothing. Miss Caudle failed to suppress a snigger.

I approached the cottage as naturally and nonchalantly as was possible with the two would-be spies tiptoeing along behind me like pantomime villains. I glanced back and saw Lady Hardcastle laughing. She waved me on.

Following my own injunction to stay clear of the windows, I ducked down and went around to the rear of the cottage, where my companions' comically inept attempts to be inconspicuous would raise fewer suspicions. And less mocking laughter.

I stopped under what I assumed to be the kitchen window and eased myself slowly up so that I could look inside. I nearly jumped out of my skin when I saw a face looking impassively back at me, and then rolled my eyes again and tutted when I realized that it was Inspector Sunderland.

I stood up and beckoned the others to do the same. He emerged from the cottage's back door.

'What are you shower of idiots doing here?' he asked. 'Were my instructions to keep well away not clear enough?'

Lady Bickle and Miss Caudle began speaking at once. While he tried to get them to shush, I walked round to the front of the cottage to signal to Lady Hardcastle that she should join us.

'Good morning, Inspector,' she said as she approached. 'Fancy seeing you here.'

'Fancy,' he said. 'I gather from your companions that you're all here on some sort of jolly outing.'

'Oh, well, you know how it is,' she said blithely. 'We couldn't just sit on our hands when there was fun to be had down by the sea.'

'Down by the estuary,' he said. 'And yes, you could. You were explicitly instructed to, after all.'

'We weren't going to get in the way – we knew you and your colleagues would have everything in hand. But how often does one get to witness the thwarting of a quarter of a million pound gold theft? We were going to observe from a safe distance.'

'You could have ruined everything – given the game away,' he said.

'But we haven't, have we? No one would ever guess the place was crawling with rozzers. You've a very good team.'

'They're invisible, all right,' he said. 'But not for the reason you think. You can't see my men because they're all back at Bristol going about their regular duties.'

'What?' we all said together.

'I was told that no one could be spared "on the word of a handful of busybodies" and that I should concentrate on catching real villains instead of wasting my time on "imaginary conspiracies".'

'And yet here you are,' said Lady Hardcastle.

'And here you are, too,' he said. 'I'm damned glad to see you, if truth be told.'

'How can we help?' asked Lady Bickle.

'Ah,' he said. 'What I meant was that I'm glad Lady Hardcastle and Miss Armstrong are here. It's not that I'm not pleased to see you, as well, but these two have skills I can use.'

'Oh, pish and blancmange!' said Lady Bickle. 'Miss Caudle and I have perfectly serviceable eyes – we can observe as well as any specially trained former agents of the Crown. No offence, dear. And, look – we're all dressed up and nowhere to go.'

The inspector thought for a moment. 'Very well,' he said at length. 'Come inside and I'll tell you what I have in mind.'

'Won't they be back?' asked Miss Caudle.

'No, they're long gone. They cleared out first thing and they'll not be hanging around to be noticed once the job's done.'

We followed him into the deserted cottage. Stansbridge's men were good. Although we knew that at least two of them had been using the place as a hideout, there was absolutely no sign that anyone had been there for years.

'At first light,' began the inspector, 'our old friend James Stansbridge—'

'The Dishonourable Jimmy,' interrupted Lady Bickle.

'Even he,' said the inspector. '—arrived on a brewer's dray with a huge crate on the back. The two men who had been holed up in here for the past few days came out to help, and between them they rolled this crate down a pair of planks and on to the road. It was already on a trolley, and from the fuss they made, it was extremely heavy.'

'About seven hundredweight?' asked Lady Hardcastle.

'That would be my guess,' he said. 'The wagon left, and all three men came in here. When they reemerged, they were dressed as Customs men. They hauled the trolley off and I've not seen them since. I didn't want to risk being seen following them, but I've a fair idea where they went.'

'To the Customs shed, presumably,' said Miss Caudle.

'Where I imagine the palms of the real Customs men have been generously greased to induce them to turn a blind eye to these strangers, and possibly to disappear at the appointed hour. By the time they work out that they've become part of the biggest gold robbery of the year, they'll be too afraid to say anything.'

'So what do you need us to do?' I asked.

'The Chilean ship arrived at about three o'clock this morning and is anchored in deep water in the middle of the estuary. Because of its special cargo, it's due to dock at the berth nearest the Customs shed in a couple of hours, as soon as the tide is high enough. I'd like us to be stationed around the shed as discreetly as possible so that we can keep an eye on exactly what happens. If we can spot how they switch the loot and what they do with it, perhaps I can finally get someone to take all this seriously enough to mount a proper raid.'

He went on to tell us exactly what he had in mind.

The Customs shed formed a gateway between the quays on one side of the sturdy chain-link fence, and England on the other. It was possible to access the various bonded warehouses from the quayside without passing through Customs, but anything that was to be directly imported had to pass through the shed, where it would be inspected.

The Chilean ship was being nudged against the dock by a tug on the seaward side of the fence, and sailors were readying themselves to make her fast with hawsers as thick as a man's leg. Meanwhile, a wagon was being nudged into place by a shunting engine on the railway tracks that ran up to a platform beside the shed on the landward side.

On the inspector's instructions, we had split into two groups, each with its own highly trained former spy. I accompanied Inspector Sunderland and Dinah Caudle as we took up position near the railway wagon. Lady Hardcastle was responsible for the safety of Lady Bickle as they crossed the tracks to lurk on the other side. Between us, we should be able to see everything that went into and came out of the Customs shed.

Once the wagon was in place, a group of eight men in dark-grey military-style tunics arrived and took up position on and around it. They were variously armed with rifles, pistols, and even one sawn-off shotgun. These were the guards hired by the engineering firms to protect their payment.

The unloading of the ship began almost immediately, and the first item of cargo to be lifted clear of the deck by one of the massive electric cranes was a pallet holding just eight smallish wooden boxes. It was swung across on to a waiting trolley, where it was immediately surrounded by six soldiers who had hurried down the gangplank to meet it. Two dock workers hauled the trolley into the shed, where it, and its armed escort, disappeared from view. Meanwhile, a small railway engine was coupled to the waiting wagon.

'Well,' said the inspector, 'that's got it inside. Now we just have to wait and see what—'

He was interrupted by the loudest explosion I had ever heard. The ground seemed to shake as all eyes turned towards the apocalyptic noise. Moments later we were hit by a wave of uncomfortably hot air. Bright orange flames danced into the sky from a shed a few hundred yards away and men began rushing towards it from every direction.

There was another colossal bang.

The guards were standing on the railway wagon trying to get a better view.

'Looks like the lamp oil store,' shouted one.

'There'll be more 'splosions if it is,' shouted another.

He was right. Two more bangs thudded into the sky.

Everywhere was pandemonium, with men running and shouting, trying to organize efforts to control the fire and minimize the damage.

Another monumental bang brought even the Customs men out of the shed. Everyone apart from the gold guards was running towards the fire. Everyone apart from the gold guards, and two Customs men who had emerged from a storage area beside the Customs shed. They entered the shed and reemerged a few minutes later, hauling the gold trolley.

They attracted the attention of the guards, who helped them drag it up the shallow ramp from the platform on to the wagon. One of the guards prised the lid from one of the boxes and gave it a cursory look to ensure that it was, indeed, the gold. He did the same with another of the boxes and then, apparently reassured that they had what they'd been sent to collect, gave the signal to go. The engine chuffed into life as the remainder of the eight armed guards scrambled to their positions on the wagon.

Within moments, the one-wagon train was gone, leaving the chaos – and the threat of robbery – behind as it set off on its journey to London.

We watched the Customs shed, but nothing else happened.

'If we were right,' said the inspector, 'and that train just steamed off with the fake gold, then what's happened to the—'

'Oi!' shouted a voice from behind us. 'What are you men doing standing about there? Can't you see there's a fire? Get to your stations. You know the drill.'

The speaker didn't stop to check that we were obeying, but it seemed that we would draw yet more unwanted attention by hanging about, so we reluctantly moved in the general direction of the burning oil shed.

We met Lady Hardcastle.

'Hello, you lot,' she said. 'It's all go here, isn't it?'

'It is,' I said. 'We think we've seen the fake gold being loaded on to the train, but we've had to come away without seeing what's happened to the real stuff.'

'Don't worry,' she said. 'We'll work it out.'

'I hope you're right,' said the inspector. 'This is beginning to look as though they might get away with it.'

'Where's Lady B?' asked Miss Caudle. 'Can't she and I sneak back and keep watch on the Customs shed?'

'She just went off to find somewhere secluded,' said Lady Hardcastle. 'Call of nature.'

'Actually,' said Miss Caudle, 'that's not a bad idea. Where did she go?'

Lady Hardcastle pointed towards two sheds built close together with a narrow passageway between them. 'She disappeared over that way. She said something about it looking like the perfect spot.'

'She's not wrong,' said Miss Caudle. 'See you in a minute.'

'Did you see anything?' I asked Lady Hardcastle. 'Of the theft,' I added quickly when I saw the twinkle in her eye and knew there'd be a joke about Lady Bickle's trip to the loo if I didn't head her off.

'Nothing more than you did, I don't think,' she said, still grinning. 'The gold went in, the gold came out. Or didn't. But like everyone else, my attention was somewhat diverted by the oil store going up in flames. One might almost think it were deliberate if one knew a competent arsonist.'

'I most definitely do think it was deliberate,' said the inspector. 'The timing was perfect. I'm not sure they could have predicted the explosions, but a call of "Fire!" would have done the trick at that moment, even without them.'

'Which means our old pal Beattie Challenger is probably around here somewhere,' I said. 'We should keep our eyes open.'

Miss Caudle returned.

'That's much better,' she said. 'But no sign of Lady B. Are you quite sure she went that way?'

'Quite sure,' said Lady Hardcastle. She began looking around. 'Where the devil can she be?'

'Gone to look at the fire?' suggested Miss Caudle.

'Perhaps. Perhaps. We should find her. I'm sure she can look after herself, but we ought to stick together.' She pointed at Inspector Sunderland and me. 'You two go that way, Miss Caudle and I will go this. We'll meet you round at the other side of the oil shed.'

◆ ◆ ◆

'Any sign of her?' asked Lady Hardcastle when we joined her at the opposite side of the shed.

'None at all,' said the inspector. 'There's a good deal of commotion to confuse things, but she's easy to spot – you're all wearing those matching jackets.'

'We didn't have time to shop for a selection,' said Lady Hardcastle. 'We had to take what was available. These were the only ones shapeless enough to conceal—'

The inspector put up his hand to stop her. 'I know what you were trying to conceal,' he said. 'But they do make you very easy to spot in a crowd, and we definitely didn't see her.'

'Any sign of Challenger?' I asked.

'No, she's long gone, I should imagine,' said Lady Hardcastle.

'You don't think she . . .' said Miss Caudle.

'Nabbed Georgie and scarpered?' I suggested.

'It certainly crossed my mind,' said Lady Hardcastle. 'Inspector, dear, can I leave Miss Caudle in your tender care? I think you two should hang around here in case she turns up. You can keep an eye on that Customs shed, too. Flo and I ought to head back into town. Challenger's got a good head start, but Georgie's Rolls goes along at a fair clip. We shouldn't be too far behind her.'

'The motor car's a mile away,' I said.

'Yes, but whatever she came in will be outside the docks somewhere,' said Lady Hardcastle. 'We have the same handicap as she does. Come on. Quicksticks.'

She clomped off at an ungainly trot in her massive work boots. I shrugged at the others and followed.

Ten minutes later we arrived at the wooded spot where we had left the Rolls-Royce. Lady Hardcastle was puffing like a train, so I invited her to settle into the driving seat while I cranked the engine to life. We set off back to Bristol at considerable speed.

'I know it adds delay,' said Lady Hardcastle once she had her breath back, 'but we have to stop at Georgie's house before we do anything else. We might end up needing to visit the ringleaders in their offices and we'll get nowhere near them dressed like this. We need to change.'

'Right you are,' I said. 'Although our next stop after that should be Challenger's flat. If she's panicking and holding Lady Bickle for any reason, that's where she'll take her. She'll want to be somewhere where she feels safe, where she's in control.'

'Agreed,' she said. 'But if that turns out to be a dud, then we'll visit Hinkley and Morefield, in that order. I can't imagine anyone going to Crane in a crisis so we'll call on him only as a last resort.'

We purred along the road. Our sudden, near silent approach startled one or two horses, but I felt the safest I'd ever felt with Lady Hardcastle at the wheel. We definitely needed a better motor car.

We saw no sign of Beattie Challenger on the way, but we had no real idea what we were looking for and there were other roads she could have taken, anyway. The journey home always seems much quicker than the journey there, but not this time. It seemed to take an age to get to Clifton and I was beginning to become a little anxious that we might have made the wrong decision in choosing to change out of our overalls before trying to hunt down Beattie Challenger and – we still assumed – her prisoner.

Williams let us in without a murmur of protest and left us alone while we got dressed in the drawing room. We were hurrying out when we all but ran into Sir Benjamin, who was returning early from the hospital.

'Hello, you two,' he said amiably. 'I thought you were off on an outing with Georgie, but then I saw the Rolls outside . . . Is everything all right?'

'Right as rain, dear,' said Lady Hardcastle as she breezed past. 'Nothing to worry about. Georgie will tell you all about it when she gets back.'

'Gets back?' he said. 'Where is she?'

'Can't stop, dear,' she said. 'Must dash. Tell you later.'

I gave an apologetic smile and followed her out to the motor car.

Once again we shot off at speed and hurtled through the streets of Redland to Beattie Challenger's flat. We parked right outside the gate and tumbled through together, paying no attention to the screeching of the gate.

Lady Hardcastle tried the door but found it locked. She rang the bell and began hammering on the knocker.

'If you'll just let me . . .' I said, reaching for the picklocks in my brooch.

The door opened to reveal a very stern-looking housekeeper.

'Just what the dickens do you mean by making all that racket?' she demanded.

Lady Hardcastle pushed her firmly in the centre of the chest and sent her staggering backwards across the hall.

'We haven't got time for any of your nonsense,' she said. 'Get out of the way.'

'Well, of all the . . .' spluttered the housekeeper, but we were already most of the way up the stairs.

Lady Hardcastle pointed at the doors and shrugged. I indicated the bedroom door, thinking it the most likely place to stash a prisoner. Surprise was lost – what with all the noise we made coming in – but there's still some shock value in a sudden, violent entrance. Lady Hardcastle burst through the door and into Challenger's bedroom with a yell. I was close behind her.

We both stopped when we saw the revolver. It was unsteady in Challenger's nervous hands, but it was unmistakably pointed at us.

'I might have known it would be you two,' she said. 'You're so clever with your amateur investigations and your codebreaking. But you've come unstuck now, haven't you? Put your hands behind your heads and don't move. I've got things to do.'

On the floor lay Lady Bickle, her wrists and ankles tied. She was gagged with a cloth. Like us, she had changed her clothes and was wearing a white dress and white boots. Unlike our change of clothes, though, hers didn't even remotely fit her. The dress was far too baggy and much too short, and her heels barely fitted inside the tops of the daisy-patterned boots.

Keeping the gun pointing in our general direction, Challenger used her free hand to slop paraffin from a bottle on to the prone figure of Lady Bickle. She also doused the bed, the rug, and the curtains.

'Even if they do work out it was me,' she said, 'Beattie Challenger will be dead. Burned to a crisp in the remains of her flat. Probably had an accident with her paraffin and matches, they'll say. She has a history of starting fires. Poor deluded creature. What? You look surprised. You didn't know about my fires, did you? I'm very good at it. I love fire. A fitting end for Bonfire Beattie.'

'You don't think they'll notice that the corpse is six inches taller than you?' I said, trying to keep her attention on me. 'Or that its hands and feet are tied together? And what about the other two bodies? Who are they supposed to be?'

'Always so clever. Always got something to say. You never did know your place, did you, you—'

The sound of the shot was no less startling for all that I knew it was coming. While Challenger had been watching me, Lady Hardcastle had been fiddling with the hat I had bought her for Christmas – the one that had been specially made and had a concealed compartment in the oversized crown to hold a derringer.

Lady Hardcastle, always a crack shot, had caught Challenger's gun arm, just below the elbow. In shock, she had dropped her own revolver.

That was all I needed. A kick here, a slap there, an elbow where it will do the most good. With a final twist and a flick, Beattie Challenger lay unconscious on the ground.

'Don't just lie there, Georgie,' said Lady Hardcastle. 'We need to get you out of those wet things. Flo, dear, could you toddle downstairs and see if the landlady knows where we might find a telephone? I think we need a little official help here.'

Keeping a wary eye on Beattie Challenger to make sure she didn't come to before Lady Hardcastle could secure her, I backed out of the room on my way to find the landlady. At the top of the stairs I turned, and my last conscious thought as I tumbled down them was, 'After all that, brought down by a fat tabby. I bloody hate cats.'

Chapter Eighteen

I awoke, groggy and aching, in an unfamiliar – but blissfully comfortable – bed. This wasn't at all what I had anticipated. As I had fallen, part of me had doubted ever waking up at all, imagining that I would almost certainly snap my neck as I reached the bottom. Even the optimist within me had imagined coming to on a stretcher in the back of an ambulance while a concerned attendant tried to reassure me that everything would be all right. A feather bed in a high-ceilinged Regency bedroom hadn't featured in even the most outrageously positive possibilities.

The door opened, and a familiar face peered round it into the room.

'Ah, you're awake,' said Lady Hardcastle. 'How wonderful. How are you feeling?'

'I feel mildly non-compos, my lady,' I croaked. 'And it's surprisingly difficult to move my left leg.'

'The befuddlement will be due to the morphine they've been putting in you to dull the pain. The immobile leg is the principal source of that pain.'

'I fell down the stairs.'

'You very did.'

'After tripping over a cat.'

'An overweight tabby that answers to the name of Mrs Merryweather.'

'And the leg?'

'I never learned the names of your legs, dear. Have you named them?'

'Is it broken?'

'In two places,' she said. 'Hence the plaster of Paris and the afore-mentioned immobility. You were never one to do things by halves.'

'I was taught always to do a thorough job. How long will I be like this?'

'Five or six weeks, according to the quack. It might slow you down a bit.'

'I'm sure I'll manage. How long have I been here? What happened at Challenger's house? Is Lady Bickle all right? And what about Inspector Sunderland and Miss Caudle? Where's the gold?'

She laughed. 'You've been here since last night – today is only Tuesday. Georgie Bickle is fine, but complains that she still smells of paraffin. I secured the Challenger woman after freeing Georgie and then managed to get hold of Simeon Gosling on the telephone. Without the inspector there, I had no idea who else to talk to, but Simeon spoke to the right people and we soon had Challenger cuffed and hauled away. The inspector and Dinah Caudle returned to town in the inspector's motor car last night. Once the hubbub had died down at the docks, he had been able to telephone the Bridewell and alert them. The train was stopped at Chippenham, where they confirmed that the "gold" wasn't gold at all. All hell, as they say, has broken loose, but there's still no sign of the real gold.'

'What about Morefield? Hinkley? Crane?'

'The inspector was shrewd enough to pick Crane up first and he crumpled immediately. He squealed on the others, and even impli-cated the inspector's chief superintendent – no wonder he couldn't get permission to investigate more thoroughly. They've all been rounded up, including the chief super.'

'Beattie Challenger?' I said. 'Have they charged her with the arson and Brookfield's murder? What's happening to Lizzie Worrel?'

'Crane gave them chapter and verse on Challenger's involvement in the whole thing. It seems that she was a very bitter, lonely woman, and was easily manipulated by a snake like Morefield. Having talked her into spying on the WSPU, it was easy to lead her to the next step, especially once Brookfield had thrown her over for Lizzie Worrel. He made some enquiries and found out that she had been suspected of arson several years ago. She was only too willing to brag about it to him when he wondered if she might be capable of carrying out some important work for him. She's still bragging now, in fact. She's been arrested, charged, and is due to take Lizzie's place at the Lent Assizes. Lizzie herself was released this morning. She's coming for dinner this evening. Everyone is, in fact. It's going to be quite the party.'

'I've nothing to wear,' I said.

'Nonsense. There's a perfectly serviceable pair of overalls downstairs. I'll have them cleaned and pressed.'

'You're too kind. But it's all over?' I asked.

'More or less,' she said. 'There's still no sign of James Stansbridge or his two hirelings. Nor the gold. The working hypothesis is that they somehow contrived to scarper with it during the commotion. A double-cross.'

'They'll not . . . get . . . far . . .' I said, but sleep overtook me before I could say any more.

◆ ◆ ◆

I woke again at around five o'clock, feeling much more like myself. I struggled out of bed and managed to wash in the fresh water that had thoughtfully been put into the jug on the washstand. There was even a smart frock on the end of the bed. I struggled into it and inspected myself in the full-length glass.

I was about to ring down to see if Lady Bickle's lady's maid might be able to let me have a needle and thread to make one or two slight alterations when there was a knock at the door.

'Are you decent?' said Lady Hardcastle.

'Please come in,' I said. 'I'm up and dressed.'

She opened the door. 'How's the dress?' she asked. 'I know it's not quite your size, but better roomy than tight, I thought.'

'It fits where it touches,' I said. 'It was a lovely thought. If you can scare up a needle and thread . . .'

'I can go one better,' she said. 'If you're happy to let her, Georgie's lady's maid – Miss Cordelia Ireland, if you please – has offered to make a few adjustments for you. She worked wonders finding a dress for someone of your diminished height, but unfortunately it seems the original wearer was a good deal wider than you.'

'You think of everything,' I said. 'Thank you.'

'One tries. I'll ask Georgie to send her up.'

An hour later, with a nip here, a tuck there, and a wide ribbon tied around the waist, the dress looked almost as though it had been made for me. I was ready to rejoin the land of the living.

I made my way clumsily down the stairs, using the crutches I found beside the bedroom door. It was an awkward journey, fraught with danger, but I made it to the bottom without falling again, and stumped across the hall to the drawing room.

I found Lady Hardcastle, Lady Bickle, and Sir Benjamin deep in conversation. Lady Hardcastle was mid-sentence as I entered.

'. . . crossed the room, put the blotting paper on the table, and said, "And that, my dear, is why you should never let the Earl of Runcorn anywhere near an anvil."'

I'd heard the story many times before and it never failed to get guffaws, though it had long since ceased to amuse me. Luckily, Sir

Benjamin was one of those unfortunate gentlemen who laughs on the in-breath so that he sounded like a sea lion barking, and I found his uninhibited joy to be thoroughly infectious. My own giggles set Lady Bickle off and we were soon all four of us helpless with mirth and quite unable to remember what we were laughing at. Sir Benjamin stood and opened his arms.

'Welcome,' he said. 'It's splendid to see you up and about.'

'Thank you for taking such good care of me,' I said. 'That bed was wonderful.'

'It's the least we could do,' he said. 'After all you went through to save Georgie from being immolated by that awful Challenger woman, we couldn't leave you to suffer one of the beds at the BRI.'

'It's much appreciated,' I said.

'Think nothing of it,' said Lady Bickle. 'I'll never be able to thank you enough for saving me. I can still smell that paraffin, you know.'

Sir Benjamin, meanwhile, had helped me across the room to a vacant chair and was propping me up with cushions.

'I often think you're wasted as a surgeon, dear,' said Lady Bickle. 'You'd make such a lovely nurse.'

He curtsied. 'Got to keep the patient comfy,' he said.

'Are you taking notes, my lady?' I asked Lady Hardcastle. 'I'll need to be entertained, too.'

'Oh,' said Sir Benjamin. 'I'm sure she can do that. Emily does have such wonderful stories to tell.'

'And at least a third of them are true,' I said.

He laughed.

'I'll deal with you later,' said Lady Hardcastle.

'But I'm poorly,' I said, and pointed to my plastered leg. Our hosts weren't in on the private joke, but it seemed to amuse them nonetheless.

The doorbell rang, and within moments the room was crowded with the new arrivals. Inspector Sunderland had brought his wife. He introduced her as Dorothea, although she insisted that we should all call her Dollie. Lizzie Worrel looked much healthier than when we had seen her last, though the slight bagginess of her dress showed how much weight she had lost during her weeks in gaol. Dinah Caudle, as always, looked as though she had been dressed for a fashion spread in a society magazine. Simeon Gosling had been invited, too.

Drinks were served and the evening began in earnest.

◆ ◆ ◆

Conversation at the dinner table was comfortable but a little guarded as we sat down. Once the food and wine began to arrive, though, things warmed up considerably. The Bickles dined extraordinarily well – it wasn't just pastry skills their cook had picked up in Paris – and Sir Benjamin kept a fine cellar.

'I feel like a bit of a Johnny Newcome,' said Dr Gosling. 'Is anyone going to bring me up to date? The last I heard, poor Lizzie here had been wrongly imprisoned, and Emily had been dragooned into helping uncover the truth. Next thing I know there's explosions at the docks, missing gold, Georgie's been rescued from a fiery death, and half the city's luminaries have been banged up in Miss Worrel's place.'

'That seems a fair summary of events,' said Lady Hardcastle. 'I'd say you were pretty much on top of things.'

'Yes, but . . .'

'What is it that you don't understand?' asked the inspector.

'You know me, Sunderland,' said Dr Gosling. 'I cut up dead bodies for a living – no one tells me anything.'

'While the ladies of the WSPU were trying to find out what had really happened at Brookfield's flat, they uncovered something of a nest of vipers,' said the inspector. 'With Councillor Morefield at its centre. He seems to have been something of a collector—'

'Of human souls?' suggested Dr Gosling.

'Needlessly poetic,' said the inspector, 'but not far off the truth. He covets power and influence above all things, it seems, and he had amassed plenty of it. Sadly for him, though, he wasn't quite as good at hanging on to his money, and the scale of his debts would make the exchequers of some small nations blanch. When he became aware of the gold shipment coming from Chile, he realized that he had the men in his pocket to pull off an audacious theft. James Stansbridge owed him a small fortune, and also happened to be a decorated ex-soldier with experience of sneaking about behind enemy lines. He'd be sure to come up with a wheeze for nicking the gold, and would have the wherewithal to pull it off. Redvers Hinkley was a crooked property developer who didn't mind using his money to get what he wanted. He'd be good for a few bob to cover the assorted expenses and disbursements of the exercise. As would Oswald Crane, the coffee magnate with whose wife Morefield has been . . . dallying. Crane's contacts at the docks would also come in handy for intelligence and—'

'Does Crane have warehouses at Avonmouth?' interrupted Lady Hardcastle.

'Of course,' said the inspector.

'Have they been searched?' she asked.

'Yes,' he said. 'This morning. Why?'

'Did they find anything?'

'Coffee beans,' he said. 'As expected. Crates and crates of the stuff.'

'When you told us about Stansbridge's arrival yesterday morning, you described the unloading of a large crate. But we know that the gold – and the fake gold – were both transported in a set of smaller boxes. So what happened to the big crate? What if – and I'm just speculating wildly here – what if the crate fitted exactly over the pallet holding the boxes of gold? What if instead of hoiking the boxes of fake gold out of the crate and putting them on a trolley, they just lifted the fake crate off the fake gold boxes and placed it over the real gold boxes? What if once it was nailed in place, it just looked like a crate of coffee beans?'

'My men opened all the crates – all full of beans.'

'What if the top half of the fake crate were filled with coffee beans, with a compartment underneath to conceal the gold boxes?'

The inspector paused for thought for a moment. 'They'd have to leave it on the trolley – they'd never lift it off.'

'That should make it easier to find, then,' said Lady Hardcastle.

'I'm so sorry, Sir Benjamin,' said the inspector. 'May I use your telephone?'

'In the hall, dear boy,' said Sir Benjamin. 'Help yourself.'

Inspector Sunderland excused himself and left the room.

'I say, Emily,' said Lady Bickle. 'You are a clever clogs.'

'That's all very well,' said Dr Gosling, 'but how does poor Miss Worrel fit into all this?'

'As well as being a thief, a scoundrel, and a peddler of influence,' said Lady Hardcastle, 'Nathaniel Morefield was also a prominent anti-suffragist. He hated the very idea of the WSPU and came up with a way of thwarting the suffragettes' plans by planting a spy in their midst. He found a likely member of the Women's National Anti-Suffrage League and employed her to join the WSPU and report on their activities. Christian Brookfield was already investigating Morefield, so he soon got wind of this new scheme. He wooed the spy – Beattie Challenger – to find out more, but then he met and fell in love with Lizzie here. He cut off his false relationship with Challenger at once. Meanwhile, Morefield *et al.* had realized Brookfield was on to them and decided he had to be done away with. It gave them a chance to kill two birds with one stone – they could kill the nosy journalist before he could unmask them in the newspaper, and they could severely damage the reputation of the suffragettes, who had supposedly ceased militant operations for the duration of the election. They had a willing volunteer in Beattie Challenger. As I said, she was lonely and easily led – eager to please. For some reason she has a passionate hatred of the idea of universal suffrage. She seems to believe wholeheartedly in the idea that the great affairs of state should be decided by wealthy men and that the rest of us should keep our beaks out. She said as much to the magistrate this morning.'

'So the job was jam all round as far as she was concerned?' I said.

'Absolutely. Not only was it an opportunity to advance her precious cause, it also gave her the chance to take revenge against her former lover and his new sweetheart by killing one and framing the other for his murder. Using her favourite method, too – it seems she has a quite impressive history of arson. The owner of the shop was a committed anti-suffragist, too, so I don't doubt he was invited to be away from home for the night with the promise of a big insurance payment. And then, of course, once we started to investigate, Challenger was on hand to keep them abreast of developments. Dinah already suggested that they must have known she had Brookfield's notebook – they broke in and tried to steal it.'

'Well I never,' said Dr Gosling. 'The things I miss while I'm slicing open corpses and weighing their internal organs.'

'Simeon, dear,' said Lady Bickle. 'Not at the dinner table, there's a good chap.'

'Right you are,' he said. 'Sorry, everyone.'

Throughout all this, Lizzie Worrel remained very quiet. She ate sparingly, and seemed somewhat overwhelmed, but she was, at least, smiling. I'd not seen her do that before. It suited her.

The inspector returned.

'I've got men heading out to Avonmouth right away,' he said. 'Thank you for the idea, my lady.'

'My pleasure,' said Lady Hardcastle. 'But you have to try this salmon pâté. It's quite the most delicious thing you'll ever eat.'

The conversation took a more conventional turn after this, with discussions on the recent election – which hadn't provided quite the mandate Mr Asquith had been looking for to pass his budget – women's suffrage, football, music, and even motor cars. Dr Gosling appeared to be getting on very well with Miss Caudle, which seemed to please Lady Bickle. And Mrs Sunderland got on very well with Lady Hardcastle, which seemed very much to please the inspector.

I tried my hardest to be sparkly and bright, but the morphine wasn't helping. It dulled the pain wonderfully, but I was ready for a return to bed. Lady Hardcastle, ever my protector, noticed that I was flagging and offered to help me upstairs once the cheese had been served.

I slept the sleep of the blessed.

◆ ◆ ◆

On Wednesday morning Lady Hardcastle and I helped Lady Bickle open up the WSPU shop. We had expected that Marisol Rojas would have opened up in Beattie's absence, but there was no sign of her. We asked around and heard from one of the neighbours that she had been seen crawling out through one of the back windows of the shop and legging it up through Berkeley Square.

'I wonder why she did that?' asked Lady Bickle. 'There was no one in the shop – she could simply have walked out through the front door.'

'No idea,' said the shopkeeper. 'I just nipped in to tell her what I'd heard. One of my regulars told me that she'd heard from her ma that her neighbour had said the Chilean gold had been stolen from the docks. We had a little chat, like, then I went back to work. I was out in the back room makin' a pot of tea, and there she was, large as life, shinnin' down a drainpipe and scootin' off through the back yard.'

'It's what I would have done,' I said.

They all looked at me blankly.

'Well, if I thought the front of the shop were being watched, and I wanted to get away, I'd go out the back. I'd have made sure I knew the way in the dark.'

'Do you think she was involved in some way?' asked Lady Bickle.

'We have no way of knowing,' I said. 'Perhaps she had been a source of information for the gang. Or perhaps she was working for the Chilean government in some capacity and was afraid of the consequences of her apparent failure to protect the gold. Or perhaps she had nothing to do with it and just thought she ought not to hang around for long enough for people to make any spurious connections. Chilean gold, Chilean suffragette – it's not a massive leap to suppose some sort of involvement.'

'I do hope she comes back,' said Lady Bickle. 'I shall miss her.'

We never saw her again.

We stayed with Lady Bickle until reinforcements arrived. We were presented with our own 'Votes for Women' badges as a token of appreciation, and were told that we would always be welcome at WSPU meetings. We both assured them that we would see them all before very long, and I promised to help with self-defence classes as soon as my leg was healed.

At about midday, we said our goodbyes and tried to fit me into the Rover for the journey home. It wasn't easy. Lady Bickle offered the use of her Rolls-Royce and her chauffeur.

'Thank you, my lady,' I said, 'but I'm going to be on the crocked list for at least another month. I've got to get used to getting about in the Rover sooner or later. I'm sure it will be fine. At least it isn't raining.'

It was uncomfortable, and highly undignified, but it wasn't too long a drive to Littleton Cotterell.

As we drove along, I had a sudden thought.

'Do we know Inspector Sunderland's first name?' I asked.

'We do,' she said. 'It's Oliver.'

'I thought so,' I said. 'So he's Ollie.'

'He is,' she said. 'Oh, and she's Dollie. I say, how utterly priceless.'

We soon arrived at Littleton Cotterell.

'Lunch at the pub?' asked Lady Hardcastle as we rounded the village green. 'I telephoned Edna not to expect us until later, so there's nothing at home.'

'I never say no to one of Old Joe's pies,' I said.

'Let's hope Holman had a meat delivery,' she said. 'Or we'll be disappointed again.'

We weren't disappointed. Pies were back on the menu, and Daisy seemed unusually pleased to see us.

'What's got into you?' I asked as she brought our food and drink to the table. 'You look like the cat that's got all the other cats' cream.'

'What's that bit from the Bible?' she asked. 'The bit about sowing and reaping?'

'"Whatsoever a man soweth, that shall he also reap",' said Lady Hardcastle.

'That's the one. And whatsoever a nasty little housemaid soweth, that shall she also reap, an' all.'

'Has some ill befallen our good friend Dora Kendrick?' I asked.

'I'll say,' said Daisy. 'While you was all off gettin' blown up and shot at—'

'To be fair,' interrupted Lady Hardcastle, 'I was the one doing the shooting.'

'Well, while all that was goin' on . . . What? You shot someone?'

'With a very tiny gun,' said Lady Hardcastle. 'It was nothing, really.'

'Right,' said Daisy doubtfully. 'Well, while you was doin' that, Dora – she as had been spreadin' false rumours about me and Lenny Leadbetter – was caught with that very man in her room up at The Grange.'

'"With" him?' I said.

'In the biblical sense,' she confirmed. 'There a'n't been a scandal like it round y'ere for years. She was sacked on the spot, my name is cleared and my honour restored, and Lenny Leadbetter daren't show his face.

Specially not now half the girls up at The Grange have seen a sight more than just his face.'

'I'm delighted to hear it,' I said. 'And is that my pie?'

'Oh, yes, my lover, sorry. You eat it up afore it gets cold.'

I'd been waiting for a pie and a pint at the Dog and Duck for weeks. I wasn't disappointed.

◆ ◆ ◆

That night, Inspector Sunderland dropped in to tell us that the Chilean gold had been retrieved.

'Was I right?' asked Lady Hardcastle eagerly.

'You were exactly right,' said the inspector. 'As always. I took a handful of men down to Avonmouth and set them to work checking the crates in Crane's warehouse. The first sweep found nothing so we had a bit of a think and then had another go. Obviously it would have to pass a cursory inspection, so just prying off the lids and having a look inside was never going to be enough. One of the lads said we should empty them all out, but the part of me that hates waste couldn't bear the thought of spoiling all that perfectly good coffee by tipping it on the floor. Then it hit me. It should have been obvious all along, really – we talked about it at some length: gold is astonishingly heavy. So I had them go round in pairs. If they could lift the crate between them, it was full of coffee. But if they couldn't get it off the ground, open it up and search it properly. They found it in no time. There were a couple of inches of beans on a false floor, and below that, thirty shiny gold bars. We were just wrapping things up when who should come bowling in, bold as brass, but James Stansbridge and his two burly minions, so we nabbed them as well.'

Lady Hardcastle tried her best not to look too smug, but she couldn't quite manage it.

The next few weeks passed extremely pleasingly. I wasn't exception-ally mobile with my broken leg, but Edna and Miss Jones stepped up and I was allowed to rest and recover. I had plenty of time to read the newspaper, too, where Dinah Caudle cemented her reputation as the rightful heir to Christian Brookfield's crown with a series of 'exposing the seamy underbelly of our corrupt city' articles.

Lady Bickle sent her car on my birthday to take Lady Hardcastle and me to dinner and a show in town. As promised, it was as soppy, trite, and syrupy as any musical ever was and I had the most splendid time. As, almost against her will, did Lady Hardcastle.

I had become used to being looked after and I wasn't entirely look-ing forward to having the plaster removed – I'd soon have no excuse for sitting down and being waited on. I needn't have worried. The doctor who removed the plaster cast told me, with – I thought – sadistic glee, that my full rehabilitation would take a long while yet. I wouldn't return to full fitness for many months, and it would take a great deal of hard work to get me there.

And speaking of getting places . . . At the end of March, Lord Riddlethorpe arrived, driving quite the most extraordinary motor car the world had ever seen. Long and sleek, like his racing cars, but with a coach-built compartment for driver and passenger to sit in, out of the wind and rain. Best of all, he had fitted an experimental electric starter motor. No more cranking.

We sold the Rover to Miss Caudle – who had broken off her engage-ment to Michael and was now walking out with Dr Gosling – and packed our bags for a trip to London to visit Lady Hardcastle's brother, Harry. I even persuaded her that we should spend a few days at the seaside when the weather was warmer. 1910 wasn't off to such a bad start, after all.

Author's Note

A little historical background.

The Women's Social and Political Union (WSPU) was formed in 1903 by Emmeline Pankhurst. She felt that the suffragists (the National Union of Women's Suffrage Societies – NUWSS) were not militant enough. She split from them with the slogan 'Deeds Not Words'.

The WSPU began demonstrations in 1906 and escalated to a campaign of window breaking in 1908. This continued, but their campaign of property damage didn't extend to arson – always of empty buildings – until July 1912.

In 1906, Charles E Hands coined the name 'suffragettes' in the *Daily Mail* to distinguish them from the other, less militant, suffragists. It was intended as a belittling term of abuse, but the suffragettes gleefully embraced it.

In April 1909, the Liberal government under Herbert Asquith put forward 'The People's Budget'. It would fund old-age pensions and other welfare programmes by increasing taxes on the wealthy. It was passed by the Commons but, in an unprecedented move, blocked by the Lords.

In January 1910, Asquith called a General Election, which ran from 15 January to 10 February. The aim was to secure another Liberal victory, giving him the mandate to pass the budget.

In January 1910, the WSPU formally suspended all militant action for the duration of the election. They continued to campaign, but window breaking and demonstrations stopped.

The result of the election was a hung parliament, with the Liberals having to get the support of Labour and the Irish National Party to secure a majority. The budget got through in April but another election was called at the end of the year, this time because the Irish wanted a law to prevent the Lords from blocking legislation again. The result was another hung parliament, but the same allegiances formed and The Parliament Act was passed in 1911.

Notes on the text

The WSPU really did rent a shop at 37 Queen's Road in Bristol in 1908 and used it as their base in the city until 1917. The shop still stands and is almost exactly as it was in 1908, except that the decorative upper-storey windows have been replaced. I wasn't able to get access to the upstairs of the shop, but the nice chaps in the barber's next door let me see the layout of their own building, which they assured me was very similar.

The objections to women's suffrage given by various characters throughout the book were genuine arguments put forward by articulate, well-educated men during the early years of the twentieth century (including the one about big hats in Parliament).

Some members of the WSPU really did learn martial arts. Edith Garrud was a suffragette who trained to become an instructor in the Japanese martial art of jiu-jitsu. By 1910 she was running courses to pass her skills on to WSPU members. Generally speaking, jiu-jitsu makes use of the principle of using an attacker's own strength and energy against him and was considered the best self-defence technique for use by women against larger, stronger opponents (until 1990, the minimum height for a police officer in England was 5'10"). Her trainees soon became known as suffrajitsus and received a good deal of press coverage as they defended themselves against attacks by the police. A few years later, thirty of these specially trained suffragettes were recruited to 'The Bodyguard' to protect Emmeline Pankhurst.

Lady Hardcastle invents the 4-4-2 formation for Association football more than seventy years before it was widely used by top-level teams. There's no reason for her to do this, it just made me laugh.

Whiteladies Road in Bristol is named after the order of white-robed Carmelite nuns who owned some of the land there. Blackboy Hill links the top of Whiteladies Road to the Downs and was probably named after a pub that once stood there. The origins of the pub's name are disputed but neither that, nor the mention of 'white ladies', has anything to do with Bristol's shameful history as a centre of the slave trade.

There really was a fish and chip shop in a half-timbered building at the bottom of Christmas Steps in 1910. It was one of the first chippies in England and, until recently, one of the longest surviving. The building itself is thought to date from the thirteenth century and there's some debate about exactly when it became a chip shop in the late nineteenth century, but it was definitely serving fish and chips by 1910. Christmas Steps are still there, and the building is still there, but at the time of writing the chip shop is closed.

The theatrical costumiers near Old Market is an invention, but the Empire Theatre on the corner of Old Market and Captain Carey's Lane was indeed Bristol's most famous music hall. Captain Carey's Lane no longer exists and no trace of the theatre nor the pub attached to it (the White Hart) remains.

Sheldon Bush and Patent Shot Company Limited is a real company and its 'new' shot tower (built in 1969) is a Grade II-listed building on Cheese Lane. The original tower was built in 1782 just down the road by William Watts, who is credited with the invention of the method of making lead shot by pouring thin streams of molten lead from a great height into a vat of water. As the lead falls, it forms droplets that solidify as they hit the water, making neatly spherical shot.

Avonmouth Docks, together with the slightly newer Royal Portbury Docks, were built to address the difficulties of navigating the River Avon to get to the old docks in the centre of the city. The Severn Estuary has the third highest tidal range in the world (15 m/48 ft) and the Avon, which drains into it, is all but empty at low tide, making it unnavigable by large vessels for great parts of the day. Incidentally, my favourite (and the most likely) explanation of the phrase 'shipshape and Bristol fashion' is a reference to the old docks in the city. Before the locks were built at Cumberland Basin to make a 'floating harbour' in the middle of town (one which wasn't affected by tides), ships in the docks would be beached at low tide and would come to rest slightly on their sides. Being merely 'shipshape' (i.e. in good order) wasn't enough – all cargo had to be carefully loaded and secured in the 'Bristol fashion' to ensure no loss or damage occurred when the ships tilted over. Thus 'shipshape and Bristol fashion' is the very acme of good order. Where was I? Ah, yes, Avonmouth Docks are real and had been fully operational for thirty years by the time of our story. The layout, though, is entirely invented to suit the purposes of the action. Just so you know.

How Emily Cracked the Code

The Vigenère cipher was the final refinement to an encryption method first proposed in the 1460s by an Italian scholar rejoicing in the name of Leon Battista Alberti. Over the next hundred years, several other people had a bash at it before the idea was perfected by French diplomat Blaise de Vigenère, who published his work in a book entitled *Traicté des Chiffres* ('A Treatise on Ciphers') in 1586.

This new encryption method takes the simple Caesar or 'shift' cipher and adds a twist which made it – for a while at least – impossible to crack, earning it the name *le chiffre indéchiffrable* – the undecipherable cipher.

Instead of using just one Caesar shift, it uses several, defined by a 'keyword'. Let's say the keyword is DOG. The first letter of the plaintext would be encrypted using a Caesar shift starting with D – a->D, b->E, c->F, etc. The second letter is encrypted using a Caesar shift starting with O – a->O, b->P, c->Q, etc. The third letter uses the letter G as its starting point, and the fourth returns to the D, then O, then G, and so on to the end of the message.

Cryptanalysts had already worked out that a Caesar cipher can be broken simply by counting up all the letters. Languages use the letters of their alphabet according to their own unique pattern. In English the most commonly used letter is E, followed by T, A, O, I, N, and so on. In French, in case you're interested, the first six most commonly used letters are E, S, A, I, T, N, while in Swedish they're E, A, N, R, T, S. Once you know the expected frequency of every letter, it's a simple matter to count up the numbers of each letter in the cipher-text and compare it with the standard pattern to see how much the alphabet has been shifted by.

Because the Vigenère cipher uses a rotating set of Caesar shifts, that frequency analysis doesn't work, leaving early cryptanalysts stumped. In 1854 (or possibly 1846), Charles Babbage (he of the mechanical computer) cracked the cipher but didn't publish his method. In 1863, a method was published by Major Friedrich Wilhelm Kasiski of the German army and it is generally assumed that Babbage did it the same way.

The method (as used by Lady Hardcastle in the story) relies on the assumption that certain groups of letters recur regularly in any given language. In English, for instance, we see groups like 'th', 'sh', 'ea', and 'ed' all the time. In a long enough plaintext, it's possible that some groups of letters will be encrypted more than once with the same part of the keyword so that they also appear in the cipher-text as repeated groups.

The Babbage/Kasiski trick is to look for repeated letter combinations in the cipher-text and note how far apart they are. If you get enough repeated groups, this gap will give you a clue as to the length of the keyword.

In Brookfield's cipher-text, for instance, the letters 'db' occur together eleven times. Some of the gaps (I confess I didn't count them all) are 33, 33, 18, 300, 228. 'lvc' crops up three times and one of the gaps is 204 characters. 'mnbi' appears twice with a gap of 72. There are many other combinations but a pattern is already beginning to emerge. With two exceptions, the largest common factor of all those gaps is 6 – there's a chance that the keyword might be six letters long. Looking at more repeated groups, the number 6 keeps coming up. Obviously that doesn't rule out 2 or 3, but Emily assumed that a two- or three-letter keyword would be too simple and plumped for 6.

You might have noticed that 33 doesn't divide neatly by 6. Looking again, though, the gap between the first and third appearance is 66 letters, so it might be safe to ignore the middle one as an unlucky coincidence.

Working from the hypothesis that the keyword is six-letters long, she broke up the text into groups of six and carried out a frequency analysis of the first letter in each group, then the second, and so on. She ended up with six frequency charts which she could compare with the chart for plaintext English.

The first group is a pretty good fit for a Caesar shift of L. The second letter seems to fit a shift to I. At this point, knowing your cryptographer can come in handy. A six-letter keyword beginning LI–, chosen by someone who was in love with Lizzie . . . It's not a massive leap to fill in the blanks with ZZIE. A quick check reveals that those letters do tally with the frequency analysis, and the business of decryption can begin.

I just thought you might like to know that it's possible to decrypt the message and that it's not just another bit of authorial flim-flam.

About the Author

Photo © 2018 Clifton Photographic Company

T E Kinsey grew up in London and read history at Bristol University. He worked for a number of years as a magazine features writer before falling into the glamorous world of the Internet, where he edited content for a very famous entertainment website for quite a few years more. After helping to raise three children, learning to scuba dive and to play the drums and the mandolin (though never, disappointingly, all at the same time), he decided the time was right to get back to writing. *The Burning Issue of the Day* is the fifth story in a series of mysteries starring Lady Hardcastle.